A DOLLAR SHORT

A Michael Christian Mystery

MIKE SAAD

ISBN 978-1-7322499-2-9
Printed in USA

Dedication

Along the way quite a few people have encouraged me to write. My high school English and Literature teacher, Sister Marie Edwards, IHM, was a perfectionist for spelling, punctuation, grammar and creative thinking. Although I didn't appreciate it at the time, I have silently thanked her over the years and I publicly do so now.

To my wife Muriel, who has celebrated every one of my successes and mourned with me over my failures. She has stood by me in this venture as she has in every endeavor of mine. Thank you.

To my young family, now adults, who must have often wondered where I was, or why I was gone so long or frequently. Maybe these stories will give you some insight as to why I was silent on many of those questions. You have managed to do quite well despite my absences, or maybe because of them. I am proud of you and write for you and your children.

In memory of Norman E. Anderson, retired Detroit Police Robbery Detective and Prosecutor's Investigator. My partner and mentor at the Wayne County Organized Crime Task Force, Norm taught me how to investigate white-collar crimes and international industrial theft. He taught me the maxim of "follow the money" and then he taught me how to do it. Occasionally, when we broke a big case, it was Norm, my senior partner, who allowed me the press interviews and credit for the bust.

And when I was in doubt about my next career move, Norm encouraged me to branch out from law enforcement into the intriguing world of corporate security. It was where I spent the next thirty years traveling the globe and "fixing" corporate problems. Thank you my friend for that well needed kick in the pants.

To Raymond Stommell, Carl Carter, Wayne Hall, Jack Knauss, Ed Ratzeburger and Arthur Kingsbury, icons of the Detroit Chapter of ASIS International, or as it was known back then, *The American Society for Industrial Security*. These men adopted me into their executive family. They were heads of security for some of the largest corporations in America, and many also served as National Society Presidents and sat on the Board of Directors of the organization. They sponsored me, advanced me to positions of opportunity and visibility, encouraged, mentored, trained and educated me. All they ever suggested was that I someday return the favor to others. Most of all, they showed me that my new career was filled with noble men and women.

Acknowledgements

Tom Kowalski, my friend since childhood, spent his early military years as a linguist, covertly monitoring the communications of Russian pilots on behalf of the United States Air Force from the northern tip of Wakkanai, Japan. Tom read and re-read my earliest drafts of this and my first book, *A Day Late*. He offered solid feedback and editing support, and recommendations for structure and character development for both, including the Russian translations and transliterations. It is no coincidence that *Special Agent Tom Koval* in this novel has a remarkably similar background.

Dave and Pat Johnson provided me valuable editing and story feedback on *A DAY LATE* and graciously agreed to do it again for *A DOLLAR SHORT*. Pat is a stickler for correct writing style and Dave shares a combined law enforcement and security background similar to mine. He contributed some astute technical observations that brought credibility to my writing.

Terri Kowal provided editorial review for *A DAY LATE* and volunteered again for A DOLLAR SHORT without any arm-twisting from me.

Laura Salanski heard about my manuscript and reached out, volunteering to Beta-read and mark it up, without any expectations other than to help. She was able to turn it around timely despite it being a larger body of work than she originally expected.

Peter and Carole O'Connor at *Bespoke Bookcovers* scored again with their excellent design work on the cover. In their first rendering, they immediately captured the essence of *A DOLLAR SHORT* and the continuing theme of Michael Christian's international adventures. I was shocked to see the shadow character on the cover standing in the very spot I stood in nineteen ninety-four.

Any error or omissions are strictly mine and some of the grammatical errors are intentional on my part to maintain conversational tone.

Table of Contents

Preface

Some of the most catastrophic declines in the value of the Russian currency interestingly occurred on a Tuesday.

October 11, 1994 was similarly one of the most significant of any collapse and was called "Black Tuesday". On that one day alone, the value of the ruble, measured against the U.S. dollar, fell by twenty-seven percent. The Russian general populace, ignorant to a great extent of the impact of inflation, was told the crash was because the United States manipulated their currency in attempts to destroy the Russian people.

A great deal of the inflation was actually driven by the rising costs of energy and food prices. The more educated felt that the "higher-ups" in the financial world intentionally manipulated the currency. Apparently, many were positioned to buy the ruble at lows and then sold it a few days later at higher prices. Financial institution investigators reported the collapse was due to incompetence and a series of bad currency decisions. The hated dollar, whether original or counterfeit, was

1

nevertheless the most valuable, stable and highly sought currency in Russia.

The Russian economy, never strong to begin with, was still staggering from Gorbachev's dissolution of the Soviet Union. The black and grey markets were becoming as powerful, if not more so, than the overt economy of Russia. And the Bratva, or *Brotherhood,* ran those underground markets. Capitalism had yet to take root and there were doubts among the wealthy oligarchs that it ever would. Many believed that former KGB officers and the mafia, by no means partners, ran just about every aspect of the local economies. To a great extent they were right. Along with nepotism and billions of illegal or diverted government dollars, the favored members of the Russian elite had begun infiltrating the highest levels of industry and energy. Self-dealing and corruption were believed to be systemic at all levels of business and government.

The Russian mafia was going through a massive growth spurt. And like any group of adolescents, they were fighting it out to establish their geographic ownership of the illegal trades. Fueled by seemingly endless supplies of cash and weapons, turf wars were common occurrences from St. Petersburg to Moscow. And territory was being claimed in nearly block-to-block fighting. Automatic gunfire in major cities, even downtown business districts, was as common as horns blaring in overcrowded intersections.

Perestroika, the restructuring of the Soviet Union, may have been underway, but the cold war with the United States was still chilly, at best. Thousands of nuclear missiles, from both sides, were still pointed at each other's countries amid a level of unprecedented political mistrust.

Western companies were sending advance teams and business start-ups to Russia to take advantage of what they thought were emerging markets. Their risk analyses grossly underestimated the level of business and economic risk and the impact of industrial espionage. And they practically ignored or undervalued the financial impact of the burgeoning Russian mafia. American employees and their families faced personal risks they could not have imagined.

It was against this backdrop that Michael Christian was sent to Moscow to "fix" another corporate problem.

CHAPTER ONE

IT ALL HAPPENED SO FAST and professionally, *just like in the movies*, he thought.

Carter Winston had deftly glided his new Mercedes into the marked parking space at the office, his name freshly lettered on the curb. As he turned off the big engine he smiled to himself, thinking about his position in life. He was a senior director of one of the largest multi-national corporations in the world. And here he was, running a foreign start-up in Russia immediately after the dissolution of the Soviet Union. In his mind's eye, he could clearly see he was on the fast track to his next promotion and another significant pay increase.

His car still smelled new and the leather felt soft and luxurious as he slid out and bent over to retrieve his briefcase off the rear seat. Before he could straighten up, he was forcefully shoved back in the car and hammered by something hard behind his right ear. His vision exploded into red and white stars and he felt an electric jolt run down through his shoulders, as his cervical spine compressed onto its discs. Then he passed out.

Carter had no idea how much time had passed while he was unconscious. He tried to lift himself off the floor, but the movement sent excruciating pain through his head. He threw up the first time he tried to kneel upright. He figured he had a concussion and was terrified he would die without proper medical attention.

He tried to inventory himself for other injuries, but he was unable to move his hands, which seemed bound tightly behind his back. His fingertips felt swollen and cold, and his ankles were bound with tape. Each time he tried to open his eyes, even the room's dim lighting riddled him with pain. He was dizzy to the point of passing out. His stiff collar had a sweet metallic smell that he recognized as his own blood, probably from where he had been struck. When he tried to lie perfectly still to avoid the intense pain, he could feel the cold floor and realized he was on rough, unsealed concrete. He began shivering as his now alert body recognized the chill. He knew he was a prisoner. No one had to tell him he had been kidnapped.

Carter had imagined scenarios all his life where he was called on to be brave. The first was when he was a boy, confronted by the school bully and told to give up his lunch money. All the kids were watching and no one would help him. He was on his own. In his fantasy, he talked the bigger kid out of hurting him. He could see himself using logic and reason to explain why he should be left alone. In Carter's moment of intellectual superiority, the befuddled oaf would laugh at him, give him a small shove and walk away, leaving Carter broke but unharmed. In reality, he gave up his money without an argument.

As a fan of his high school teams, he would stand in the bleachers and watch the athletes bang it out on the field. In this fantasy, Carter was lined up against the biggest, meanest kid on the defensive line. Just before the ball was snapped, Carter would whisper into his opponent's helmeted facemask, "Just fall down when I hit you and it won't hurt as much." To his deep satisfaction, the larger football player would take a dive when he was hit, creating a hole large enough for the halfback to run through and score the winning touchdown. His teammates would lift Carter on to their shoulders and cheer his well-delivered block, bravely rendered against all odds.

As a young man sitting in his cubicle at work, Carter imagined the office manager assigning him the most difficult work and then taking all the credit. At the leadership meeting Carter would look his manager daringly in the eye, then hoist himself from his chair and tell the department head that the report he was reviewing was Carter's and not that of his manager. The department director would admire Carter's boldness as well as his creative work product. Of course, Carter would get the promotion and the raise.

Truth be told, Carter was not that brave of a guy. But he was quite intelligent and not afraid of hard work. He was determined to get ahead and he advanced rapidly. In time, he became the department director. He spun failing operations into efficient, profitable entities. He was known for turning around sluggish processes and saving significant amounts of money in re-investment costs or plant closings.

He then helped his company's start-up businesses in emerging markets. He was doing exactly that in Moscow, in post-Soviet Union Russia. Now he wished he had all the bravery of his fantasies.

Before his transfer, the company had someone brief him about situations like this. He was told that corporate kidnappings had become commonplace throughout Russian metropolitan areas and Moscow in particular. He had been given the background on the power of the Russian Mafia and the fact that they were regularly kidnapping western businessmen and extorting their companies or their families.

The security expert had told him that he must be vigilant, keep a low profile, build a security plan, avoid the train stations, and not hire taxis off the curb. Carter thought the briefing was exaggerated. He pegged the guy as one who had no real role in performing business risk analysis, someone who was frightening him just to make himself look important.

The lawyers and finance guys had already done their risk assessments, leading Carter to believe the company would not knowingly send him to a place that was really as dangerous as the security guy warned. But there was also something else about the security briefing that was causing Carter to feel sick to his stomach now. He was told the United States government had an official and immutable policy that it doesn't pay ransoms and it would not allow ransom demands to be paid to foreign kidnappers. He had also been told that the

FBI had no official role in Russia should something like this happen to a U.S. citizen.

So when they came for him in his cell the first time, he concluded his best opportunity was to be brave and rational. Carter thought himself a very smart man. He decided he would logically explain that ransom attempts would be futile. He told them the U.S. government would not pay and his company could not pay. He explained to them that the best solution would be to blindfold him and return him to his workplace – no harm, no foul. He never finished his explanation.

His abductors laughed at him. Then they beat him with a rolled-up newspaper. After only three solid punches to the face, he passed out from the pain in his head. He awoke lying in his own cold vomit. So, rather than calling his office to make a kidnap demand, they forced him to give them his home phone number in the States. That call to his wife ended horribly and now he was again on the floor of the warehouse. Bleeding and broken, Carter feared desperately for his life. He would have to figure something else out to avoid further beatings and to get out of there alive, wherever *there* was.

The call to his wife had not gone as Carter had expected. Once his wife, Carol, realized he had been taken, she sounded terrified and unintelligible in the phone. Her hysteric words ran together, her sobs drowning out her answers. They had been married for eight years, yet he could barely understand what she was trying to say. The Russians had a harder time. They became angry and frustrated, and hung up on her without any assurances she even understood their instructions for the ransom payment. They were, however, able to warn her not to notify the police or the FBI. They couldn't take their exasperation out on his wife, so they took it out on Carter.

They started on his face with their bare fists, knocking out a tooth. The swelling of his cut lips was so painful he couldn't form his own words. He passed out within the first few minutes but they doused him with water and woke him. They taunted him in Russian while they beat him again - this time on his ribs. Each breath he took caused such sharp pain Carter thought he would die of suffocation or a punctured lung as the beating continued.

Carter realized he would never be able to talk or fight his way out of this. He was now worried that they might kill him even if his wife did pay the ransom.

■ ■ ■ ■ ■

Carol Winston listened intently as he spoke. Jonathan's words were somehow comforting in a world that had just been turned totally upside down by a phone call.

"The first thing we should do is write down everything you remember about what they said. You need to recall exactly what makes you think it was Carter on the other end of the call. Didn't you say you weren't even sure it was him with all the yelling and screaming going on? Let's make sure one way or another. Was it him or not? We need to decide quickly if this is real or just a way to scam money from you. We need to be certain it's Carter.

And Carol, if it is, we need to act right away to get him out of there."

Jonathan's steady voice was one of the attractive things about him. The fact that he was handsome, treated her wonderfully, and was an excellent lover helped too. But right now, she needed someone she could trust to help her figure this all out. She trusted Jonathan.

When Carter took the Moscow assignment it was for four years. Carol had told him right up front she would not go to Russia and didn't want him to go either. Not only was it a geographically dull and dirty country, but the living conditions for U.S. expatriates were abysmal. There was no shopping to speak of and dining-out was so limited that it wasn't worth going. Besides, the company security executive had told them it was dangerous.

Carol had grown accustomed to the comforts of being moderately wealthy, with the Country Club, the social parties, the high-end restaurants, and being able to buy her clothes at boutique shops. These were the benefits she had earned by being married to Carter. She wasn't ready to give them up for a term in Moscow.

Carol also felt their marriage was drifting apart with Carter traveling all over the world. She felt they needed to be together if they were going to try to salvage the marriage, assuming that was even possible. But that wasn't going to happen in Moscow. She wasn't going and that was that. She had expected her refusal would deter Carter from accepting the assignment. When Carter agreed to the posting in Russia, she made up her mind. She wasn't waiting four years for him to return and she wasn't planning on remaining celibate for four years either. Enter Jonathan Drews.

Jonathan made the days go by easily and the nights were wonderfully long. She wouldn't call her attraction to Jonathan love but the bond was certainly strong. She looked forward to each day with him. She felt alive and young again, though she was by no means an old or unattractive woman. She knew she had a desirable body and she worked out to keep it that way. But you can be a forty-something girl and feel like your life has passed you by. And Carol had definitely fallen into a boring routine with Carter.

Over the years, she spent many nights in bed alone. And when she and her husband tried to be intimate, it was over quickly for Carter and not quickly enough for Carol. So she joined some clubs in the neighborhood. They kept her busy, but deep down she felt unfulfilled emotionally, intellectually and especially physically. Jonathan made her feel *alive* and excitingly wicked. And he gave her shuddering orgasms that rushed through her entire body. She didn't recall ever having a real orgasm with a partner before Jonathan. And now she was craving them daily, several times a day. Having Jonathan nearby was handy for her in the short term. Of late, he'd been asking her to spend nights and weekends at his apartment downtown. She hadn't given in to that yet, but she was close. The thought of being able to have sex whenever she wanted was a powerful aphrodisiac. Yet Jonathan also seemed to be genuinely concerned for Carter's safety, even though he was making love to his wife.

She had now fallen completely out of love with Carter and was planning their divorce. Her attorney was going to serve him the papers on his next visit home to the States. Now she faced a moral dilemma. She didn't love Carter. And she didn't want to remain married to him any longer. She dreaded his return into her life. A question began to form in her mind. Perhaps it was more the inkling of an answer. Her uncertainty was keeping her from giving a response to the Russians. It was this impasse that was making it difficult to answer Jonathan's well-intentioned questions. She wondered privately, *what would happen if she didn't pay?*

When they called the first time, she heard them better than she had let on. Between real fear and feigned fright, she was trying to buy time from them. She tried to convince them she couldn't understand them, much less respond, hoping they would call back. Before they hung up they gave her a clear message. *Do not call the authorities,* they had said. *Do so and he will die,* they said. The second time they called, they gave her another clear message. It was a demand. They wanted one million U.S. dollars in cash, delivered by a courier in Moscow. Carol knew she could raise the money. It would take a few days, but she could do it. She also knew it would practically drain their retirement investments. And she wasn't sure she wanted Carter back at all, much less with both of them broke and starting over financially.

Besides, she didn't even know how to begin such a transaction. There was so much to consider. Would she fly the cash overseas? She didn't think that was possible, or even legal, in amounts that large. Would she have to set up a wire transfer? Were the Russian banks trustworthy? Would her bankers ask questions? What would their investment planner think? Who would be her courier? How does one hire such a person? Would they even return Carter? Was he already dead? Did she care?

Right now Carol had more questions than answers. But one thing was certain, it was definitely Carter crying and screaming on the other end of the line. She would recognize that whiny voice anywhere. She decided to hold off telling that to Jonathan. Being certain about that would force her to make a decision right away, a decision about Carter and a decision about Jonathan.

Carol Winston needed more time to think it through. She wasn't going to respond to Jonathan just yet. And no way in hell was she going to respond to the Russians.

■ ■ ■ ■ ■

Fedor was proud of his rank in the Bratva, or the *Brotherhood*, as the Russian Mafia was commonly known. His job was to generate money upwards to Sergei Miloradov, his *Pakhan,* through various criminal activities. Given the emerging strength of the mafia and its place in the country's economy, nearly any activity he engaged in was foolproof and protected. There would be no interference or investigation by the police.

Fedor's specialties were kidnapping for ransom and extortion. His people were good at it and generated large sums of untraceable cash. The victims were usually western businessmen or their families who made easy targets. After a few months in Russia the targets became lax. They stopped being vigilant or worrying about being tailed. Truth was, they were followed from the day they arrived. The businessmen also got comfortable working with their Russian counterparts day in and day out, not realizing that their partners had their habits and movements under surveillance.

Fedor's only problems usually revolved around keeping his subordinate members under control until the ransom was paid. Each of those thugs was trying to become a *Vor* 'made member.' And killing the victims was seen, at least at their low level, as proving their prowess and loyalty to the family. There was competition to kill, and each *shestyorka* wanted to prove he was capable of a more horrendous murder than the next guy. *Yes*, Fedor thought, *being a manager of people was not as easy as some made it out to be*.

And so it was a bit difficult with this latest one, Carter Winston. This arrogant American had really pissed off his men by trying to outsmart them. He was trying to reason his way out of paying and of being harmed. He came across as someone trying to show he was more intelligent than the boys and they resented it. Winston was playing a dangerous game with risk-takers who had nothing to lose. They enjoyed beating him. It had become a game of beating him to unconsciousness and then letting him recover enough to beat him again without killing him.

15

But it was getting out of hand. Winston was not a physically strong man. After only two days, he was showing signs of emotional frailty as well. He was likely to die too soon if Fedor allowed the beatings to go on at the current pace. And what was wrong with the wife? Why was she not paying or even taking their calls? He would have to make a decision quickly. Winston had not reported to work in two days and for sure he would be reported missing by now. On the other hand, the local police had not reported to Fedor that a complaint had been filed about Winston's absence. Yes, this one was different. He assembled his men and addressed them, his *moi mal chiki*.

"Boys, I know you are having fun with this American. But this is about money, always the money. And this is not my money. It belongs to Sergei." He paused for effect. Sergei Miloradov was the leader of the largest crime syndicate in Russia. "And if your fun goes too far, if he dies before I get paid, that would not be such a good thing. So I warn you in good faith. The punishment for killing off my asset will be extreme. Do you understand?"

They nodded without saying a word. "So give him a rest. Give him some water and keep him alive. If he can eat, give him soup. I want him to at least appear to be healthy for the next talks with his wife. If she does not pay next time, we try another approach. We talk to the company, not the wife. I cannot wait for her to make up her mind. Bring him to me tonight around six. I have things to do now." And with that Fedor waived them out of his warehouse office.

16

As the men exited, Fedor called out, "Grigor, stay with me."

The two of them had shared a cell in *Vladimirski Central*, 'Vladimir Prison.' The penitentiary, about one hundred miles northeast of central Moscow, housed dangerous criminals serving a minimum of ten years. With the dissolution of the Soviet Union, Sergei Miloradov arranged for their sentences for *military crimes* to be commuted. As soon as they were released, Sergei recruited them into the higher ranks of the Bratva. Sergei had been a ranking officer in the Eighth Guards Army Group in historic Naumburg, Germany. There Fedor and Grigor made their mark with Sergei as smugglers of art, antiquities, precious metals and chemical drugs. After their military arrest for smuggling, they served three of their ten-year sentences, until freed into Sergei's custody.

"Grigor, we have to move quickly. I fear that Winston will die soon. Before we lose him, we must convince the wife to pay. First we must convince her we have him and he is alive. Tonight you will bring him here to my office. I want you to video record his proof of life and how serious my intent is to be paid. Is that clear? Have him hold today's newspaper to the camera and make sure it shows today's date. Record what we will do if she does not pay right away. And Grigor, make sure whatever you do, that he does not die. That would not be good. Then have Vaclav put the video cassette in the Diplomatic Pouch to the United States. It must reach the wife tomorrow. Understood?" Fedor was making direct eye contact with his most trusted lieutenant. It probably wasn't necessary with Grigor, but Fedor wanted to make sure that Grigor understood the consequences if it went wrong.

"Yes, Fedor. I understand. Do you want to see a copy of the video before we send it?" Grigor asked.

"Of course. What would be the fun of not witnessing it? But be sure to have your boys clean up any mess they make." With that Fedor nodded Grigor out of the office.

Fedor had a meeting coming up with another member of his team about another American manager. This one was foolish enough to bring his lovely wife and pretty young daughter to live here in Mother Russia.

■ ■ ■ ■ ■

Carol Winston had quickly made up her mind. When the first call came in, her routine abruptly changed. She was no longer meeting Jonathan for their lunchtime quickie before he headed back to his office. Their liaisons had become fraught with worry and concern over taking the appropriate action. Jonathan was as solid a friend as she could have hoped for and Carol did not want to come across to him as cold and conniving. She felt that would scare him off while she really needed him.

Her plan had taken shape. She would stall and delay the kidnappers, making it seem to Jonathan that she was struggling to find the proper thing to do. She would delay telling the police or the FBI about the kidnapping and would wait a day or two to report it to the company, if they did not call her first. Given the beating she heard them giving to

Carter, she knew they were serious and she knew he would not last very long under those circumstances.

Her plan was simple. They were threatening Carter with death if she did not pay. It wasn't like she wasn't going to pay. At least that is what she wanted Jonathan and the authorities to believe. It was just that she wasn't planning to pay on time. If all went according to plan, her problem with Carter would solve itself. Jonathan would see her as a poor martyred wife who would need plenty of consoling.

Time was her friend.

CHAPTER TWO

I WALKED CASUALLY DOWN THE corridor that joined our company fitness center to the corporate wing. My mind was already processing my calendar for the day and it looked like it was going to be a light one. My written report, covering my trip to Germany last month, had been rewritten a half dozen times in response to constant questions from the General Counsel's office. Some of those answers were never going to end up in a report. My boss had been verbally briefed and he was satisfied. The less I put in writing, the better for both of us.

I enjoyed getting in about five in the morning, before the crowds arrived at the gym. It only took about forty-five minutes to cover the thirty-five miles of my commute. I could get in a good workout, take my shower, and be dressed and in the cafeteria just about the time they began serving breakfast. If I waited any longer to head out in the morning, the commute was two hours or more in New Jersey traffic.

My office was on the ground floor in the northwest corner of the administrative headquarters building on the campus. It was an expansive setting and would have been desirable to any executive, except it was too far from the CEO's office. There was a pecking order that suggested the closer you were to the sun, the higher your rank. I guess most of the hot shots hadn't read about Icarus.

There was a hedonistic side of me that reveled in the spacious paneled office with its tall walls and floor-to-ceiling windows. The glass panes were coated with a metal reflectorized glaze that looked mirrored from the outside. In reality, the skin was an acoustically protective screen that prevented electronic eavesdropping from the outside. But I spent very little time in my office. Mostly I used it for entertaining outsiders, either security contractors or government investigators of one sort or another.

I spent most of my time in meetings or on airplanes bound for destinations in the States or in foreign countries. As the global head of security for a Fortune Fifty company with three divisions, travel had become an increasingly regular part of my routine and a growing part of my job duties.

I was the corporate "problem solver". And the problems always involved some type of ethics violation or criminal malfeasance committed by our employees, or against them or the company. I had become a guy who was constantly on the go. It was starting to wear on my home life and the stress on my body was mounting. I was as equally involved in responding to crises occurring in real time as I was in responding to issues that had already occurred. In any case, my job was to *fix* things.

Although most of what I did was considered confidential, word of my successes leaked out. As more of our managers around the world heard about my *escapades*, as they were dubbed, they began calling on me in greater numbers to help solve their security troubles. I only employed a small staff of investigators, but spent a multi-million dollar budget on a raft of outside consultants, fully capable of helping me anywhere in the world. And they too were always busy.

Depending on the problem, I could beckon a surveillance crew in Germany, a handwriting analyst in London, or a data forensic investigator in China. They represented a significant force projection anywhere in the world. But limited staff didn't slow the requests from group presidents around the globe. They wanted me to be on site personally, to provide the same skills I brought to bear on other seemingly insurmountable problems.

It wasn't that the company was ethically void. It was just that with over one hundred thousand employees there were bound to be some bad apples and we, Transeget Industries, did business in some places conducive to criminal behavior.

Then there was the one-off espionage case that came up nearly every month, as a competitor or foreign government tried to gain unauthorized access to company secrets. There was a lot on my plate and the servings kept growing.

My good friend, who is also the company chief medical officer, had prescribed regular exercise to relieve the stress and to build up my resistance to physical and psychological fatigue. So a year ago I joined the company fitness program and was working out daily with a cardiac fitness coach in the executive gym. I was his first client of the day. I was also working out on alternate days with a strength conditioning and a Tae Kwan Do coach. I guess I had rebuilt my rough form from years ago, and I was secretly feeding my ego with that knowledge. In my late thirties, I was as fit as when I was a cop in my twenties. I smiled in satisfaction. I was fit. I felt it and looked it. And working out at five o'clock each morning seemed to fit my lifestyle just fine.

"Michael!" A voice called out to me from behind. I recognized it without turning around.

I stopped and looked over my shoulder. "Hi Marianne, what's up?"

Marianne Callucci was the executive administrative assistant to the Chief Executive Officer of Transeget Industries. There were executive vice presidents making ten times her salary, but none was more powerful. The fact that Marianne was walking the halls looking for me before seven o'clock in the morning told me that something was in the works.

"Barry wants to see you right away, in his private office." It didn't surprise me that my boss was already at work. He was over sixty years old, seemed to work twenty-four hours a day and never looked tired. Barry Brinton was one of the most respected businessmen in the world. He had singlehandedly taken this sixty billion dollar company and turned it from a marginal performer to a winner. Our stock price soared.

His group presidents lived in a mixture of loyalty, fear and awe of him. He was a corporate ass-kicker and a Wall Street favorite. When Barry Brinton talked, investors around the world listened for clues about where to place their money or when to remove it. He had singlehandedly and forcefully managed a stock-split and brought TI's price back up to its original position in one year.

Brinton had no time for small talk and usually had minions to handle just about anything that came up. Asking me to join him in his private office had me a bit curious because Brinton had another, more public office where he met with just about everyone. True to his status as a corporate magnate, that office was tastefully decorated to establish his role as an executive who ranked in the top layer of his peers around the world. But his most private conversations were in an office whose security I had personally overseen, including the soundproofing of the room at the level of *Sensitive Compartmented Information Facility*, according to U.S. government standards. A *SCIF*, as it was called, was rarely seen at corporate executive levels. Although Brinton was big on corporate privacy, a SCIF was a significant investment and went a bit farther than one had to go to protect private company information.

TI was publicly known as a government contractor and often participated voluntarily in "special projects" or "requests for assistance", as some agencies referred to them. Although a SCIF wasn't required, that's what he wanted, so that's what I gave him.

"Private office Marianne? What I am walking into?" I asked.

"Sorry, Mike. He just said to find you and get you there immediately. I guess I can tell you that he's not alone though." She turned and began walking back to the executive wing.

While she did not have me by the elbow, she might just as well have grabbed me. She was very self-confident and had earned the right to be. I liked working with her. Although, she was the ultimate professional and totally committed to her boss, she favored me with tidbits of information to make my life a bit easier with Brinton. Trusting that level of confidence, I pressed on as we walked.

"Who's there Marianne? Anybody I should be aware of?"

"I think you may know at least one of them Mike, but they are not *ours*." I knew she meant they were outsiders, neither board members, corporate executives or other employees. The suspense of a meeting with outsiders in Brinton's secure office was intoxicating to me. It was the kind of thing that made this job so exciting. I couldn't wait to get up there.

As we got on the private elevator to the top floor I asked, "Do you think you could have someone rustle up a bite for me to eat? I'm famished and was on my way to the dining room when you caught me." I was very careful not to presume that Marianne's job description included schlepping coffee for anyone, including Brinton.

"I've already had someone see to that. There should be a warm breakfast for you all when you get there," she replied. I felt a bit foolish. I should have known. Marianne would have already anticipated and provided for that, just like she managed all of Brinton's business, personal and social calendar requirements. It didn't matter who you were, you couldn't get to see the boss without approval from Marianne.

The elevator door opened quietly and Bill Jennings nodded to us. The plain clothed executive protection agent had seen us approach on the computer screen that monitored the camera in the executive elevator. Jennings was a former United States Secret Service agent that I had hired from active service. He had been in the field, serving on a protection detail for the wife of a former vice president, and he was an alternate instructor on advanced executive protection techniques at the Service's academy in Georgia. A friend of mine in the FBI had recommended Jennings based on personal experiences when the two agencies actually played nice together.

"Mr. Christian. Good to see you sir. Mr. Brinton is waiting for you and asked that you go right in." He swiped an electronic ID card in front of the sensor, pressed his personal five-digit code into the touchpad and opened the door to Brinton's office. He stepped part way inside and quietly stated, "Mr. Christian is here sir," and then he stepped aside. I entered and the door closed behind me with a solid but quiet thud and the snap of a heavy-duty lock. An electronic deadbolt imbedded two and a half inches into a steel frame, and a magnet capable of withstanding nine hundred pounds of force sealed the door shut along the top doorframe.

■ ■ ■ ■ ■

Brinton's private office also served as his safe hiding room. It wasn't a secret space but with other security embellishments, it was virtually penetration proof. There was independent backup power, separate telecommunications, a satellite phone always charging and food and drink for a week. It also had its own bathroom equipped with a personal, walkthrough shower. It was a soundproofed, mini war room which suited Brinton's style just fine.

The six hundred square foot suite was neatly, but not spartanly outfitted. A Telluride executive desk with a leather writing-surface sat off to the left side of the room in front of a matching cabinet-front hutch. Paired lateral files and credenzas neatly lined the walls under Old-English countryside lithographs. A large, out-of-context Remington bronze of "Coming Through the Rye" sat on a table.

A news reporter had once called Brinton a cowboy, referring to his rough and ready style. Marianne arranged for the bronze horseback-riding cowboys to be in his office the following week, despite the advertised requirement for a significant deposit and a projected timeline of four to five weeks for a personal casting. No one but Marianne knew the final price tag on the work of art.

There was a small conference table in the room and more casual seating on several leather armchairs and a small loveseat. Persian rugs covered the black mahogany floors and not a board squeaked when I crossed the room to greet my boss.

"Mr. Brinton." I greeted my CEO formally, out of respect while in the presence of others. Brinton replied, "You can dispense with the formalities Mike. I believe you know Cam Cross."

Cameron Cross was with the Central Intelligence Agency and was a corporate liaison officer. TI was his *account*. We had met on several occasions when I was briefed into certain events. I doubted that Cross was the government official's real name. The agent rose from his seat, walked across the room and extended his hand. "Good to see you again Michael. I'd like you to meet an associate of mine, William Walters." It was all I could do to keep from chuckling out loud. *William Walters.* Whether that was his real name or not, it seemed too hokey to be real. I nodded, "Walters."

Brinton started right in. "Help yourself to some coffee or breakfast while we get you up to speed."

I stood at the breakfast bar, laid out on a credenza at the back wall, and poured myself a cup of robust smelling black coffee. I opted away from the fruit, muffins, cereal and warming chafers for now. I had been read into a few programs already and all of the briefings had been a bit intense. Having a stranger in the room led me to believe it was about to happen again. I didn't want to be distracted by eating. Walters began, quite formally and that's not usually a good sign.

"I am sure it's not necessary to remind you, but I will do so anyway, Mr. Christian. You are still sworn to secrecy under the National Security Act, the Espionage Act and CNWDI. There is no end to the term of your oath of secrecy unless we specifically and in writing advise you accordingly." He then made a notation into a notebook he was carrying, as if checking off an obligation he had fulfilled.

"Wait a minute." I interrupted. "The Critical Nuclear Weapons Design Information level applies to this conversation?" I was playing a little bit dumb because I wanted clarification before allowing Walters to just blow through the secrecy requirements. I already knew that TI was involved in the government's Plowshares initiative with Russia. Basically, the U.S. would buy Russian weapons-grade nuclear material to reduce their arsenal. TI and others held contracts to convert it into energy grade uranium and sell it back to Russia and other countries. They in turn would use it in their nuclear energy programs. The fact that a couple CIA agents were here talking about it was interesting, but a bit unsettling, especially given that I was being pulled into their conversation.

Walters continued, "Don't worry. We'll keep this at a high level Mr. Christian. For the moment we do not have an assignment that includes you specifically. But we may need your insight or the benefits of your observations on an upcoming trip. You are aware of the Plowshares program I presume."

I nodded but said nothing. I guessed our conversation was being covertly recorded by one or both of the agents.

"The program has hit a few snags and you may be aware of some of them. A few have even made world news. The Russians are playing fast and loose with us. The NATO contract calls for a fixed purchase price from the Russians. In turn the contract specifies a fixed sell-back price. There is a little room for profit, with a small margin of error for delays, process breakdowns and the like. But the margins are slim."

I glanced over at Brinton who raised his eyebrows as if to say *profits are not as good as I would like.*

Walters proceeded, "Recently two things have happened that put the program more at risk. One is simply a matter of economics and was predictable. The Russians have raised the selling price to the Plowshares companies and have demanded lower buy-back prices. We do not know if they are serious about the pricing as a long-term rule, or if they are using it as negotiating power for some other issue altogether.

"Regardless, the private corporations servicing the program, including yours, are being squeezed at both ends and the program is at risk. Obviously, so is national security if the Russian nuclear arsenal is not depleted under this initiative. We continue to draw down our arsenal according to our responsibilities, but the Russians are now behind schedule. Unfortunately, I can also assure you that neither our government energy agencies, nor the participants of the accord, are willing to subsidize your company for losses, even if that was a workable solution."

I saw this as another example of bad decision-making. Whether it was made to look like patriotism or not, it was either corporate greed or corporate profit-taking that got TI involved. This was business and it was always about the money. There also had to be a secret assumption that the government had too much at stake to let the partner companies go bust over the deal. They were in it because there was presumably a buck to be made and for no other reason.

And now, predictably, the deal was going sour. Dealing with the Russians was always risky as was dealing with the Agency. The Russians didn't even understand much less respect the word *partnership*. On the other hand, TI had made other business decisions that caused Brinton to shut down an operation when profitability went too far south. I knew my boss wouldn't hesitate to pull the trigger again if he felt it was necessary. I also had been involved with similar cases enough times to know I was not there to solve a profitability problem. Brinton must have already indicated he was willing to explore other solutions. He looked at Walters and said, "You want to tell him the *other* reason the program is in jeopardy, or should I?"

Walters looked from Brinton to Cross to me, then continued, "Without going into specific inventory numbers, suffice it to say we have a very accurate count of the number of warheads and other materials that should have been brought into the program. The Russian nuclear commissioner and international inspectors have identified specific components to be decommissioned and their nuclear payloads re-purposed. From their launch sites around the Former Soviet Union Countries, missiles are shipped to and then disassembled at only three points in Russia. The warheads are removed, and the payloads are securely repackaged and crated for shipment to the States. The entire process is under intense international monitoring during disassembly, containerization and transport.

"Less known, but of equal concern are the *suitcase* bombs. You may have heard them referred to as *dirty* bombs. But these are also nuclear weapons and there are about forty of them covered in our agreement. We have been reprocessing them in accord with a sub-rosa clause in a separate and secret codicil to the contract. This one is specifically between the Russian government and ours."

I had heard of suitcase bombs. They were the topic of much official and unofficial speculation as to whether they really existed. This was the first time I felt they were real. I looked at Brinton. I thought I was privy to most of the government contract terms, especially where there was a high-risk security requirement. Brinton looked away as if to say, *this is not the time or place for me to explain to you why you weren't included.*

Walters went on, "But when those shipments arrived at our reprocessing plants, the inventory count was short. Initially the Russians denied that they were shorting the sale and they refused to acknowledge the next obvious conclusion."

"And what's that?" I asked.

Walters looked at Cross then continued, "Somewhere out there, low-grade, weaponized uranium is floating around unaccounted for, in the form of nuclear bombs small enough to fit in a suitcase." He seemed to pause for effect but needn't have bothered. The silence in the room grew deeper and if it was possible, the air seemed to become heavier. Almost imperceptibly, Brinton stirred in his seat. I thought I should be relieved to know that nuclear missiles weren't missing. But the idea that someone could carry a nuclear bomb around in a suitcase was deeply disturbing. The fact that we were dealing with the Russians made it even more so.

Walters continued, "As you can imagine, our government needs to make the world aware the program is at risk, but we cannot be talking in public about missing nuclear weapons, even if they *are* low yield."

I interrupted, "What do you consider low yield?" Walters replied as if it were a mere statistic, "Only about a kiloton."

He moved on as if a thousand tons of explosive force was nothing. "We need to do all we can to find out where those suitcases are and bring them back into the program. An added bonus would be to interdict those persons involved as well."

When it came to the agency, *interdicting someone* could mean anything at all. I could see where this was going and didn't like it one bit. "And what does this have to do with us," I asked, "other than our profits are being reduced? This seems to be an intelligence community problem or diplomatic or military issue. And if I may be so blunt, what does this have to do with me? Why am I being read into this level of the program?"

I looked over at Brinton who was deliberately not returning my glance. Walters and Cross were also looking at Brinton who stood and went to the coffee setup. Pouring himself a cup of the rich black brew, he spoke quietly.

"I'll be sending you over to Moscow, Mike. We have another problem that was just brought to my attention, a serious internal issue. While there, I presume you will likely use your access to Russian resources, entirely off the record, to help you solve that problem. I am guessing these will be people you trust and have worked with in the past. We have more than our Plowshares operations at risk here. Some of our people have gotten involved with the Russian mafia, it seems."

Cam Cross took over from there. "And while you are solving that problem, we would like you to use your relationships and connections and see if you can learn what is going on with the nuclear program. You may get only rumor, hearsay, innuendo, denial or even false leads. But we need everything you can get. In fact, some of the rumors may have their basis in fact.

"We have our own people pulling in and analyzing every lead and contact they have, but we also want to use less obvious avenues. We want to include every civilian resource at our disposal. And that is where you come in. We'll leave the information gathering methods up to you. You will not be working for us. This is strictly a back-channel initiative, more of an informal request for assistance. You'll be working as an employee of TI solving an internal matter. But we need you to dig as far as you can without exposing your involvement with us. Make it purely a financial-loss issue. We know you'll be conducting a business investigation. But if you happen to run across any information of value, and if you think you can share it, we would appreciate it."

Walters interjected, "And Mr. Christian, as you would expect, if something should go wrong, anything, you are entirely on your own and can expect no support from the Agency or the United States government. We will deny this conversation ever took place and deny you work in conjunction with us. Understood?"

I believed him. Not only was there no sound leaving this room. There was no recorded evidence of the conversation ever taking place, except in the hands of the agency itself. And I was sure Jennings would never say a word about who came to visit Brinton, if he even knew.

I looked again at Brinton, who this time was looking me straight in the eye.

The silver-haired CEO looked almost grandfatherly as he said, "Mike, you can certainly say *No*. You can go over, solve our other problem, come straight home and there will be no corporate repercussions. Of course, we stand to lose millions if we cannot get the program on track or establish a business case for extracting ourselves from Plowshares. I would be grateful if you could help with that any way you and your people can. But the call is yours."

In front of the Agency guys, Brinton practically told me, *you don't have to do this*. And at the same time, he made it solely my decision if I chose to go ahead with it. He had deftly established complete deniability if the shit hit the fan. I was screwed and knew it. Everyone in the room knew it. But this was the price I paid for playing the game at this level.

As Walters and Cross stood and handshakes were passed around, Cross whispered silently to me, "Sorry about this Michael. I know this isn't as clean as you like it when we ask for assistance. But we are pulling out all the stops. I am afraid I spoke too highly of you based on other things you have done. When the FBI got the tip on your problem in Moscow, they notified us and here we are."

There it was again. It seemed everyone knew but me. "What is the problem in Moscow? What do you know about it Cam?"

Cross backed off. "I'll leave that for you and Mr. Brinton." With that, he and Walters left.

■ ■ ■ ■ ■

Brinton and I waited for the big door to close securely. I turned to Brinton, but before I could speak, he said, "I know you must have many questions, but first let's refill our coffees. This is going to take a while."

I filled his cup and this time I grabbed a banana nut muffin and filled a small bowl with yogurt, berries and nuts. I had no idea where they came from, but every item seemed like it had been handpicked, washed and chilled to perfection that morning.

I sat leaning forward at the coffee table opposite Brinton who said, "I am going to keep this simple, Mike. You can fill in the details later with our internal audit guys. They have been looking into one of our ventures in Russia. This one is under the umbrella of our parts distribution division. Seems there is an unexplained shortage in that business. There should be no reason for losses of this nature. The venture was well thought out before we engaged as to market, sales, distribution and operations. Every detail suggested we should be very profitable there, even in the startup phase."

I had heard that litany of bad rationale before. Missing from every financial risk assessment was a map of the security risk and its associated costs. Although I was well equipped to elaborate on contemporary geopolitical security risk, I was not welcome to the table of finance guys and lawyers doing the assessment. They only called after something serious, that could have been predicted if only they asked, went all to hell. "But what does that have to do with security, Barry?" I asked.

Brinton replied, "On its face, it would seem like there was nothing for you to look at. Nothing that is until we got the call from the FBI."

"FBI in Russia?" I knew there were limits of their authority. The FBI was primarily a domestic law enforcement agency, but they did get around, especially when crimes had been committed involving Americans or their companies, or regarding U.S. government contracts abroad, whether they were victims or perpetrators. "Who is the Special Agent?" I asked.

"No one I knew offhand," Brinton replied. "But I didn't speak to the Russian Field Office agent. I was contacted by Jerry Maniaci, the Newark SAC."

I knew the Special Agent in Charge of the Newark Office very well. While a Detroit Police Sergeant, I had been the Liaison Officer between the Wayne County Organized Crime Task Force and the Detroit Office of the FBI Organized Crime Unit, as well as the liaison to the prosecuting attorney's office on the U.S. Strike Force.

I had been working undercover when, during an FBI surveillance being run by Maniaci, they discovered me in the regular presence of a Detroit mobster. It finally came to light that I was an on-duty officer at the Task Force and had made deep inroads into the organized crime structure in Detroit. Maniaci agreed to merge resources with the Task Force to bring the case to a good conclusion. That high visibility investigation resulted not only in promotions for both of us, but also in a long-lasting relationship of deep trust. It was only the coincidence of job changes and transfers that brought Maniaci and me together again in New Jersey.

We also worked together to trace the actions of one of the nineteen ninety-three World Trade Center bombers. That guy ordered the chemicals used in the bomb that went into the white van they parked in the basement at the World Trade Center. I covertly assisted the Bureau with mapping the chemical ordering and delivery processes and determined how the chemicals were diverted from a vendor of theirs. And the bond deepened. That was why I found it odd that Maniaci had not contacted me directly and had gone to Brinton instead.

"Before you ask, I should let you know that he called for you while you were still in Germany. Whatever he said to Joanne caused her to forward the call my office. Good thing she did." Brinton said.

Joanne was my admin manager. She was a damn good one and I valued her decisions, but I was surprised that she didn't mention to me that Maniaci had called while I was out. I decided it was not worth mentioning to her. If she didn't see fit to let me know, there would be a good reason anyway. I'd mention to her that I had met with some Feds and see what she had to say.

"Maniaci was contacted by the Russian field office. It seems one of our employees may have got tangled up with the Russian mafia." I looked up from my coffee at that, waiting for more. Brinton continued. "Actually, our internal audit identified that he has been paying money out of our

39

corporate accounts to an unknown vendor for consulting services. Our manager, Alex Weiner, insisted to our audit team that the business transactions were legitimate. The Feds were monitoring some Russian accounts and saw the money moving into them in equal amounts as to what our guy was depositing. They surmised he was paying off the mob for some reason, or he was complicit in some larger scheme. We doubt it. Weiner seems like a straight up guy, but you never know."

I made a mental note to background check our manager, Weiner.

"We're concerned perhaps he's making illegal facilitating payments in violation of the Foreign Corrupt Practices Act. That would put the business at risk. And frankly, my name is at the top on the board of director's ethics committee. It's my hide at risk if Weiner is violating the FCPA. I need you to go find out what the hell is going on. All the details I have are in the internal audit report. And that's why you will be going to Russia immediately. As a favor to us, the Bureau is staying out of it until you get there. It's a corporate crime and we will deal with it as an internal issue until we are ready to involve the Feds. They are fine with that, given that all their resources are apparently dedicated to finding the nukes. I expect you to find out what is going on with our guy. I want you to put a stop to it. I want to make sure that our employee and his family are safe too. Basically Mike, I want you to find out what is going on over there and to *fix this*." Brinton paused and waited for my reaction. The most he got was a head nod. Then he shifted gears.

"Given the intelligence cross-connect between the Bureau and the Agency on the Plowshares thing and our past experiences with them, I expect they figured we were trustworthy enough to be read into their problem. And frankly, I think the agency was selfish enough to think that our financial concerns would goad us into cooperating with their intelligence gathering requirements. So yes, go fix the mafia thing, if that's the issue. And if you have a chance, inquire about those goddamn missing suitcases. I don't need to know the details of who you talk with or how you come by any information. But listen to me Michael, I do not want you to put yourself in danger with the Russian government or the mafia. And I especially do not want you to put our business name at risk. Do you understand me?"

I understood all right. In essence, Brinton was laying out the rules of engagement for this assignment. Business comes first. Agency needs come second. But I knew from past experience that often those needs overlapped. And when I was in the field, the decisions became mine. If my call went right, I could be a hero. If it went wrong, I would definitely be the goat. I would be out on a limb all by myself. I also knew that Brinton played in the very big leagues and had a global reputation to protect. I had a sense that all the big CEOs ran backroom ventures like this in cooperation with the government. But I knew Brinton could not have his name associated with anything I said or did on this matter.

"Got it." I said. "Where do I go for the details on our guy?"

"See Marianne on your way out. She has a file from Internal Audit that identifies the financial discrepancies and the cash withdrawals from our accounts. They are significant. She will also give you our file on Alexander Weiner, our manager in charge over there. Then give your FBI friend, Maniaci, a call. I'm sure he will read you in on more details than he gave me. Then I want you to leave immediately. And Mike, no notes about today's meeting, right?"

I knew that Brinton would never settle for a "smoking gun" about working with the Agency. "Understood," I replied and headed for the door.

"And Mike, one more thing. When you're explaining to Alice why you are leaving so quickly on your trip, let's leave out the more salient details. Okay?"

"I always do, Barry. And she is wise enough not to press me for information." I knew that this was not about sheltering my wife from fear and anxiety. It was all about Brinton making sure there were no unnecessary witnesses to conversations better left unheard. Besides, I would never share classified information, even with Alice.

■ ■ ■ ■ ■

I left Brinton alone in his office and walked past Jennings, nodding as I went. Although I had hired Bill Jennings, and he still worked for me, he was now a dedicated Brinton soldier, as he should be. He returned the nod as I headed across the short hallway to Marianne's office. Her door was open but I knocked anyway before stepping inside. She looked up and reached across to the corner of her desk. "This is for you," she said.

I wondered just how much she really knew about the trouble in Moscow. I guessed she knew just enough to make her efficient for Brinton, but not much more. "You will find the internal audit report in here, as well as a personnel file on Alexander Weiner and his family. We moved them over to Moscow less than a year ago."

I took the folder from Marianne, thanked her and headed for the door. From the heft of it, I knew I had a lot of reading ahead of me. Marianne stopped me. "Mike, I've met Alex a few times in meetings with Barry. He is a sincere and hard working guy and loves his family. He's right for the assignment but may be a bit naïve. And from what you've told us about the conditions in Moscow, he may be in over his head. I also know Rachel Weiner. She is a good woman and Sarah is an adorable little girl. Please make them safe."

I nodded. There wasn't much I could say. I preferred cases where I was dealing with suspects and thugs. Those lines were pretty clear and I could remain coldly objective. But when I was dealing with victims, it got tougher. And when kids were at risk, I felt an added sense of responsibility and urgency. "I'll do all I can Marianne." Then I turned and walked out – with purpose.

I decided not to open the envelope in the elevator and just held it by my side as if it was merely another file. I knew, given the briefings I had just gone through, that it was better if no one had an inkling of just what was at stake, even if it was just an inference from a recorded elevator camera.

Exiting the elevator, I walked the two hundred feet of carpeted hallway back to my office to find Joanne waiting for me.

"Marianne called and said you were on your way back." She said.

I wondered just how fast the informal network passed along information, or gossip, for that matter. She continued, "I need a few minutes with you before you start something new. Marianne suggested I clear your morning calendar, so that's done. I won't be but five minutes unless you have more for me."

These ladies run my life, I mused to myself. Probably just as well. It was better left to them anyway, given my haste to change some things on my own and forgetting to change others, I thought.

"Sure, come on in." I replied as she walked into my office.

Joanne was the single mother of two teen children. She had been single quite a while and seemed comfortable with her circumstances. She wasn't on the make or searching for a man "to complete her life." She was an attractive woman with a good head on her shoulders, active with her lady friends and dedicated to her children. And she was smart, very smart.

Because she had been around a while, she was also connected to just about every executive's administrative assistant in the company, both at headquarters and in most of the branch offices around the world. Her standing with them was impeccable which made her invaluable. When I first came over to the company, she had been recently divorced and was relegated to a clerical position in the security department, trying to make ends meet in a very high rent part of the country.

I immediately saw her potential and promoted her two levels to be my administrative assistant. Her knowledge of the inner workings of the company and her relationships with the more powerful admins in the company, including Marianne, provided just the edge I needed to keep me ahead of the game. Joanne also proved to be trustworthy, a quality that I valued above many others. She could keep a confidence or know just how much was okay to share to get me the resources I needed, like access to the corporate air fleet, or booking at the last minute on international flights.

And Joanne was a multi-tasker, capable of handling complex assignments without ever looking fatigued or overworked. I promoted her again recently, making her my administrative manager and putting her in the salaried ranks with annual performance benefits. This improved her lifestyle and gave her girls advantages they may never have had. I occasionally brought back token gifts for her and the girls when I returned from my travels. Not only was she trustworthy, she was also very loyal.

Joanne closed the door behind her and as she turned and walked toward me, I noticed she was carrying a manila envelope with no apparent markings on it. *It must be the day for unmarked envelopes*, I thought.

She sat across from me with the packet held gingerly on her lap. Her eye contact told me she was deliberately delaying giving me the envelope. "Jerry Maniaci stopped by to see you yesterday afternoon just before closing. When I told him you weren't due until this morning, he explained that he was trying to set up a meeting with you and Mr. Brinton and a couple of *boys from across the street.*" I knew that was Fed-speak for the Agency, even though they were located in Langley, Virginia and the Bureau was in DC.

She continued, "I suggested I could reach out to you and clear your calendar for last night if necessary. He said first thing this morning was fine, but he would not be attending the meeting. He then gave me this envelope and said to wait until you got back from your meeting this morning to give it to you."

Several thoughts were speeding through my mind at this point. Jerry had not waited to meet personally with me. Then he gave an envelope to Joanne to be delivered after the meeting. Jerry knew the meeting was with Cross and Walters but still chose not to attend, or maybe he wasn't invited. It wouldn't be the first time an FBI agent provided key information or support to the CIA and was then cut out of any further involvement. But the Bureau also played the same game with other agencies and especially with civilians.

These twists and turns did not surprise me anymore. I took them in stride and let them unfold in their own time. I also guessed that Maniaci didn't want Joanne to know who from the agency was going to be at the meeting. But Joanne held a Top-Secret clearance, as did Marianne, who did know who was at the meeting. Getting this all cleared up would have to wait until I could talk personally with Jerry and that was going to be my first outside call of the day.

Joanne continued while I was processing my thoughts. "You know I would normally give you a heads-up on these things. But Jerry specifically asked me not to tell you until he had a chance to talk with Marianne. That was the last I heard from him before I went home last night. So, when Marianne called me this morning to let me know you were already in Brinton's private office, it was the first time I knew the meeting had been scheduled. I asked her to call me when you got out of it. I wanted to be sure you didn't jump on a plane before coming back here to get this."

With that, Joanne placed the envelope on my desk and slid it over to me, pushing it only with the tips of her fingernails, as if she didn't want to have her prints on the envelope. But it was already too late for that.

"So, what's in the envelope Joanne? And why all the cloak and dagger?"

Joanne looked a bit crestfallen. "I don't really know what is going on Mike and I have no clue what is in the envelope. You know I would tell you if I did."

"Don't take this the wrong way Joanne. I know you'd tell me. It just seems a bit odd. Jerry has my home number and my mobile number. He could just as well have called me. I am just trying to figure this out. I'll call him in a bit." I tried to reassure her.

Then I continued, "I am not sure of the departure times, but see if you can book me a first-class seat, non-stop through to Sheremetyevo International Airport outside Moscow, but not leaving until after seven this evening. Get me a couple time options through midnight. If nothing works, see if we can get a corporate flight on the Gulfstream over there.

47

If necessary clear that through Marianne rather than going straight through the aviation unit but check on all the other options first. Only pull that favor if we have no other choices. Leave the return dates open."

I knew that using a corporate jet to fly to Moscow would be an expensive venture, but it would certainly be faster, much more comfortable and left no easily discoverable public paper trail. "My passport is good so no worries there but have Marianne check to see if we can fast track a Russian visa for me with a generic business case. My old visa to Russia may still be good, but I am running out of trip days and returns on it. I also want you to book me a room at the Metropol in downtown Moscow. Get me on the second floor if you can, but no higher than the fourth. I don't want to be a mistaken victim of a stray bullet over there. I especially do not want to stay at the Novotel at the airport. That place is a dive. Get me at least two weeks in town. It is easier to extend my stay if they see me as a long-term guest and I can always cancel early if I finish in less time."

Joanne cocked her head to the side with her eyebrows raised at the reference to the Metropol. She knew it was a five-star hotel and way above the level of normal corporate lodging for business trips, even for me. The Novotel, dive or not, was the recommended lodging for routine company travel to Moscow. She smiled inwardly as she recalled me telling her the story of being at the Novotel with Russian agents sitting in a cubby space between every two occupied rooms, watching and listening to the activities of the occupants. I could hear my watchers talking and moving their chairs about as they *secretly* spied on me.

Finally, I had waved at the stippled wall and said out loud *Spakoynoy nochi* 'good night.' Shortly I heard the shuffling of chairs and the middle door open and close shut. It was quiet in the listening room after that.

Joanne would get me the room at the Metropol, no matter what strings needed pulling. It wouldn't be the first time I ignored the travel rules. The accounting department no longer bothered to forward the expense account overages to my boss, because Brinton always approved them.

I continued, "Besides, if I stayed out there, I'd have to have a different driver pick me up each morning and navigate that miserable Russian traffic, every day and night at rush hour, to get me around from the airport. I'd lose hours of productivity during that ride. It is like a demolition derby." Joanne knew that I was just grousing out loud. I would stay at the Metropol, as planned, and I would have a private driver and car just as I always had whenever I asked.

I felt the need to explain again, "I don't use the taxi service in Moscow because they're all corrupt and I don't particularly trust the Russian fleet drivers at the airport curbs. So use the same agency as last time I was there. And see if Sasha is still there. He may be willing to take me around. Hopefully his driving and language skills have improved."

Joanne knew that I was making a solid business case for my upgrades in the unlikely event corporate travel challenged my accommodations going out or my expenses upon my return. "And one more thing." I continued. "Keep corporate travel out of this as long as you can. I want you to make the inquiries directly yourself please. And arrange to get me a cash advance of about five thousand dollars in large bills, hundreds. You might want to do that first. Let's have those here in the office after lunch. And find out what the current exchange rate is for the ruble, on the dollar." Russian rubles were nearly worthless as interest rates there fell regularly, and most Russians did not trust their own currency. Our dollars spent very easily, but exchange rates were sharply negotiated, even by street vendors.

The Russian people were propagandized into believing that their unemployment rate and the falling value of the ruble were directly the fault of the United States and their monetary policy, not the fault of the Russian government or their economy. The average Russian hated the U.S. dollar but coveted it. "Have someone run out and get me five cartons of Marlboros and a dozen Hershey chocolate bars, big ones. See if the public relations folks can spare a couple dozen fountain pens, the good ones, with our corporate logos on them, and a dozen of our Zippo lighters with the red TI logo."

I recalled that Levi blue jeans were also a black-market currency that could be given as gifts to my driver, the translator and others, without having to spend cash. I decided I did not want to lug jeans around in another bag on this trip. I paused as I thought what else Joanne could be doing for me before I cut her loose. She didn't add anything, so I closed. "OK. I think that will do it for now." I picked the envelope off the desk and Joanne left me alone.

I had to read through the internal auditor's notes, and I needed to read Maniaci's notes to reduce the need to ask him questions that he already answered. So I poured myself a cup of coffee from the fresh pot and got started.

■ ■ ■ ■ ■

The first item in the envelope was a redacted copy of a "For Official Use Only" telex coversheet from the Russian Field office to the New Jersey Special Agent in Charge, Maniaci.

FOUO
To: Maniaci, Newark, NJ SAC
From: [XXXX], LEGAT Moscow Field Office
Re: Possible Intelligence Breach – Plowshares Company

The second page was also redacted.

FOUO
U.S. Company - Transeget Industries (TI) is a corporation in your jurisdiction.

TI employee and U.S. citizen, Alexander Weiner is seen on several occasions associating with [XXX] a Mafia shestyorka - street-tough.

Surveillance IDs same Bratva street operative associating with [XXX], a Bratva Avtoritet – Mafia brigadier.

Surveillance details included in attached full report. See RUSBRAT [XXX] 93-SRV -22-[XXX]

[XXX] Brigadier is known extortionist and kidnapper.

Is also known previous narcotics and arms smuggler.

Considered multi-millionaire of suspect financial resources.

Owns several business fronts, including heavy stock investments in Russian energy companies. See FOUO Financial Report RUSBRAT 93-22-[XXX].

Weiner moving cash into [XXX] Brigadier dummy business account in Panama.

Q: Weiner – Bratv – TI = Plowshares Risk?

R: Request you initiate and provide full intelligence background report on Weiner.

R: Request you initiate and provide full intelligence report on TI. Details of our request included in attached full report.

Q: Do you have cleared POC at TI? Provide contact info.

Brigadier [XXX] and his organizational chart included in attached full report.

Awaiting your returns as requested above to begin development of local action plan

[XXX], LEGAT Moscow Field Office
FOUO

Given this morning's briefing by the Agency, none of this made any sense. The Agency guys had coordinated with the Bureau before coming to the briefing meeting. They must have known about the potential intelligence risk raised by the Bureau's Field Office in Moscow. If there was a Plowshares risk, wouldn't the agency be all over this themselves? If there was a link between our guy and an arms smuggler from the Russian Mafia, both the Agency and the Bureau would be investigating this, although they may not likely be sharing investigation results. And Weiner would already have been scooped up by one or both of the agencies for questioning. At a minimum he would be under constant surveillance. Why would they allow TI to conduct its own investigation, given the risk?

I looked in the envelope. There were no attached reports. I didn't think there would be. I shook the envelope. There was one more piece of paper. It was a sticky note stuck to the inside of the envelope. I recognized the handwriting. It belonged to Jerry Maniaci, Special Agent In Charge of the Newark, New Jersey Office of the Federal Bureau of Investigation. It simply said, "Call me".

I decided to call Jerry before I finished the internal audit report. This way I had honest deniability if he asked questions I didn't feel right answering.

I swiveled my chair around to face my credenza, lifted the handset receiver to my third generation

Secure Telephone Unit, or STU III, and called Maniaci's counterpart phone number. It rang only once. I recognized Jerry's voice and said only, "Let's do a secure connection." Within only a few seconds an encrypted connection was made, scrambling the communications in such a way that only Maniaci and I could hear in the clear. A sixty-four-bit encryption algorithm was encoding each sound I made and it was decrypted on Maniaci's end. The same process worked when the Special Agent In Charge spoke. Not even the Chinese had been able to break the code.

Maniaci began apologetically, "Listen Mike, before you say anything, let me explain. I would rather have briefed you in person. But since I knew I wouldn't have time before you met with Cross and his man, I figured I better get a briefing package together for you. I'm sure Joanne told you I came by in person and didn't just courier the packet over to you. I also guessed that Brinton would have you on a plane as fast as he could, once your meeting was over. So I hope you forgive the method and consider the intent."

I was immediately appeased. "Actually Jerry, I'm fine. First of all, I didn't get a "package". It was merely the coversheet and a two-page redacted memo to you, and your sticky-note. The other thing is, I need to know what is really going on. Three different parties are sending me out on two seemingly unrelated assignments. On the one hand I have my company wanting answers to questions and a resolution to the problem of our plant manager making payments for some mafia types.

"They also want me to look into our Plowshares venture and see what I can find out relative to price fixing and missing inventory. And that appears to be the only interest of the Agency. They want me to press my sources for information on missing nuke suitcases. And I suppose your Bureau wants some kind of resolution and answers to both issues as well. Given the sense of urgency I get from both your groups, why are you guys not taking extreme measures to contain Weiner? Why are you giving us a free hand to do an internal first? OK. I'm done. Does that about sum it up?"

Jerry paused and asked, "Well aren't you the master of the *Cliff's Notes* version? Yes, that's it in a nutshell. I have a few things I want to go over with you before you go. As you must have guessed by now, when it comes to dealing with us or the other guys, there is always more than meets the eye. Can you give me about an hour of your time? How about a quick lunch? I have some things I want to go over with you so you are not heading over there in the blind. And you are right. There were only those two pieces in your envelope. I had planned on dropping off more but decided not to leave too much paper out in the clear."

I would have preferred not to lose any time eating off-property and I was anxious as hell to find out what else could have gone into that envelope but didn't make it. The cafeteria on campus was a fine place to grab a good meal. And my good friend Merritt McDuff ran the food services business for our three thousand employees like a five-star restaurant, especially in the executive dining room. But it would do neither of us any good to be seen together on-property just before a business trip to

Russia. "Sure, lunch is fine and the earlier the better. Do you have a place in mind?"

"Yeah, I know a great little deli that's been around since the forties and if we get there before the lunch crowd, we can have some time to talk quietly. We are very unlikely to be recognized there anyway. Do you know the Town Hall Delicatessen? It's on South Orange Avenue in town just down the street from the performing arts center."

I knew it. "I've heard folks talk about it, but I've never been there. To be honest with you Jerry, I'm starved. I worked out this morning and had only a snack in my meeting. So, the sooner we can get there, the better for me. I have a file from my auditing department I want to read before we meet. You have a street address?"

It was obvious Maniaci had been there before. He knew the address without looking it up. "Eighteen South Orange, right in town. What time works for you, Mike?"

I now knew the location exactly and figured there were three routes there and each was about twenty-five minutes once I got off my massive headquarters property. "See you in an hour Jerry. That should give me time to go over the file and get there. If you arrive before me, get me a large ice water to start. And thanks. I always appreciate the heads up when walking into something new. Especially if it has to do with the Russians."

We made our good-byes, I disconnected the secure encryption key to the STU, and hit my intercom button. "Joanne, hold all my calls and don't let anyone put anything on my calendar today. Put everything else out about ten days. I am running out to meet Maniaci and when I get back, hopefully you will have my travel package ready. I doubt I'll have time to get home before I head to Newark Airport." Joanne answered with a simple "Have done that and will do the rest." Then she hung up. Total efficiency.

It would have been nice to get home and personally bid my wife goodbye. But the nature of my work often called on me to leave immediately to solve a problem of high value, high risk, high visibility, or potential harm to employees. This case was all of that and I was leaving as soon as I was able. I had a "go bag" in the office and that would get me through the first several days. Anything else I needed, I could buy.

Alice would understand. I speed-dialed my home number and got my wife's lilting and happy recorded voice on the answering machine, *"We're not able to come to the phone right now, please leave a message."* Perfect – crisp, efficient, didn't reveal too much about who was home or not. Every time I heard her voice, I could see her face. I realized how lucky I was on so many levels to have Alice for a wife. I reflected briefly on my past and wondered how I deserved such good fortune. "Honey, I have to head out this afternoon on an overseas emergency." I thought to myself, all my apologies started that way. It was as if I was saying, everyone else is more important than you. I really hoped she understood, especially since I could rarely explain where I was or what I was doing. "I'll call you later, probably from the airport. I'll grab my go-bag from here but I'm thinking I could be a few days at least. Will call when I know more. Love you." And I hung up.

I cleared my head and returned to the auditor's report. There was something specific I wanted to get from it before I met with Maniaci. It was to know who the payees were on those fund transfers. I knew the Feds would already have the intelligence reports on those companies and their players and I wanted to be sure they weren't holding anything back. I also wanted the complete "book" on the mafia members the Russian office had identified, including their companies, their organization charts and their turfs. That would be a good starting point for me. If Jerry didn't come across with that info voluntarily, I was going to push for it before I left the country. They owed me at least that much. I also wanted to know why the Feds were holding off taking over the investigation. That still didn't make any sense. I had very little time left this afternoon and something told me it would be another sleepless transatlantic flight.

CHAPTER THREE

I SPOTTED JERRY MANIACI ALMOST immediately. The head of Newark's FBI office wasn't hard to find. He was one of the easiest going guys I had ever met yet he stood out in a crowd. People may not know who Maniaci was, but they couldn't help but notice him in a room. He stood about six foot two, was lean and physically fit. His dark black hair and olive skin spoke to his Italian lineage, but it was his manner of dress that set him apart. Jerry was impeccably attired. Tailored was probably the best way to describe him.

His Italian made, Egyptian cotton, bright white shirt, was personally measured for his form. The European cut collar pointed straight up to his face, as did his tie from the New York Metropolitan Museum reflecting a Renaissance armor collection on display there. His charcoal black suit, fitted in his office in Newark, was custom cut for him by Capelli Adoni's. He could have modeled for GQ. Although he was quiet, personable and unassuming, he exuded power, as befitting the head of the FBI in a state notorious for its mob strongholds and for being the home of the World Trade Center bombers. He may have looked it, but Jerry was no pretty boy. He was the real thing as a crime fighter and worked his way up the hard way, running up the numbers of mafia members he sent to prison.

I made eye contact with him, nodded and made my way to the table in the back. Jerry rose partially from his seat as we shook hands.

I noticed the glass of ice water already on the table next to a perspiring aluminum pitcher filled with more.

"You said you were pressed for time. I figured you were already mentally on a flight overseas, so I took the liberty of ordering for you." Jerry opened. "We're both having their traditional corned beef on rye. They are famous for their sloppy Joe, but..." With that Maniaci pointed from his chest to his lap with his fingers, indicating there was no way he was taking the chance of dripping tomato sauce onto his thousand dollars' worth of clothes. "I'm Sicilian and I can't talk without moving my hands. It will be bad enough with the sandwich as it is."

I noted that Maniaci referred to himself as Sicilian and not Italian. How does a guy get to be the head of the FBI in a mob-infested area when he is one hundred percent Sicilian? I was half Sicilian myself, and it posed a similar problem when I was invited to join the illustrious Wayne County Organized Crime Task Force. I knew the answer was that Maniaci had made his own bones with the Bureau by aggressively pursuing mob characters and locking up Detroit Mafia leaders in the late seventies and early eighties. Assigned to the U.S.

Strike force, he went after political corruption and mob activity at the higher levels with equal passion. It was like shooting ducks in a barrel back then.

Maniaci got us on track immediately. He leaned in and began quietly, "Let's agree that your summary is correct and on point. I have two issues of interest to you here. One is that your man is making payments to Russian bad guys. And I mean some serious bad guys, not just greasy street punks. And the question is why? Is he acting alone, or is your company up to something?"

I was about to object to the inference that my corporation was in cahoots with the mob for any reason. But Maniaci held his hand palm up and interrupted me. "Let me continue. We both know that you're not likely involved. But I need positive affirmation with proof. As far as I'm concerned, your word would be good enough. But since this incident is obviously news to you, then we both need proof."

"The other problem I have is that our friends at the Agency are worried that some weapons grade uranium is in the wrong hands or making its way here. We both want to identify who is involved, where the weapons are, recover them and interdict any further movement of them. From an intelligence and national security perspective, the Agency wants control of investigation management. From evidence recovery, investigation and prosecution perspectives, we want it."

I knew there was a formal separation of powers when it came to the two strongest investigative units in the world. Generally, the CIA was not permitted to conduct investigations or gather intelligence on our citizens or businesses in the States. The FBI was prohibited from doing the same overseas. But both organizations could find legal reasons or covert justification for blurring the lines. And both would jump at the chance to "resolve" illegal activity.

One group worked through the courts and the other settled their cases privately and sometimes with extreme prejudice. One had rules of criminal law to follow and one had practically no rules at all. Whether it was informal agreements to "work together" or one agency needing the resources of the other, it happened. Sometimes they had to play nice.

I had met with the Agency that morning for breakfast and now I was meeting with the FBI over a sandwich. But I did not know how far their mutual cooperation had gone and what they might have in mind for me.

I also noted that Maniaci had also suggested the bombs might be secretly on their way to be hidden in the U.S.

Maniaci continued. "So here is what I have for you. The Mafia guys you will be up against in Moscow are Fedor Davydov, his boss, Sergei Miloradov and a couple underlings, Grigor Koshkin and Vadim Mirski. It looks like your fellow, Weiner, is dealing with Mirski who is a direct report to Davydov. Mirski is a smart cookie and a confidant of Davydov's. Koshkin also works for Davydov, but he is considered muscle. Not very smart but by no mean stupid. He's trusted to independently carry out tough assignments."

As the information began flowing, I asked, "Should I be writing this down?" But Maniaci waved the remark away. He reached alongside his seat and revealed a thin, sealed manila envelope.

Another one, I noted. "There is a single sheet in here. Familiarize yourself with it then get rid of it." Maniaci said, then he continued.

"Fedor Davydov is not the top guy. By all accounts, Sergei Miloradov is. He is the top guy for all of Moscow and its environs, We believe he's positioning himself for the role of top boss for all of Russia. His reach is multinational even to major cities in the States. Several other mafia leaders have tried to take him down in power struggles and it didn't go well for them. Miloradov is still here and they aren't.

"Davydov, on the other hand, is a very powerful brigadier in his own right. He is extraordinarily wealthy and a pretty good businessman, considering his line of work. Miloradov trusts Davydov, but mostly because the Davydov enterprise donates millions to Miloradov."

I asked for clarification. "How many millions a year?"

"Millions a month." Jerry replied.

I was a bit taken aback. "Drugs?" I asked

"No, extortion and kidnapping." It began dawning on me how extensive crime really was and what Weiner's problem might be. Given Marianne's affinity for the Weiner family, it all made more sense. Weiner wasn't a mobster or trying to make a quick buck. He had gotten himself crosswise with these guys and was paying to stay safe. But I also knew Maniaci wasn't going to take my word for it. I needed to get over there fast and verify it for myself. What was especially generous, as well as curious, was that the FBI wasn't interjecting itself into the investigation yet.

I understood how the Feds worked. They always developed their intelligence first, followed by the investigative facts before they presented their case to the U.S. Attorney. When there was a suspect, like Weiner, they started their methodical process rolling. It seemed like they were waiting for a complaint from TI or from Weiner. Neither had happened yet. And TI surely wasn't going to file a complaint until I said so. The question was, *why hadn't Weiner called for help or filed a complaint?*

Maniaci continued, "Davydov runs a front company called Industrial Partners Consulting Company. In its Cyrillic translation its initials are PPKK. They call it P2K2. Davydov runs all his finances through this Panamanian registered business. Cash deposits, wire transfers, and the buying and selling of legitimate businesses run through there to clean the money and get it back in circulation. All that money isn't any good to them if they can't spend or reinvest it.

"Davydov is very handsomely rewarded for his larger kick up to Miloradov. Our Moscow office estimates that Davydov is a multi-millionaire. Miloradov is believed to have dozens of *Davydovs* running around Russia and the United States and may very well be a billionaire."

I knew the numbers were big but I had no idea that local mafia lords were billionaires. That kind of money seemed obscene compared to the *lower paid* mafia kingpins in the States.

"Besides kidnapping for ransom, Davydov operates a white slave trade. Women, young girls and boys are taken from families in Russia, as are the wives and children of western businessmen. If the ransom isn't paid, the more attractive of them, at any age, are taken and sold into prostitution and pornography. This is just one business line of our friend Davydov and his minions Koshkin and Mirski."

Maniaci paused to let it all settle in. Then he continued without missing a beat. "When you get to Moscow, take a ride by our office there and visit with our Station Chief, Tom Koval. Koval runs a brand-new position over there as the Legal Attaché in partnership with the Ministry of Internal Affairs and the FSK, the Russian Counter Intelligence Unit in Moscow. He has his hands full. Some of the FSK are not trustworthy and he has to decipher both their intelligence and their motives. Besides being a good guy and very knowledgeable, Tom is extraordinarily well connected to other countries' law enforcement counterparts who are also stationed in Moscow.

"He hasn't been there a long time, given the iron curtain just came down a couple years ago. He keeps an arm's length with the guys across the street, but they respect him. Tom will be a sharp ally to have and he will fill you in on any further developments from our end. Once you walk into our office there, by the way, you will likely be marked for surveillance."

I assumed Jerry meant watched by the Russians and I knew how that went. I almost always checked in with the State Department or the FBI on arrival in a foreign country. It was something every business traveler should do in hostile countries, but most never did. I did it for selfish purposes, not for traveler safety. Very often these guys knew very much about the crime situation and proved invaluable assets in "problem solving" for me.

"I'll hook up with him. Do you have contact information for Koval?" I asked.

"It's in there," replied Maniaci pointing to the envelope.

I had been drinking the ice water while Maniaci talked. I was refilling my glass and topping off Jerry's when the sandwiches came. They were monsters. Huge slices of homemade dark rye bread were stuffed with a mountain of deep, thinly sliced, pink corned beef. A brown mustard was slathered over the mounds of meat and two thick slices of Swiss cheese were stuffed in there too. There was a garnish of a whole fresh dill pickle with a strong hint of garlic. I knew I would have to brush and gargle before I spent hours on an international flight. Otherwise some poor bastard in the seat next to me would end up enjoying a deli lunch by aromatic proxy. Homemade potato chips fell off the plate as it was plopped in front of me.

We dug in and ate quietly for a few minutes before Maniaci continued. I kept right on eating as I listened to him begin anew. "It is on the weapons side that I am light on information Mike. That whole mess is being primarily handled by the Agency. I am sure you can imagine, but this is very high visibility in Washington. Our friends are responsible to a congressional arms subcommittee, the Nuclear Regulatory Agency, the Defense Security Agency and the Chairman of the Joint Chiefs, who is already developing a plan of how to respond if someone detonates one of those things in the United States.

"The Agency is working out of the State Department offices in Moscow, but they may not want to talk with you. In fact, many of the missing units are believed to be from locations outside Moscow. So, this could go anywhere. They are barely talking with us about this in any detail, so I don't know how much they have already or what they don't have. They are not sharing leads and they are not asking for our input any longer. If I had to bet Mike, I would say they have tapped out their leads and are hoping for a break, maybe from private industry. Your trip and your reputation play fortuitously into their goal of working the private sector."

I hadn't heard all the facts yet but the more I learned, the less fortuitous it sounded for me.

"Once our guy sent me the signal about Weiner," he continued, "the Agency guys got the flag. They immediately reached out to me about Weiner and TI. That's when your name came up from me. Cross seemed to already have some experience with you as well, so it seemed like a good fit to reach out to TI. They asked me to arrange the meeting with you, since we have an established relationship."

That caught me off guard. I didn't say anything to Jerry about it because I had secrecy requirements about acknowledging working with the Agency and I wasn't sure Maniaci was officially aware. It made me wonder why Cross didn't just pick up the phone and ask for the meeting himself. I wondered if I would ever find out the answer to that one.

"Mike, I am guessing that on the civilian side, you are not likely to get any information they don't already know. While we want every effort you can muster up, I'd like to offer some personal advice."

I encouraged Maniaci to continue, "Sure, go ahead. I won't be offended."

"Be very careful over there. The mafia is ruthless and a bit out of control. The gang wars are escalating among smaller factions and people are innocently becoming victims of stray gunshots. The mafia guys are a suspicious lot, even within their own ranks. None of them can be trusted. And they are very powerful, controlling banks, the courts, large private industry and law enforcement, even into the military. I know you have to "fix" something for Brinton and Transeget Industries. I know that's what you do. But my advice to you, when you start snooping around is ...", Maniaci paused to make sure he had my full attention, "don't get yourself killed over this. Even our own team treads lightly when it comes to the mob over there."

I slowly chewed my sandwich, as much to clear my throat as to think it through before responding. I had been in some really tough situations before. Just a few weeks ago I was in a small shipping village on the Baltic Sea breaking up a smuggling operation that ended in a few deaths. I had been in South America a couple years prior making a ransom payoff, only to learn that our employee had already been killed, but the FARC rebels wanted the money I was carrying anyway.

I didn't go out seeking trouble, but it certainly wasn't far around the corner in my line of work. Having survived several shootouts on the Police Department, I didn't want to be a victim of innocent gunfire, much less the target of a Bratva contract killing. "I'll stay as clear of the mob as I can." I replied.

Maniaci replied, "It's not just the mob I am worried about, Mike. It's the other thing too. Missing nuclear material is a very big deal. I would suspect that merely asking about it would cause the people involved to become very nervous. And nervous people make *extreme* judgments." I noted that Maniaci emphasized the word "extreme". It was code among intelligence officers who are authorized to kill, whether to maintain the secrecy of a mission, in retribution, or sometimes just to make a point. It was a practice utilized by both sides – the good guys and the bad. And both sides thought they were the good guys.

"I get it Jerry. And thanks for caring, brother." Maniaci shrugged. "If you get your ass shot up over there, I am going to have to fill out a ton of paperwork. And you know how I hate paperwork." We looked quietly at each other for a moment. Then the moment passed. "I'll be careful." I promised.

The bill came before we finished eating. I reached for it. I had a nearly bottomless corporate expense account. But Maniaci shook his head. "We pay cash and we go Dutch. You know I can't accept a bribe from a corporate guy." I almost choked on that. We had eaten at each other's homes but could not officially share even a sandwich, in case it was perceived that something corrupt was occurring. "You've got a deal," I said.

With the bill paid and the last crumbs cleaned from our lips, I rose holding my third manila envelope of the day. I offered Maniaci my other hand. "Gotta run, Jerry. I have a hectic day and a long evening flight ahead of me. Thanks for the meeting and the gab session. I'll give you a call when I get back. And of course, I'll check in with Koval if you'll give him a heads up. He'll be my first stop when I get to Moscow tomorrow morning. I'm hoping to stay at the Metropol."

As we headed for the door, Maniaci shook my hand and said, "That's a hell of a lot better than the Novotel at Sheremetyevo." I wondered how the head of the FBI office in Newark knew about the Metropol or the Novotel, but didn't ask.

I fingered the envelope as I walked to my car and wondered what was in it. Whatever it was, I hoped it wasn't redacted to the point of being worthless. I had seen so many redacted reports that they were a bureaucratic waste of time to prepare them. I'd read it when I got back to my office and destroy it before I boarded my flight. One did not need a foreign government finding such documentation on a business traveler. Especially a foreign government that presumed everyone who entered was a spy of the CIA. Although at this point, I wondered if perhaps I already was one.

■ ■ ■ ■ ■

Joanne was waiting for me when I arrived. It was as if the woman never ate or slept. I walked with her into my office.

She began without waiting for informal chatting, "Let's start with air transportation. The earliest flight I could get you on leaves around midnight and isn't a first-class ticket. It is a nine-hour flight that stops in Amsterdam. The flight from Amsterdam to Moscow is another three hours on top of the Amsterdam layover, and that was another three hours. So by the time you got into Moscow it would be seven pm tomorrow night. There is no non-stop available." I was about to object, when Joanne held up her hand and continued before I could interrupt.

"I called Marianne. She has authorized you to use the Gulfstream. You can leave in a couple hours. Your connection will be in Heathrow, rather than Amsterdam. It is a tight connection to Moscow at that point. You'll have about an hour to deplane the Gulfstream and get from the FBO to the gate." I knew that getting from the Fixed Base Operator to the main gate at Heathrow would be no problem. I would be taxied across the airfield in a VIP vehicle to the gate. Since I was going to be carrying only an overnight bag and a briefcase, I just needed a first-class ticket to Moscow to avoid the long lines. Joanne continued.

"That will save you about eight hours and get you into Moscow ..." I interjected, "Early morning and enough time to get downtown and checked in." It went without saying that Joanne got me the reservations at the Metropol.

"Yes," Joanne affirmed. "We have a first-class ticket for you from Heathrow to Moscow, so that should help get you on board on time. I have a driver waiting for you outside baggage claim, just beyond the customs checkpoint. It will be Sasha, as you requested. He hopes you will recognize him, but he will have a small sign that simply states *TI*. He will convey you to the Metropol. We also have a room reserved for you in your name, not the company's. The deposit is prepaid, as is the

71

following week. They will want you to present a credit card. Use your company card rather than your personal." I knew that my habit of using my personal card for some business expenses was frowned on.

Even though I have all my corporate travel points linked to my personal card, on occasion I did not want my identity linked to the company. In Russia it wouldn't matter. As soon as my passport was processed at Heathrow for arrival in Moscow, an agent of the Russian FSK, the newly formed Federal Counterintelligence Agency, would be assigned to track me upon landing.

I nodded my understanding. With that, Joanne handed me my paperwork. "Your Visa is still good. Your work purpose is *site operational inspections and goodwill*. You have your passport. Here is your first class ticket and a boarding pass from Heathrow to Moscow. You have been assigned the window seat, three-A." I had no issues about being trapped against the wall. Although it wasn't going to be a long flight, I preferred not having to get up and down for someone with a bladder control issue.

"Here is your Metropol hotel room confirmation. We have asked that it not be above the fourth floor." I glanced down at it as Joanne passed it across to me. It was a suite, which I preferred in case I had to have a meeting in the room. I did not like the idea of someone seeing my unmade bed for some reason. And I also preferred a lower floor, in case there was a fire, so the fire truck ladders and hoses could reach my room. One could get a wonderful view of downtown Moscow from the top floors of the Metropol, but it wasn't worth it, given the lack of fire safety measures in this nearly third world country.

"Here is the number to the American Embassy and their street address. Gary O'Chadwick is their security officer, in case you want to meet with him." I had been to the small "temporary" embassy location during my trip last year. The new Embassy was still being built after a congressional review established that the Russians, during eight years of construction, had placed hundreds of bugs throughout the building process. They were in the walls, ceilings, and fixtures. They had even been placed in the concrete of the floors and pillars. It would be a while before the embassy staff moved into a permanent location in Moscow. And there was no doubt that even the current venue was bugged as well. I might stop in there, but if I did, our conversation would be superficial.

"I've arranged for a car to take you to Teterboro airfield to get you aboard the Gulfstream. It will be here in about an hour and a half. That way you won't have to park your car at Teterboro for a week or more. In fact, they prefer it that way. Your pilots will be Ankers and Walny." I knew both these guys. They were extraordinarily qualified pilots, hired away from commercial flying to wing Brinton and his team around the world at lower altitudes, but at a much higher rate of pay.

"Your flight attendant will be Kathy Stillman. I think you've flown with her before as well."

I knew her. She was a quiet, polite, professional attendant who could anticipate just about any travel comfort a passenger could want. It usually was already stocked on board. And when Stillman

73

wasn't seeing to something, she was otherwise invisible on the flight.

I knew that traveling on the Gulfstream IV was expensive. The plane was spared no corporate extravagance and Marianne had personally seen to the interior decor relative to floor and wall color, fabric and woods. With a base price tag of about twenty-five million, it was no corporate toy. Brinton had this one outfitted with a full standup shower that could allow each traveler a brief but refreshing hot water shower before landing after a long transcontinental flight. It also had a complete operating galley, separate luggage storage and a small data center running off a telephone system capable of international dialing.

Originally outfitted to seat fourteen, he had the sideways bench seats taken out and retrofitted with full loungers, converting the seating to eight. The chairs could be swiveled one hundred eighty degrees and positioned such that a conference table could be inserted for team discussions and workspace on either aisle. Traveling at fifty mph faster than most commercial airlines, it was also more efficient on a four-thousand mile journey, time-wise. I didn't relish the travel aspect of my job, at least not the time wasted between point A and B. I estimated it cost about twenty-five hundred dollars or more per hour to fly this thing. And the cost was the same returning, even though it would fly back empty.

The company was spending over ten-thousand dollars one way to get me there in a day. It wouldn't be the first time. Given the circumstances and the risk associated with delay, this was the way to go. I smiled to myself, thinking how lucky I was. I came from a lower-income family in a poor area of Detroit, and now I was flying in world-class luxury. It was a remarkable turn around of fortune and I never tired of it.

I thanked Joanne and she left. I then dialed Marianne. "It's Christian," I said, when she picked up. "I wanted to thank you for clearing the Gulfstream. I know it is not inexpensive."

"No, it is not." She said. "And I had to bump three VPs off the plane to get you that arrangement. They were quite upset and wanted to know who had bumped them. I just told them it was a corporate emergency and they let it go at that." I knew that once Marianne gave someone an answer, regardless of their rank in the corporation, it wouldn't do anyone any good to press her for more. Then she added, "Mr. Brinton says you better bring him back some results."

Given what was discussed in my briefing I wondered if Brinton was hinting that I should press hard on the issue of the bombs. I shrugged it off. If the cards played out, I would. "Tell him I'll bring him back some Russian babushka stacking dolls."

"Was there anything else?" I knew Marianne was a busy executive in her own right and not one with a long sense of humor. "No, Just wanted to personally say thanks."

"Travel safely." And with that she rang off.

I dialed home again wanting to talk personally with Alice before I took off. And again, the call rang over to our answering machine. "Hi Hon. Just trying again. Look, I'm taking off from Teterboro in a couple hours and could likely be gone a week. I really want to talk with you in person, so I will call when I get to the airport. Otherwise, it could be another ten or twelve hours before I am able to call again." That was as close as I would likely get to tell her where I was going without talking to her in person. I hung up and turned back to my desk and opened Jerry's envelope.

It contained one typewritten page and no sticky note. At the bottom of the page was a phone number with a Moscow area code, followed by the words *Tom Koval.*

At the top was an org chart showing the relationships between Miloradov and his people. There were lines that tailed off without additional subordinates. The chart showed the details of just one branch. Beneath him was Davydov. Then on equal planes below Davydov were Mirski and Koshkin, nothing new there. But what was of particular interest to me was the range of activity they suspected of Miloradov. Beneath the small chart was a bulleted list of "businesses" and their "markets". Manufacture, sale and distribution of drugs, and beneath that a secondary list of types - Opioid, counterfeit pharmaceutical and chemical drugs in Russia, western Europe, and in North and South America.

Then there was the kidnapping of westerners for ransom and taking of human beings for forced prostitution in Russia, Eurasia, the Middle East, Israel, Western Europe and the United States. This was followed by theft, and the commercial and black-market resale of home appliances, furniture, new and used automotive parts and other manufacturing assets through burglary, armed robbery and hijacking of land-based cargo, all for redistribution throughout European major markets.

What also caught my eye was the extortion of businesses through protection rackets, blackmail for inappropriate behavior through entrapment, and extortion extracting payment in exchange for a promise not to kill or kidnap a loved one. And I was stopped in my tracks when I saw the smuggling of arms into the international black market and the sale of weapons on the open market. I wondered if this was a link to anything bigger, or of interest to the boys across the street. If so, I thought, the Agency would already be all over it.

Following the "accusations" list of illegal activities was another list. This one dealt mostly with business enterprises by name, but not so much by type of business. Since the list was titled "Fronts", I did not put much stock into any name resembling an actual business. So, when I saw *P2K2* I gave no credence to them being a legitimate consulting company. I felt these companies were all established as shells to move illegal money. Then I saw the legitimate names and that threw me.

Miloradov and Davydov separately were owners or majority shareholders in coal and electric companies, in grain cooperatives, banks and in retail chain stores throughout Russia and many former Soviet Union countries. And several of Davydov's companies were chartered in the elusive and secretive Panamanian registries. This level of ownership and sophistication was too big for them to have achieved on their own. There had to be powerful government connections to allow this to happen, and powerful businessmen sharing in or directing their activities and profits. I felt, for the first time, that I just might be over my head on this trip.

With this kind of horsepower at their disposal, how could I overcome their pressure on our company? I knew there must be a way. I just had to figure it out. No matter how big the bully, there was always someone *bigger and badder*. I thought about asking Jerry, but there came a point where it was better if the government did not know how certain issues got fixed. I would work it out once I got there, then I'd tell them only what was absolutely necessary. After all this was still an internal matter, even if the Feds already knew about it.

I knew a couple of security execs who had been doing business in Russia for a decade, even when it was not proper to do so. I'd ring them up when I got to Moscow if I had to. And there was always Koval. I'd check-in right away with him and see if there was anything of value he could offer. The rest would be up to my own ingenuity and the resources I could muster.

■ ■ ■ ■ ■

I sat in the back of the black Lincoln Continental as it cruised silently to Teterboro Airport. I had the partition window up between the driver and me. Not so much as a personal barrier, but because I had tried calling Alice one more time and wanted a private conversation with her. Unfortunately, I got the answering machine again.

I knew not to be upset or worried. Alice was an independent woman who filled her time with her lady friends playing golf or tennis and volunteering in community services. She was practically as busy as I was without having to endure the travel. I left another brief message and hung up.

I turned to the itinerary materials Joanne had given me and leafed superficially through them. For the first leg of the journey it wouldn't matter. Just before we arrived at Heathrow, either the pilot or Kathy Stillman would alert me in enough time to take a shower and shave if I pleased. At that time we'd confirm that my flight arrangements out of Heathrow were still good. Those could change twice in the next several hours, so there was no need to pore over them now. My thoughts were elsewhere. In Russia.

I had brushes with some of Miloradov's mafia minions before. Or at least what we believed to be their arms supplier, in Germany.

German federal investigators had been working under the assumption that cigarettes and liquor, without German tax stamps, were being stolen and smuggled to Poland using TI's customs documents, company drivers and trucks.

While indeed that was going on without our permission, it seemed that one of Miloradov's minions had gone rogue and was smuggling handguns, automatic Kalashnikov rifles, ammo and grenades from an East German armory whose inventory draw-down he was managing. He had learned about the smuggling route and commandeered it for his purposes. He was stashing some guns for himself and was also selling others to Miloradov's operation. I broke the case, which resulted in the capture of a few low level Russians, likely Davydov's guys, and some

Poles. The arms smuggler, Pavel Oveshkin, got away.

I had also been in Russia before, although only briefly. Our company had established a small engine repair service to support servicing airline electronic and hydraulic luggage carts at Sheremetyevo airport. It was much easier to have a local base of operations than to fly in parts and service teams every time a unit was put out of commission or needed an annual servicing. I had been invited over to perform the security assessment and recommendations for the building they were going to lease for our IT and administration teams. I hadn't been back since it was occupied. I planned to make goodwill visit on this trip and see how things were going. My visa aptly described that purpose.

I fingered one of the business cards I brought along for this occasion. They were printed in English on the front and in Russian Cyrillic on the reverse. There was one subtle change on the back of my card that no one had challenged. Where my title should have read "Global Head of Security", I had it changed to read "Corporate Diplomat". I chuckled as I thought how each time some subordinate foreign bureaucrat would read that title he might back down from an inspection or search. Besides, broadcasting that you were a security executive could have negative ramification in many places around the world, especially Russia. I had found Russia to be a dirty place where everyone in government dealt in dirty practices, and I was on my way back.

My driver stopped outside the security gate at the Fixed Base Operator's entrance to Teterboro's corporate airport area and rolled down his electric window. After he ran a security access card through the reader and the gate opened, he drove straight to the TI hangar. Our plane was already out of the hangar and on the tarmac. The number on the tail and rear fuselage of the beautiful chrome and white Gulfstream was the only marking. After the World Trade Center bombing, I had our corporate logos removed from all air fleet equipment that flew overseas, as a security precaution.

The stairway was already down, and I could see a flight crewmember sitting inside the cockpit. I waved at Ankers who smiled and nodded back. As I entered the hangar, Stillman greeted me immediately.

"Welcome Mr. Christian, it is good to see you again."

"Kathy, nice to see you too. And please, call me Mike."

"Thank you, Mr. Christian," she smiled. "We are actually ready to board when you are. So, if you need to freshen up in the lounge, please do so." I smiled at how deftly she deflected my attempt to personalize the long trip. She was another consummate professional. She was very attractive and that worked against her in some respects. She was by no means unintelligent and she didn't get to this position merely on her looks.

Brinton could have had any number of beautiful women on his aircraft if he chose, but that was not his style. If Stillman didn't have the skills to manage the hospitality arrangements for each individual boarding this craft and to work well with the flight crew, she wouldn't have been chosen to be on it. This was her business and she was very good at it.

I knew there would be no food or beverage service until we reached a safe cruising altitude when Stillman could prepare a hot dinner, so I grabbed a sports nutrition bar of fruit and nuts and two bottles of water from the FBO courtesy desk and tossed them into my briefcase. Carrying my go-bag of clothes and gifts over my shoulder, I walked out onto the apron and to the rear of the jet.

The tail hatch was open and the crew's bags were on the ground at the base of the ladder. A member of the FBO team was walking out to load the bags onto the jet. I decided to watch the process out of habit. Nothing unusual was loaded from the FBO office onto the plane. Once the tail storage door was secured, I boarded.

Walny, the other pilot, was walking back from inside the tail cargo area toward the cockpit and greeted me. "Hey, Mike. Saw you monitoring the loading. Thanks."

I smiled almost sheepishly. I knew that Walny was personally loading the gear onto the plane as it was handed up. He too was following a security protocol of only taking onboard approved and known packages. "Old habits." I quipped.

Walny, continued, "You know we would have taken you all the way in to Moscow if we could have, Mike. We've made that flight before. But we didn't really have enough time for our clearances and to file an acceptable flight plan. With a little more notice, we might have been able to pull it off for you. Anyway, once we get leveled off, feel free to come up front, if you like." he offered.

I actually was like a kid in that regard. On big commercial airlines, I had no interest in the goings-on of the pilots. But on the company fleet, the perspective of the sky and ground as seen above the equipment dashboard, and out the window of these jets, never failed to move me. "Thanks, I just might pop in to say hi."

I took a forward-facing seat that converted into a lounger and strapped myself in. I heard Kathy moving about the galley, so I opened a bottle of water and started the hydration process I followed on every long flight. I had no notes from Maniaci, having shredded them in my Department of Defense crosscut shredder for classified information. I would wait until I was airborne to re-read the internal audit report, but that wouldn't be necessary either. I already knew what was in there and who the players were. My job would be to unravel the truth and put a stop to whatever was going on. That was what was expected of me, nothing less.

Facilitating payments, bribes, kickbacks, theft by conversion, self-dealing of all kinds, these were the bread and butter investigations of my trade. Eventually it got down to matching the paper trail to the perpetrators. And internal audit had already done their part.

It was obvious that Weiner, or someone with his access was making seemingly improper payments. Whether or not Weiner knew that his payments were made to a mob organization remained to be seen. But that was well within my wheelhouse of discovery. An interview with Weiner was one of the first orders of business at his office. And that interview could turn into an interrogation quickly, if

83

the facts began to show that Weiner was complicit in some illegal scheme.

But I might have to deal with different ramifications if Weiner was being extorted by the mob. Calling off those dogs would be a bit more challenging. I wondered if Weiner had set up a secret partnership for the Moscow parts business and if so, who were his partners?

The bigger problem I had to address was that of the missing nukes. And it surely wasn't going to be resolved as easily as having an interview with a thief. I had half a day to chew on that and a plan was already forming in my mind. One thing was certain. I wasn't sticking my neck out unless the cards fell right for me. I was accustomed to pushing the limits. But these stakes were pretty high. And the only skin in the game was that of corporate profit. I wasn't about to lose my own skin over that.

I started to doze as I relaxed for the long flight over. I would get in a power nap before Stillman came by with refreshments.

■ ■ ■ ■ ■

Alice threw her keys on the hallstand and saw she had three voice messages on the answering machine. Her afternoon round of golf with her lady friends ended with light sandwiches in the clubhouse dining room and she had just gotten home.

She listened to all three of her husband's vague messages and realized he was likely onboard some airplane again on his way to another adventure. She knew that eventually she would find out where he had gone and possibly even why. She doubted he would tell her the complete story. He never did. She recognized his need for confidentiality and respected it.

She remembered being attracted to his stories when they were first dating. He had just been hired as their company's first security executive. He was fresh from eleven years as a cop in the Detroit Police Department. But not just a street cop anymore. He was a corporate crimes investigator, had arrested some big-time organized crime figures, and had broken up some international theft rings.

At first she never believed his stories because they were so far removed from her own frame of reference. Truth be told, they seemed almost like the fiction of her paperback mystery novels or of TV shows. He was such a good storyteller and although she knew he was never telling the *whole* story, the tales she and their friends were hearing were intriguing. So much so that she found herself drawn to the mystery and to the danger and excitement that at one time must have been a part of his life. What she didn't know was they would marry, and she would learn firsthand how the excitement of his work-life was real and enduring.

She hoped his trip was not dangerous and that he was not going to be gone long. But he had said it was an "emergency". *Weren't they all*, she thought? Alice sighed and concluded that she couldn't speculate. She would learn more when they finally talked.

After three corporate moves with him and working for four international companies, she knew her husband's job involved more than its share of danger and intrigue. She had learned to focus on the thought of his returning, not the danger he might face. She whispered a silent prayer for his safety and began preparing herself another dinner at home, alone.

■ ■ ■ ■ ■

Stillman had already brought me my in-flight meal, and I was slicing a garlic roasted, new-potato to chase down a morsel of filet mignon, when Ankers came out of the cockpit and sat opposite me.

"Walny has the stick right now, Mike. I don't know if this is good news or bad, but we are taking advantage of a powerful jet stream and we can arrive almost two hours early into England. We have a choice to reduce speed and save fuel, still arriving at the originally scheduled time. Or we can maintain our airspeed, ride the jet stream and approach supersonic ground speed. That would get us into Heathrow way ahead of your forecasted arrival.

"We have checked flight schedules. If we maintain our speed, we can get you there with about forty-five minutes to spare to connect to an earlier Aeroflot flight into Sheremetyevo. That flight time is only three and a half hours. We talked with Joanne from the cockpit and she has confirmed that your driver can make an adjustment and meet you in Moscow, but we would need to let them know right away. It's your call."

I mulled it over briefly. "Running it flat out is a lot of fuel to burn unnecessarily." I said.

Ankers smiled and replied, "Not a problem for us Mike. You are being charged for the fuel, whether we use it or not."

"Then burn it. Let's get the connections confirmed first and make sure my driver can be there. The last thing I want to do is fool with the taxi hacks or wait a few hours at that dirty airport for him."

"Roger that. I'll let you know either way." With that Ankers rose and walked back toward the galley.

Although I knew no one would object, I decided not to call Alice from the phone connection on the plane. The calls were expensive and reserved for business purposes. I would try to ring her from Heathrow, but my flight connection times would be close. If I missed her then, I would call her from my hotel in Moscow, if it wasn't too late back in the States. I returned to my case strategy.

I usually worked from a notepad, writing out my investigation strategy in a series of flow chart boxes, lines and arrows. But I didn't want to enter customs in Russia with a bunch of field notes relative to the mafia or anyone else. My luggage and briefcase would be searched overtly and covertly at least a couple times over the next few days, if not daily. I would have to organize my plan in my head.

The first thing I'd do would be to check-in at the Metropol and have Sasha, my driver, wait for me. I'd have my go-bag sent to the room where it would certainly be searched. I'd carry my briefcase with me and call the FBI legate, Koval. I'd set up that appointment to meet with him, right away, if possible. If Maniaci had called ahead, that should be no problem. Jerry held some serious horsepower.

After my meeting with Koval I'd interview Weiner. But first I had to get an updated lay of the land about the Bureau's intelligence on Weiner and his new "friends".

Normally I'd also check in with the Resident Security Officer at the Embassy. Usually the average John Doe that walks in off the street can get a meeting and receive a plain vanilla briefing on country conditions. The information is diluted as it comes from the CIA "Fact Book" and is made palatable for the average citizen.

Over the years, I had been able to receive deeper briefings, given my role as head of security for one of the largest companies in the world. It didn't hurt either that guys like Cam Cross would vouch for me if necessary. But I wouldn't meet with the RSO on this trip.

I didn't trust the sanctity of the Embassy temporary offices either and did not want to be on record with the Russians, much less the Agency, as asking dangerous questions.

With plenty of flight time left, I decided to take another run at the internal audit report. Not so much from the perspective of the payments to an offshore corporation, but I wanted to review the amounts, timing, frequency and method of transferring the money from the corporate account to a foreign business account. When did they start? Who authorized them from the bank? Were two party signatures required? Could the authorized parties from the foreign corporation be identified?

If I passed along the Transeget Industries payment logs to the Feds, could I get information from them as to the amounts in the offshore accounts and where the money might be subsequently transferred?

I could work all that out before interviewing Weiner. If he was up to something, I wanted all the ducks in my row, not his.

I knew that every unethical or illegal act I had investigated was capable of being mapped, just like any quality assurance process. Since I already read the files and received the federal briefings, I mentally mapped out the people and their relationships. Somehow money was moved from our accounts to an outside account. I wanted that documentation. It was my version of the old investigative maxim "follow the money". In this case it was more like "find the vulnerability points in the process and the people who can exploit them." My friend and mentor in the Organized Crime Task Force, first pointed this approach out to me when he broke me in on investigating criminal conspiracies.

These *maps* pointed out gaps in internal controls or identified controls that, if circumvented, provided the greatest opportunities for abuse. I knew that even the business of crime was still a business when broken down to its simplest elements. I had unraveled it before, and it was often not easy. But it was a logic that had to be worked through. Over the next few hours, I would commit this fundamental framework of my investigation to memory. It would do no good to have an FSK agent find my notes. I remembered Maniaci's warning, *trust no one.*

The big question remained, *how does one overcome the power and might of the burgeoning Bratva*? I thought I might have a plan for that too.

■ ■ ■ ■ ■

Kathy Stillman stood in the back of the executive aircraft and quietly watched Christian work. They had been on many flights together and despite him trying to become politely sociable with her, she always kept her professional distance.

Everyone knew he was the company problem solver and it was said that some of the challenges he faced were matters of life and death, not merely dollars and cents. She was sure she overheard Ankers and Walny whisper there had been shooting on his last mission in Germany.

But Christian frightened her in a way that thrilled her. Kathy was drawn to his confident, quiet energy and to the very danger in his life that he seemed to handle so adroitly. Other corporate executives exuded power, but not like Christian.

And then there was his physicality. She found his dark hair and brown eyes handsomely attractive, and she could see that he was muscular and fit under his tailored clothes.

She had been on hundreds of corporate flights and never once let her personal feelings get out of control. More importantly, she knew he was a married man and nothing good could come of letting her feelings grow. Nevertheless, she could feel her body warm as she allowed her mind to wander. *What are you up to now, Michael*

Christian? She sighed and prayed silently for his safety.

CHAPTER FOUR

RACHEL WEINER LOOKED ACROSS THE table at her husband with concern written on her face. Alexander was losing weight and had not been sleeping well for months. He resisted all her encouragement to go see a doctor. She was certain he had cancer. Not prone to wild guesses about health issues, her worry had nevertheless made her obsessive, thinking about him being terminally ill. She had never seen him like this in their twelve years of marriage. He was quiet and withdrawn. When she asked about his health, his lack of appetite and his sleeplessness, he mumbled "*it will get better,*" and then refused to move forward with her in conversation about it. She worried that if he became seriously ill, he could not get adequate medical treatment here in Russia.

"Do you want me to reheat that for you?" she asked, pointing to a cold rib eye steak. He had barely touched it.

"No, really. It's ok. I'll put it in the fridge. Maybe I can eat it later." Weiner rose from the table with his plate and set it on the kitchen counter. Absentmindedly, he left it sitting there and strode from the kitchen, kissing Sarah on the forehead as he passed his daughter. He walked into his den and closed the door behind him.

Weiner had never encountered a problem that he couldn't resolve. And as difficult as a dilemma could be, it was always the company's assets that were at risk. This, however, was personal. Closely personal. It consumed his every waking thought. And there was no way out.

Weiner knew the audit team didn't buy his excuse about paying consultants such an exorbitant amount of money. He knew the company would be sending someone over, probably an attorney, to meet with him about it. He would just have to continue lying.

The Russians made it very clear that the money must continue or they would carry out their threats. They also went into great detail to explain that their reach went all the way into the United States, so there was no escaping them. Fleeing home was not an option.

He recalled the pictures they showed him of the women and the young girls. All with listless eyes and dressed for sex. He just couldn't imagine this might possibly be the fate of his wife and daughter. The fear consumed him, robbed him of his appetite, his sleep and his ability to think in the present.

Complicating matters were the hijackings. He never told corporate how his first weeks were fraught with armed hijackings of their trucks as they left his central warehouse.

Thugs with greasy hair and dirty leather coats had visited him. Armed ruffians who told him that

94

the robberies would continue if he did not pay them. They literally wanted to be paid for protection against their own violence. Weiner was reminded of early Chicago and Detroit when the mobs ran protection rackets.

He told the guys that the company was prohibited from making such payments. They seemed at first very accustomed to being told no. In fact, one of the men merely shrugged his shoulders and said, "You say no? You say no to us? OK. Then no it is." And they left.

Weiner didn't know what to make of that harmless response. But he quickly found out what it meant. The next day, one of his local Russian drivers was pulled over at gunpoint after leaving the warehouse. A truck full of their parts was stolen and then their driver was shot in both legs. Weiner had been able to cover the losses of trucks and inventory. Some financial slop was built into the calculations for the first six months of operations due to expected economic and market uncertainties.

But the shooting took a bit more to cover up. Everyone in the warehouse was talking about it and speculation included every imaginable crime scenario. But most guesses centered on the reality of contemporary Moscow. The mob was moving in and they were sending a message.

When word of the shooting got back to his office, Weiner called the police, as did a passing motorist, anonymously. Their driver had been conveyed to a local Moscow hospital and would recover but he told Weiner he would never return to work there. He was convinced he would be killed if he did.

When the translator told the police what had happened, and how a mob representative had visited Weiner, the police officer merely shrugged his shoulders and said *"Chto vy khotite ot menya sdelat?"* *What do you want me to do about it?* He refused to even take a report, telling Weiner that it would only make the crime statistics go up if Weiner filed a complaint.

Weiner thought long and hard about whether to pay the protection fee. Before he could make up his mind however, he received another delegation from the mafia, different guys this time with different demands. Their message was much more serious and terribly personal. They were threatening his wife and daughter.

They came without shame, without compunction. Simply stated, he would have to pay to keep them from taking his wife and daughter and making whores of them. They were calmly bold and brazen, matter of fact in every respect, like it was a daily occurrence for them to steal human beings. He was shown surveillance photographs of his wife and daughter at home, while shopping and at his daughter's school. He was also shown the other photos. Weiner was unnerved because they seemed so confident. He lost his poise and his resolve to argue. They had succeeded in making their point almost within minutes.

Weiner did not have the kind of money being demanded of him. The price for his family's protection was obscene – two-hundred-fifty thousand dollars a month, every month, forever. And they made it clear. There was nowhere to turn, no one to go to who could help him. Not the company, not the Russian authorities and not the

American authorities. Any attempt, they said, would guarantee that before a police investigator even arrived to speak with him, Weiner's wife and daughter would be taken away. And although he would never see them again, he would know they were being drug addicted before being sold as sex slaves. There was no attempt to physically strong-arm him, no other indication of other intimidation, just simple statements of immutable fact.

For Weiner, the choice was obvious. The choice had been made for him. He had control over that kind of money. It just wasn't his.

He was provided the name of a business, masquerading as a consulting company, and its offshore bank routing information. All he had to do was wire the money into their business account every month, without fail. If he missed a payment, there would be no collections phone calls, no letters of reminder in the mail. They would simply take their collateral and he would never see them again. There would be no further contact from the Russians. There would be no negotiations, no conversation, no late payments with interest penalties, just a final settlement.

Weiner had acted to protect his wife and daughter and he never told them of the threat. It was gnawing away at him from the inside and it showed on the outside.

■ ■ ■ ■ ■

FEDOR DAVYDOV LOVED BEING seen at the Hotel Metropol. There was a time in his youth when the doormen would not even let him enter the lobby. Now his call for a dinner reservation at the Savva, inside the hotel, was warmly greeted where they knew him by name. Yes, they would move another reservation to accommodate Fedor Davydov, Bratva Brigadier. Fedor had been assured they would seat him at the table against the back wall with the large mirror behind him. From there he could see anyone entering and he would surely be seen as a celebrity.

Upon his arrival in the doorway, the Maitre D' effusively saluted him and proudly walked him to his chosen table. Heads turned and people whispered as he walked through the restaurant, but no one made eye contact with him. He was impeccably dressed in a Saville Row bespoke suit of four-inch squares, patterned of a rich navy blue he had personally selected. The exquisitely tailored fabric draped perfectly over his handmade, crisp, open collared white shirt. He wore a honey smooth, golden cravat of fine satin that covered the folds of his full neck.

He knew he was a large man, some would say fat, but he did present as a well-groomed, attractive man of means. He loved his change of appearance from convict to gentleman. If one didn't know Fedor's background, one would never believe it. He was the master of his own image and no one would dare challenge it. It was amazing what money could buy, even credibility.

Fedor rewarded his host with a one-hundred-dollar bill in American currency. It didn't matter that it was counterfeit. It would spend equally well anywhere in Russia.

A bottle of Dom Perignon, a gift from the house, appeared tableside without him ordering. He sent the sommelier away before the champagne was opened. He wanted it fresh when his guest arrived.

Fedor was a big man and indulged his appetites with anything he pleased. And he could afford it, whether food, alcohol or the pale young girls that drove him wild. This evening it would be the pork chop, followed by standing lamb chops. He would enjoy the olives, soft white cheeses, grapes and Beluga caviar between his servings while he discussed the business at hand. With business out of the way, he would move on to his other appetite.

Fedor was not a common street thug and did not like being portrayed as one, regardless of how his minions carried out his orders. He was a businessman, managing several dozen employees and millions in British and U.S. currency. He would not trade in rubles because, as far as he was concerned, they were worthless. He was adroit at working with international bankers and with managing wire transfers. And he enjoyed the mental gymnastics of international investment managers who laundered the money he took as his own profits.

This evening he was meeting one of his middle managers. They had been discussing the direction of his next investment. They had progressed beyond whether to proceed. It was now merely a matter of which course to follow. Fedor would give his decision to Vadim when he arrived, but only after they spent some moments exchanging a few pleasantries over champagne and good food. He was after all a businessman and there was no need to discuss extortion in an alley.

In Fedor's mind the fundamentals of income streaming were basic. Recurring monthly revenue was more important than one-time *sales*. Someone who could pay two hundred fifty thousand dollars per month for twelve months, year-after-year, was much more valuable than someone who could pay a million dollars once. Fedor's initial investment cost was about the same either way. Therefore, his margins were better in a recurring revenue model.

In fact, it was somewhat less expensive to maintain a long-term relationship with someone, than resorting to one-time payments. In the latter case, Fedor's crew faced business risk each time. Properly extorting someone for recurring payments was cheaper and more profitable than kidnapping three or four people a year.

It was much easier to explain that to Vadim than to Grigor and his crew. Grigor would obey of course, but he just didn't get the principles of good business. And Grigor much preferred the rough end of the business. It satisfied his need to live on the edge.

Fedor smiled wistfully to himself. What a shame he didn't have a chance to develop a real business of his own. He would have been a megastar. Then he chuckled to himself. He was a megastar and he was a businessman, just not the type of business most people could appreciate. And as Vadim Mirski approached Fedor's table, their next victim's destiny became a fait accompli.

As befitting a man of elevated means, Fedor did not stand when Mirski approached and said, "*Moi lider.*" Vadim bowed slightly then waited until Fedor offered an extended hand. They shook briefly and Vadim waited again. Fedor motioned for him to take the seat that would face Vadim to the mirror and away from the room. Fedor was still fully in view for all to see. "*Dobro pozhalovat', moy khoroshiy drug*, Welcome, my good friend." Fedor knew that Vadim, even as a trusted confidant, was respectful more out of fear than loyalty. Yet he greeted all the subordinates in his direct chain of command as "friends."

Fedor motioned for the wine steward who was standing attentively out of earshot, but nearby. With deft fingers, he lifted the bottle from its nest of ice, draped it in a white linen towel and peeled back the foil wrapper, slipping it unobtrusively in his pocket. With three quick twists, he partially opened the wire cage and firmly lifted the tight cork from the throat of the bottle, not allowing it to fly through the air. The quiet pop spoke to the sommelier's expertise as the bottle exhaled a soft white mist from the bubbling golden liquid. He poured a taste and offered it to Fedor to sample.

Fedor motioned it away with a flick of acceptance. He knew it was Dom Perignon and that was enough for him. He would have been even more impressed had he known it was from nineteen seventy-one, the last time this white vintage was produced in alternating years. The sommelier's effort to impress was wasted on Fedor. Once his crystal flute was topped off, Fedor raised it to Vadim and toasted, "*Na mat' Rossiyu, pust' shlyukha prodolzhit otdavat' nam vse svoi den'gi* 'To mother Russia, may the whore continue to give us all her money.' " Vadim chuckled, tipped the brim of his glass to Fedor and sipped in agreement.

A platter of oysters was their first serving and Fedor and Vadim made a show of slurping the tasteless, phlegmy liquid into their mouths while wiping their wet lips and chins with the napkins they had tucked into their shirt collars. In moments, they had established their virility for all to see and the plate of empty half-shells was whisked away. A warm, silver bowl of escargot was devoured in similar style and soon the empty tub was wiped clean of its garlic-buttered juices with crusty white bread. Fedor waved away the salad and French onion soup, and ordered the chops to be brought out right away. He had become impatient with the ritual of his meal and was hungry for the main courses. They dipped crackers into the Beluga caviar while they waited.

As requested, both the lamb and pork chops materialized almost instantly. It was obvious that someone else would wait a little longer for their meal, which was now being served to Fedor's table. In a matter of moments, Fedor and Vadim had the bones to their teeth and soon pulled the last shards clean. Wiping his face with his napkin with one hand, Fedor motioned to the headwaiter with his other. "Clear these away and bring us Stolichnaya 4.12." Fedor knew that all Russian Vodka tasted about the same, but he preferred the Stoli that harkened to a day when a bottle cost four rubbles and twelve kopecks.

As the meal wound down, Fedor cleared his throat of a crust of zavarnoy bread and washed it down with a shot of Stoli. "Before we begin Vadim, what about this Winston? Has his wife paid yet?"

Mirski knew that this one was a bit sticky. The wife had hesitated and the boys were getting heavy handed with Winston. It was not going as planned and so he told Davydov. "Be sure not to kill him yet.

Perhaps we should go to his company and not the wife. Is it time?"

Mirski thought it over a bit before he replied, "It could be time. We are waiting feedback from her as we speak. If we do not hear soon, we should try to get the money from his company. They must be concerned by now." They both knew that the responsibility for collecting the ransom was not Vadim's directly. It had been handed over to Trofim and Grigor. This was the dirty end of the business that Mirski no longer cared for.

He was unhappy with the news, but sometimes waiting was a good alternative to killing the victim and starting all over again with another. Davydov continued, "Now tell me about this Alex Weiner. Is he still paying? Does he stay in line? Do I have any reason to worry?"

Vadim was much more comfortable with this answer. Even if things hadn't gone as planned with a *client,* he had to portray to Fedor that all was well for the time being. Failure was not a welcome option. But in Weiner's case, all was going as planned. Weiner had too much at stake. Besides a beautiful wife, he had an eleven-year-old daughter in Moscow. After initial hesitation about getting the money, his will collapsed when he saw the photos of the other girls who had been taken, and he fell right into the plan. It worked that way each time the target hesitated. When the wives or daughters were threatened, Vadim produced the pictures. It never failed.

Fedor had a front company set up expressly for taking deposits such as this. *Promyshlennyye Partnery Konsaltingovaya Kompaniya*, Industrial Partners Consulting Company or P2K2.

Incorporated in Panama, the company wasn't subject to income, corporate or local taxes and the owner's privacy was vigorously protected under Panamanian bank secrecy laws. There were no tax treaties to worry about, and subpoenas would never be a worry. Vadim had to admit, Fedor had a handle on the money side of things.

He pulled a piece of paper from his jacket pocket and laid it on the table. There were no other notations than dollar amounts. He pushed it toward Fedor who read it without touching it. In a single column there was a number repeated three times. Fedor smiled as he read it, *two-hundred-fifty thousand dollars* a month for the last three months. "All from the same depositor?" he asked.

"Yes boss, all from Transeget Industries. To anyone checking, these are payments for consulting services on doing business in Russia and on using the proper means of exporting product from the country. Weiner is schooled on how to reply to inquiries, especially from his internal audit department. He assures us he has the authority to hire such consultants as us. This one can go on indefinitely. Transeget Industries is valued in the billons and their operation here is a multimillion-dollar investment. Our payments would seem in line if anyone should inquire."

"No Vadim," Fedor cautioned calmly. "These payments do not go on indefinitely. Sooner or later Weiner will be exposed as making unnecessary payments over time. He may try to move his wife and daughter home, or he may be transferred or die. Nothing is forever Vadim. So, we monitor his payments closely. If there is any discrepancy, let me know immediately. If necessary, we can take the wife or the daughter to show we mean business. Keep me posted at all times." Fedor did not like to use that hammer unless necessary. Although a mature woman in her thirties may be worth fifty thousand dollars, a young pretty child almost old enough for sex was worth three times that. But those were one-time payments and that did not appeal to Fedor. "And the others? They are all paying on time?"

Vadim smiled. He was managing three more westerners living under the constant threat that a spouse or child would be taken into the white slave trade. This was a dream come true. As long as naïve companies sent their families here, there would be an income stream. He turned the paper over and showed a similar series of amounts. Vadim thought the math through in his head. From this line of business alone, his monthly take for Fedor was nearly a million dollars, and this next project would just add to that.

Vadim preferred this to Grigor's line of work, where they snatched someone and extorted a ransom payment. There was too much that could go wrong. And each of Grigor's cases ended in some kind of mess because Grigor's teams were brutes who enjoyed the thrill of danger and of blood. Even when they snatched women and children off the streets, there was always some kind of violence. That was a dirty side of the business and was where Vadim began his career. He no longer stood guard or beat the prisoners to ensure payment. He was glad to be out of that end of it now. He much preferred extortion or selling the women and children. He was out of it as long as Fedor felt he was doing his current job well.

Fedor was pleased with Vadim's update, and knew Sergei would be pleased as well. The thought of not pleasing Sergei passed through his mind, making him shudder inwardly. At that point he announced to Vadim that dinner was over. Now it was time for Fedor to satisfy his other appetite.

■ ■ ■ ■ ■

Carter heard them coming. He was hoping they were coming to tell him that Carol had agreed to the ransom.

Why had she taken so long? If she had responded sooner, he would have been spared his last beating.

They hadn't let him go to the bathroom and they wouldn't clean him up either. The blood oozing from his back didn't seem to matter anymore.

He was so weak from worry he no longer thought about eating or drinking. When he was awake his head throbbed constantly. Truth be told, he was beginning to welcome the respite from pain when they would finally knock him unconscious. He could barely breathe, and he was so dehydrated he could no longer urinate. The last time he did it on the floor it was red with blood.

The door to his cell opened.

Gloved hands dragged him to his feet, and he moaned in pain. Carter could not get his legs to support his weight, so they dragged him along the corridor to a janitor's closet. There they turned on the water to a hose that had been hooked up to the cold-water faucet. They dropped him to the floor

106

and began hosing him off. They seemed to be cleaning him, because they focused the frigid stream on his face and back and the crotch of his pants.

Then two of his captors reached under his armpits and hauled him to his feet. While he was still dripping, they pulled him listlessly down a hallway and into another room. He did not recognize this one. It seemed more like an office than a cell. He saw a wooden desk, chairs, a sofa and file cabinets. All the lights were on in the room and the brightness hurt when he tried to squint through his swollen eyelids.

They pushed him down into a plastic armchair and tied his legs to its legs, and his wrists to the chair's armrests. *Thank God they're not tying me to face the back of the chair,* he thought. Then he noticed it through his slitted eyes. Facing him was a video camera on a large tripod. The lone red light above the lens stared back at him. One of the Russians, a man with a completely shaved head, pushed a coffee table close to Carter's knees.

He opened his eyes again and the sight terrified him. Sitting on the table, without a sheath, was a Soviet Shaitan. The combat knife could inflict deep, wide wounds and it had a serrated blade capable of sawing through even mountaineering rope. Next to the knife were a thick folded towel and a current, English version of the Moscow Times.

Carter thought he understood why they had a current dated newspaper, but he dreaded why they had the Shaitan. He couldn't take his eyes from it and though it didn't seem possible, Carter became even sicker to his stomach. He began writhing in his chair, trying to escape his bonds as a sound, more like a wail than a moan, escaped him.

In broken English one of the men shouted at him, shook his shoulders and slapped his face trying to get his attention. "Carter, Carter. Your wife, why she no pay? She does not love you? Maybe she wants get rid of you. Yes? Maybe she think you not really in bad company." The man turned to one of his compatriots and said something in Russian that Carter could not understand.

The other guy reached behind the camera and pushed a button. On the front, the red eye of the Cyclops began winking at him and Carter seemed mesmerized by it, as if he were in a dream. The man then picked up the newspaper, walked behind Carter and held it under Carter's chin. They were showing that Carter was alive on today's date.

The man in charge said to him, "Tell your wife you are alive Carter. Say to her she is to pay us and stop fooling around." With that, he took the newspaper, rolled it tightly and punched Carter on the side of the head with it. The thud would surely be heard on the recording. Carter thought he would pass out, but the man behind him held his neck and began violently shaking his head. The pain was excruciating, and he cried out, "For God's sake Carol, pay them. Get me out of here. I can't take it anymore. Please God, pay them." The guy let go of his jaw. Then the leader picked up the Shaitan. The other one held down Carter's right wrist and isolated his baby finger. The red eye watched unsympathetically.

CHAPTER FIVE

I MADE THE CONNECTION IN Heathrow on time and the flight into Sheremetyevo was uneventful. The fact that I only had a briefcase and a carry-on bag and was sitting in first class put me nearly first in line at the immigration clearance checkpoint. From behind a smoked glass window an unseen hand switched my lane light to green. I approached the secure desk of the agent.

The guy working immigration looked to be about twenty years old. The bland features on a pale face changed to a sneer when he saw the Eagle of the United States of America on my passport booklet. He opened the book and began very slowly leafing through the pages. Every now and then he would pause and look back to the photo page and then back at me. The booklet read like an international travel log with some date-stamps nearly back-to-back. He recognized that I was a seasoned world traveler and must have figured I was wise to the ways of immigration officials. He might also have assumed that I knew the darker ways of how things were done in some countries.

He leaned toward me and whispered in a coarse, heavily accented English, "You have cigarettes for me?" U.S. cigarettes were a currency of their own in Russia and could be traded like dollars. There it was. The first sign of corruption and I wasn't even out of the airport. These small bribes were considered extra gravy for the agents who were usually some shirttail relative of a bureaucrat somewhere. It was how they got these jobs, and why they were coveted. I smiled innocently at the agent and leaned into the window space and whispered, "I don't smoke, but you can have my pen." With that, I reached into my jacket pocket, pulled out a company pen and handed it to the agent.

The agent felt it wasn't enough. He put the entry stamp aside and was about to hand me a red customs inspection card. Seeing what was coming I sternly whispered "Nyet" and pointed to the Great Seal of the United States on the passport cover, as if it was a magic talisman. The agent looked down, but not at the logo. He flipped the cover open and noticed the point of origin of the passport, Chicago.

He stared at it a moment as if trying to understand something important that escaped him. "Cheecago?" the agent asked, then answered his own question. "Da, Cheecago." Then he made an unmistakable stuttering sound, "duh duh duh duh duh," mimicking an automatic weapon and holding his hands as if he was cradling a Thompson sub machine gun. It worked. He must have thought I was from the Chicago mob. He nodded at me in a knowing way, stamped my passport, and then handed me a red card anyway. As if to show he was still in charge, he gruffly pointed me to the inspection line.

Even on a good day, going through Russian customs inspections could be problematic. The corruption and incompetence were on display everywhere.

A small queue had formed at two of the three red-card inspection lanes. There was another lane, but no one was getting into it. I looked around the corner and looked at the agents. They were equally as young as my immigration officer and they seemed to be paying absolutely no attention to the conveyor belt for incoming passenger luggage. I decided to take a chance with these guys. I loudly threw my carryon bag and briefcase onto the conveyor and they began their slow crawl toward the inspection end. Those two dolts never looked up.

I walked up to my bags and the agents. Wearing uniforms that were way too big for their youthful frames, they both had eyes that were half closed. They could barely hold their heads up. One leaned back in his aluminum chair, his eyes half closed. He seemed to be contemplating the meaning of life by staring at the ceiling without blinking. The other leaned forward and, folding his arms across the railing of the conveyor, placed his head in the cradle of his arms. I stood there a moment, cleared my throat loudly and waited. They were both so high on some drug or another that they never looked up. I grabbed my bags, threw the red card into the lap of one of the officers and left the immigration area without hesitation. No one called out to stop me.

The long, dingy white corridor from customs to the passenger pick up area was practically empty as most of the coach class passengers had yet to clear customs. I walked past the luggage carousel towards the transportation area. Many foreign travelers make the mistake of thinking a local taxi, randomly waiting in the cue at the curb, was a good bet to get them to their hotels. That may have been so in other countries, but not here.

It's common for most big-city, Russian cab drivers to "double-fare". That's a practice where the driver loads the passenger into the cab then leaves the airport. Somewhere along the route the driver stops and picks up another passenger. No amount of arguing with the driver can dissuade him from picking up the other fare.

Then after a few minutes on the road, the driver pulls over to "drop off" the second fare. At that point, this passenger pulls a knife or gun and robs the first passenger of money, luggage and credit cards. The driver pleads that he knew nothing of the intention of the second passenger. When asked to call the police, the driver says that will be the passenger's responsibility once they get to their destination. Then the police do not come, once they realize the victim is a foreigner.

Here in Moscow, the practice was so commonplace that the State Department warned travelers to Russia's major cities not to take the taxis anywhere, and to arrange for a private driver. Many companies do not want to incur the additional expense and there are still travelers who attest they had never been robbed and that it is safe. Regardless, when the consular travel warnings include the info, it makes good sense to pay heed.

Besides, I find Russian cabbies to be lousy drivers and surly to their passengers, especially Americans.

I looked around the area and saw Sasha standing there with a sign that simply said *TI*. It was innocuous and misleading enough that I didn't mind my company name being displayed like that. Besides, I figured the FSK already knew I was coming, based on my visa and passport information.

Sasha saw me, smiled and approached. "*Privet, gospodin* 'Hello, Christian,' " he said as he reached for my carryon. I shifted the carryon from my right hand to my left and grabbed Sasha's extended hand, shaking it. "I will take this Sasha. Thank you. Before we get in the car, I have to telephone someone. Where can I get some coins for a local phone call?"

Sasha reached into his jacket pocket, pulled out a thin, Dunhill leather wallet and extracted an American Express credit card. "We will use this, and I will bill your company. That way, your name does not show up too soon with your credit card number. Yes? You can exchange money at the hotel." Again, I wondered about the Americanization that Sasha demonstrated.

"No thanks Sasha. I will use this instead." I produced a Sprint calling card that I purchased from a supermarket in New Jersey. It was very untraceable. I also didn't want to give Sasha or anyone else a heads up on calls I was making before I had to.

I closed myself into the phone booth, entered the sixteen digits and dialed the number Maniaci gave me to reach Koval. The agent was expecting the call and we agreed to meet in two hours at a coffee shop not far from his office. Koval described himself – big guy, black T shirt and jeans under a short black leather coat. I thought to myself, *is this how a legal attaché dresses?*

I described myself and realized I looked like so many other non-descript vanilla businessmen. Close cropped hair, dark suit, white shirt, tie, blah blah blah. I made a note to myself. I would have to do something about that, someday.

■ ■ ■ ■ ■

Sasha led me to the limousine standing area. There was his cream colored, personally owned Mercedes E-Five Hundred sedan, the same one as last time and it still looked brand new. I knew that only a limited number of these had ever been imported to the States and wondered how Sasha had gotten one in Moscow. I didn't ask. I figured Sasha had a full-time and very lucrative contract with various American companies to haul their executives around and could charge them whatever the going rate was, or more. I knew that Sasha's wife drove for him as well. I felt fortunate that Transeget Industries afforded me that perk. Or at least they never challenged my expense account. *Same thing*, I thought.

"This is all I have, Sasha," I said, pointing to my carryon bag and briefcase. "Take me first to the Metropol, let me get checked in and I will drop this stuff off. Then I want you to take me to another location in downtown Moscow."

Sasha wanted me to sit in the back seat as befitting an executive, but I knew better. If I looked important enough, we might become a mark for a hijacking or an extortion attempt by local Moscow police. I sat in the front passenger seat and fastened my seatbelt.

"You still do not trust my driving Mr. Christian?" Sasha asked, looking genuinely concerned. I knew I ran the risk of offending him but I was taking no chances on Moscow roads and highways.

"It isn't you Sasha. It is the other drivers I don't trust." And with that I snapped my harness firmly in place. I had read about and seen countless, crazy examples of head on collisions and intersection T-bones, caused by drunken or careless drivers in Russia. Vehicle cadavers littered Russian roadsides, and flower-covered, makeshift crosses stood testament to the many automobile deaths. They were a sad example of a nation of drivers too inexperienced or too inebriated to be behind a wheel, or too arrogant to yield to oncoming traffic, regardless of traffic control lights and signs. I wanted to give myself every advantage to survive, especially on the road systems of Russia.

The ride to the Metropol was not a scenic one. We crossed over rivers of black water that looked unsafe for recreational use, in contrast to my home state of Michigan that designates nearly every public body of water for recreational use. There was plenty of public housing along the way, but if not for the cars in the parking lots, I would have thought the cold grey buildings were unoccupied.

We passed a road crew consisting of old men slamming pick axes into the concrete while babushka grandmothers walked behind them with pikes they used to break the concrete chunks into smaller pieces. Another group of old men bent and stooped to pick up or shovel the pieces and toss them into a pickup truck. Younger men used brooms made of twigs to sweep the smaller pieces to the side of the road. If the holes were going to be repaired, it wasn't going to be done right away. There was no gravel or tar truck anywhere to be seen.

Sasha noted, "They do not put up warning signs about the holes they just made. That would be someone else's job. The cars behind us will soon be driving through those holes and losing hubcaps and tires. Young boys will hide on the side of the road and steal the wheel covers, as they are jolted off the cars. Everyone must make money, no?"

We made it almost to the Metropol hotel without being hassled and then it happened.

At a major intersection only a few blocks from the hotel we spotted a half dozen Moscow city police officers standing in the middle of the street. Motorcycle officers straddled their bikes with the engines running and wore Kalashnikov rifles slung over their shoulders. A Moscow Police Officer, barely eighteen years old, pointed his striped baton at Sasha's Mercedes. "*Sukin syn* 'Son of a bitch!' " Sasha said. "We must pull over."

I wanted nothing to do with being stopped by the local police. They were all corrupt. It was how they augmented their income. "Drive on Sasha." I said.

"No, we must stop. The officer on the bike will pull us over or shoot us if we do not." Sasha pulled the vehicle to the curb. I was reaching for my wallet when Sasha objected, "No. I will handle this. If they find out you are an American, they will take everything you have, including your money, your bag and briefcase. Do not let them see that you are the one with money. I will take care of this little *khuy* 'prick.' It gets tiresome for everyone."

Sasha got out of the car and walked towards the approaching officer, shouting loudly. A heated argument ensued and one of the motorcycle officers began slowly cruising over. Just before the motor cop could cross the street, Sasha seemed to relent and reached into his pocket, pulling some cash out and stuffing it into the officer's hand. The kid quickly pocketed it before the motorcycle cop arrived. Sasha was waving his hands angrily in the air as he walked back to the car.

"Are you OK?" I asked.

"Of course," Sasha answered. "It is all part of the show we must put on. I could not let the officer question you or ask you for a separate contribution. It would be too dangerous for us both. And he did not want to share with the motorcycle cop, so I had to time the payment for him. It goes on all the time. It is the cost of owning a car and driving in Moscow. If you do not have a government vehicle, you will be pulled over for sure, sometimes twice within six blocks."

I reached for my wallet. "Let me pay you back. I can write this all off."

"Do not worry, Mr. Christian. I will bill your company and maybe mark it up for the inconvenience. Yes?"

I smiled at Sasha, "Yes. Bill them."

On the way to the hotel, I looked through my carryon and briefcase to make sure there was nothing incriminating. I would be leaving the bags in my room before the meeting with Koval. The

117

small box of gifts that Joanne had prepared for me was still wrapped in brown paper and taped inside my duffel. I would ask the hotel clerk to put that in a safe for me. While it would likely be inspected and possibly X-rayed by the FSK, it was not likely to be opened. If I left it in the room, it stood a greater chance of being stolen.

We drove the next few blocks without further incident. Sasha told me he would circle the block but could not wait in front of the Metropol. Those spaces were reserved for the mafia. My ears perked up at that, and while I wanted to explore that further with Sasha, I also needed to put my things in my room and then go over to see Koval. First things first.

The check-in process went smoothly. It always irked me to have to give up my passport to a hotel clerk overseas. And although I had never gotten used to the practice, I reluctantly acquiesced. They checked my package for me as well, but I got no receipt. "Just produce your hotel key to redeem your package sir." It was all very perfunctory, as if it happened that way every day. It probably did.

I asked for and got a room on the third floor. It was far enough up from the street to be relatively removed from road noise. But more importantly, it was close enough to the street that fire truck ladders could reach it if necessary. I didn't expect a hotel as staid as the Metropol to burn down again. The last time it happened there was in 1901. It didn't matter what era it was, because I wasn't taking any chances.

I wasn't disappointed with my small suite and knew I wouldn't spend much time in the simple room, other than to sleep and review my notes. The only thing that made this a suite was the separation of the bedroom from the main lounging area by a small half-wall.

From this point forward, I would always keep any notes with me rather than run the risk of someone taking them. I took a small sheet of luxurious linen hotel stationary from the desk drawer and scribbled a small note on it – *9:30 am - meet downstairs for breakfast*. The note was drivel, but it was a marker. I then set the note casually on the desk next to my briefcase, noting the position of the lower right corner relative to a clock face at four-twenty-five. I then left the room, securing the door behind me.

■ ■ ■ ■ ■

Sasha was not at the curb when I got downstairs. I paused to give myself a moment to recall the lay of the land. I smiled as I realized I was only a block from the Bolshoi Theater and within four blocks, depending on how I walked there, of Red Square.

I smiled as I thought about how interesting and historic the seat of the cold war enemy was, but I was immediately jolted from my reverie by the sounds of nearby automatic weapons fire. It was so close and loud that my reaction was to duck and hunch my shoulders. My hand instinctively moved to my hip where I grabbed a fistful of air. I hadn't regularly carried a weapon in over a decade.

Nearby, at the bottom of the steps, three men in hip length leather jackets observed me and laughed at my reaction. One of the men opened his jacket to reveal a Kalashnikov hanging from a strap. He chuckled, dropped the jacket closed and turned away from me to resume his conversation as if it was the most natural thing to be packing an automatic rifle and listening to the sound of gun battles in the heart of downtown Moscow. It reminded me of my days as a cop in Detroit, when gunfire was as common as automobile accidents. I had aged ten years and traveled forty-six hundred miles just to experience it all over again. I knew though, that bullets knew no cultural barriers and was thankful when Sasha pulled to the curb.

I dropped in the front seat, closing the door behind me. "Did you hear that?" I asked.

"Hear what?" Sasha replied.

"The automatic weapons. It sounded like a gun fight."

"Oh, that. Yes Mr. Christian. It probably *was* a gunfight. It is so commonplace any more that most people do not even notice. There is no way to avoid the shooting in any neighborhood, especially down here."

"Drugs?" I asked.

"The mafia controls everything here in Russia. Everything. But it is a very large organization with many leaders. Their turf is supposedly well defined but there are constant battles over ownership of every block, and every business on every block. This is why I do not register my business. I do not want a bureaucrat knowing what I am doing. If they did, they would tell a Bratva leader. His people would find me and make me pay for the privilege of doing business in their area. You see, everyone must pay the mafia. It is called building a roof, of

120

protection as it were, over my business. Without a roof, I would be assaulted, intimidated until I paid, or killed if I didn't. As you can imagine, I travel through all kinds of areas. I would be paying out more than I take in, just to bring you here from the airport. It is also why my only employee is my wife. We must keep it all a secret. It is why I do not object with you in the front seat of my car. It is safer for us both."

With the mob's fingers in so much, I wondered, *how is it that Sasha has not yet been found out and made to pay*? I would have to ask Koval how that was possible.

It wasn't long before Sasha pulled us in front of the coffee shop. I told him to come back in an hour and stepped onto the curb. In the distance I could still hear gunshots, but not so close that I felt the need to duck.

The coffee shop had a nice outdoor seating area enclosed by a small, steel half-fence. Although it was a relatively nice day, if you didn't mind the constant oily smog that hung like a pall in the sky, there was no one sitting outside. I pulled open the door and looked inside before entering all the way. This was going to be a problem.

Except for the women in there, nearly everyone was wearing a black T-shirt, jeans and a leather jacket. Was this some kind of joke Koval was playing? A guy carrying two cups of coffee was trying to walk around me to get out when I realized I was still blocking the doorway. As I stepped aside the man whispered in an American accent, "Christian? Wait a few seconds for me to leave, then follow me."

As instructed, I waited then followed Koval down the sidewalk and around the corner. Koval had picked a bench across from a street vendor selling cigarettes, vodka and re-used bottles of water at a kiosk. He sat and motioned for me to do likewise. From where we were sitting, we could see the entrance of the coffee shop. No one followed us out.

■ ■ ■ ■ ■

"Christian, I'm Tom Koval. Sorry for all the cloak and dagger stuff. I'll explain in a minute. Sit, join me." And with that he handed me a black coffee.

I sipped from the paper cup. It was a dark and hearty roast. Just the way I liked it. "I can't be the only guy in a suit that ever frequents that place. How did you know it was me?"

"Oh, that was easy," Koval chuckled. "Jerry wired me a photo of you right after he called." Koval shifted gears sociably. "How was your flight?"

"Actually, the flights were fine. Thanks, and please call me Michael. I was lucky enough to grab a company Gulfstream that got me to London way ahead of schedule and that got me here early as well." I enjoyed the pleasantries but wanted to get down to business. I knew this friendly chatter was a social process that had to be gone through. It was the same just about anywhere I traveled. When you were asking someone for help, it was important they got to know you, to feel they could trust you and to feel you were worthy of their assistance. The fact that Maniaci vouched for me eased the process, but it wasn't enough. I decided I would be the social one.

"So, Tom, Jerry tells me you have quite a background."

Koval briefly summarized. He seemed almost embarrassed by talking about it. Or maybe he just didn't like revealing what he had done. "Well, I had a little military experience and did some things in a war zone or two. I joined the Bureau after partnering with them on an assignment and have never looked back. But for the most part, I have been a desk jockey."

I pressed on, doubting the last part but expressing an honest interest. "Well, what does a legal attaché from the FBI do in Russia? Isn't that a bit of a challenge, given they are spying on you and you are spying on them?"

"Actually, Michael, it is working out better than you might think, better than any of us thought. As soon as I got over here, we found we had a mutual interest, terrorists. We started sharing information and knocking down cells before they were able to cause real damage."

I was recalling the work Maniaci and I had done gathering evidence just a year previous on one of the nineteen ninety-three World Trade Center bombers. I wondered how the blind sheikh, Omar Abdel-Rahman, managed to pass through everyone's intelligence radar and pull that one off.

As Koval explained, most of the work the legate was doing, to support the Russians, had to do with terrorists who were politically opposed to the Russian government's agenda. They were truly terrorists, but with a mission against the Russians. In years past, the terrorists might have been our political allies against the Russians. On the other hand, Koval revealed that he had approached the Russians for Intel on various Pakistani terrorist training camps and the attendees, and the Russians had been very forthcoming. It seems there was a link between the terrorists attacking both countries. The Intel allowed the bureau to interdict or put under surveillance numerous terrorists who were returning to the United States to set up autonomous cells there. These terrorist training camp graduates were bringing back skills in bomb making, cell development and the radicalization of our citizens. What Koval was sharing was information I had already surmised, but no one in authority had attested to it so openly. Koval must have sensed my wonderment.

"Don't look so surprised. This is open information among Federal law enforcement agencies, including Interpol. It's also pretty common knowledge within various House and Senate committees. Folks back home think I am a boy wonder of some kind because we got off to such a fast and significant start. Truth of the matter is someone somewhere knew ahead of time that the Russians needed our help and we needed theirs. This play was set in motion long before I got here. I think we may have a friend or two on the inside of the FSK, probably some old time KGB guys who have been around a long time. Regardless, it is working quite well for me and for both our countries. I suppose that brings us to *why we are meeting*?"

The abrupt change of topic caught me off guard. But I hoped I was smooth enough not to show it.

"Well yes. But first I have to tell you Tom. I'm impressed. You've been here less than a year and are making significant strides as the first FBI legate in what I would consider hostile territory. Congratulations."

Koval could tell I was buttering him up, nodded slightly and let me continue.

"So, let me give you a quick summary of what I know and why I am here."

"One of our managers seems to have somehow gotten himself involved with the Russian mafia. He is making regular payments from one of our business accounts in exorbitant amounts. He is embezzling the money and the company is not a part of this. We have not authorized facilitating payments of any kind, in fact the practice is prohibited. You need to know that up front."

I paused to gage Koval's reaction. If the Feds believed Transeget Industries was involved in prohibited payments, there would be Federal indictments that would not stop with Weiner. They could go all the way to Brinton.

Koval nodded as if he understood and agreed. But he gave no other affirmative indication that he felt TI was in the clear. He was playing that hand close to the vest until the last card was turned.

I continued, "My office personally briefed Weiner when he came over here, so he knows the rules and the security risks. Our General Counsel in France also briefed him separately about doing business in Russia. So, I expect whatever he is up to, he is acting without company authorization. In fact, I am sure of it. Feedback I get from those who know him indicates he is a pretty straight shooter and a good family man.

"So, although the evidence points to it, I am going on the assumption that this is something other than what it appears. But I am not sure yet what it might be. I promise that once I get it cleared up, I'll let you know. The company and the law department have a policy about not involving law enforcement without it going through counsel. But I'll get back with you, even if off the record."

Koval replied, "That's fine, Michael. Jerry says you are a straight up guy. That works for me. Now what can I do for you?"

"Actually Tom, I do have a question for you. I am curious about this roof-building business with the mafia."

Koval smiled and paused before answering. "Why? Are you interested in building a roof over something here? You know that might be considered a facilitating payment in some circles."

I did not want to be misinterpreted, especially by a Federal law enforcement officer.

"No, not at all. I have this driver I use, Sasha. He runs a private limousine service and our corporation uses him for our executives here also. He seems very above board. He bills on proper invoices and seems protective of our people while he drives for them. But today he mentioned that everyone in business, in all of Moscow, has to pay this rapidly burgeoning mafia. It's kind of like the old Chicago protection rackets. But he also said he does not pay and can't afford to pay. He called the protection *a roof*. He says he hides his business from them. Is that possible?"

"Well, let me clarify a few things here, Michael. First of all, the Russian mafia is very real, but it is not newly emerging. It dates back to the Czars.

And their tentacles reach not just into Moscow, but throughout all of Russia. In fact, the Bureau has traced them into New York City, Miami and Atlanta. They already have a monopoly on the drug trade there as well as prostitution, white slavery, and protection rackets. They are also deep into the South American drug trade and provide weapons to the cartels. And speaking of weapons, they are believed to have access to unlimited personal weapons and some heavy military-type artillery." Koval paused, as if waiting for me to intervene. I sensed it too but wasn't yet ready to talk with Koval about the nuclear issue. *Let him bring it up*, I thought to myself.

I tried to get Koval back on track. "But can he hide his business from the mafia? Is that possible? How can he avoid paying them? I am worried that he might get killed. His wife is in business with him as well. They both drive the car." I explained.

"It is possible he can hide the business by just not documenting it. But he would be running the risk of not paying business tax, and that is both a mob and government regulated operation anyway. It would also be hard to keep it from his neighbors and friends. Nearly everyone must be suspected of being a spy for the mob. It's just like in the old days of the Soviet Union. Every friend or neighbor might be a spy for the political officer of the house.

"But there is another way that I have heard of to protect oneself from the mob. You just have to find someone more fearful, someone more ruthless than the mob." He stopped.

I asked, "Is there someone tougher than the mob? Not from what I hear."

Koval replied, "There are rumors that there are still some old warriors of the KGB around. Perhaps that is what people refer to as more fearsome than the Mafia."

I was surprised. "You think a KGB guy is protecting Sasha? I thought they had been disbanded and reconstituted as the FSK and the GRU?"

"I can't speak to what Sasha is doing to cover himself. I am only telling you what I hear." Koval said. "I'm not sure I am giving you the answers you're looking for relative to Sasha. But a couple things you'll want to be aware of. The guys that Weiner is paying are real bad actors. We know them to be involved in kidnaps, extortions, hijackings, and white slave trade. They have a ton of money and launder it through what used to be legitimate businesses. These guys are multimillionaires and sit on the boards of directors of manufacturing companies, banks and energy companies. They are believed to have infiltrated nearly every major company in Russia and have the ears, if not the wallets, of every major politician in Russia – every politician – if you know what I am getting at. And every one of them is believed to be a murderer."

I guess I suspected this was going on. But to hear Koval say it with such emphasis seemed to bring it home even harder.

"Listen, Michael, you are going to be making inquiries into matters involving the businesses of Sergei Miloradov and Fedor Davydov. The moment you start asking questions, these guys are going to find out. They do not tolerate interference. My recommendation to you is to move fast and keep moving. You might want to line up alternative places to stay while you are here, just so they can't find you if they start looking.

"If you have to pull your guy out, do it as fast as you can and go out with him. I can't protect you. But if you find out what he is up to and it is a Federal violation, I expect you to let me in on it. Maybe we can then scoop up the bad guys, and get Weiner and his family out of here before Miloradov can react. Otherwise, it can be tough. Remember, we have no law enforcement clout over here. Just relationships. And they might not be enough, given we are dealing with Miloradov. It is not like I can summon an army here. And Sergei can – in a minute."

I asked, "Don't you have an inside man in the mob, someone undercover, an informant? Where do you get your Intel?"

"This isn't like a drug operation where we bust a guy and flip him into introducing an undercover guy. To get into the Bratva, you have to be vouched for by a fellow prisoner."

"Prisoner?"

"Yes, prisoner. Each of these guys, going back decades have served time in prison with each other or with someone inside the organization who can vouch for them. They do not betray each other, ever. They live by their *code*. Even at great risk, they will admit to the police to being Bratva, when asked. But they refuse to cooperate with any form of government. There is no getting inside this organization Michael."

I didn't like what I was hearing. I'd been hoping for something more positive from Koval. I was hoping he could use his legate standing to put some pressure on the bad guys. But it didn't look like that was going to happen. In fact, it looked like the Feds were powerless against the mob. It seemed more like they were holding back, waiting to bring Weiner in for making illegal payments, if I couldn't build their case for them. And that would not make Brinton happy at all.

"Well," I said, "It looks like I better get started. Just so you know, I will begin interviewing Weiner in the morning. He doesn't know I am in town, so I am hoping he'll be here and available to me."

Koval replied, "He's here. Don't let him or his people tell you otherwise. If he doesn't come in tomorrow morning or if he makes personal contact with the bad guys, I'll let you know." I knew right away then that the Feds had Weiner under some kind of surveillance. It was now entirely possible that I was under surveillance too.

I rose. "Well thanks for the coffee. I'll keep you posted and will take your advice. I'll try to wrap this up as quickly as possible. Just one request, do you think you could chase down a few more details about how Sasha might be protecting himself? Do you really think the KGB is making a business of offering a roof from the protection racket of the mafia?"

Koval rose and shook my hand. "I'll ask quietly of people I think I can trust. Keep in mind, even my counterparts and I do not feel secure from the mob here. They are very powerful."

I nodded my thanks and Koval walked away down the sidewalk and around the corner out of sight. I followed him a short way back, but Koval was already nowhere to be seen.

■ ■ ■ ■ ■

I took my coffee back to the coffee shop and sat outside waiting for Sasha. How did he avoid paying off the mob? Could I expect a straight answer from Sasha? Did I even want to push that button?

Besides, it wasn't the reason I was here anyway. I was here to resolve questions about a possible federal criminal offense and maybe to help the boys across the street with their missing material. In fact, it seemed odd to me that Koval never mentioned anything about helping with the search for the missing nuclear weapons. It seemed so strange in fact that I decided not to mention it if Koval didn't.

I wondered if my observation was real or just an overreaction on my part. Either way, I was uneasy. Usually after a meeting with the local law enforcement types, I was well on my way to solving my investigation. Not this time. It seemed I was still at square one. I also knew that once I started making waves, my window of opportunity would be very short.

I made up my mind that I was not going to call Weiner and request time with him tomorrow. I was just going to show up at the office in the morning. Weiner would just have to cancel anything he had going on and the interrogation would begin. They already had Weiner dirty. But key questions needed answers, like *why was Weiner doing this*? Another was *what kind of exposure did the company have?* And *what was it going to take to keep our business running without mafia interference?*

Brinton, Koval, and the lawyers would want answers. Then there was the matter of the nukes. I hadn't even begun down that path yet. And given my limited window of opportunity, I might never get there. My first priority was Weiner. This was becoming frustrating. Maybe it was just jet leg, but I began to feel overwhelmed.

Sasha pulled up while I was deciding what to do next.

I had some time on my hands and decided to take a drive over to our small information technology and administrative office. I gave Sasha the address, but he said he was familiar with it, having brought several executives there in the past.

It was becoming late in the afternoon and traffic was getting heavy. As we drove out of town, I noticed a car pulled over on the side of the road with its trunk open. A police officer was there talking to the driver.

"Is he getting a traffic citation?" I asked?

"No," Sasha replied. "The officer is being paid to protect the driver."

"Protect him from what?" I asked.

"The driver is selling water, petrol and auto parts out of his trunk. He is there every day. People pull up to see what new items he may have. Maybe one day he has extra spark plugs or a distributor cap or brake pads. Some say you can place an order for parts, and he will get them for you. His price is less expensive than trying to order them or find a parts store. You could wait for months if you order from a dealership."

I knew that people could own cars in Russia, but if a part went bad, a car could sit idle forever because of the lack of a replacement part. Once the iron curtain fell and capitalism was introduced, Transeget Industries' auto parts division rushed to fill that gap. I also knew that the parts being sold out of the trunk were likely stolen from the parts business that Weiner ran. "And the cop," I asked, "What is he protecting the guy from?"

"Strong-arm men will come and demand that the driver pays them for protection from thieves. Of course, the thieves would be the strong-arm men. The cop is there to tell the thieves that the driver is already paying. The driver must pay someone, the strong-arm men or the police, and a cut goes to the mafia. It seems that no one can make money without the mafia getting a piece of it."

"And you Sasha, how do you avoid it?" I asked.

Sasha drove a while in silence, and then said, "I do not tell anyone what I do. So, they do not come after me." I was beginning to doubt Sasha's word. I didn't know if I could trust Koval, and now I was unsure about Sasha. I recalled Maniaci's warning. *Don't trust anyone.*

We rode the rest of the way to our office in silence.

CHAPTER SIX

CAROL WINSTON WAS JARRED FROM her sleep by the incessant knocking on her front door. Disoriented, she looked over at her dressing table clock. The green analog numbers read eleven twenty-two pm. She had barely been asleep an hour and Jonathan had been gone less than two. Her bed still smelled like their sex and the scent aroused her immediately. She smiled and her nipples hardened as her mind drifted, but the pounding on the door roused her back to reality.

Could it be Jonathan? Was something wrong? Her anxiety took the place of pleasant memories and she threw a robe around her bare shoulders, fastening it as she hurried to the door. Looking through the viewer she saw a uniformed woman holding a small shipping box in her hand as she raised the other to knock again.

"Just a minute," Carol called through the door. She looked around on the porch and saw no one else around. She fastened the chain and partially opened the door.

"Carol Winston?" the courier asked. Carol nodded but said nothing, still wary. "I have an immediate delivery parcel for you, but your signature is required." She handed a delivery confirmation slip through the slit in the door for Carol's signature and followed it with an uncapped ballpoint pen. Carol jotted down a fast scribble and the parcel was handed to her. The driver turned without another word and got in her truck, without giving Carol a delivery receipt. She then drove out of the driveway and down the street.

Carol's first inclination was that this intrusion was a nuisance, so late at night, and tossed the small box on the coat tree table by the front door. Then in the half-light she could see the package had no postage or any other markings. She began tearing at it, looking for a seam to open it. It resisted being stripped in such a rough handed manner. Carol examined it further, more slowly, and found a zipper strip that would allow her to get at what was inside.

It was simply a videocassette from a camcorder, nothing else, and Carol had no way to play it. She called Jonathan immediately. He said he had a playback machine, but it was at his office in Union. He offered to play it for her in the morning, but when she told him it might be from Russia, he drew the same conclusion and said he would meet her at his office right away. If she hurried, she could be there in twenty minutes.

Jonathan was waiting for her in the lobby doorway when she arrived. He went to kiss her, but she ignored the offering. "Where is the machine Jonathan? We have to see this right away." Feeling snubbed but recognizing the gravity of the situation, he walked down the half-lit corridor. "This way," he said.

He walked her into their audio videoconference room where a camcorder was set up on a tripod. "I don't know how to project this onto the screen, but I do know we can view it on the camera itself." He pushed the power button on the camcorder and a red light on the front glowed steadily, indicating it stood ready to mindlessly respond to its master's beckoning. Jonathan inserted the cassette into the machine and hit the play button. They huddled around the three-inch display screen.

Carol had expected the worst, expecting to see Carter's dead body. But there was Carter, alive though barely so. It was obvious he had been beaten repeatedly. His eyelids were purple and swollen nearly shut. His lips were so puffed from bruising it hardly looked like him.

But Carol knew it was Carter, despite the deep black and blue of his eyes and the deep red welts on his cheeks and chin. The shirt he wore looked like an old rag, stained dark red and shredded. She could tell he had been whipped, just by the nature of the damage to the fabric.

Then she saw a man walk behind Carter and hold up a paper with a date on it. Two days ago. Then he folded it and delivered a crushing blow to the side of Carter's head. His head snapped so hard Carol was sure his neck had to be broken.

They then grabbed Carter's face and held it to the camera and screamed something at him. Soon Carter was screaming in pain "For God's sake Carol, pay them. Get me out of here. I can't take it anymore. Please God, pay them." Then he was blocked from view as two men stood in front of him.

When Carol saw him again, she thought two men were holding down his arm, and then saw they were struggling to hold his hand still. When she realized what they were about to do, she screamed to the unhearing men in the video. "Oh God no! Please don't!" Carter was struggling with all his might. His body convulsed in the chair, but there was no escaping. Carol was unable to look away and Jonathan was spellbound as well. They watched as one of the men picked up a fearsome knife with a large steel blade and in three aggressive cuts bloodily sawed off Carter's baby finger at the base of his hand. Carol fainted and missed the next part of the video.

Jonathan was sickened to the point of nausea but could not stop watching. Carter had passed out as a man wrapped his hand in a white towel. It immediately soaked through in a deep, dark red. He bound the towel tightly with what looked like a strip of inner tube, and the soaking seemed to abate.

The big Russian then positioned himself in front of the camera and spoke in slow, clear, broken English. He looked right into the camera and Jonathan Drews could swear the Russian was looking right at him.

"And now, Mrs. Winston, you see that we mean business. We demand to be paid and we want our cash within four days of the date on this newspaper. Your husband has many body parts, but we are no longer patient with your delays. There will be no more conversation. You will soon see on screen, information about our account in Panama. Do not try anything funny with your FBI. The account is protected. You will deposit two hundred fifty thousand dollars into the account before the end of the fourth day. In the meanwhile, we will take another part of your husband, just because you have pissed us off. Maybe next time not his finger.

"If we do not receive the payment by the end of day four, we will kill your precious Carter Winston and you will be at fault. There will be no more conversation and there will be no more delays. Pay us and we will drop your husband off at his office that very day. Do not pay us and we will drop off his dead body. The choice is yours."

The video cut off for a brief moment and then on the small screen Drews could see a plain white piece of paper come into focus. On it was printed the name of a Russian company, a bank routing number and a bank account number. Without shame or fear of exposure, the kidnappers clearly named Promyshlennyye Partnery Konsaltingovaya Kompaniya.

Jonathan froze the frame and wrote down all the information. He had no idea if Carol and Carter had this kind of money or how long it would take to access it. But the least he could do was facilitate the payment information for Carol so she would not have to watch the video again.

Then the guilt hit him. Only a few hours ago he had been naked with Carter's wife in their bed. He had spent a couple of hours sweating and doing things in private with her that should have been reserved for Carter. He did for Carol all the things she said Carter would never do for her, things that she hungered for with Jonathan. God, he felt low. Remorse swept over him as he recalled Carol's naked body over his, and their grunting and moaning.

But even in his shame he began to feel arousal at the mental image. He was confused by the feelings and disgusted with himself. He gave up trying to resolve his feelings. He wasn't sure he could stay away from Carol, regardless of what happened.

There was a side of him that wished he hadn't been able to play the video. Maybe it would have been too late to save Carter by the time Carol could figure out how to decode its contents. His mind was awash with conflicting thoughts and none of them were noble. He turned his attention to Carol, still in a fugue on an office sofa.

He brought her a glass of cold water, raised her ankles over the armrest of the couch, and laid a wet paper towel on her forehead and another behind her neck. In moments she awakened. Then she screamed again and tried to wrest herself away from Jonathan as the image flooded back of Carter's beaten body and bloody hand. At that moment she made up her mind. She had to do all she could to get Carter back alive, even if it broke them financially. It was her duty.

Then she felt Jonathan's comforting arms around her, smelled his musky scent, could feel the heat rising from him and she became aroused, deeply aroused at the basest level. At that moment Jonathan and Carol decided Carter's fate and it wasn't good. They sealed their agreement on Drews' conference room floor.

■ ■ ■ ■ ■

Fedor enjoyed this part of his evenings. A good meal was behind him and after-dinner cordials were complete. He had enjoyed a spa plunge in the basement and was relaxing naked, except for a warm white robe that anyone else might call a tent. But no one would dare say such a thing.

He was not alone. There were several teenaged girls in various forms of nakedness in the room with him. They were from his own stables, and hand picked for him. The girls looked younger than they were, with their waif-thin bodies, blonde hair and blue eyes. He liked his girls very white and pale skinned, no tan lines. All the girls were at one time or another stolen from their families. Most no longer remembered their parents and most no longer cared. He frowned when his phone rang. He had left orders not to be disturbed. This was his private time and there would be hell to pay for this. "Da," was all he gruffly said.

It was Grigor.

"There has been a development, *ser*." Fedor knew right away it was serious. Grigor never called him sir unless something bad had happened. "Speak," was all Fedor said.

"It is the American, Winston. He is dead."

Fedor's immediate reaction was rage. Then he cooled almost immediately. "Did I not tell you, Grigor, that Winston was an asset to be protected?"

"Yes sir, but," Davydov cut him off. "And did I not tell you that this was not my asset and that it was Sergei's? Did I not tell you that it was his revenue stream? Not for me Grigor, but for Sergei?"

"Yes, Fedor. Yes, you did, but ..."

Fedor Davydov was not going to be interrupted. "And did I not tell you there would be serious consequences if anything happened to this asset? Did I not look you in your eyes, Grigor, to make sure you understood?"

"Yes, Fedor, you did. I understand." Grigor realized that his life was now in Fedor's hands. Long standing relationships no longer mattered. This was likely also outside of his boss's hands. No matter who was to decide what happened next, it would not be good for Fedor and would be worse for Grigor. He tried to mitigate the fall-out.

"I have already dealt with it, Fedor. It is taken care of. Trofim and his boys were to see to the American's care and watching. You saw the video. He was alive and energetic enough to lash out in pain until he passed out. Once we took his finger on the video, we took him back to his cell. After that he did not awaken. Trofim thought Winston was just passed out from the pain and shock. So, he let him sleep. The American did not wake up. When Trofim went to check on him again several hours later, Winston was in the same position on the floor. The shock may have killed him, or sheer exhaustion, or he may have bled out from his finger. There was a lot of blood on the floor. Either way, he was a weak man and did not do well. Trofim tried to revive him. But he was already dead."

Fedor was unmoved and remained silent. He was planning how to tell Sergei that he had lost a quarter of a million dollars by Fedor's team being too rough on the asset.

Grigor tried to explain further. "Everyone was aware of the importance of keeping him alive, Fedor. Everyone. I was very clear about that."

"Yes, well apparently I did not make myself clear enough to you Grigor. You have lost my asset. Tell me, how did you *deal with it?*"

Grigor measured his words carefully. He needed to be certain that he conveyed that he was appropriately hard on Trofim without giving Fedor any ideas about how to deal with Grigor himself.

"Once I learned that Winston was dead, I myself went to the cell to make certain. Yes, he was indeed dead and seemed to have been for several hours. I cleared the room of everyone but Trofim and interrogated him loudly so the others could hear. I asked how this could have happened when we made it clear he had to be kept alive. I told him you would be displeased, Fedor. He was trembling and began begging for leniency. He said it wasn't his fault and that Winston was weaker than we thought. He said it wasn't his idea to take his finger and we should have just beat him and maybe he wouldn't have died."

Fedor was tiring of this explanation and thought Grigor was now protecting himself rather than providing any valuable input. He stood from his lounge chair and motioned the girls from the room, watching in frustration as the naked nubile bodies gathered flimsy lingerie pieces and hurriedly left.

"Enough. Enough. It does not matter. Meet me at my office in two hours. I am not sure I can protect you Grigor. I am not sure I can even protect myself. Pack a bag. I must get you out of town right away. It may be the best I can do, for old times' sake, Grigor."

"But Fedor, can we not just explain to Sergei that it was not our fault. That we gave very clear orders and they were not carried out?"

Fedor thought to himself, *this is why Grigor can never rise in the ranks of my organization. He does not understand that this is a business. And in a well-run business, the manager takes responsibility for the actions of his subordinates.*

"No, Grigor. Pack the bag and I will see you as I said – two hours, my office. But tell me, Grigor, how *did* you handle Trofim?"

Grigor knew he had done the right thing, but he sensed Fedor was not ready for any puffery. "I called the team together in Winston's cell and stood them around his dead body, with Trofim at my side. I reminded them that we were charged with keeping the asset alive and now he was dead. Each man sensed the gravity of their collective failure, but they were all looking at Trofim. They were waiting for him to take the blame. He did not." Grigor paused to see if Fedor had any comment. Hearing none, he continued, "I told Trofim this had occurred under his supervision and that he must say a prayer for Winston's soul, since we were to keep him alive. I made Trofim kneel next to the body to pray. As Trofim closed his eyes to pray, I took the Shaitan he used to take Winston's finger and I slit Trofim's throat."

Fedor would hate to lose this one. Grigor understood the use of force so well. Without commenting on Trofim's fate he said, "Meet me.

144

Tell no one you are leaving, my friend. And I mean no one, especially that girlfriend of yours. She will be the death of you Grigor. She cannot keep a secret. She thinks she is a movie star because she is dating you and you bought her new breasts. But she is a talkative one. For now, I must deal with Sergei to buy us some time. This cannot wait."

Fedor gently replaced the handset in the cradle. His anger had passed, and he was calculating his next moves carefully. One misstep and he would be dead, just as his friend Grigor would soon be.

Fedor knew he would have a hole in his organization that must be filled with someone of complete competence, someone who understood business better than Grigor. Sergei would be watching closely how Fedor handled this. He took a deep breath and dialed Sergei's number.

■ ■ ■ ■ ■

Transeget Industry's administrative office was situated in a small, wooded office park of two-story, yellow brick buildings. In English and Cyrillic, the lettering on the door merely said *Transeget Industries*, nothing about the nature of the work that went on in there.

I asked Sasha to wait in the car. This was merely a courtesy c+all where I would introduce myself to the manager and see if there was anything the manager wanted to talk about security-wise. Either way I would leave a business card and head out. There would be no deep conversations about crime, extortion, or the

145

challenges of doing business with Russian partners who owned a controlling interest in the joint venture.

When I entered at the ground floor, I found the doors to the individual offices locked and most of the lights out. There was no alarm control panel that I could see in the halls. I walked up the steps to the second level and found the office doors also locked. Looking into our space through the glass panes of one of the doors I could see this was our computer server area. I was dismayed there was a clear view into the room from the hallway. The glass should have been opaque, if not a solid door. There were no electronic door locks and no camera systems monitoring the halls and entryway. These were among the minimum-security requirements at all Transeget Industries data centers.

A woman approached me, listlessly pushing a bucket on wheels and holding a mop inside it. She looked at me suspiciously, then put her head down subserviently as she walked by.

I removed one of my TI business cards from my pocket and held it out to her. I only knew a few Russian words. "*Pozhaluysta*," I said, 'please'. She looked up and then at my card. It was written in English on one side and in Cyrillic on the other. She read the card, saw the word *Diplomat* and bowed deeply. It had the intended affect.

I made a motion with my hand as if I was opening a door with a key and pointed at the door to the server room. My pantomime worked. She took her key chain from her pocket and opened the door for me and stood aside, allowing me to enter. *Spasibo* "Thank you," I said, smiling. I had breached the perimeter barrier by using social engineering, a fake scrawl on a business card, a polite word and a smile. *So much for the lock and key aspect of security.*

I wanted to take a look around, even though I didn't know what to expect or what I would find. Reaching along the wall in the dim illumination, I found the light switch and turned on the fluorescents that came on in stages down the aisles of server racks. The thought occurred to me that there was a lot more computing power here than our repair centers normally had. Still with no one to ask, I didn't know what to make of it, if anything.

"Who's there?" A voice called out from behind the wall of servers.

"My name is Michael Christian and I am with TI," I replied.

A figure walked out from around the corner. "How did you get in here?" he asked.

I didn't like being put on anyone's hot seat. "I am the global head of security for Transeget Industries and I used a key." I replied, "Who are you?"

The man looked at the card and then warily at me and replied, "I am the admin data manager, Jason Torrey, and I run these machines. My Russian counterpart has gone home already. What are you doing here? I mean, what can I do for you?"

I replied, "I didn't know you were closed this early. I came by to meet your VP and introduce myself. But since you are here, I do have a question for you."

Jason nodded as if to say *okay*.

"Given that this is the service group's local data function, what are all these servers doing here? I mean for God's sake, you could run an entire division's processing requirements on these machines. If you're the admin manager, how do you keep the Russian's out of our trade secret knickers with all this gear?"

Jason seemed enthused to talk about his business. "Well you're right about the amount of horsepower we are running here. But when we brought the repair and service business over, our Russian partners invited us to make a Eurasian hub of this center. It made good sense since we were planning to branch out the repair service to all the former Soviet countries anyway. Rather than build individual administrative data centers, we built just this one and plan to remotely provide data services and software to the others.

"As for trade secret security, we built a firewall to protect our stuff. If there was any crash through that wall, the system would notify me."

I had seen server rooms before and the investment of gear in this one far exceeded any need for this division, especially since it was barely off the ground. Something was not right about this. It was time to hold Torrey's feet to the fire.

"Walk me over to your office while we talk, Jason. So, did Transeget Industries have a security blueprint? You know, for the load-up and software requirements, for the access control and data-rights protocols? If so, I haven't seen it."

Jason stopped and turned to me. "Why would you see the data security blueprint? You're not in IT."

I was sensing the beginning of resistance. "No, Jason, I'm not. But all foreign data services start-ups are to be presented to me and my teams so we can review their adherence to corporate security policy, including IT security policy, which I co-authored with your vice president. Furthermore, there are Export Control Act and the ITAR's bill of munitions requirements governing the types of physical security and encryption technology allowed out of the States, especially to Russia. I didn't see the bill of materials for any of this gear."

Jason stammered briefly as he tried to frame a response. "I don't know why you weren't read in to our plans. That call would have been above my pay grade. And frankly, a lot changed once we got over here. For example, we projected the need for only one rack of three servers and central processors, and a primary, a backup and an overflow server in case we got jammed up in a denial of service attack. It was our partners who asked for and got these other five rows."

"Doesn't it seem odd to you that they want all this extra processing and storage power? Are they paying for it, or are we?" I asked.

"There's no doubt that it's overkill and we said so in a board meeting of this joint venture. But keep in mind that the Russians control fifty-two percent of the votes on all matters. Once they have an agenda, we are powerless to stop them. And the funding for all this stuff was a non-budgeted expense paid for out of the venture's proceeds." Jason was warming to the conversation and seemed glad to have a sympathetic ear about the partners running roughshod over the IT group.

I pushed on. "Are you running Intrusion Detection and Prevention systems on your firewall? Have you set a cyber-attack threshold and are you notified in real time or via a report of any attempts?" I wanted Torrey to know that I knew about cyber security measures, even if my knowledge was only at the policy level.

Torrey wasn't sure he should be providing this kind of detail to a stranger, but I seemed too well informed to be a fraud. He explained, "We're using IPS combined with IDS. If there are more than two hundred attempts from a single source, I am notified by email. If an attack crosses five hundred attempts, that IP address is reported out and blocked to prevent further attempts. Most attempts number fewer than a couple dozen and most all of them are unsuccessful."

"*Most* are unsuccessful? What do you mean most? Do some manage to hack their way in? I'd like those transaction histories, where they went and what they were after. I want to have them examined forensically by my team." I said.

Torrey was visibly coloring as he thought about his reply. Someone he didn't even know was challenging his authority and skills. He wasn't even sure I was an actual employee. He decided not to provide any more information without some further kind of credential. "Do you mind if I see some identification, before we go any further? And I think I need to call my boss," he said.

While I was fishing a business card out of its leather folio, I looked around the office and Torrey's open space desk configuration. I handed my business card and corporate ID card to Torrey to examine then took my ID card back. "Call your boss if you want to Jason. In fact, I'd like to meet him. I want to ask him if those are re-built desktop PCs meeting company export standards, or if they're new-in-the-box and shipped here for configuration."

"No," Torrey responded. "These were all shipped here new and I configured each one myself. The Russians haven't touched these."

"That wasn't my concern Jason. These PCs contain 1024-bit encryption keys and as such are still restricted under the munitions list. This is exactly what I was talking about earlier. How the hell did they end up here?"

I was looking at the equipment and felt the internal conflict that Torrey must have been going through. But the kid's personal feelings didn't matter. I knew that someone back in the states felt it necessary to encrypt certain data to keep the Russians from seeing some trade secret information. But they made the wrong equipment call. This is why my department was to see all technology being exported to foreign operations. The lawyers were going to have a tough time with this one.

"Jason, where's your boss's office?"

Torrey walked to the only room in the suite that had a door and unlocked it. *Interesting,* I thought. *The IT guy has a key to the manager's office. I wondered who else had one – besides the janitor?*

The office was quite large, and the manager's PC was sitting on a credenza wall behind the manager's chair. I walked over to the machine and pulled it from the wall. There it was, just as I expected. Clipped between the keyboard cable and its connection to the PC hard drive was a keystroke logger. Someone was monitoring every keystroke, and presumably the logon ID and passwords, of every one of the branch manager's accounts.

Customer lists, equipment configurations, purchase prices of customer gear, warranty information and extended warranty costs, customer equipment logs and driver data. This was more than the Russian partners were entitled to and the breach had happened on Torrey's watch. He was screwed.

I held my finger to my lips, indicating I wanted silence. Torrey seemed confused until I pointed out the logging device. Torrey seemed about to comment when I held up my finger again.

"Let's go grab a smoke," I said. And we walked from the office.

When we got downstairs, Sasha saw us coming and began exiting the driver's seat of the Mercedes. I motioned for him to stay in the car and wait.

The two of us continued down the sidewalk a bit before I spoke. "You do not need to be running IDS or IPS software on your gear. Your partners now have access to anything they want. And their transactions will appear as having been authorized under your manager's logon address, including his emails and the authoring of email as if it was from him. I presume you keep engineering prints of all our gear and our detailed repair manuals online as well. All our proprietary data is certainly in their possession. Your firewall is useless as far as separating us from them. Your *partners* could open a competitive business of their own and undercut our own pricing and it would appear to be our own company doing it.

"I am also guessing all our strategic plans for Eurasian growth were on the machines, as were progress reports to your group heads back in the States. Would that be right?"

Torrey just nodded his head, couldn't even look up. He looked like he was going to be sick. The strategic plans were any company's crown jewels and they were now very likely in the hands of the Russians.

"Here is what we are going to do, Jason. We are going to leave that keystroke logger right where it is. And we are going to have a chat this evening with your manager. I want you to drive to his home, explain to him what we have discovered, explain about the illegal machines in your office and tell him that we are to meet at my hotel in forty-five minutes. I am staying at the Metropol. Whatever you do, do not discuss any of this in the office or on the phone. Just meet me in forty-five minutes. I don't care if he is at dinner with the Russian President. You grab him and meet me. Do you understand Jason?"

"Yes, nothing over the phone. Meet you at the Metropol in forty-five minutes. No exceptions."

"Right. No exceptions. I will be waiting for you on the steps of the lobby."

With that, I turned back to my car and got in the front seat, strapping myself in. I reflected on the past few minutes, *between arrogance, carelessness and corruption, could there be a worse place on earth to conduct business?*

"Sasha, how long will it take to drive me to our parts warehouse and then back to my hotel?"

"About thirty minutes if we do not have to go inside to visit. Traffic could still be heavy and then it could take an hour." He replied.

I thought it over. I really wanted to see the place before I met Weiner, but I could not afford to miss my meeting with Torrey and his boss, especially after insisting we meet, *no exceptions*. I had to be on time.

"Listen Sasha, I just want to ride by the place, front and back and then head back to the Metropol. Can you do that in about a half hour?"

Sasha was already putting the car in gear and his foot to the pedal when he answered, "Dah."

■ ■ ■ ■ ■

The ride to the warehouse was like riding in a dodge-em car at an amusement park. Rush hour traffic was well over. Although there should have been a quieter pace to the flow of vehicles on the M10 that connected Moscow to Novgorod to St. Petersburg, it seemed to me that everyone was late getting somewhere. Sasha was not slowing anyone down. He was driving over ninety-five miles per hour, as it was. And that worried me. But we were relegated to the right hand of the three lanes, as cars raced by us.

I was getting the impression that the one hundred fifty kilometers per hour signs were more like a recommendation to be multiplied by a factor of two. If turn indicators were available on the cars, no one used them, and drivers seemed unable or unwilling to stay within their lanes. Cars without headlights or taillights in the early evening hours swerved back and forth with regularity.

"Too much vodka," Sasha observed. Drunken drivers were pushing their Ladas and Trabants beyond their limits, as if some death wish was hurrying them on their way to a fatal accident somewhere.

As they drove, tall telephone poles stood sentry, guarding the roadside. Electric cables branched off them through sparse woods into tall apartment complexes. The high-tension wires to the buildings were run through the crotches of trees rather than on poles. It appeared that any heavy storm could topple a branch and plunge hundreds of households into frigid darkness.

And we feared this nation, I thought. Their only claim to international power and might seemed to be their stolen missile technology, espionage being their stock in trade.

We slowed as we approached the exit to the warehouse district north of Sheremetyevo airport. I told Sasha, "When we get there, drive around the rear first."

The rear driveway was narrow with wooden pallets strewn along the path leading to our facility's rear doors. The delineation between the other tenants and Transeget Industries' facility was obvious. Where junk was littered everywhere else, TI's property was nearly immaculate by comparison. Excess skids were neatly stacked out of the way, along the perimeter fence. Entrances to pedestrian and dock doors were clear of debris and visual obstructions and they were well illuminated. Two Transeget Industries trucks labeled in Russian were backed tight to the walls in front of dock doors. It was immediately obvious that although this may have been a Russian owned company, this was not a Russian-run company.

Sasha slowed and as my eyes adjusted for distance, I observed a parked car facing us from down the alley and across the street. Exhaust streamed up from the rear tailpipe and hung like a shroud over the top of the car. It was occupied.

Sasha turned right onto the street in front of the car. As our headlights lit up the occupants, three men stared back with unblinking eyes.

"Mafia guys?" I asked. Sasha answered, "I don't really know boss." But in the pit of my stomach, I thought I knew the answer to the question. They sure looked like it. But why would they be here?

As Sasha turned right again onto the street fronting the office entrance, I noticed another occupied car, this one a black Volvo, parked to our left facing our entrance. Sasha noticed it too. "More bad guys." He mumbled. It didn't make sense to me. The place was empty, yet it seemed to be guarded by two vehicles. And by the looks of the occupants, they seemed capable of roughhousing if necessary. I didn't like it one bit and wondered what I might encounter when I came in the morning.

The front of the building, in contrast to all the other buildings in the area, was well illuminated. High-intensity lights mounted on the building roof, brightening the sidewalks and street. Our car was clearly visible, I noted. "OK, Sasha, let's get out of here and get me back as fast as you can. Safely." I added.

Sasha tromped on the gas as I looked out my side view mirror. The Volvo was not following.

■ ■ ■ ■ ■

Sergei Miloradov kept a measured pace about himself. Everything he did, every business decision he made, was calmly and coldly calculated. Every person who reported to him directly had been handpicked for his unique qualifications. These men were experienced in criminal undertakings and each had a specialty. Some, like Fedor had several. Every one of them had served time in a Moscow prison. Since there were thousands to choose from, Sergei only selected the exceptional ones. He intentionally chose former military officers or educated gang leaders, or KGB members who somehow offended their leader and ended up in the infamous *Vladimirski Tsentral*, The Vladimir Central Prison. It was no use trying to recruit from Lubyanka prison. No one ever escaped or had their freedom bought from there.

He was particularly interested in men who were from his old neighborhood where he knew their parents or relatives. These men had loyalty and a code whose rules of understanding, their *Ponyatiya*, bound them together. They must be willing to die for each other and where their obedience became doubtful, Sergei would casually mention the name of a loved one as if recalling a boyhood memory. Each soldier in his command knew it was a death threat and they lined right up. But some like Fedor were special and became Sergei's direct reports.

Fedor rarely bothered Sergei. He was a stream of income for Sergei and rarely posed a problem. In fact, Fedor provided the most generous share of all Sergei's subordinates. If he allowed himself to, Sergei could almost trust Fedor. But Sergei would never allow that to happen. They both knew and respected a higher relationship – this was all about the money. And business was business after all.

So, when Fedor called and said he needed to speak with him right away, Sergei agreed. It was unusual for Fedor to request an immediate audience, so Sergei cancelled his lunch and meeting with the Russian Minister of Energy. It didn't matter to Sergei. He would simply reschedule. The minister was on Sergei's payroll anyway and Sergei sat on the board of directors.

Sergei enjoyed the infrequent but long conversations with Fedor about skimming on bulk sales of oil to western markets or increasing mining production of their raw alumina for export to Poland. Together they took advantage of insider tips to buy shares in privatized, undervalued Russian assets, and then watching their share prices rise when the oligarchs announced open trading or asset valuations. And they were equally as comfortable talking about the less sophisticated but equally lucrative side of their business, kidnapping and extortion.

Fedor was indeed the best *Avtoritet* of Sergei's cells.

Fedor dreaded the meeting with Sergei. His boss had called him on the carpet in the past but never for anything as serious as this. By Grigor ruining the value of this asset, Sergei was going to be out a quarter of a million dollars. Sergei monitored his revenue daily. And even though it was in the millions each day, this was a significant loss and it was on Fedor's watch.

On the other hand, Fedor didn't get where he was by being either afraid or unimaginative. He had been with Sergei almost seven years now. He was *vor* a 'loyal member'. Although thousands of vory had died during the decades-long *Bitch Wars*, he and Sergei had survived the last of those turf battles together. They emerged from it rich and powerful. Fedor knew that his own success and wealth could only have happened, as it did, under Sergei's tough and brilliant leadership. Sergei was cold and unemotional about his business and Fedor wanted to survive this likely fatal failure. For that he drew on his intimate knowledge of what drove Sergei - money and absolute obedience.

When Fedor entered Sergei's front door and nodded to the bodyguards, they both eyed the large, dirty canvas sack in Fedor's hand. "Open it," one said. Fedor opened the bag. The other man searched his person. Fedor did not carry a weapon to business meetings with his boss. He knew there was no way he was going to be allowed past the guards with an uninspected package or a weapon.

Sergei's life hung in the balance each time he met with someone, loyal comrade or not. Everything and everyone who came into his home or business was searched. Everyone, every time. Although there was a look of surprise on his face, the guard who inspected his bag allowed Fedor to retain it. He merely said, "He is upstairs." Fedor pulled the drawstrings shut on the top of the bag, securing its contents from further review, and walked across the polished marble floor.

He climbed the winding stairway with its hand-carved, polished mahogany bannister. A crystal chandelier hung in the arch of the stairway and every crystal was immaculately clean. Fedor thought about the image Segei's lifestyle conveyed. It was more to impress others than about the way Sergei cared to live. Had this building, in the heart of Moscow's government district, not been given to Sergei to settle a debt, he likely would not have chosen it. If he chose, all his residences here and around the Mediterranean would be Frank Lloyd Wright architecture. Sergei loved the western modern influence, not this ornate gold guilt style of Russian bourgeoisie.

The door to Sergei's office was open, but he knocked twice anyway and waited. "Come in Fedor, come in," Sergei called out. Fedor took a deep breath and entered.

Sergei rose from his desk and the two shook hands. He motioned for Fedor to sit opposite him and took the lead without pleasantries. "So, tell me. Why am I cancelling meetings for you, Fedor Davydov? What is so important?"

Fedor sat straight in his chair. Without interruption he narrated the whole chain of events from the selection of Winston, the demands on the wife and her failure to pay or listen. He told of them using more extreme measures on Winston and sending the video to the wife. He told how Winston had died, either from his wounds, internal injuries or just fatigue and shock. He stopped there without mentioning Grigor. A deep frown appeared on Sergei's face as the story ended with the loss of his money-maker.

"Has she sent the money?" He asked.

"Not yet Sergei. Honestly, I do not believe she wants to redeem her husband."

"Have you approached the company for a ransom?"

This was the flaw in Fedor's initial strategy. He knew they should have gone that route first. It was their standard operating procedure to make the demand of the company because they inevitably had Kidnap and Ransom insurance coverage. But Winston had convinced them the company would not use the K&R policy to pay. He had been told that before he came to Russia. He had insisted his wife could come up with the money. Winston had not counted on the fact his wife may not want to pay. Neither had Fedor. He explained his rationale, but the frown did not leave Sergei. His mood blackened and Fedor became a bit unnerved.

"How much was the demand?" Sergei asked. Fedor knew Sergei was calculating his loss in U.S. dollars, the only currency that mattered. He also felt no need to mention that their initial demand was for a million, and when it seemed the wife was hesitant, they lowered the price on Carter's head.

Without waiting for any additional comment from Sergei, Fedor followed with his ace-in-the hole and tossed the canvas bag on Sergei's desk.

"Two-hundred-fifty thousand dollars Sergei. I am sorry for the inconvenience." With that, he pointed to the bag. "This is from my own account. It is all there, in cash. Please accept my apology."

Sergei was at first taken aback. Then he pointed to the bag. "Open it." He said.

Fedor pulled the leather drawstrings open and dropped a few wrapped packets of hundred-dollar bills on the desk. "These are all real Sergei, no counterfeit."

Sergei looked at the cash on his desk and paused a long time before responding. Fedor knew that Sergei was pondering his next move, the move that would decide Fedor's fate. He bit his tongue and maintained his silence. He had made his case and made his atonement. There was nothing left to say. He was prepared regardless of what Sergei decided. This final outcome was a risk he knew he would someday have to face.

Sergei took the bundles of cash and slipped them back into the bag, pointing to it. "Put the bag on the floor behind the coffee table, Fedor."

Fedor knew the move would require him to turn his back to his *Pakhan*. He knew his boss was capable of it and feared the worst - a shot in the back from a silenced weapon. He hoped it was to the head so the end would come quickly.

He took his first step and heard Sergei's desk drawer pull open. He stopped dead in his tracks and waited.

■ ■ ■ ■ ■

"Go ahead Fedor, put it behind the table."

The Brigadier took the next two steps, dropped the bag as told and turned to face his boss. Sergei was standing behind the desk holding a bottle of Askaig seventeen-year-old single malt liquor.

"Fedor. A simple explanation would have sufficed. You did not need to make me whole. I thank you for it however, and will keep your offering in the spirit of friendship. Have a drink with me my loyal friend and explain to me how you have handled this lapse."

Fedor was perspiring profusely under his suit, and he hoped the tension in his muscles wasn't showing. He wanted to appear nonchalant about the circumstances, but he knew that Sergei had spent a moment contemplating killing him. It appeared his gamble had worked. Now he had to figure out if Grigor was salvageable.

"The boys had been clearly instructed that we needed Winston alive. I held a special meeting of the team – with Grigor and he had a further meeting with his *shestyorka*. I had asked him to have a separate talk with his guys to warn them not to be too aggressive.

"Winston had been punched around pretty well before that, especially when his wife began hesitating with payments. He was weaker than we thought."

Sergei interrupted him. "We have gone over that Fedor. Tell me how you handled it after."

"The man in charge of his day-to-day care, Trofim, has been made an example for his carelessness. His throat was slit in front of his team members. It was done as a reminder that we must follow orders. It also showed the importance of the value of the asset. Grigor was in charge of this group, so he saw to it personally." Fedor paused. He did not want to over explain, and he wanted validation from Sergei that he was on the right course. He also hoped that killing Trofim alone would satisfy Sergei.

"And what of Grigor. How did you handle him?" There it was. Sergei wanted more. The rules were absolute. Disobedience would not be tolerated, even by accident.

"I had him pack a bag, Sergei. He must leave Russia. I have a meeting with him this evening. He has told no one. His people will think he has been disposed of, but he is exiled. Grigor and I have known each other a long time Sergei and he is good on the street. He sees lucrative opportunities for you and me. This is his first error and that is no easy feat managing those ruffians on a day-to-day basis. Of course, if you have other thoughts on how I should handle Grigor, just say it."

Sergei had been sipping the golden-brown nectar and set the glass down. Fedor's had remained untouched. "Drink Fedor. Let me explain something to you.

"An efficient organization is like a complex piece of equipment. The value of the machine is that it can produce parts faster than a single individual. Optimally, the appliance will run with low costs to operate, and low cost to maintain and repair it. It will stay within tolerance, producing quality output, one after the other, without error. Over time several things can happen that impair that efficiency. Its parts become tired or worn. Slack occurs between parts when they run a long time. And that affects efficiency and inefficiency affects profitability.

"It is therefore important, Fedor, to have a good operations manager to ensure that things run smoothly, without fail. Yes?"

Fedor was about to answer when Sergei cut him off. "And the hard-working employees look to the boss for assurance that their work is valued, Yes? And when someone is not pulling their fair share of the load, the others know it, Yes? And they expect the manager to address it properly or they will become loose parts in the system also, Yes?" This time Sergei paused, both to ensure Fedor was paying close attention as well as to get a commitment from him.

"Yes, Sergei." Fedor was now being circumspect. He knew he was being set up for the point Sergei wanted to make.

"If that is the case, you still have a couple inefficiencies to address. What is your plan?"

Fedor knew whatever he told Sergei had to be weighed as a satisfactory response to his organizational problem. But it might also give Sergei ideas on how to deal with Fedor himself. Sergei prized Fedor and both men knew it. But Fedor was merely a cog in Sergei's machine. If he was viewed as broken, he could be replaced instead of repaired. He needed to be careful here. He answered confidently.

"Grigor must disappear. He plans to meet me at my office shortly. He is expecting that I will ship him to Minsk, to another operation, and have him take it over. I can arrange that, but I have deeper concerns. I have a young organization and each of my new men is trying to become vor. They are headstrong, cocky and hard to tame. That was a weakness of Grigor's. He could be hard on the assets but was not so good keeping his men in line. That is how we lost Winston. I am afraid I may have to make an example of Grigor also."

Sergei interrupted him. "There is no doubt about making an example and I am glad you brought it up. Tell, me Fedor. What do you have in mind?"

"Frankly, Sergei, while you know I am capable of this, I would like to keep my hands out of it. I would like to have one of your men go to my office, meet Grigor there and handle it. And I would prefer no mess, so that it looked like Grigor just disappeared. Everyone will understand but will have no proof."

Sergei turned his back to Fedor and picked up the phone. He spoke so lowly that Fedor could barely hear him. But he did make out some of the conversation, "...Fedor's office. Make it quick but make it clean." Then his words were indiscernible again. He spoke a few more moments then turned back to Fedor.

"It is done. But now let us turn to your other problem. You now have a hole in your management ranks. How will you fill it? Is anyone in your group ready to move upward?"

"No Sergei. I have Mirski handling a very large load now and I am pushing his limits. There is no one with the experience to take on all that Grigor had managed for us. I have two people that I can use to each take part of the load. They can manage for a while. One of them may rise to the top and take over for Grigor, but it could be possibly a year or two."

"That won't work Fedor. I might have an alternative for you, however."

Fedor knew this was not up for debate, so he merely nodded his understanding and waited for Sergei to continue.

"I have someone whose expertise I am trying to broaden. I have done business with him outside our group. You may know his name, but perhaps not. I do not expose him and his work where others may see him. You, I can share with. I need his revenue stream under my direct control rather than merely taking a piece of his action or buying from him. He is a shrewd businessman, a former junior officer in the East German Stasi."

Fedor stammered, "A German in our group? What ...?"

Segei held up his hand. "He is not German Fedor, He is one of us. He was placed in the Stasi leadership to monitor and manage East German and Russian troops. He managed inventory in the Berlin armory and when the Union was dissolved, he was responsible for repatriating those weapons to Mother Russia. I will tell you more about him in time. But for now, I want him under your management. I will have him join us in a few days. I believe he is currently traveling.

He will fill Grigor's slot for now. You will be responsible for teaching him how we operate, for explaining our code. I want you to make sure that your men accept him. There is to be no doubt among your people that he is my pick and that this is my doing, not yours. That will help smooth the transition. Use him as if you have known him for decades, as I have. We must make him *vor* as soon as he is ready. Someday I will make him a brigadier. Fedor, groom him to become your ally or at least indebted to you. His name is Pavel Oveshkin."

■ ■ ■ ■ ■

Grigor felt sick to his stomach. He knew he was lucky to get out with his life and to begin somewhere else, safely. There was a side of him that thought it was wrong for Fedor to ban him from the area. Yes, the American was killed by his men, but he had warned them to be careful and he had taken the most drastic measures when he was disobeyed. That should have been enough to lessen the punishment he faced. But there was a side of him that understood where Fedor was coming from. Fedor had to account to Miloradov, who would surely have killed Grigor. He was thankful that Fedor was his friend as well as his boss. Anyone else might have killed him just to serve as an example. He contemplated all this as he waited in Fedor's office.

It wasn't that Grigor was afraid to die if that had been Fedor's decision. He wasn't. It was just that he wasn't ready yet. So, he was grateful to Fedor for a chance to start over. He had a full life to lead and he had a young wife.

It wasn't as if they were really married. They had just been together a while and neither was seeing anyone else. She was a pretty girl, just twenty, but wise for her years. And she was feisty. She had been one of their inside *prostitutki* and served higher-end clientele who liked the new ones who looked younger.

Although she had been sold repeatedly for four years, Grigor became obsessed with her. In time he was able to slowly move her away from the regular schedule of a high-end call girl. He then bought out her contract under the guise of moving her to another venue. That was when he moved her into his apartment, and they became lovers.

Truth be told, Grigor liked his women just a bit older, but this one had the attributes of a young one with the attitude of a girl much more mature. He had no idea at the moment what to do about her. When he got re-established, he would send for her. He had very specific instructions not to tell her he was leaving, so he would have to leave that communication to Fedor.

Grigor was awakened from his musing by the opening of the inner door to Fedor's office. It wasn't his boss. Grigor barely had time to process what was unfolding in front of him. He had no time to ask what was going on and when he realized what was about to happen, he had no time to beg for mercy or pray. He wouldn't have anyway.

It was over in a few seconds. One instant he was watching as the first man of three pulled a silenced small caliber weapon from his jacket and took aim at Grigor's face. The next moment it was dark. And then there was nothing.

The two other men rushed to Grigor and held him up before he fell completely to the floor. One pulled a blue plastic tarp from inside a duffle bag and laid Grigor's still warm corpse on it. Not a drop got on the floor, not even back splatter. Using the tarp to carry him, two of them lifted the body, carried it out of the building and into the back of their van. Meanwhile the shooter grabbed Grigor's suitcase, extended the handle and rolled it from the room. He looked back carefully. The ashtray was empty and there was no glass or bottle out of place. The room was perfectly clean. He gently pulled the door shut and, using Fedor's key, locked it behind him. It was as if Grigor never existed.

CHAPTER SEVEN

JASON TORREY AND HIS BOSS stood at the top of the wide marble entrance staircase in the lobby of the Metropol. The place reeked money and elegantly and ornate interior design. Brass railings, tray ceilings and gold-gilt pillars shouted stability and power, and gave testimony a culture of another time. Mirrors reflected vanity at every turn. "Isn't this place amazing?" Torrey asked.

His boss, Ron Crandall looked around. Men in brown and black leather coats ran up and down the stairs, in and out the front doors. The liveried doormen ignored them. The smell of cigarette smoke hung on the cold air behind them as they moved in and out of the entry. He sensed low-life self-importance about them, and maybe something sinister. It unnerved him.

"Amazing? No. I think the place is over-rated. Look at these guys. You know they are mafia thugs, right?"

Torrey was impressed, nevertheless. *The Metropol.* He had never been here, despite having lived in Moscow almost a year now. But the place was famous, and Jason knew it. Business executives, politicians, and the elite of the European entertainment world all stayed here. And Christian called the meeting here. He wondered if Christian had a room here. *No, he mused, not a security guy. No way.*

When I pushed through the Metropol doors at ground level, I saw them standing at the top of the stairs, just as instructed. Torrey waved a small gesture to make sure I saw him. We made eye contact and I could see him struggling to figure out what I was doing at such a place. I climbed the stairs deliberately, keeping them waiting a few more seconds.

"Mr. Christian, this is my boss, Ron Crandall. Ron is the vice president of IT for our Russian ventures. Ron, Michael Christian." We shook hands and I said, "Gentlemen, excuse me just a moment," as I walked to the front desk and picked up my key.

Torrey was watching in disbelief as I asked the clerk to find me a quiet place to have a private conversation. The desk clerk picked up the phone and dialed. A brief conversation ensued, and the clerk hung up and whispered to me. He then pointed to an elevator.

I returned to Crandall and Torrey and said, "We have a small sitting area where we can talk," and I turned to the elevators with them trailing behind.

The second floor's wide, straight corridor was edged with a polished brass railing that looked down over the registration area below. The hall was lined with glossy mahogany tables. Arranged around each were four solid, cushioned chairs. Clean ashtrays adorned every table, and each had a phone. I moved to the center of the long room and selected a table along the railing overlooking an atrium area. We pulled out chairs and sat. Torrey's amazement was showing. "Are you staying here?" he asked.

I started right in. "Yes, I have a room upstairs. But let us begin. I know you will want to get home, and I have some things we need to go over immediately. There are things you will need to set in motion tonight."

"Just a minute!" Crandall interrupted. "We don't even know who you are, and we have our own agenda that keeps us busy day and night. Before you begin adding to it, you have some explaining to do. Like what gives you the right to walk in here and start giving orders?"

Before I answered, I picked up the table telephone set, turned it upside down and examined the cable leading to it. I reached down and unplugged the cable from the base of the phone. I figured every phone in the place was wired to a central recording system and was very likely being monitored live whether the handset was lifted or not. I had to be clear with these guys, but I also had to be careful.

I began, "I am the global head of security for Transeget Industries. I have been sent here under orders from Barry Brinton. I report directly to him and no one else. There seems to be a problem with some of the operations here. I was making a courtesy call at your facility when I noticed some things out of the ordinary."

Crandall interrupted again, "That may be so, but from what I understand, you broke into our space uninvited and began snooping around. I object and will be reporting your rude and intrusive behavior to my boss and to *your* boss!"

I was becoming frustrated with this distraction from my primary mission. What had started out as a mere courtesy call had morphed into another investigation. I had to resolve it, but I didn't have any time to spare. I knew exactly how I was going to handle them.

"Not a problem," I replied. I opened my business card wallet and pulled out one of my cards. On the back, where my name was printed in Cyrillic, I wrote a phone number from memory, including the international dialing sequence. I handed the card to Crandall.

"What's this?" Crandall asked after only a cursory examination, flipping the card on the table.

I enjoyed this part. "This is the personal mobile phone number for Barry Brinton. Call him now. It is only about one o'clock a.m. in New Jersey. Let's get this resolved so we can move on. Call him."

Crandall blanched. His bluff was called. Once he realized that I actually had the horsepower, Crandall was now on the hot spot. These next few seconds would determine his future whether he knew it or not. His best option was to try to get out of this gracefully, and also to maybe save his job.

"OK, Christian. You win. I hope you can see how I would be skeptical of a stranger just showing up in Moscow, unannounced and sneaking into our facility. And surely you can tell how it sounded to me when you started giving orders without me knowing for sure if I should even be listening to you, much less following your direction. What is it you need and what do you want from us?"

I had seen this play out before. In other cases, I actually forced the arrogant party to call Brinton. It usually resulted in an ass chewing from Brinton. It often resulted in a job re-assignment or at least a demotion for the calling party. Now that I had made my point to Crandall, I needed to convince him that we needed to move fast, tonight. I made up my mind to move on.

"I do understand Crandall, but I hope when I'm through, you'll see why we're moving so fast to resolve some open issues. This conversation is not going to be documented in writing. No follow up memos, from either of us. Understand?" Crandall nodded.

I continued, "You have brought over computers from the States that contain prohibited encryption standards. Your machines are specifically listed as unauthorized into Russia, which makes them, and you for that matter, in violation of U.S. Export Guidelines. Your export and joint venture data materials list was not submitted to my office for review before this gear got here. Perhaps someone knew that if my department saw that list, we would have insisted it be modified. That's a violation of company policy and a violation of internal audit guidelines, including your division's own security policy. It's very likely a violation of some statutory requirement as well". I saw a small twitch in Crandall's eyelid and figured it was Crandall himself who gave the order to circumvent corporate security.

I went on, "Your joint venture partners have loaded up our server room with more equipment processing power than you need for this business, even with a Eurasian expansion. And we are paying for that. I am guessing we have no access to the information or applications stored on your partners' partitions on those servers. Would that all be about right?" Crandall's head lowered just a touch as he framed his answer. There was no longer any arrogance or hostility in his carriage.

I moved on without an answer. "I don't expect you to answer, Crandall. It's a moot point at this juncture. And confirming my suspicions and probably yours, I found a keystroke logger attached to your key board cable."

With that, Crandall turned to Torrey, "How is that possible? You are supposed to be our data security guy here. Aren't you checking these things? Aren't you tracking attempts to steal information from us? This is one of the things we talk about all the time!"

Torrey tried to answer, "I have IDS and IPS software running. I am not seeing ..."

"Obviously that has not been good enough!" Crandall shouted.

I hissed, "Keep your voices down. This is closing the barn door after the horse is gone. Not only are your Russian partners duping you into financing and equipping some larger, unknown operation of theirs. They are spying on you. It will not surprise me to find that they have all our customer lists, our state-side pricing schemes, our engineering designs, our prototype drawings, our five-year divisional plans and your global passwords Crandall."

Crandall was turning grey. He knew it was probably true. I could see it written all over him. Crandall was seeing his career go right down the drain. This would be an irrevocable mistake. Torrey knew he was riding on the same horse as Crandall and was silently depressed as well.

I hated this part of my job. But I had repeatedly caught arrogant people who made rogue decisions, thinking their rationale superseded the rules. These were guys who thought they knew better and therefore the rules didn't apply to them. They moved in their little circles thinking all was well. And it was, as long as they didn't get caught.

These two had made some decisions that exposed the company and its proprietary information, and the value of shareholder investments, to economic and foreign industrial espionage. God only knows what the Russians were doing with all those servers and the encryption software they had access to. I would let Crandall's and Torrey's chips fall where they may. But I needed these two guys to take some action and try to salvage or mitigate any loss that had already occurred.

I paused, looking hard into their eyes before beginning. "Torrey, I want you to leave the keystroke logger in place. They already have what they want and if you remove it, they'll think they have been burned and will likely try to cover their tracks. Take another PC off the shelf and set Crandall up with another master account and don't use his real credentials.

"Crandall, I want you to stay off internal mail for a while except for completely innocuous correspondence. Use the compromised system for those simple emails. If you think you need to mark something confidential, then use a third-party phone and dictate your email to someone in our French General Counsel's office to send for you.

Nothing confidential or private can ever be sent on your current machine again, unless it is blatantly false, intended to misdirect, and our recipient knows it." I had something else in mind for Crandall.

"I want you to fly to France this week, tomorrow would be best, and meet with our counsel. They may have you begin a disinformation program. But we must also begin a market impact analysis on our compromised data.

"Torrey, I want you to begin a plan for an immediate transition of computers used in your operation to those that have a fifty-six-bit encryption key. That must happen within the next day or two. And it has to happen out of view of your partners. The water may be already over the dam on this one. I am guessing they already have the key software code and are using it to decrypt our information and to encrypt all theirs. This is a first priority. Work tomorrow with the general counsel. They will handle all the logistic aspects for your communications needs. You might want to consider calling them from a public phone.

"And I want you to begin planning a software virus attack on those damn Russian servers tonight. As soon as you are sure you can pull it off, get to work planting it and let it run. Make it look like it was dropped on them in an online attack. You don't need anyone else's permission or authority to do this. If the shit ever hits the fan on it, blame it directly on me.

"I also want you to set up your most robust machine, maybe two, to begin a dedicated denial of service attack on the Russian servers, all of them. I want them so overloaded with attacks they cannot use their own equipment to search you out. The goal would be for them to make a decision to take all their gear off line. Better still, if they ask you for help, make that your recommendation until they can clean their servers.

"And if they do clean them, I want you to re-infect them. Mask your attack IP addresses and point them to North Korea or China. Better still, if you can find a backdoor access to one of those servers, turn it into a machine that attacks the others. And while you are mucking around in their systems, I want you to download all their stored files, even if they are encrypted, and see what we have lost to them. Send whatever you find to our general counsel in France.

"If you can't do that for ethical or technical reasons, tell me now and I'll have someone here tomorrow who can. We are only going to do this until we can gather enough evidence to prove what they have been up to, and get our machines and data clear of theirs. Then we will litigate them into separating us from the venture. Meanwhile, I'll be talking to our European attorneys tonight to fill them in on the plan.

"Crandall, Torrey, is this something you can do, or should I bring in someone else to handle it?" I knew they could handle most of the demands. But I was unsure of Torrey's technical skills as a hacker. I was also relying on the fact they would try to do anything they could to save their jobs.

Crandall answered first. "I can do these things and I can get to France right away. I may have some trouble working off a new computer though. All my reporting software is linked to privileges associated with that processing unit. I will ..."

Torrey interrupted him, "It won't be a problem. I will clone a clean device and work it off a new VPN connection. And I can keep it from reporting to the logs and local registry. But we will have to let New Jersey know somehow what the new ID is that you'll be using to communicate with them."

"Do it by phone," I interrupted. "Not all communication has to be by a computer, just because it is sitting there. Now what about the hacking? Can you handle it or not?"

Torrey nodded. "Yes, I can handle it. I guess I may have been a bit of a hacker before I got this job. And I have been building defenses against them for quite a while." Then he stopped. He seemed to realize that he wasn't as good at cyber security as he thought. "Maybe I am a better hacker than a security person?"

"Let's hope so," I answered.

I rose from the table. I had made my point about the risk these two had exposed the company to. I had given them direction and distracted them, for the moment, about their careers. And I bought some time before I had to call the General Counsel and start that process rolling. I made up my mind to spare the general counsel my suggestions for a counter-attack on the Russian equipment. They'd find out soon enough. What a mess, I thought to myself. And I hadn't even begun resolving the issue I was sent here for in the first place.

All my intelligence-gathering efforts pointed to the fact it was too early to be doing business with the Russians. Their economy was unstable, and early Russian joint ventures had already developed a history of going belly up within months of their inception. The Russians needed just enough time in the relationship to clone, copy, counterfeit and steal all the information they wanted to set up their own competitive business.

The ruble was unstable as hell, the banking system was untrustworthy, and Russia refused to acknowledge the World Court as a body to adjudicate contractual differences. Making matters worse, local judges consistently ruled in favor of the Russian side of all joint venture disputes and often found the western counterparts guilty of some trumped up criminal offense, forcing them to leave the country or face imprisonment.

But the smell of money for TI's global marketing executives had overcome any sense of reason when it came to risk management. Corporate financial risk assessments tended to ignore or minimize the threat from criminal enterprise. On the one hand, finance managers seemed to think that corporate espionage was a myth made up by government officials and security executives. And on the other, they had trouble quantifying the impact of lost intellectual proprietary. Therefore, they often ignored it or downplayed it in market risk assessments.

And now these decisions by Crandall and Torrey were sure to delay the timeline for profitability on this side of our business.

As we stood together, I waited for the IT guys to make the first move. Crandall extended his hand. "I'm sorry we got off on the wrong foot. I can see where I am screwed no matter what. Thanks for making the revelation at least somewhat palatable. Is there anything we can do to save Torrey here?"

I doubted it. "I'll leave that to you and the attorneys. Why don't you ask them that question?

They have a lot more experience with this kind of thing. I also imagine it will depend on how well you guys do in the next few days creating havoc for your Russian friends and limiting any further exposure. You might want to save sharing that last tidbit for a while."

I had a twinge of disappointment that young Jason Torrey's career was about to come to an end, but this story would give him something to talk about at a later time. As for their Russian partners, screw them. I just wished I could be around to see the chaos when their computers crashed time after time.

We shook hands around and the two computer wizards walked to the elevator. I waited for them to enter and head downstairs before I summoned an elevator of my own.

■ ■ ■ ■ ■

My footfall was quiet on the thick, rich carpet as I walked to my room. The sound and feel were lush and comforting. I knew that a thousand royalty and literati had walked these same halls for almost a hundred years. It felt strangely good and odd at the same time.

I was from a truly humble background and would have never believed in my lifetime that I would be in Russia and staying in the Metropol. My mother had passed away before I joined the security profession. My dad just smiled in pride when he heard stories of my escapades. My father-in-law, an educator, wondered how I earned my credentials and never understood what any security person did, other than a guard. He certainly couldn't reconcile, with his academic background, what I did on my travels, and I am sure he doubted many of the stories I related to him.

And just what was I doing here? Investigating a Russian mob connection with an employee of our company? Authorizing a hack into a Russian joint venture? And what about the *other thing*? Would I even have the time or the connections to be of value to Cam Cross? I wasn't so sure. That effort was a Gordian knot without a single loose end to tug as a starting point.

The oversized brass key fob, that read *Metropol,* clinked as I slid the key into the lock and turned it. The mechanical click was not as solid as one might expect. It almost seemed flimsy as a lockset for such an auspicious lodging. I walked into the room, letting the door close on its own. The light was already on inside. Maybe room service left it on when they turned down my bed. Then I looked across the room to my briefcase. It wasn't just that the stationary I had meticulously placed at the corner of my briefcase had been moved. The whole damned case was opened, and its contents were strewn about.

It wasn't the first time my briefcase had been tossed as I traveled around the world. It was just that this was so blatant and obvious. It seemed either that the crew that did this were rank amateurs, didn't care, or were deliberately sending me a message, *we are watching you*. If the latter message was true, then whoever was sending the message was confident in doing so. It would certainly complicate all I was sent here to do.

My message light was lit on my phone, so I called the front desk. "Mr. Christian, we have a message for you to call a Mr. Koval when you get in. He left a number." The desk clerk passed along the local number, which I dialed right away. Koval answered on the first ring.

"Michael, I have some information for you about how someone ensures their business is safe from local risk. It is interesting and may be of value to you. Can you come by in the morning, first thing? I have somewhere to be, but I would like to pass this along to you in person. Would seven o'clock be too early, maybe for coffee at the same place?"

I thought about the proposed meeting time and immediately felt the jet lag hit me. It seemed like I had been up for days, and in international time zones, I guess I had been. If it were possible, I would have slept until noon the next day. "Sure, seven is fine. And thanks, I'll see you then." With that, we rang off. Maybe I should have told Koval about the search of my briefcase, but I left that as an agenda item for the morning. First, I had to call Paris and get things rolling there.

■ ■ ■ ■ ■

Despite being exhausted, or maybe because of it, I had a fitful night. I felt groggy and unrested when the alarm went off at five in the morning and the cold shower did nothing to revive me. I would have to rely on caffeine and excitement to keep me going all day. I wasn't hungry but knew I had to get some fuel in me before I started. No telling when I might eat again.

I dressed in an open collared button-down shirt, clean slacks and my black leather jacket. Good enough for business in Russia I thought. I grabbed my briefcase and tossed in some small things for Sasha and his wife and headed for the door. I left my duffle bag in the room.

I rode down the elevator trying to organize my day but this one seemed elusive. I knew I would eat first and then grab that cup of coffee with Koval. From there I would have Sasha take me over to the warehouse office to meet Weiner. At that point everything seemed to unravel. Whether it was fatigue or confusion, I could not seem to develop a clear plan of attack. And I preferred to always have a plan.

By the time the elevator reached the Buffet Mezzanine, I decided that I would treat Weiner as a suspect, rather than a witness to some misadventure. He was embezzling company funds and funneling it to some mob guys, and according to Maniaci, some seriously bad gangsters. Regardless of what Marianne said, nice guy or not, I had to decide how to handle my meeting with Weiner and this was an approach that was not only appropriate but would give me direction. I would take what I learned from interrogating Weiner and go from there.

If I was good at anything, it was getting people to tell me the truth, no matter what they thought they had to lose by doing so. The process was pretty straightforward. And things began to finally gel in my mind.

I would start out slowly with simple but probative questions. I'd watch Weiner's body language with the easy ones that we both knew the answers to. I would check how Weiner recalled truthful information. I'd watch the movement of his eyes. Was he being truthful or deceptive? Then I would look for deviations from that pattern when asking him difficult and challenging questions designed to prove guilty actions or guilty knowledge.

I had spent years fine-tuning my formal interview training against real-life experiences. The amount of time it took for me to get to the truth of the matter depended not so much on how strong-willed a subject was, but how long it took me to get convince he he had more to fear more by lying to me, than by being honest.

As I stood in line for the luxurious Metropol buffet I began to feel better about the way the day might go. I looked at the tables arrayed before me. I could have been on a cruise ship.

Ice carvings, floral arrangements and fruit-art graced every table. Everything was fresh and not a morsel fell off a serving platter without it being scooped up and carried away in a moment. The spread could satisfy anyone, if they had a European appetite, that is. There were fresh processed meats and cold fish of all kinds, cheeses, olives, fresh and pickled tomatoes, cucumbers, baby corns and more. Cold hard-boiled eggs were in abundance as were dozens of assortments of freshly baked small breads, crusty buns and croissants. Notably absent were the American traveler's favorites of toasted white bread and breakfast sausage and bacon. In their stead were the wonderful, light pastries and a European breakfast sausage that resembled more of a small bratwurst. I noticed that the cold cuts were the breakfast meat of choice for the European guests, so I decided to follow suit.

I started out with only a sample of a few things but before I was halfway through the buffet, my plate was full. As a waiter appeared from nowhere to carry my plate to my table, a voice from over my shoulder said, "You going to eat all that Christian or are you hosting a party?"

I was startled. I wasn't expecting anyone I knew to be here. I turned, looking surprised, as I tried to place the face of the Yank standing behind me in line. "It's me, Kenny Stiles. TelcoCom? Kansas City?"

It took a moment, and then it registered. Stiles was not a co-worker, but he and I had served on a couple executive committees for a previous employer. I was Director of Security and had worked my way onto several total quality and future planning committees. Stiles was from the General Counsel's office but was almost invisible among the nearly one hundred attorneys that supported the company in one way or another.

"Kenny, what the ... What are you doing here?" I didn't mean it to sound as if Stiles shouldn't be there, but it probably came off that way. "No, I didn't mean ..." He must have seen the confusion on my face and didn't seem offended, seeming more amused than anything. He replied good naturedly, "I know, right? What are the chances we would meet in Moscow? What are you doing here? Some more spy stuff?"

That put me off balance. Many thoughts were going through my head. What *were* the chances I would meet someone in Moscow, especially Stiles from Kansas, and standing right behind me in line? And what was that crack about *spy stuff*?

The moment seemed awkward for both of us. Stiles mentioned something about having guests waiting at another table, suggesting maybe we could hook up for dinner some time, and began edging his way out of the conversation.

For a moment, I felt bad that the encounter had gone so awkwardly and was about to chalk it up to fatigue. But the more I thought about it, the more Maniaci's words came back to me *trust no one.* I really didn't like this aspect of the job, the side of me that took even friendly encounters with a grain of salt.

I had become a guy who said *I will be your friend when you prove yourself worthy of my trust.* I was no longer the guy who said *I will be your friend until you prove yourself unworthy.* The less sensitive approach served me in my line of work, but I knew it sometimes grated people the wrong way. *The hell with it* I thought. *I've got things to do.* I pushed those thoughts to the back of my mind as I walked to my table to eat my breakfast.

■ ■ ■ ■ ■

Sasha was standing by the Mercedes as I walked to the curb and slid into the front passenger seat. "Good morning Sasha. Thanks for joining me so early."

Sasha did not respond to the greeting. Instead he slid the big car into traffic, turned right alongside the hotel and asked, "Are you expecting company? Did you hire someone to join us?"

"No, why do you ask?" I answered as he turned in his seat.

"I believe there is a car that has been following me from the petrol station this morning."

There was little traffic coming from the front of the hotel and not too much on Revolyutsii as we pulled north onto it. Sure enough, a car pulled slowly around the corner lagging behind us. I did not want to over-react. The car could be anyone. "Black Volvo," I observed.

"Yes. Wasn't it also a black Volvo at the warehouse last night?" Sasha recalled.

It was, but this was Moscow. Black Volvos, BMWs and Mercedes were commonplace. "Is that the car you think was following you this morning?" I asked.

"It is the same car and the same guys as this morning. It was dark last night, but I think it is also the same car and those boys from your warehouse."

I wasn't sure about that but wasn't taking any chances. And regardless of who was following, I didn't want them to see me meeting with an FBI agent. "Turn right up here at Tealtranyy and then take your first left. It is a quieter street. Let's see if they follow."

Sasha negotiated the turn smoothly using his turn indicator. As he approached Neglinnaya he made an abrupt and unannounced left turn. The Volvo sped up and followed but stayed about ten car lengths back.

Sasha was flying along a small side street now and I had a fleeting thought about being stopped by the Moscow police. It would not be easy to explain why we were speeding and might even require a bribe to keep out of jail. But the thought passed quickly as Sasha noted "They are still with us."

Sasha turned right onto Pushechnaya across heavy oncoming traffic and accelerated. I could hear the throaty rumble of the Mercedes and was pleased he had the larger engine. Traffic was heavy at the next intersection also, but we caught the left turn lane empty with nothing but oncoming traffic to slow us. Sasha ignored the approaching cars and turned directly into them, amidst blaring horns and screeching brakes. He raced up to the next corner and made a sharp left into the quiet street and followed the curve of the road back south. At the intersection he ran through the stop sign and turned right for a block, then north blocks and then west onto Bolshoy Kiselnyy. Sasha watched his rear view-mirror a while. "They are gone," he said and returned to keep pace with traffic.

"Where did you learn to drive like that?" I asked.

"It is Russia," Sasha answered. "Everyone drives like this." We shared a nervous laugh at his humor.

"Bring me back to the coffee shop where you took me yesterday Sasha. Drop me off about a block away and wait for me in the area. I won't be long, maybe ten minutes, I would think. Will waiting at the curb be a problem?"

"No problem, boss."

It took less time than we both thought to get there and as Sasha pulled to the curb about a block away, I wondered if I was going to be early.

Koval was walking from the shop with two coffees in hand as I approached the front door. "Let's sit over here," Koval pointed to an empty table under a tree on the patio as he handed me a black coffee. The air was cool but not damp, and the morning sun seemed to partner with the pollutants as it tried to warm the air.

Koval started right in, without any social chitchat, "I only have a few minutes, but this won't take long. As I told you, the mafia here has been around a long time, hundreds of years. But they have really grown in the last few years since the dissolution of the Union, in great part due to the government's attempts to privatize and capitalize business. The mafia runs just about every aspect of the country's underground market. Many believe it is with the permission of the highest levels of the oligarchy. We think so too.

"Millionaires are being made here monthly, as power is wrested from failed government bureaucrats or from those who have fallen out of favor. We think mob leaders are significantly investing in the banking and energy sectors, especially oil and electricity. Rampant nepotism, cronyism and favoritism are filling the upper echelons of business.

"Back home, the drug lords and the mafia have to clean their money. They invest in small obscure businesses and use them for money laundering. They even invest in casinos and resorts. But over here we are not talking millions, Christian. We are talking billions. Owning a furniture store or a dry-cleaning business is not going to clean that kind of money.

"In the States, the mob used to buy a privately-owned business, uses it as a front for spending money and sells off the assets before running it into the ground and moving on. Not anymore and not in Russia. Now the businesses must succeed. They buy thousands of shares of class A stock, or in some cases, they are gifted their shares, or they provide loans to the business in exchange for shares. It doesn't matter to anyone if the money originated from extortion or kidnapping, or if it is real or counterfeit.

"They then own either influencing or majority voting rights. New, legitimate cash is pulled in through earnings on shares of stock and dividends or corporate assets can be purchased with hot money and resold for legitimate cash. Now they use clean cash to expand into new markets that would have been inaccessible in the old days of government waste, bureaucratic nepotism and inefficiency. It's big business Christian. And it actually bolsters their economy."

I got it. I understood money laundering. I had been in the organized crime task force, investigating dozens of mob guys and their finances, where the maxim was always, *follow the money*. Besides, Maniaci had already explained the Russian mob subtleties to me. I wasn't sure where Koval was going with this history lesson.

"So how does a little guy like Sasha or any other business protect itself from mob influence or extortion?" I asked.

"It's not just small businesses Christian. Everyone doing business here is at risk. Think about this when you go see Weiner this morning.

"The Bratva has an expression." Koval continued. "It is *Krishi.* It refers to a roofer who builds protection over your house from the elements. I recalled Sasha's similar explanation. No home is safe from nature without a roof of some kind. The same goes for all business here. If you are going to start a business, you must contract with a roofer to protect your investment. Otherwise, you may start to have problems, like drivers not showing up for work, or regular break-ins at your building, or trucks being hijacked at gunpoint and loads commandeered. The list of harassment can range from nuisance to life threatening. Your roof protects from all that."

I stopped him there. "Look Koval, you and I both know that shit happens in foreign countries. And we both know that sometimes the only way around that is by paying someone off. But you, especially, should know that the Federal Foreign Corrupt Practices Act prohibits us from making that type of payment to government officials. I have conducted plenty of investigations into such allegations for Transeget Industries, as has every security executive working for a multi-national company. The last thing anyone wants is for the Feds to come breathing down our necks. Are you suggesting or advising that we make an extortion payoff for the sake of doing business unmolested?"

Koval smiled with an open and unassuming grin. "Oh, God no. Don't get me wrong Christian. You're the one who asked how Sasha might be getting around the problem. I have no idea who he knows or what he has done to operate freely and as visibly as he does."

I chewed on that for a moment. Both of us knew my question about Sasha had to do with the larger issue of Weiner's payments to the mob. I wanted to begin laying the groundwork with him for a more plausible explanation than bribery or collusion. Koval seemed like a nice enough guy, professional and trying to help me, but keeping his distance. I preferred straight talkers, but maybe we hadn't built that bond yet. It surely wasn't my intention to agitate him, since I might need him later. "I get it Koval. Sorry if I offended you. This one has me a bit puzzled. Everything I hear about Weiner is that he is a straight arrow. So, his being involved with the mob has me crosswise. If he is making protection payments for the business, he should have gotten ahold of me right away. We deal with that kind of pressure from locals all the time. But the first we heard about it was through an audit and almost simultaneously from your team in the States. I am thinking it is entirely possible that our company failed to build that roof. But again, Weiner should have let me know.

"So, let me ask you." I continued, "Let's assume for a moment that we are being screwed over by the mob. How does one get out from under that? Or don't we? If I have to recommend we close the business, I'll need to show that it is unrecoverable and unsafe at any investment cost."

Koval smiled again as if he had been waiting for this moment in the conversation. "That's why we are here Christian, instead of in my office. There is a way around this dilemma, if that's what this is all about. But it's a bit unorthodox. I want to make it clear that I am not recommending this alternative.

Just letting you know that it exists. So, let's just stick with the analogy of Sasha's business.

"There is only one group in all of Russia that is believed to be more powerful than the Bratva." Koval paused for effect. He wanted to make sure that the entire concept sank in with me before he proceeded.

I was getting a bit impatient with the theatrics. "And that group is...?"

"The KGB, or as it is now known, the FSK or GRU."

I did not know what to say. Frankly, I was stunned. The relationship between the mafia and their KGB bedfellows was incestuous. They greased each other's palms when need be and cut each other's hands off when advantageous. Were they partners in crime or independent contractors? And how does one become more ruthless in business than the seemingly protected, all-pervasive and vicious Bratva?

"Don't be confused by all this Christian. It is actually clearer than it seems," Koval started. "Certain members of the KGB are in the *insurance* business for companies that have been struck by disaster, so to speak. A business that gets itself crosswise with the mob has recourse. And that is to buy an insurance policy that acts as a new roof over a troubled business."

If it wasn't so tragically corrupt, I could almost see the humor in the way business was conducted in Russia. I could also see why, after corporate America's investment of billions, the Russian economy was still in a shambles and its average citizens were still living on the government dole.

"Look Christian. I haven't got much more time. I have passed your name along to an insurance agent I know. Here is his business card. And here is a list of some Corporate Security executives for companies doing business here in Russia, in case you want an independent referral. You probably know some of these guys. Call them."

I looked at the card, *Vladimir Takhoyev*. Executive Director of Risk Management. There was no business name, just a local Moscow mobile number. No address.

"Thanks, Koval, I am not going to ask you how you got Takhoyev's card, but I do have another question for you. Can you think of anyone who would want to be following me? Sasha and I had a tail this morning on our way here."

"You were followed here?" Koval's head didn't spasm about, but his eyes began looking furtively in all directions, the street, the sidewalks, doorways, the tables and paths in the park. "Did they follow you here? What were they driving? Did you get a look at them or their plate?"

I was glad I didn't bring it up at the beginning of the meeting. I doubted Koval would have hung around for it. "It was the black Volvo you see everywhere here. The answer to all your other questions is *no*. But Sasha said he was followed this morning from his home to the hotel and they were definitely following us as evidenced by their pursuit when we tried to shake them. We lost them a few miles before we got here, and I had Sasha drop me off away from here. I walked over and saw no one following me."

"Well if it was mafia guys, then you dusted them. Not a problem. But if it was the KGB or FSK they made you and are likely watching now. They are too good to shake and would have used more than one car. But that wouldn't be a problem, obviously. We are actually working off a referral of one of their own."

"Wait a minute," I interrupted. "Not a problem? That means they would have been watching me before they knew I was meeting you. Right?"

Koval thought a moment. "Look, you registered to get into Russia. As soon as they saw you were a Plowshares employee and the head of security, they would have been on you, probably from the airport. I wouldn't worry about it. Happens all the time."

I thought back to the prior evening. "Someone tossed my briefcase in my hotel room last night."

"That's not odd either, Christian. Haven't you had your stuff searched before?"

Maybe I was being a bit overly worried. Koval was right. My belongings had been surreptitiously searched in Saigon, Taiwan, Singapore, Shanghai, and on my prior trip to Moscow. Someone had even tried to steal my briefcase out of the backseat of my car while I was stopped at a traffic light in London. It troubled me that Koval was taking it all so nonchalantly, the surveillance this morning and the search last night. I wasn't going to get any further with him, so I let it go.

"Listen, thanks Koval. I appreciate you taking the time to meet me today and for the introduction to this insurance agent. If I have to call him, I'll be sure to mention you, so you get the commission." I said it as a joke, but I could tell by the look on Koval's face that it fell flat.

"You're welcome," Koval said as he stood to leave. "Look Christian, I know this is a bit unnerving. But don't let it get to you. This is the new Moscow. It is a bit rougher than the last time you were here, and the players are different. Don't be surprised to find that the guys who were on the opposite team ten years ago may be your allies now, even if only covertly. Call me if you need me. You have my mobile number."

I now had another question. *How did Koval know I had been to Moscow before?* I didn't think I would get a straight answer from Koval and I had to get going. We shook hands and I walked down the sidewalk and around the corner from the coffee shop. There was Sasha's car about a block away. As I approached, I could see the car was empty. I looked around but didn't see my driver.

As I walked up, Sasha came out from a small store across the street. "Cigarettes," he said and held up a pack.

"I forgot you smoked, Sasha."

"Not too much and only outside the car, boss." And that explained why there was no residual smoke odor in the car, that and the air freshener hanging from the mirror.

I walked back into the store and approached the counter. Not knowing much Russian, I pointed to the cartons of Marlboros and held up two fingers. The shopkeeper reached for two packs of cigarettes. I said "Nyet" and pointed to the cartons and again held up the two fingers. The store clerk raised his eyebrows as if to ask *are you sure?* And I nodded, again showed the two fingers.

Then I pointed to a stack of Rossiya chocolate candies. These were highly desirable in Russia, but usually not available to the common people because of the cost. The candy company had recently received an infusion of investment capital from Nestle and now produced high quality chocolates. I held up ten fingers and pointed to the chocolate bars. The shopkeeper quickly filled a small white paper bag with the treats, almost as if he feared I might change my mind about the quantity.

I paid for my purchase and handed the bags to Sasha. "For you and your wife," I said. *So many simple things we often take for granted are often thought of as special by others*, I thought to myself.

Sasha seemed deeply moved and lost for words. Before things got too mopey, I said, "Sasha, take me back to the warehouse. And keep an eye out for the tail. Let me know if you see anything. We won't try to shake them this time because they seem to be watching the warehouse anyway. But I just want to know."

"Ok, boss," he said, checking his rear-view mirror. He then looked at the chocolates and smiled, but I could see a trace of inexplicable sadness as well.

■ ■ ■ ■ ■

We no longer had a tail on us, but when we pulled up the street, I saw the black Volvo sitting at the curb, just like the previous evening. It was the same car and crew from the Metropol. One or both of us was definitely being watched.

As Sasha drove by, the occupants stared at us without expression. I had to admit, it was a bit unsettling. Sasha proceeded about a hundred yards up the road and nosed the Mercedes into a parking slot on an angle across the street from the building. "Wait here for me Sasha. And if these guys approach you, just leave. Don't try to engage them," I cautioned. Sasha nodded his understanding, as his eyes remained glued to the rear-view mirror.

I exited the car and walked across the street to the pedestrian entrance. It was locked. I pressed the buzzer, all the while watching to see if anyone approached me. A voice over the intercom said, "*Ya mogu vam pomoch* 'Can I help you?' "

I replied, "Can you repeat that in English, please?" I heard a buzzer and the snap of an electronic lock release. I pulled on the door and entered a narrow stairway to a second-floor walk-up office.

Two men stood there waiting. One was definitely of Slavic ancestry, the other must have been Weiner. He seemed in charge and spoke first, in English.

"Christian? Michael Christian. Right?"

I replied, "Yes, Alex Weiner?"

Weiner nodded and extended his hand in greeting. "I recognize you from some of the risk management seminars you put on in Morristown. A woman from your team briefed my wife and I before we came over here."

I shook Weiner's hand and said, "Yes, that would have been Joanne, my admin manager. Look, Weiner, I am afraid I am here on official business. This is not a courtesy call..."

Weiner interrupted me. "I can't say I am sad to hear that, or I am glad. Let's go into my office." As we passed the other man, Weiner merely nodded toward him and said, "This is my counterpart, Nikolay Kuznetsov," And with that he kept walking. No handshake, no pleasantries.

Weiner locked the door behind him as we entered his office. He pointed to either of two chairs motioning for me to take a seat as he walked behind the desk. I stood by one and said, "Sit with me," and motioned to the other seat in front of the desk.

In the hierarchy of interviews and interrogations, the investigator never relinquishes the power position to the subject. Peerage or dominance are the favored positions. I settled for peerage in this case. Weiner seemed taken aback for a moment and then took the chair next to me, as I adjusted my chair to face him directly.

Weiner said, "You're probably wondering why I didn't introduce you to Kuznetsov more formally, but frankly, I don't trust him and don't like him, either. I have the distinct impression that he and our majority partners are stealing us blind and there is nothing I can do to stop them. We are experiencing other difficulties and I believe Kuznetsov is the inside man, providing information to outsiders who are ripping us off."

"Whoa, stop." I said. Weiner was getting way ahead of himself and of my order of business. I couldn't be sure if Weiner was trying to distract me, set a false flag for me to follow, or if there were indeed other things going on that I needed to address. Weiner was bringing forth some interesting information. I would let him run a bit, but with some controls. "One thing at a time. Let's start with Kuznetsov and his partners stealing you blind. What do you mean by that?"

Weiner looked at the locked door before answering. Then he leaned in to me, "I believe they are setting up a company to compete with us. Two weeks ago, a local customer called to confirm the details of a parts order. The order number he gave us was out of sequence from our current runs. The parts numbers were all the same as ours, of course. So, when I pressed him for details, he seemed to get confused, apologized and hung up.

"One of our Russian sales reps, who's not an employee, is the lead on that account. When I asked him about the order, he seemed flustered and was unable to refer to any specifics about it, including costs or invoicing information. When I showed him a copy of the fax the customer sent us, the rep claimed not to have sold the parts to the customer. When I called the customer back, he was unavailable to take my call. Then I got an email asking us to disregard his call, that it had all been a mistake.

"Then there is the matter of the hijackings and burglaries."

"We're being robbed on the road?" I interjected.

"Yes. Our drivers have been having trouble on their routes. They claim our trucks are being broken into while the driver is in with a customer or on a lunch break. Other drivers are claiming to have been held up at gunpoint and their loads stolen." Weiner paused to see if I was keeping up with it, or maybe just checking to see if his story was being believed.

I checked, "You mean the skids and their contents are being offloaded from the trucks? Wouldn't that require a forklift or hi-boy of some kind? How is that possible on such a short time-line as a lunch break or while our guy is in the customer lounge or a roadside restaurant? And if that's the case, why aren't we investigating the customer loading dock guys? I guess more importantly Weiner, why was my office not notified?"

Weiner could see that his explanation was causing more questions than answers. "Look. I have tried reporting these incidents to the police. Frankly, they are all corrupt or in collusion. They refuse to take my reports, something about it being bad for crime statistics. I have even had a contract driver shot in the legs during a robbery and the police wouldn't take the report. The driver quit and hasn't been back for me to even get a statement from him or to collect his final paycheck."

"Wait a minute Weiner," I interjected. "Any one of these things, whether reported to the police or not, is a crime against the business. You still haven't answered why you haven't reported these incidents to my office. And an internal audit team was just out here a couple weeks ago. How did you handle those missing shipments?"

"Simple really. I told them, honestly, that the shipments went missing in transit. I explained the state of law enforcement here. They simply shook their shoulders, nodded in agreement and moved on from there."

"That's not going to fly Weiner. Are you telling me that neither member of the audit team told you these were reportable offenses? They know damn well you had an obligation to report these robberies."

It was obvious Weiner wasn't used to being talked to like this and was about to object loudly. He opened his mouth as if to offer a retort then stopped. He started again to reply, then stopped again. "Listen, Christian. You and I both know what is going on here. Let's not try to kid each other."

"Why don't you just tell me what's going on, Weiner? I am tired of listening to you verbally dance around your obligations and I am getting to the point where I don't believe you are telling me the truth, at least not all the truth. Last chance. What the hell are you hiding?"

"Honestly, Christian..."

I sharply interrupted, "Stop with the *honestly* or the *frankly* Weiner. Just answer the question. I am at the point where your honesty is in serious doubt. What are you not telling me?"

Weiner began anew. "Internal audit is aware. The finance department is aware, and my group president is aware that doing business here requires us to assume certain risks. We are not naïve to the cost of crime here in Russia and especially Moscow. We've read the travel briefings you've given to others and agree with them. There is an economic cost associated with crime. My division has made a decision to factor that in. With that being taken into consideration, we are on track this month to make our projected margins, regardless of what we have lost to the criminal element. And we have been on track for the last six months I have been setting this business up. The phrase "lost in transit" is my way of coding to our group president that the cost of crime is included in the financial reports on that line item."

I was doing a slow boil inwardly. This team had decided crime losses were considered a line item and by budgeting for them, they could show a profit. That was some screwed-up accounting. I wondered if Brinton knew.

"What are your losses, exactly," I asked. I was trying to recall the data from the audit report I was given. The losses were significant, but there was black ink in the lower right-hand corner of the financial report, a sign the business should be profitable.

"We are averaging about one hundred thirty thousand dollars a month in such losses. We budgeted a couple million in "cost of crime" costs for the startup year. In fact, this month we are on track to report a significant reduction in crime losses and next month, I expect that number to break even or be eliminated."

And there it was. It was time to drive it home with Weiner.

"I can't argue with what your group thinks is profitable or not Weiner. But I can tell you that a shrinkage loss in excess of one percent per month is considered unacceptable in most circles. That's twelve percent per year. If I had heard of this on my own, I would already be initiating an investigation into these costs. And are you telling me that Barry Brinton is aware of the *cost of crime* assumptions you and your team have put together? That he is good with losing millions to the cost of crime?" *And even if he is*, I thought, *I'm not.*

Weiner was choosing his words carefully now, "Brinton was made aware that there were risks associated with the startup and he was very assertive about wanting to be in this market. How he was made aware, or what the details were in my boss's briefing to him, I don't know."

"And are you telling me, Weiner, that Brinton is aware of the other unbudgeted expenses you are incurring?"

Weiner sat back in his chair. To me it almost seemed like he was trying to press himself into the softness of the leather cushion and hide. "What unbudgeted expenses are you talking about?"

I was pacing myself. I wasn't yet to the confrontational stage with him, but I had now moved from being conversational to being coldly direct. "Look Weiner, we have moved from this being a courtesy call to it being an investigation. If you don't stop bullshitting me, things are going to get ugly and you are rapidly moving from being a witness to being a suspect. We know you are making payments to a Russian consulting company, P2K2. And they are exorbitant amounts. Audit called them to our attention. When we asked your uplink management, they waffled on the answers and basically mumbled something along the lines that you know what you are doing. Your bosses may be greedy, and they may turn a blind eye to you violating the Foreign Corrupt Practices Act, but we don't. And Brinton doesn't want to go to jail for your misdeeds. So, now's the time to come clean. What the hell is going on?"

Weiner had turned grey and his skin looked clammy. As he gripped and released the armrests on the chair, he left wet marks under his fingers and palms. I recognized the obvious signs that Weiner wasn't a good liar, at least not under pressure. Either he was guilty of some act or he had guilty knowledge, especially as to the payments. It was at this point most suspects hedged their answer before making any full admission. They always wanted to know how much the investigator already knew before spilling any unnecessary beans.

"I am telling you, my bosses know how difficult it is getting started up here," he repeated. "They know that in order to get ahead of our competition we have to have a fast and smooth introduction to the market. This is a rapidly emerging economy and we needed someone capable of navigating the twists of bringing our parts to market here. P2K2 is that company for us. This is money well spent." When Weiner said the words *P2K2*, his tongue stuck to the roof of his mouth. His adrenalin had kicked in and he was barely producing any saliva. It was as if his entire body was revolting against saying those words out loud.

I set the trap. "Show me the consulting reports. Get them for me. I'll wait."

Weiner didn't move from his chair. "Get them for me now, Weiner."

"I don't have them here." Weiner whispered.

I made him say it again, made him reinforce the lie. "What did you say? I couldn't hear you."

"I said I don't have them here."

I moved my chair so that my knees were nearly touching Weiner's. I was taking it to the next level, tightening the lines on a sailboat that was not going where Weiner wanted. "I know you don't have another office. Are they at your home, in your car? Where are the reports? I will go with you to get them. I want to see drafts, interim reports and any final reports that are worth a quarter of a million dollars a month. I want to be able to clear you of suspicion and put this matter to bed."

Weiner just sat there, seemingly immobilized.

"I would also like you to tell me how you were introduced to the consultants. Who introduced you and where did you meet for the first time? I want you to give me the addresses and phone numbers for that company and your contacts, and I want to see all your correspondence between you and them, including all calendar appointments for meetings, emails and phone calls. Let's start with their names. What are the names of the consultants you dealt with directly?"

I couldn't tell yet, if Weiner was choosing not to respond or he couldn't. Either way he just sat there, wiping his moist hands over and over on his slacks. I knew that Weiner could not produce any such documentation. No mob works that way. About the only thing real would be the foreign deposit wire transfer numbers and I already knew Maniaci or Koval would provide those if necessary. Given the lack of any other evidence, this was starting to smell seriously like a bribe.

It was my job to get the details nailed down and an admission from Weiner in order to keep my boss out of jail, our company's name off the front pages and their stock price stable. I saw Weiner glance up at the clock on the wall in his office. It was only nine in the morning. We had been together less than a half hour. It must have seemed an eternity to Weiner.

"What are their names Weiner?"

I had to be careful here. I closed in on Weiner's personal space and placed a hand gently on the back of his wrist, establishing a contact point of trust. "What are their names?"

"I don't know," Weiner answered.

I still didn't know if I believed him. "Does the name Mirski sound familiar?"

"Yes, Vadim Mirski. He is the consultant." Weiner could not look up and seemed to be talking to the floor.

"Stop, Alex. You know he's not a consultant. He's a mid-level mob member. You don't have any reports either, do you? There's nothing for me to see, is there?"

"No, nothing." Weiner said. His head was bent so low I could not see his eyes. Weiner's damp hands unconsciously moved from his pant legs where he folded them to form a protective shield between his legs. I could see his fingertips trembling. I opened the space between us again and sat upright as I challenged Weiner.

"What did you say? I couldn't hear you."

"I said no, there is nothing. No reports."

I had cracked open the lid on the box of secrecy and out came a general admission of some cover up. Now I needed the details. "Okay Weiner. Let's go over this in detail. I want you to start from the beginning and tell me how you met these guys, what specific political obstacles they have overcome for you, what inspectors have been taken care of, what licenses and permits they have facilitated and anything else your bribe money is providing. And I have to be honest with you. When you are through answering all my questions, we are going to write it all down as an admission and then you are going to sign it."

Weiner nodded his head in agreement but with so little movement I could hardly tell.

"And just so you know, when we are through this morning, I am going to have you and your wife and daughter packed up and sent home, likely on the first plane tomorrow."

"No!" Weiner sprang from his chair and shouted. "You can't do that!"

"Oh yes I can. You are through here."

"No, we can't be moved. I mean you can do what you want with me, but you cannot move my family. You don't understand."

■ ■ ■ ■ ■

I saw the look of panic on Weiner's face and knew it wasn't just about losing his job. It was something bigger and it had to do with P2K2. I could just sense it, but I had to be careful. I had gotten the improper payments admission, but no details. And Weiner hadn't signed an admission yet. The lawyers always wanted a signed admission from executives being terminated for cause. It kept the company from being boxed-in and then having to pay some obscure separation bonus to a guy who was a thief. It also served as a deterrent for follow-up lawsuits for wrongful discharge.

"Sit back down. What are you talking about? You know I can have you removed. What aren't you telling me, Weiner? Either I get an explanation and help you out of whatever trouble you are in, or we start packing."

Weiner wavered between standing and sitting. He looked at other chairs, as if moving somewhere else would possibly provide him an escape route. I pointed to Weiner's chair as if to remove the options. "Sit."

Weiner sat back into his chair. "Start at the beginning, Alex. Tell me what really happened to you and your family." I used Weiner's first name. It was time to build a bridge, rather than isolate him. The transition had occurred. He now feared not telling the truth more than the outcome of admitting he had screwed up somehow. He seemed to be reaching out for a lifeline, rather than making an admission.

Weiner began slowly at first, and then it all came tumbling out.

At first, Weiner said, it was just parts being stolen from the warehouse, then several trucks were hijacked and then the driver was shot. He then told me about the first visit from two tough looking strangers who said that the robbing would continue unless Transeget Industries paid for protection. He related their promise to make it all go away once the payment was posted to an account, which they would provide the next day. Then Weiner explained how he never saw the first two guys again. Instead two different men came. One of them was Vadim Mirski. He never knew the other's name. Weiner described how it went.

"Mirski said that the terms of the agreement had changed and that I was no longer buying protection from the thefts. I told him I didn't understand. I actually hoped we were off the hook. But the guy Mirski was with pulled out pictures of my wife and daughter, there must have been a dozen of them.

He slowly showed them to me, one after the other while Mirski talked."

"They were close-up pictures of Rachel and Sarah shopping at the grocer's, at clothing stores, having a lunch inside a restaurant, and of my daughter at school, in my back yard, in the driveway in our gated community. Christian, they had pictures of her in the car with my driver. It seemed they could get near her any time they wanted. I was terrified. You have to understand. Losing assets is one thing, especially, since we budgeted for loss. But my wife and daughter ..."

"What did they say Alex? Try to remember the exact words."

"I don't know if I can recall exactly, but the message was clear. Mirski told me I was going to be buying insurance from them to make sure my wife and daughter were safe. So many thoughts were going through my mind. I didn't want them kidnapped and have to pay a ransom anyway, and I knew I couldn't count on the government for help. I knew we had kidnap and ransom insurance for me, but I didn't think it extended to my family. I was so confused while they were talking. And all the while, I just kept looking at their pictures. They must have thought I was hesitating because Mirski told the other guy to show me the other pictures."

"What other pictures?" I asked.

"There were a dozen pictures of women my wife's age, and of boys and girls my daughter's age. And they were all posed in sex scenes. Mirski said they were all now prostitutes but had formerly been relatives of westerners who didn't pay. These poor people had been addicted into a life of sex for money, just like Rachel and Sarah would be if I didn't pay. They said they would get Rachel hooked on drugs and shipped to the Middle East and I would never see her again. Sarah would be in child porn and then repeatedly prostituted to some wealthy men in Belarus or Turkmenistan or Russia.

"Christian, they were so coldly objective about it, and they just kept shuffling through the pictures of my girls and of the others, until my girls seemed like they were part of their photo album. It scared the hell out of me!"

I felt terribly sorry for Weiner, but I needed to move him through this. "What were their demands to keep your girls safe Alex?"

"It was insane! I knew I didn't have the money they were asking for! I was in a panic!"

"How much did they ask you to pay?"

"It was two hundred fifty thousand a month! A month, Christian! If I emptied all my personal accounts, I couldn't keep them safe for more than a few months. I told them I didn't have that kind of money, but they were ready for that."

"What do you mean, they were ready, Alex?"

"They said they knew I didn't have that kind of money, but Transeget Industries did. They knew what our annual budget was for our operations here. That was when they talked about the phony consulting scam and it all came together for me. I knew I had no choice and I knew we had the money budgeted, at least for a few years. It would give me time to figure out what to do."

"Why didn't you call me or the FBI, Alex? We could have intervened."

"Really Christian? You can stop the Russian mafia? They were so damn confident about their ability to move around the police. They sounded like the police were part of all this."

"They said they could snatch Rachel and Sarah before we could even get to the airport. And they said the FBI would be powerless to investigate anything over here. Blame me if you will, but I believed them. Honestly Christian, I know I should have reported this, but I felt boxed in, like I had nowhere to go. And I was not going to risk my family on the chance that somehow the FBI or you had the means to save us over here."

Things were falling into place for me. The suggestions of bribery had shifted to extortion and all the facts made more sense now. Brinton would be off the hook for a FCPA violation. It was incumbent on me to resolve the matter of getting Weiner and his family to some safe position, whatever that meant. I also had to stop the ongoing threat somehow so TI could stay in business here. Lacking that, I'd have to develop a risk analysis that justified putting employees in harm's way. I wasn't about to do that. I'd wait to call Brinton until I had something further to add about resolving the issue.

"OK, Alex. I am glad you told me. And don't worry. I don't plan to take any action or make any moves that put you or your family in danger. I want you to keep my knowledge of this between you and me. When did you make the last payment? Or more importantly, when is the next one due?"

Weiner gathered his thoughts before replying, "The next payment is due before close of business Friday. But please remember that I can't miss a payment, not one. And it had to be all the money and they specifically warned me, not a dollar short. They said if it was even one dollar short, they would just take the girls. No warning, no second chance. The girls would just disappear, and I would never see them again."

End of the day Friday I thought. That was only two business days. Not that much time.

"OK Alex, here's the plan. I am heading out to meet someone later this morning. Stay here as you normally would and run the business. If there are any hold-ups or hijackings, or if you have any reason to be concerned about your family, call me at this mobile number." I jotted Koval's number down on a memo pad on Weiner's desk.

"It is safe to leave a message but keep it short and simple. I hope to be back after lunch, so eat if you can. If you need a fall back to reach me, leave a message at the Hotel Metropol desk. I am staying there. But it is not safe to be specific if you leave a message. I am sure I am being monitored. Now give me your contact numbers, including your home phone and I will get going. And I promise you Alex, if I have nothing in place by then, we will make that payment on Friday."

With that, I walked downstairs and out the front door. Sasha was sitting in his car parked across the street with the Mercedes facing away. I took a moment to look up and down the street. The black Volvo was parked about seventy-five yards to the east. I could see two men in it. The windows were clear, so they must have been running the engine and the windshield defrosters. They were definitely watching. But who were they watching?

As I approached the car, Sasha must have seen me in the rear-view mirrors because the front door lock opened electronically. He had the engine

215

running too and had it in gear before I could fasten my seatbelt.

"They are still down the street boss. Should I lose them?"

"Let's see what they do. I want you to take me downtown to the park near the coffee shop. But I have to find a payphone first." I ordered.

"No problem, boss." The Volvo remained at the curb as Sasha pulled away. "Hey boss ..."

"Yes, Sasha, I see them. It looks like their interest is in the business and not in me in particularly. That's good news."

Sasha found an outdoor phone box just a few miles down near the airport entrance road. I got out and dialed the number.

CHAPTER EIGHT

"HELLO?" THE VOICE SPOKE PERFECT, unaccented English.

"Who am I speaking with?" I asked.

"Whom did you call?" came the answer. No hostility, in fact the reply was civil and conversational.

"I am trying to reach Vladimir Takhoyev."

"This is Vladimir Takhoyev. And with whom do I have the pleasure of speaking?" I noted that the words were textbook English. It was a perfectly structured sentence and correct use of the objective pronoun.

"My name is Michael Christian and I have been referred to you by ..."

"By Tom Koval. Yes, Yes. He told me you might call. A good man, Mr. Koval, no?" And I noted a lapse into a Russian style of speaking and negative use of the word "no". I wondered which was Vladimir Takhoyev's most comfortable language.

I knew I was taking a huge step into uncharted territory. Takhoyev may be an "insurance agent" but there was no doubt that he was KGB or

217

whatever they called themselves nowadays. And I also heard they fancied themselves like our Marines, in that there is no such thing as an *ex* KGB officer. There was plenty of downside risk merely being associated with a guy like Takhoyev, much less doing business with him. My decision would be second-guessed over and over if it didn't work, and possibly even if it did.

"I was hoping we could meet somewhere, soon, Mr. Takhoyev. I would like to discuss purchasing some insurance coverage. It appears our business manager may have chosen the wrong agents and purchased inadequate coverage for an enterprise we have in your country." I was hoping that I was being specific enough to be understood and vague enough to avoid some later scrutiny.

"Certainly, certainly, Michael. And please call me Vladimir. I may have some free time next week, perhaps early in the week. Does that work?"

"No, Vladimir, I am afraid that won't work. My need for insurance is urgent and I am leaving town soon. I won't be here next week." I needed to move right away on Weiner's behalf and couldn't wait indefinitely to get him and his family to a position of safety. "I was hoping I could meet you this afternoon." I knew my sense of urgency might encourage Takhoyev to inflate his price. On the other hand, I didn't want to make a payment to the mob on Friday and then make a similar payment to Takhoyev a few days later. But I was past that point already, considering how much Weiner had already paid to P2K2. We had to meet now.

"Well, certainly Michael. I may be able to accommodate you." And without taking the time to look at any calendar, Takhoyev said, "Meet me at my office. If you can be here within the hour, I can see you today." And he proceeded to give me the address.

I thanked Takhoyev promising to be there shortly and returned to the car, reciting the address to Sasha. "Do you know where this is?"

Sasha replied, "Of course. It is off Leninski Street in the residential district near the Novodevichy Convent. Actually just a few blocks down."

On my last trip, I visited the convent as a tourist. The Russian Orthodox Church took in exiled royal women and rape victims, birthed the babies, then placed them for adoption. They sheltered the royal ladies and educated the poorer mothers to be nuns. Thus, they all became *new virgins*, as the name translates.

"Is the address a private home, do you think?" I asked.

"Well it was surely a home at one time or another. I doubt if it is anymore." Sasha offered. "This area was known for large commune-style homes with often six to eight families in each. Within the last two years, the families were offered a forced choice of other housing, none of it nearby. It seems the space near the central district was more valuable as office space than housing. Each building has been divided into individual offices, which would make roughly two-thousand American dollars a square meter."

I was doing the calculation in my head while Sasha went on to describe the history of the area renovation. It was just about a hundred eighty six dollars a square foot. Even by our standards, that was pretty high for office space. In rubles, no average Russian could afford to live in such homes any longer. A single square foot would be equal to roughly half of a month's living wage for the local Muscovite. I thought it best not to tell Sasha who would be attending my meeting, by name, title, business, and especially past history.

Less than thirty minutes later we pulled up in front of the address. Sasha found a parking space at the curb a little-way down and said, "I will wait here, boss."

The large, two-story, red brick home looked Italianate in architecture and recently had a sandblasting to give it a clean face-lift. New windowpanes were fit in old, freshly painted gloss-black frames. Given the space the property-line occupied, all beneath one roof, there were almost twenty-two hundred square feet on each floor, in a prime location. *This insurance company must be mighty profitable* I thought to myself as I dropped the brass doorknocker a few times.

A fifty-something year old man in a black, bespoke, silk suit, perfectly tailored to his frame, swung the door open widely. His thick head of white hair was trimly cropped in a military-style brush cut. One of his manicured fingers sported a gold ring with a diamond that I estimated to be at least two karats.

Vladimir Takhoyev smiled with perfectly straight white teeth and said, "Michael. Welcome, please come in, come in." He held the door and gestured broadly to the inside. There was no question in his voice as to my identity.

I extended my hand, "Mr. Takhoyev, a pleasure to meet you."

"Vladimir, please. Have a seat Michael. Let us see what you are in such a hurry about and how I may be of service."

The foyer opened to a large, carpeted sitting room with solid oak chairs and tables gathered in several small groups. I figured this to be a lobby for the company offices.

Without asking, Takhoyev proceeded to a bar on the wall of the sitting room and pulled down a bottle of Crown Royal. He grabbed two tumblers and added a few cubes of ice to each. He then poured a proper two fingers of Crown and handed one of the full glasses to me. "I believe this is your preference."

I was unnerved at the level of intimate knowledge Takhoyev possessed about me, and said so.

"Vladimir, you have me at a disadvantage. I have been in town less than two days and you already know my drinking habits. Am I to believe I am under some kind of surveillance?" I thought about the guys in the Volvo.

Takhoyev smiled that personable smile and said with confidence, "Of course you are. It is Russia and you are a U.S. businessman. Not to mention a security executive of one of our largest Plowshares partners. Did you expect less?"

I mulled it over briefly, but knew the answer already. Koval was right. I had suspected I would be under government surveillance the moment I arrived. But how could Takhoyev learn that so quickly? And what was the connection?

Vladimir added, "Do not worry. Your friend at the FBI told me you like Crown Royal. I just happened to have it on the shelf for you when you arrived.

"And yes, I do know about you Michael. It seems you have quite a reputation among some of my former counterparts in western intelligence. Your own FBI seems to hold you in high regard. And my friends at Scotland Yard's Special Branch recommend your skills as does Sir James Fairweather at MI5. Don't worry. When Koval said you might be calling on me, I did some inquiring of my own. One can never be too sure. Right, Michael?" Takhoyev obviously meant it as a rhetorical question, because he continued uninterrupted.

"And before you ask, it wasn't Tom Koval who pointed me to the Crown Royal. It was our mutual friend Jerry Maniaci."

I was trying to keep up with all of it. It wasn't the first time I had been vetted by government officials before they agreed to work with me. But Takhoyev had managed to do it all in a matter of a few hours, and as a *former* KGB agent for god's sake. Why do the U.S. agencies even talk with them?

"And your friend Felder, from the German prosecutor's office, says your capabilities amazed him. But he wondered if perhaps you weren't a *spy*. Don't you find that an interesting recommendation?"

I had no trouble imagining how Felder might conclude that. I had just solved a case for him involving German, Polish and Russian smugglers and it was a messy resolution.

Felder had agreed to give me some room to work. The team I assembled had unique capabilities when under pressure. And in solving our mutual problem, we left Felder the matter of a small body count to deal with. Nevertheless, it bothered me that a KGB agent might think I was a spy.

"Don't worry Michael. I know you are not a spy. Besides, do not be surprised if your enemies from yesterday are your friends today. It is a new world, is it not?" Hadn't I just heard that from both Koval and Maniaci? I wondered if this was exactly what they were talking about.

I decided it was not time to be coy or cute with Takhoyev. I needed the insurance agent and I had to move fast.

I tried to keep it politely sociable, "Thank you. May we move to your office? I have some things I would like to discuss with you in private."

And flashing that bright open smile and, with wide open arms that seemed to engulf the entire room, Takhoyev replied, "This *is* my office and it is also my home. And we are alone."

I was surprised again. There were easily twenty four hundred feet of space on each of the two floors, maybe more. It had to have cost Takhoyev over seven hundred thousand dollars for the place, and that didn't include the furnishings. Not bad for a retired agent, insurance or otherwise.

We may have been alone, but I didn't doubt for a moment that the conversation was being recorded. Takhoyev didn't get where he was by being careless.

I courteously tipped the rim of my tumbler toward Takhoyev in a toast, took a sip and began.

"My company has opened a small business importing and distributing electrical and replacement parts, which are in short supply in your country."

Takhoyev added, "Yes, Transeget Industries replacement and OEM parts division. I am aware of it. You have a warehouse near Sheremetyevo, but it seems to be a building with a weak roof. If it falls in, someone might get hurt, No?"

I was glad Takhoyev was playing the word game, for both our sakes.

"Yes, Vladimir. And that is why I am here. It may be too late to rebuild that roof, so I am seeking insurance against such catastrophic risk."

"You have come to the right place Michael. I am sure we can help you. We are well aware of the risks western businesses face trying to make a go of it here. We all face the same risk. Yet as you know, risk is a manageable component, and what cannot be managed, can be either assumed or financed, No?"

"Yes," I answered. "And we have assumed about all the risk we can tolerate. I am here about a risk alternative and I understand your company is in that business."

"Would you like some music while we talk?" Takhoyev didn't wait for an answer. He rose and turned on a stereo system mounted flush to the wall. A symphony quietly filled the room as it began with an acoustically balanced, quiet overture.

I listened for a moment before I heard anything distinctly, then it all made sense. It was the prelude to the great Russian composer's most famous piece. It was Tchaikovsky's *1812 Overture*. I knew if it continued to be played at this ambient sound level, the music would soon drown out all conversation unless you were lips to ear with the other person. Takhoyev knew the process perfectly and waited a few stanzas before he continued.

"Let us be frank, Michael. The mafia is extorting your business. Specifically, Vadim Mirski is pressuring your man Weiner, likely with threats to his family. I know Mirski. But more importantly, I know his boss's boss, Sergei Miloradov. Miloradov is cold and ruthless. He is addicted to money and he can never have enough. Perhaps that is what makes him so wealthy. But Vadim's boss and I, well we have an understanding about business, we say, *inogda on moyet mne ruki, a inogda ya umyvayu yego* 'sometimes he washes my hands and sometimes I wash his.' Some may say a partnership, but I like to think not. I will not spend a favor at Miloradov's level on something as mundane as extortion. I must save that for bigger things. But as for Davydov, I do not often ask him to wash my hands. More often than not it is the other way around. So, perhaps he owes me."

Takhoyev paused and sipped. "This is so smooth, no?" Again, it was merely rhetorical. I noticed the fingers holding the sweating crystal tumbler. They were strong and powerful as if the hands were accustomed to lifting great weights or laying bricks.

He continued, "So tell me, Michael. What is your company paying for that sagging roof of yours? What is Mirski charging to keep Weiner's wife and daughter from becoming the next whores exported from Russia?"

I noted how seamlessly Takhoyev had slipped from sophisticated businessman to cold-hearted mercenary.

"Two fifty a month."

Takhoyev lifted his eyebrows ever so slightly. "That is a bit steep, I think. But there are two girls

225

and Sarah is still so young. I can see why the extra expense. Rachel must be very pretty."

I didn't rise to the bait. I merely nodded as if to say, *yes, she is.* I knew that Takhoyev was establishing that these were going to be tough negotiations. More importantly, Takhoyev was telling me there was nothing he didn't know about Weiner's problem. His intelligence was perfect.

"We have a policy that can cover you Christian. It can go into effect as soon as the premium payment is made. We might call it *same day coverage.*"

It all seemed too simple, too choreographed.

"Well that is most encouraging Vladimir, but we are fearful of any mistake. Weiner has been warned. Any failure to pay will result in the immediate taking of his wife and daughter, and they will never be seen again. He was specifically warned that there was nothing the authorities can do, that any investigation would be stopped in its tracks and the girls would be taken. It is too big a risk to take based on our general conversation. Specifically, what safeguards does your policy provide?"

"So, my question Michael, he was warned not to go to any authorities, but was your Mr. Weiner warned not to speak with Vladimir Takhoyev? I am joking, forgive me. You are here because people whose reputations you trust have recommended that you see me about such specific problems. I am, as they say, *the man.* So, let us get to the heart of the service.

"You buy an insurance policy from me and I provide a new roof for you. It specifically protects you from the threats and risks you are currently facing and any other threats as well. There is no waiting period because the coverage is immediate, within hours let us say. Is that specific enough for you?" Takhoyev's countenance was cloudy now. He was no longer the pink-faced, manicured insurance agent. He was formidable and just short of bristling with dark energy.

I had seen angry people before and was not intimidated. But this was different. It was the eyes. Takhoyev's eyes told a deep and dangerous story and I was sure it was no fairy tale. I did not blanche though and kept the negotiations going.

"What is this policy going to cost us?"

"You are currently paying what, two hundred fifty thousand a month. That is three million a year. No. You will not pay them anymore. You will pay me two hundred fifty thousand..."

I objected, "Hang on there, Takhoyev. I have no intention of changing one extortionist for another..."

"Michael, Michael, take it easy. You offend me. I am not an extortionist. I am an insurance agent in the business of risk management. Mine is a one-time insurance premium of two hundred fifty thousand. One time, that is all." With that he began writing on a single piece of stationary that he withdrew from a leather tray.

"Here is my banking information." I was looking down at a thirty-four-digit, wire transfer code Takhoyev had written from memory. He had matter-of-factly inscribed it on a linen, Pineider notecard from Italy. That simple gesture cost him three bucks when it could just as easily have been written on the back of a matchbook cover. If Takhoyev was a fake, he had gone to great lengths to promote his image. He was even using an FBI agent as a broker.

He continued uninterrupted, "A direct deposit will do. You will receive no receipt. There will be no insurance binder and no record of coverage. What you *will* get is the protection this policy provides. Do you think Koval would send you here if I could not do what I say I can do? Did you not call the references he provided you to verify my services?" I had not, but now I knew where Koval had gotten the list.

"I presume you are able to speak for your company. So, before you leave, tell me, Michael Christian. Do we have a deal or not?"

I had to act on gut instinct because I had nothing else. I made my decision. "You will have your deposit by the end of the day Vladimir. And I want proof positive that the coverage is in effect." I rose as if to leave.

"Do not go just yet, Michael." And with that, Takhoyev grabbed me by the elbow. It wasn't a rough gesture, but it was firm and unyielding and made with powerful hands. I wasn't going anywhere. Once I relaxed, he let go his grip. "Now that we have concluded our business, let me show you my home."

Takhoyev took me on a room-by-room tour, showing off beautiful antique furnishings and original art that reflected a fortune in investments. It was designed to impress a visitor, and it should. It was all lost on me though.

My mind was a jumble of thoughts about art on the one hand, and the mechanics of making another massive and traceable payment from our

Moscow account to a shadowy person, whose receipt of the money may likely be untraceable.

When we got to the top floor, Takhoyev led me to a small doorway that opened to a short, well-lit flight of stairs leading to the roof. We exited together and Takhoyev guided me to the edge. The balustrade was only about two feet off the roof. In essence we were standing on the edge. "Look out here," pointed Takhoyev. He was showing me the domes of Our Lady of Smolensk and the Novodevichy Convent.

The view of the red and white buildings and gold domes was spectacular and only added to the value of his property. But that wasn't the message Takhoyev was delivering. He had his arm around my shoulder now, and a strong hand on me. It was as if to say *one could fall from the roof quite easily.* "This mother Russia," Takhoyev said, "She can be both beautiful and deadly, No?"

I replied, "Then it makes sense to have an insurance agent as a good friend, No?"

Takhoyev chuckled, patted me on the back and we headed back inside.

As he walked me to the front door, Takhoyev whispered, "I am also good at finding things people think are lost. Call me if you think I can be of service." With that, Takhoyev stepped back inside the door as it closed with a quiet mechanical click.

I just stood there staring blankly into space. Could Takhoyev be talking about the nuclear material? How the hell could he know? And what made him think I would have anything to do with that? Would the Feds be telling a KGB agent that I might be on a mission? I doubted it.

The sound of Sasha honking the horn jolted me back to reality. The day was wearing on and if I was going to generate a deposit, it had to happen fast – today, before the end of business.

We encountered no delays on the trip back to Weiner's office and that was just as well. I had a lot on my mind. I was about to make a payoff to a former KGB agent. I was paying for protection as if I was paying the mob, only I was paying for protection from the mob. I had only Koval's assurances that it would work, and I was betting a quarter of a million dollars on that hunch. I was alone again with this decision. My judgment would doubtless be called into question, if the money spent did not produce the intended results. Hell, my judgment deserved to be called into question.

Although I could justify it in my own mind, there would be no easy way to explain it in the sterile environment of a Federal Courthouse, if necessary. I was sure Koval would deny all knowledge. Certainly, if push came to shove, he would deny recommending that Takhoyev and I do business together. It was just how things got done at this level.

I recalled Maniaci's two warnings. *You are on your own* and *Trust no one*. Did that apply to Koval as well? It surely applied to Takhoyev, but I knew that going in.

And what about my new *friend*? Just what the hell did he mean that he could help find things people thought were lost? In the context of what I was doing in Russia, I could come to only one conclusion. Takhoyev knew about my other interest and may be of some service to me. Or he was part of the problem and was setting a trap for Transeget Industries and me.

One thing at a time I thought. Let's clear Weiner's family from danger first and protect the ongoing business. Anything else I managed to accomplish this trip was gravy.

■ ■ ■ ■ ■

Weiner was less than excited by the plan to buy more protection. In fact, he was adamantly opposed to it, particularly since I was not giving him any details about where the other payment was going. I merely stated that I had negotiated an alternative payment plan that would be paid in full with the next installment.

He was terrified that if he stopped making payments, without assurances from Mirski, then the girls would be taken as threatened. He wanted to talk with Mirski before he made a commitment of funds to me. I knew I had to draw a hard line.

"Look Alex. This can go my way and my way only. I am making that payment for you. You have a couple days leeway to see if there is relief from Mirski. If not, we can take it from there. But I can assure you that we will not authorize any future payments, regardless of your phony budget allocation for losses in transit. And you may not know it, but the FBI has had your payments, and you, under surveillance for about two months already and the mob has done nothing to you or your girls. The Bureau thinks you are in some kind of bribery scheme involving FCPA violations. They are giving me the courtesy of working this out or they will lock you up. Either way, your payments stop. This is not negotiable. We're making the final payment and I have you, Rachel and Sarah covered. So, what do we have to do to get this payment made right now?"

Weiner's original opposition had melted away. I didn't think for a moment that he had seen the logic. He merely folded under the exhaustive fatigue of worry. He needed someone to throw him a safety line, and my deal was all he got. He could take it or sink his whole family. He made the only choice, even if he was unhappy with it.

"It is not that complicated," he said. "We will go to our bank and execute the transfer on my signature. Kuznetsov is not necessary for the transfer, and I would prefer to keep him completely out of this."

"We'll take my car." I said as we stood and walked out.

The payment went easier than I thought. By having both accounts' information and Weiner being a known signatory on the account, the process was as easy as making a deposit. One thing I noted was the Panamanian registry of Takhoyev's account. I added one codicil to the deposit before it was made and asked if I could use a private phone to make a call.

Given a private office at the bank, I dialed Takhoyev who picked it up on the first ring. "Vladimir, this is Michael Christian. The insurance premium has been deposited as directed, except for one thing." I paused for effect. There was no response from Takhoyev.

"We have put a twenty four hour hold on the funds. I want to see demonstrable results before we free the funds. I want to see them by tomorrow morning, as you said was possible. If you cannot do this, we will withdraw the payment. Given the local market conditions, I am sure there are other insurance agencies in town willing to underwrite the risk. If we see irrevocable results, I will free the funds immediately."

I paused again. This time I would not continue without a reply.

"Michael, Michael. The freeze is not necessary. Did I not say I would provide the service we discussed? Trust me. I can do it."

Trust no one.

"People have faith in you Vladimir. Faith is a belief in something when there is no objective or logical proof. But trust is not given like faith. Trust is earned. Once you deliver as promised, then I will trust you in matters like these."

"Ah, you want to negotiate with an insurance company. Is that something you Americans are used to? I doubt it. It is a good thing you are so well recommended Michael. You see, I *trust* you will release the funds as you promise, once I deliver as I say I can. I have faith I will earn your trust in return. I will talk with you tomorrow." With that, Takhoyev dropped the call.

The next call I made was to the States, to Maniaci's private cell phone. He picked it up on its first ring. "Maniaci," he said.

"Jerry, it's Christian. I haven't got much time and I am calling from inside a bank in Moscow. Hopefully the line is relatively secure."

"Sure. What's up?"

233

I thought Maniaci was being rather casual in his response, given the mission I was on and the call he must have received from Takhoyev. "Jerry there are a lot of things going on here and I have to admit, this is the first time I can recall being totally out of my element and controlled by outside forces, including you and the Bureau. Maybe you can tell *me* what's up?"

"What are you talking about Michael? What do you mean *controlling* you?"

"So Koval gives me Takhoyev's name as a guy I can deal with. Takhoyev calls you about me and you even give him my brand of whiskey. But I don't get any feedback from you or Tom Koval about the back-office chatter about me. Now I am doing business with a guy who infers in a vague way that he can help me *find things that are lost*! What the hell Jerry? Is he in on the missing materials investigation?"

Maniaci was as unflappable as ever when it came to his work. It was likely why he was the Bureau's agent in charge of a major city. "Think about it Michael. Vladimir is a well-regarded source of information to the Bureau and to other agencies in our government. He was likely contacted multiple times long before he had any idea of who you are. He also knows that you are the head of security for a Plowshares company. It is only logical to assume that you would be on the hunt for the materials too."

I wasn't having any of it. "C'mon Jerry. Hell, I didn't even know about the missing materials until two days ago and I have spent most of my time since then on airplanes. I guess you are answering my question by talking around it. But I was hoping for a direct answer. I thought we knew each other better than that. Does he know or not, that I am on a *goodwill* mission here."

Maniaci answered, "Look Michael. He called me to vet you and I gave him the usual glowing report without going into too many details. I told him about our work together fighting organized crime in Detroit. I told him about you and me working together on the ninety-three World Trade Center bombing suspect. And I told him he was not the first foreign agency to inquire about you. I pointed him to Fairweather in Great Britain and to Felder in Germany, who also called me in the past. I have no idea what they told him.

"But you know the ropes, Michael. We vouch for each other or not, based on trust. I have done enough things with him that I trust Takhoyev on certain matters. But one thing is certain. I did not tell him about your having any knowledge of materials being missing. If he heard that, it wasn't from me and it wasn't from Koval."

I listened and had calmed by the time Maniaci was through. I believed Jerry and above all, I trusted him. I just didn't like being left in the dark. We rang off, not coldly, but with a sense of edge anyway.

I called Koval next but there was no answer. I wondered if Maniaci had speed dialed him first, so I left a voice message. "Tom Koval, this is Michael Christian. I need to see you tomorrow morning to update you. My business here may be wrapping up very quickly. Can you leave me a message at the hotel this evening relative to time and place? I may also want to send a package home and need some advice." I hung up and joined Weiner and the wire transfer manager in the main lobby. We made our goodbyes and walked from the bank. "What was that all about?" Weiner asked.

I explained, "I was buying time with the Feds. I think we are good with them for now, but I still need full disclosure from you in more detail about Mirski and P2K2. Remember, all I have is your word about why you are giving mafia guys our money. And while I am inclined to believe you, I will need more than a believable story. I want to know dates of contact, who was present, full physical descriptions, and your detailed recall about what you saw in those photographs, not only of Rachel and Sarah but of the other women, girls and boys. I want physical descriptions, what you saw in the backgrounds, clothing styles, and geography, if any. This can take a while, so we better go back to your office and get started.

We headed out to the waiting car where Sasha started the journey back to the Transeget Industries warehouse.

■ ■ ■ ■ ■

I was already thinking about preparing a verbal summary for Brinton. If I got results from Takhoyev, I would call Brinton. If not, we were not just at square-one, we were behind the eight-ball and I'd have to try another approach to helping Weiner.

Kuznetsov was not at the office when we returned. I invited Sasha in, but he seemed comfortable waiting with the car, even for long periods of time. I told him, "Sasha, I am going to be here at least a couple hours. Come inside and relax."

"No thanks, boss. I will wait with the car. If I leave it unattended for too long, it will be stolen, and if not the entire car, then the tires for sure. It is best if I stay with the car."

I was curious. "What do you do in the evenings when you are home for the day? Surely you do not sleep in your car?"

Sasha snorted a laugh, "Oh, no. I do not sleep in the car and neither does my wife. We have a metal garage. It is just big enough to drive into. I close a drop-down metal door and it has a very sturdy lock. My dogs would alert me if someone came walking too close to the garage. It is not a problem."

Inside Weiner's locked office I began the tedious task of documentation. The process was not simply a series of questions and answers. I led Weiner down a methodical path of visualizing what had occurred when Mirski and the other man showed him the frightening photographs.

As Weiner struggled to objectively bring back the images, I could see the emotional conflict to his memory because of what was associated with them – women and children in forced sexual bondage. And I knew as he reconstructed the details, he was superimposing the images of his wife and daughter into the worst of the photos. It must have been pure hell, but we had to get through it.

Initially I took no notes other than minor marginalia. I didn't want to interrupt his honest attempts to remember. It wasn't until Weiner was in the flow of recalling clearly, that I began taking detailed notes that would form the basis for his admission statement. It took hours before we finished. Weiner declined a dinner invitation with me, choosing to go straight home. I couldn't blame him.

I gathered my notes while making my goodbyes. I tried to calm him about the new payment, but I could tell he would only get to that point when he saw some kind of proof that it was working. I felt the same way.

Sasha got me back to the Metropol in record time. I sent him home with a request to be picked up no later than eight a.m.

I found two messages awaiting me when I picked up my key at the front desk.

The first was from Weiner. It simply said *Thank you.* The second was from Koval. It said *Cannot meet in morning. How about dinner tonight? Call me.*

CHAPTER NINE

IN A VERY BRIEF PHONE call, Koval suggested we meet at Yar on Leningradsky Prospect. It was nearby but too far to walk comfortably, not to mention safely. So Koval offered to pick me up in about forty-five minutes – enough time for me to get cleaned up.

When I exited the elevator to the main floor, Koval was waiting for me. He had a taxi standing at the front door, engine running. "He's my regular," was all that Koval said and we hopped in.

The ride to Yar was brief, maybe ten minutes. We barely had time in the car for meaningful conversation, but Koval was able to explain that Yar was a historic restaurant, with the chef and owner keeping alive a tradition of fine dining, dating back to the eighteen hundreds. I recognized the nervous small talk Koval was making and wondered when we would be able to get to the heart of my problem.

I had to admit I was impressed as we entered the lobby. It was what some might call elegant, with gold gilt walls and ceilings and mirrored panels everywhere. Seating at most of the linen covered tables was set for six with larger booths along the windows. Koval had a reservation and the maître de mentioned that Koval's other guest had already arrived. I looked sharply at Koval, as if to say *there's another guest and you didn't tell me?*

Koval said, "I didn't want to give you the chance to decline until we had a chance to talk." Rising to greet us as we were escorted to our table was Vladimir Takhoyev, KGB or FSK or insurance agent, whatever he was. To say that I was pissed, was to put it mildly.

Yet there was that warm smile, trained to be welcoming and disarming and an outreaching hand gestured in greeting. It did have the effect of taking some of the edge off. I shook it without enthusiasm.

Koval said, "Michael, I know this is a surprise and I apologize. We both apologize, but this wasn't our idea. Jerry suggested we three meet and break some bread together." And there it was. *Don't be surprised if the guys who were on the opposite side ten years ago ...*

Takhoyev opened the conversation. "First of all, Michael, let me thank you for doing business with my agency." Now I began to wonder just exactly which agency Takhoyev was talking about. "I have confirmed that you have made the premium payment, even if there is a hold on it. I have made some calls to ensure the coverage is in effect. I assure you, it is."

I was going to ask how he could be sure but decided to hold back on any comments that might seem antagonistic, even if that was the way I felt.

Koval added, "I know several of your corporate security counterparts in Moscow, Michael. I have spoken with them about the roofs they have built over their businesses. They are quite comfortable talking about their insurance programs and the effectiveness of their coverage. Did you talk with anyone on the list I gave you?"

I felt foolish. In my rush to solve the problem, I had skipped the fact-checking process. "I really didn't have time, given what I had learned." Turning to Takhoyev I said, "And given what the two of you seemed to have known all along."

Takhoyev responded to the jab. "Michael, you have your facts wrong, at least the order of occurrence. Tom did not explain to me the nature of your problem, and only let me know that you might be calling. He also only referenced your company operation by name, as the reason for your being in Moscow. If he did know, he didn't let on to me. My job is to do the underwriting and risk assessment. It wasn't difficult for me to get the facts surrounding your Mr. Weiner's dilemma. And that is how I was so well informed when you came to see me. Not through any breach of trust you may have assumed about Tom."

Again, I felt like a bird in a tornado. I was there, but inconsequential in some larger, swirling scheme of things. And I was hearing from a former KGB agent that his FBI confidant was trustworthy. Furthermore, my friend Maniaci had orchestrated this meeting without telling me. It all seemed backward and it troubled me. Now I was wondering if Koval was in deeper than Maniaci knew about, and had he used the follow up phone call to suggest we three meet?

Koval took over. "I sent Jerry a message that you and Vladimir had met through me. I also told him you and I were meeting for dinner tonight. He suggested I include Vladimir in the invitation. It was sort of a way to build the trust relationship faster and more solidly. He said he would call you, but I told him we were only a few minutes apart. And frankly I told him that you might not come if you knew Vladimir was going to be here. Jerry has known both you and Vladimir a long time. But he deferred to me. Not calling you in advance wasn't his first choice. Since I am in-country and he isn't, it was my call, Michael. So, go easy on him."

It was beginning to seem logical to me. I also knew that the brotherhood between FBI agents would override anything Jerry and I had, and Koval and I had only known each other a day or so.

I shouldn't have been disappointed or surprised by it.

I decided I had nothing to gain by being resistive and extended my hand to Takhoyev saying, "Let's start over. Vladimir, how nice to see you. Tom, what a pleasant surprise and thank you for arranging it."

Smiles broke out all around and the waiters, sensing the tension had melted from the table, brought fresh bottled water. Koval watched over them breaking the seals on each container before they poured. He knew there was a large black market in tap water being poured into non-sanitized bottles as if it were fresh-filtered, even in commercial establishments. Although it didn't seem to bother the other two, I had my water without ice.

Wanting to know more about these two characters, I opened the conversation. "You two have me at a disadvantage. You both seem to know about me, and you also seem to know each other comfortably. Perhaps you can tell me a bit about yourselves. Tom, why don't you tell me a bit more about your background? Just how is it that you came to be stationed in Moscow?"

Koval tried to keep it short because his story spanned decades. "It's pretty simple, really. I went into the Air Force during the height of the Vietnam era and was sure I'd end up in country there. Apparently, I have an aptitude for languages, so instead they sent me to a unique program at Syracuse University for immersive training in Russian. Before I knew it, I was in Wakkanai, Japan listening to Russian bomber and fighter pilots, translating their chatter and sending it back to the States for analysis. When my tour was up, I was nabbed by the National Security Agency and asked to stay on a bit as a special analyst, since I seemed to do well with technical translations, in addition to common idioms and colloquialisms.

"After that, I was searching for something to do when I exited government service. One of my supervisors suggested that with my Russian language background and my experiences in analysis, the Bureau might find me an interesting candidate. I was accepted immediately and attended the Academy in Quantico. From there I was assigned to a team that specifically investigates the activities of the Russian mafia in the States. Years later, when the Attaché position opened, I was considered a natural and transferred here. That's pretty much it."

Koval looked back and forth between Vladimir and me, indicating he was through.

Takhoyev spoke right up. "My background is simple also, Michael. By the time I retired from military service I spoke four languages fluently, much like our friend Tom. Mine were the languages of international business, especially English. I have what you would call Masters Degrees in Business, International Finance and Economics. My superiors found I had an aptitude for risk financing and furthered my education. When I completed my years with the military, I became an insurance agent with some others I had previously worked with. Business is *booming*. And yes, I intended the pun. That is how you and I met."

Takhoyev stopped and looked to me as if to say, *I am done.* No mention of his role in the KGB, or in its other services since their reorganization. Not a word about whether he was officially or unofficially serving the new FSK for counter intelligence services or the SVR for foreign intelligence services. It irked me for some reason that Takhoyev was playing smug with me. It must have shown on my face.

Takhoyev added, "I would love to tell you more about my background in depth, but much of what I did is still classified under our states secrets act. I could be shot for merely mentioning it."

Koval picked it up from there. "We can tell you that Vladimir appeared on the FBI charts as a senior member of the KGB for foreign intelligence services. It is public information in the States, at least among our agencies." And here they go, involving me in their agency secrets. I thought. *Damn, I wish they wouldn't do that.* Koval continued, "He has been most beneficial to us in several joint ventures as an advisor." Koval nodded toward Takhoyev and continued, "We have likewise reciprocated as consultants to Vladimir on issues where he needed our assistance. Jerry and I both know him as a friend."

I thought it was my turn to explain my background when Takhoyev said, "We are aware of your experiences Michael. For a civilian it is most impressive, given what we find in your file, some older press releases and Jerry's recounting of some tall tales about you."

"What file?" I asked.

Takhoyev repressed a small laugh and smiled. "Michael, you should feel proud. Anyone who is anyone and enters Russia has a file. Think about it. You are head of security for Transeget Industries and have been here before. You conducted an investigation on our soil. Quite effectively, I might add. And you represent a Plowshares company. Did you think you would not have a file?"

I suspected I had been under surveillance the last time I was here. And I was sure I had come under the watchful eye of the KGB in the past, even on this trip. But to have it said so boldly and without rancor or bragging threw me off guard for a moment. I repressed the urge to feel offended or violated. "I guess it does make sense, but it surprises me that you are so open about it."

"Ah, yes. But there is fast-becoming a relationship here, no?" Perhaps Takhoyev was right.

The banter continued as a bottle of Smirnoff Vodka was brought to the table along with three tumblers. Smirnoff had only recently been re-introduced as a Russian product after a few decades of it being outsourced to U.S. companies. Rumor was that it was owned and operated in Russia under the direction of some Greek mafioso personage. Koval poured while Takhoyev and I waited.

Koval raised his glass of Vodka and held it forth, "To fast-becoming relationships!" Takhoyev and I lifted our glasses also, nodded the rims towards each other and we all downed it straight, *Na Zdorovya*.

Dinner was more of the same. Light-hearted conversation intended to warm the relationship. My grandmother used to say, *always feed your company, it makes them feel special*. My grandfather would just roll his eyes.to

I really wanted some alone time with Koval, but it was obvious it wasn't going to happen this evening during dinner. I was desperate to learn whether or not we could get Weiner out of the country in a hurry if need be.

Conversation moved from the weather to the capitalizing of the Russian economy, more aptly described as privatization, and its success or failure. Interestingly, Takhoyev mostly wanted to talk about baseball. American baseball.

"How is it possible that there is no World Series this year? For God's sake Christian this is baseball!" Takhoyev was referring to the strike that idled the Major Leagues for over two hundred days and disrupted the game like never before.

"Ah, now you see how bargaining as a collective works. Or not." I answered.

Takhoyev did not rise to my bait to turn the conversation into a discussion of communism. He just continued on, "But it is baseball, no? It is Hot Dogs, Apple Pie, America! There must be baseball!"

He seemed in a particularly good mood and it seemed genuine. His grasp of American expressions was spot on.

I found myself relaxing a bit. As I sipped, I realized I was exhausted. Jet lag was catching up with me and adrenaline was no longer enough to keep me going without fatigue. The meal came and went, as did a dessert of petite chocolate cream cakes and coffee liquors, but our conversation never slowed. We all participated and seemed at ease with each other as the evening wore on.

Finally, Koval said, "I need to get going. I have a full day tomorrow, and I imagine you do as well Michael."

I took it as my cue to stand. Koval asked Vladimir, "Can I drop you off somewhere?"

"Yes, thank you, I'd like that. To my office would be fine." So, we all exited to Koval's waiting taxi and driver.

Once in the car, with Koval in the front, Takhoyev asked the driver to take him to St. Basil's Cathedral instead. The driver proceeded directly there, bypassing my hotel. As the driver pulled in front of one of the most famous landmarks in the world, Lenin's Tomb, Takhoyev leaned in to me and said, "I would like you to walk with me. We can head back to your hotel together. I know a shortcut."

I was about to say I would rather ride with Koval but knew it would sound rude. And it did seem like Takhoyev was up to something that was going to be strictly between the two of us. Maybe it was an update on Weiner's protective plan. So, I agreed.

■ ■ ■ ■ ■

We had said goodbye to Koval and were slowly walking north through the Square. Takhoyev had set a deliberately slow pace enhancing the majesty of this place. The slow gait reminded me of my beat-walking days as a rookie cop.

I had been to Red Square before, but the place never ceased to amaze me. Here was the center of Russian might, the power of one of the largest militaries in the world, and the seat of a still hostile government. Lenin's tomb was directly across the brick-paved walkway from me. Behind it loomed the tall, dark wall enclosing the Kremlin. Just up from us, St. Basil's spires stood majestically against the black night sky. Even in the darkness, the onion-shaped domes still looked beautiful. I thought back across the different phases of my life and recalled seeing newsreels of Russian military troops in full parade, rolling tanks and nuclear missiles through this very courtyard where I now stood.

Takhoyev sensing my thoughts said, "It still impresses me too and I have been around a long time. I have marched in military formation here and I have stood on the reviewing stand as well. For all our might and for all we aspire to, our people will always be impoverished. And knowing that, we must keep them drunk and docile.

"Russia is a big country with too many mouths to feed. And being formerly responsible for the entire Soviet Union any chance we had for global greatness was diminished by trying to retain control over these warlord mentalities. We were constantly suppressing rebellions everywhere.

"We cannot grow enough food because our farming methods are archaic, and our equipment is old and broken down. What we do grow, we cannot transport to the people economically. There will always be rebellions and insurgencies for us to stamp out. Radical groups that appeal to the unemployed, the uneducated and the hopeless will always be there to rise up against us. Our common enemies finance them. Sometimes your government supports them against us and sometimes we support them against you. It is a mistake that will haunt us both in the future. And thus, there will never be peace."

He continued, "For a thousand years we have known that we could not allow the populace to blame us for their sad state. Otherwise there would be more revolutions and we could not allow that either. When the people rail against us, we divert their anger to a different enemy. So, whom do we blame? Anyone else we can, but never ourselves. For decades we blamed the bourgeoisie and the Russian Royal families."

"And under communism, we blame America of course. It is easy to demonize you. As you can see though, we are all just people. When we meet each other face to face, without having to worry if we are trying to kill each other, we can be very civilized."

"It must be sad to live a lifetime of despair, Vladimir." I offered.

"Yes, I imagine so. But that is not my worry. I do okay as a humble insurance man."

I was smiling to myself at that when Takhoyev added, "But I did not ask you to join me as your tour guide or history teacher."

I had no retort, so I waited for Takhoyev to give me the update on Weiner. We walked without speaking out the north end of the Square through the archway of the State Historical Museum and were heading east along the north frontage of the Metro Train Station in the general direction of the Metropol. It was only a few paces away.

Takhoyev stopped and said, "Tomorrow morning you will learn that all is as I told you it would be. Your threat is over, and Mr. Weiner and his girls are safe from now on. They can move about unmolested. Your business can operate without fear. That means no more robberies or hijackings, no more burglaries and no more driver harassment. It doesn't protect you from some low-life trying to steal scrap metal. But you are free from major worries."

I wasn't sure how to respond but was trying to formulate a *thank you* of sorts, when Takhoyev continued. "There is no need to thank me Michael. You bought a roof and we built it. It is simple as that. I deliver on my promises." I gave him a simple *thank you.*

We continued to walk again in silence. We neared the front entrance to the Metropol when Takhoyev pulled up, tugged my elbow again and turned me back toward the Square. "There is another matter Michael. I have given a great deal of thought about sharing this with you. It is best we both become a bit circumspect. Are you familiar with St. Anthony of Padua?" he asked.

I was, but Takhoyev answered his own question for me, "He is the patron saint of lost items. People pray to St. Anthony when something seems hopelessly lost, no?"

Another rhetorical question. There seemed to be a lot of that going on.

"Perhaps your company is looking for something that is missing. Maybe it is merely lost. It seems that a lot of people are looking for something missing lately. Your Agency boys have feelers out everywhere for something missing. Maybe they are wanting you to help find it. No?"

I was still trying to figure out Takhoyev's easy use of the American language and how he slipped back and forth between perfect English grammar and low Russian. And more importantly how he assumed I might be somehow involved in the Agency mission.

His demeanor had gone cold. "Are you, Michael Christian? Are you too looking for something missing? Maybe you are a spy. Is that why you are really here?"

Takhoyev held up a hand. "Do not answer. Just listen to me. There is no sense getting off on the wrong foot when we have just had a nice dinner together. If you thought you were playing with some tough mafia characters you were mistaken. Those are merely well organized, low-life thugs without a conscience. They play with lives as if people were bottle caps, cheap and disposable. And their bosses are worse. But if you were looking for something else Christian, you might likely encounter a group more cruel and more deadly, the likes of which you have never experienced.

251

"I am not saying that you are, Christian. But let us assume that your Mr. Brinton sent you here to help find missing nuclear materials. Do you really have any means of helping in that regard? You realize you are totally out of your league, don't you?"

I was dumbfounded and didn't know how to respond. If it was Takhoyev's goal to catch me off guard, he had succeeded. In a few simple sentences, he had summed up my position and I firmly agreed that I was totally unable to pursue that line of inquiry on my own. And at this juncture, I was being confronted by a former KGB agent. I was damned no matter what I said. Someone had briefed Takhoyev thoroughly or he had access to highly confidential government information. Was there a leak in the Agency? Was his source Koval or Maniaci, or both? Did the intelligence ministries have a line on this, given all the inquiries that the Agency and maybe even the Bureau had made? Were the Russians complicit in the thefts in an effort to hide their own materials from being dismantled? Or worse. Were they seeking an alibi for using them somewhere and claiming these were stolen from them? I was afraid that if I made just one slip of the tongue, I might be feeding information to the Russian intelligence services, and then be found alongside a slightly-used country road outside Moscow. I was being forced into the position of *good listener* again and thank goodness. I had no spy craft skills whatsoever. I decided that my only response was not to respond.

Takhoyev continued, "So here are some facts for you Christian. It seems no one is exactly sure where the material is. But one thing is certain.

Neither of our governments wants to help the other find it without assurances of some kind. For all the partnerships that are being deployed at our level, there is no concurrence at the executive levels of our governments about how to handle the materials if they are found. Another thing is certain. Neither of our governments wants this kind of power in the hands of terrorists.

"So, there is pressure at the top of both our governments to find the material, yet there is an unspoken expectation that whoever finds it will not tell the other. It makes for a difficult intelligence-sharing partnership at our level, does it not?" Another damn question where he did not expect an answer from me.

"But let me ask you, Michael. What if someone thought they knew where the material was, or at least knew in general where to start looking for it? To whom would they go with the information? The opportunity for misuse of that knowledge is too great. Maybe it is better lost?"

I got in my two cents on that. "If the material works its way into the hands of terrorists, that would be catastrophic regardless of who it was used against. If someone knew where it was, wouldn't it be better to just go to his or her agency leaders and let them recover it? It seems to be the goal of both our countries. If you have a handle on where it is, just go get it."

"If only it was that easy, Christian. You see there are people in our government and even in my agency who would just as soon privately own that material. They would profit enormously from repositioning it in the hands of Iran, Pakistan, Syria or Hezbollah. Then there is the mafia. They too have a cook in the kitchen, so to speak. What if they got their hands on it? Would they foment insurrection? Could they hold governments or companies hostage? Would they sell to terrorists or to the Georgians or the Chechens? We are afraid the answers to those questions are all *yes*. The bottom line is, this is all about greed and personal wealth, not our government hiding inventory to protect it from your country.

"So, let me ask you again, Christian. Are you looking for it? More importantly, could you use a guide to help you navigate these byzantine waters? You see, while I too want to grow my personal wealth, I cannot imagine the disaster it would be if this got into the wrong hands, even to my agency who lost it to begin with. Frankly, I would prefer to see it re-introduced to a Plowshares company for disposition."

Now I was concerned that regardless of what he was saying, Takhoyev may want the material for his own personal gain and was merely using me. I asked dubiously, "Are you telling me Vladimir that you know where it is and are willing to turn it over to me?" I thought it was insane that I would catch a break like this, given all the efforts of the CIA and FBI, and God only knew who else was looking for this stuff.

"No, Michael. I am asking if you would consider a guide who might help *you* look for the material. I have it from reliable sources that it may be in the hands of someone known to deal in weapons of all kinds. I do not know exactly where he is. It seems no one does right now. But he fits the profile and has the contacts. He may be coming to Moscow as we speak.

"If that is the case, we may catch a break. If not, you go home with some raw intelligence that makes you look very good to your government friends. But you must promise me. If we find what you are looking for, you must develop a way to get it directly to your reprocessing plant in the States without going through my government's hands. If that were the case, it would merely move from the devil you know to the one you don't want to know. And it just might get me killed."

I had felt I was in way over my head since I got here, just like Takhoyev had said. Now I was in even deeper. I was unsure how to proceed and unsure even how to answer. But a plan was beginning to formulate. I decided that being honest was my best course. It would satisfy Takhoyev and it would give me some time to think this all through.

"You have overwhelmed me with innuendo and with choices, Vladimir. You know I could not tell you if I was doing government work, even if I was. We both know that would make me a spy. And I have done nothing of that nature." I knew I was playing with words there. If I had a chance, I would definitely nose around. But Takhoyev was right. I didn't even know where to start.

I continued, "If you have this information Vladimir, why not just pass it along to Koval or Maniaci and work with them? My mind is whirling with questions that I cannot process. I don't know what is trustworthy or not. I need some time to think about it."

Takhoyev responded, "To answer your question about working with the Bureau, I cannot appear to be officially or unofficially working with a foreign government's intelligence agencies on this particular matter and still maintain my status in Russia. Like you, I am only a former government worker, now in private business. Sometimes, like you, I am asked to be observant or to act for my government as well. You know I cannot give the Bureau rough information without being willing to help them develop it into actionable evidence. And I cannot, as I mentioned before, go to my own agency or around them. So, time and options are things we do not have at our disposal, no?

"Michael, if all goes well tomorrow with Weiner, how would you justify any additional time here in Russia? You might gain a day, but anything beyond that would raise questions about you. Even if you found a way to rationalize remaining here longer, as a sightseer let us say, where would you begin on your own? You have no leads and no contacts. You might as well go home, because without help you are done here."

I knew he was right about that and had reached the same conclusion myself.

"This man who is coming, who may have the weapons, may be coming to stay or he may be meeting a buyer, which would be a bad thing. Or he may be merely passing through and would become invisible again. Michael, I think we need each other. We do not have time to dance around a decision. And I think you may have a personal interest in moving forward with me. We cannot give Oveshkin a chance to slip through our fingers."

I was jolted from indecision! "Oveshkin? *Pavel Oveshkin*?"

"Yes. *Your* Pavel Oveshkin."

Oveshkin was a man I knew very well, or at least by reputation. I had just broken a gun smuggling case in Germany involving Pavel Oveshkin.

Information I developed led the authorities to believe he was selling to the mafia, to terrorists, to insurgents and rogue regimes around Eurasia and the Middle East.

Nearly everyone in that investigation was captured in the net I had woven. Everyone was detained except Oveshkin. He got clean away. To think that he, with his connections to the wrong people, may have nuclear material was frightening. There was also a sense of ego involved since I hadn't cleaned up that gun smuggling case as nicely as I like to. Someone had gotten clean away, and it was Oveshkin! I made up my mind in that instant.

"I'm in," I said. And I briefed Takhoyev on my background with Oveshkin and his network. We walked around the Square as I explained my case from Germany, our informants, our interdiction of them, and the smuggling routes, even the use of a Russian trawler to bring some of the weapons from northeast Germany to St. Petersburg. Takhoyev could sense my frustration as I explained how Oveshkin eluded us. Takhoyev's bait was tasty and I bit. So, we talked about next steps.

We walked back to Red Square, circling its mall for another hour before we broke up for the evening. I returned to the Metropol and the comfort of my room. I was exhausted but too wired to sleep. That disturbed me, as did the fact that my briefcase was open on my bed again. So was my carryon bag of gifts, but only the remaining chocolate was missing.

■ ■ ■ ■ ■

Fedor thought nothing of it when Sergei called him in for a meeting. Nor was he surprised when Sergei told him that it was time to take the pressure off Weiner. These things happened. At times there would be a meeting of the minds between two competing forces and an agreement would be worked out. It was a matter of one party never pushing too hard on the other, and of knowing that if one agreed to back off a venture, the other might become indebted.

Fedor didn't know who owed whom, but he did know that someone from the KGB or the GRU had met with Sergei, and he had his ideas about just who that might be. Someone had built a roof over Weiner who was now out of reach. There would be no slip-ups, no attempt to squeeze a last payment out of him. It was finished the moment Sergei said it was.

Fedor's job was to ensure that Sergei's orders were carried out immediately and he did. This came so closely on the heels of his team accidently killing Carter Winston, followed by Trofim being killed for allowing the mistake to happen on his watch, and Grigor being made to disappear. If he screwed this up with Weiner, it would be Fedor's head on the block, and this time, Sergei would show him no mercy.

So, that very afternoon Fedor met with his entire team and explained that Weiner was never again to be threatened, harassed or intimidated. The plant surveillance was shut down and the crews watching Weiner's wife and daughter were removed. He told them that the business would be left untouched now, including the small office downtown. That it had a bigger roof over it. And every single man in the room knew what that meant. Some scoffed in rebuke, but they did so silently. No one would dare challenge that authority out loud.

Fedor did not know who the small-time limousine driver was who was also protected under that edict, but he added Sasha's name to the list of untouchable people and businesses.

Fedor knew that Sergei was getting a cut of some other pie, but it wasn't the same as receiving a monthly pot of cash. Nevertheless, if Sergei thought it was a good deal for him, then that was how it was to be regardless of what Fedor thought. He leaned back in his chair and decided to accelerate the extortion of his next victim.

That was when he saw the shadow move across the glass in his office door. But before he could react to it, the door opened. He was reaching for his gun in the holster fastened to the inside of his desk when he was told, "You are not that fast, and you are not that good. Besides, you wouldn't shoot an old friend, would you?" And there stood Vladimir Takhoyev.

"*Mudak* 'you asshole.' You scared me to death. I almost shot you."

"No, you didn't almost shoot me Fedor Davydov. Your face was still in shock when I walked in. Had I intended to kill you, you would already be dead. You need to sharpen your skills."

259

Fedor stared at his friend and made a mental note, "You are right. I was careless. But you can trust it won't happen again. You better knock next time."

Takhoyev settled into a chair. "We must talk and then I must leave before someone sees us. This is about your new friend who is coming to town, Oveshkin."

Davydov leaned forward in his chair and whispered, "You know the code Vladimir Takhoyev. We do not tell on our own. And we do not cooperate with the government. The rule is simple, and it cannot be changed."

"Don't talk to me about codes Fedor. Oveshkin is not a made member of the Bratva and we both know it. If anything, he is more government, even if he has left the service. And do you really think that he will merely come here and work beside you? I know Sergei better than you do and I have known him longer. He is rebuilding his organization and Oveshkin will soon be a Brigadier, just like you, and maybe over you. And we both know you will have trouble with your men accepting an outsider. We both know what you worry about."

"And what is that?" Davydov asked.

"You wonder if you are training your replacement. And you know if that were the case, then there is nowhere for you to go. You wonder if your days are numbered, or if you can prove to Sergei that you are worth not killing. You have probably already figured out that Sergei will never allow you to end up in someone else's organization."

"So, let us not talk about your *Code*. You already told me Oveshkin is going to be running the arms dealing business for Sergei and I need to have a direct line on him. I want to know when he is coming and going, where he is staying and who he is meeting at all times. And yes, right now I am asking nicely, Fedor, as a friend. I do not want to have to go to the next level of asking."

There it was, the threat. *It is always the same with the fucking KGB*, Fedor thought. They ask nicely, but only once. Then they give the veiled threat. There is no mistaking it.

Fedor was tough. His people were vicious and equally as capable of instilling fear as delivering pain or death. But they were just amateurs compared with the KGB.

"*Chyort poberi* 'damn it', Vladimir. You do not have to threaten me. We can talk like businessmen, like friends. Am I not the one who told you about Oveshkin to begin with? Do you think I will not help you if I can? It is just that we need to figure out a way for us to meet and talk. It is dangerous for you to be here."

"Dangerous for whom, Fedor?"

"Dangerous for me, Vladimir. If we are seen together, the word will get to Sergei before you can walk across the street. You may be able to get away with anything, but not the rest of us. You and I can talk but let us be safe."

Vladimir rose and straightened his coat. "Yes, you are right. I will go now and let you know when I want to see you again. In the meanwhile, answer me some things Fedor. When is Oveshkin expected and where will he be staying? I presume you will be making arrangements?"

"He is staying at the Hotel Ukraina. And he is here already. He came just today. I will be having breakfast with him there in the morning before we head over to meet with Sergei. In a few weeks, Sergei will post him in a home he is acquiring for him."

"And will you be showing him the business, introducing him around, explaining the territory boundaries and tutoring him on the Code, Fedor?"

"He will be my shadow, Vladimir. I will keep you posted."

"Remember Fedor, I do not want to know afterward. I want to know before he does anything, meets anyone. Before. Do you understand?"

Fedor was boiling inside. He had planned to offer Vladimir Takhoyev a tidbit to show that he was helpful. Instead he had become an informant. He hated that role. He had killed people for such a violation of the code and now here he was. "Yes, Vladimir. I understand. But why is he so important to you?"

Vladimir chuckled as he buttoned his jacket. "There is an old American movie expression my friend. *If I told you, I'd have to kill you.*" He turned and saw himself out.

There was no doubt in Fedor's mind that Vladimir was serious, dead serious.

CHAPTER TEN

I WALKED OUT INTO WHAT looked like a bright Moscow morning and down the steps of the Metropol just as Sasha pulled to the curb in front. Then, as I looked around, I realized that for all the light, I couldn't see the blue of the sky or the sun itself. It seemed like the sun couldn't make its way through the haze. It was as if even the firmament was telling the same lie to the Russian people, *everything is beautiful and there is no need to worry.* Or maybe it was just speaking to me.

That pervasive greasy substance still hung in the air, settling on the buildings, the cars and the streets. Maybe it was my imagination, but even the people walking about at this early hour seemed to have a sheen on their skin and hair. The very oxygen I was breathing smelled and tasted electrical. The black cables of the outdated trolleys reached up and clung to overhead wires, sparking and popping as if that would help keep Muscovites from smashing into their overcrowded cars.

Once I directed Sasha to Weiner's warehouse, he said, "My wife was very excited by the chocolate. Thank you, boss."

"I am glad, Sasha. Hopefully she won't eat it all at once."

"Oh no, she won't. I only gave her some. Later I will give her more and she will be happy all over again." Sasha said. I enjoyed the simple wisdom of his relationship with his wife.

I felt I should spend more time talking with Sasha about things personal to him, but I was formulating multiple tactics on a different level. I had an inkling of how to deal with Weiner's safety if our "roof" collapsed. Although I hoped Takhoyev would deliver, I couldn't rely simply on that. I needed to have a strategy in place if I had to get the Weiners out of Russia in a hurry. I had an idea, but I hadn't worked it all out yet.

I had slipped into a higher gear, now that Takhoyev and I had struck an agreement. And for the time being, it was just the two of us. Koval wasn't in, not just yet. As congenial as Koval was and as well connected as he was, it was premature to let him know I was working another angle. Besides, Koval may have tried to prohibit such an arrangement if he knew a civilian was working alone with a former KGB agent on something as high stakes as this.

Sasha guided the Mercedes to the curb across the street from the warehouse entrance and parked. He turned the engine off and said. "I will come with you boss." We had both noticed the two large men standing in front of the building's main door.

"No Sasha, wait here. I'll be ok." I hoped I was right about that.

As I exited the car and walked toward the front door, I saw the men staring intently at me. Slowly I reached into my left shirt pocket to extract my business card. At the movement of my hand inside my jacket, the two men simultaneously opened their leather car-coats, revealing that each had an automatic rifle hanging from a sling. I had seen that dress code before. Their eyes were black as night as they leveled the muzzles at me, and the look on their faces showed cold, deadly and willing capability. It didn't look like the first time they pulled their guns and might not have been the first time they chose to shoot someone. I hesitated but did not stop my advance. Holding the card far in front of me, I continued to walk, holding my other hand above my head in the universal sign of surrender.

When I was an arm's length away from the pair, I stopped, leaned forward and handed the card to the gunman on the right. He looked at it quizzically, so I motioned for him to turn it over. Flipping it from the English version to the rear of the card, the guard read the Cyrillic script, and then showed it to his partner. They let the machineguns drop to their sides and gave me a crisp coordinated salute. The guy on the left then held the door open for me. That was the first sign that Takhoyev's insurance was at work.

I scaled the stairs quietly and entered the workspace to find Weiner bent over a conference table sorting through stacks of paperwork. He looked up when the door opened, the look of surprise obvious on his face. Then he looked pleased. "Come in, come in," he said, motioning to

265

his office. Again he closed the door behind us as he took the chair alongside me.

"I don't know what you did yesterday Christian, but it must have worked. The guys down the street are gone. My drivers on the early routes have reported no cars following them. No one has been hijacked or stopped. And most importantly of all, Rachel tells me they were not followed when she took Sarah to school today.

"The only difference is that there are two gunmen in front of the building instead of in a car down the street. We are using the back entrances for everything. They are so fearsome, that people approaching our building cross the street and walk on the other sidewalk. I thought you were going to get rid of them."

And there it was. Warehouse operations were running smoothly, and the drivers were reporting no intimidating people along the routes. All in one day. Just like Takhoyev said.

I answered Weiner, "The two guys in front are our guys. Consider it a better insurance policy. But do not interact with them. I'd keep using the back door a few more days. I am sure once we are convinced that all is permanently well, they will be told to stand down." I handed Weiner another of my business cards. "In the meanwhile, if I were you, I'd keep this in your pocket for them, in case they ask."

"Are you saying it is safe? Does this mean I will not have to make another deposit into their account? Are you sure Christian? Are you certain? What if we don't make a payment and they take my girls? I couldn't bear it." Weiner started ramping up his own anxiety again.

"I am saying that we have taken care of this problem and you do not have to make another payment. But I am warning you. If you are approached again, you must contact me immediately. No side payments and no delays. You are not equipped to handle threats like this on your own. You are out of your league in matters like these." Out of *his* league? My thoughts immediately went back to my conversation with Takhoyev last night.

"I can't thank you enough, Christian. Thank you."

"Don't think you are completely out of hot water yet, Alex. You still made illegal payments from company funds. But if what you say is true about your division president authorizing you to make contingency payments, it may soften the blow for you, maybe not so much for him though. I will look into that when I return to the States. I am staying at the Metropol for a few more days. If anything out of the ordinary comes up, *anything*, reach out to me there."

Weiner offered me some coffee and fresh pastries, but I declined and headed back down the front stairs. The guards heard me coming and one of them sprang to open the door for me. They were talking and sharing a smoke with Sasha who, when he saw me, snuffed the hot ash of his cigarette onto the street. Together we walked back to his car. Sasha was grinning a huge Cheshire Cat smile.

We got in the car and I fastened myself in. "What are you smiling about, Sasha? What's so funny?"

267

"You pretty big shot, boss." And with that he gave me a good-natured nudge with his elbow and hooked his thumb at me repeating, "You big shot, boss." Then Sasha pointed that thumb at him and said, "You big shot. Me big shot!" I wondered what brought that on and asked.

Sasha then nodded his head backwards towards the guards and said "Bad guys. You own mafia bad guys. You pretty damn big shot." Then he smiled that big grin again and said proudly, "Me big shot!"

I said, "No Sasha. Nyet mafia."

Sasha didn't get it. "Da, boss. Mafia bad guys,"

And I repeated and explained, "Nyet Mafia, Sasha. KGB."

That slapped the smile right off Sasha's face. His color went pale and his eyes widened. I recognized the signs of fight or flight that overtake you when you are great fear. I wasn't sure what I had said to cause that reaction.

"Nyet, boss. Nyet. No KGB." Sasha insisted. He seemed almost pleading for it not to be true.

"Yes, Sasha, KGB. They are helping me with a problem."

Sasha seemed lost in his thoughts. He was trying to get a cigarette from his pack, but his fingers were shaking so badly he dropped several of them onto the floor under the steering wheel. He repeated the words ever so softly that I could hardly hear him. "Nyet KGB, Nyet KGB."

I had never seen Sasha react like this, even when he thought the mafia might be following us. Finally, I took the pack from Sasha and shook out a cigarette, took his lighter from the center console, lit the cigarette and held it to him. Sasha took it and put it in his lips. He dragged on it deeply and before he could exhale, he dragged on it again. He let out the smoke in a long, protracted breath and repeated the process. The red end glowed angrily.

"Are you okay Sasha? Do you want me to drive?"

Sasha did not answer. His pallor had turned gray and I feared he might have a heart attack right there in the driver's seat. He looked unblinkingly at me for several seconds and asked "KGB? You hire KGB?"

I knew I needed to explain, but only superficially. "I have a friend who is helping me solve a problem."

Sasha was still in shock. "This is Russia. No one has friend who is KGB. *Mother of God.*" He seemed to be praying.

I knew the KGB was feared in Russia but didn't know the mere mention of their name was terrifying, much more so than the mafia. I began to wonder what my driver had shared with the guards in conversation. Hoping Sasha had calmed down enough to continue driving, I asked again. "Are you okay to drive?"

When I got an affirmative answer, I told him to take me back to Takhoyev's office. I didn't know if Sasha made the connection, but it didn't matter. He would likely never tell anyone about this morning, maybe not even his wife.

■ ■ ■ ■ ■

Takhoyev greeted me before I had a chance to knock on the door. "Come in Michael. I have been waiting for you. I trust all went well at your office this morning?" It was as much a statement as a question.

"Yes, Vladimir. It went very well. From all reports, there are no issues and the thugs down the street were gone."

"And my men?"

"Yes," I answered, "They were out front brandishing guns at me as I approached. That's a pretty efficient way to keep the other bad guys at a distance." If he noticed my inference that his were bad guys too, he didn't indicate it.

Takhoyev chuckled. "Very well, then. You are safe."

"Weiner is very worried that if he misses the next payment perhaps the wires will get accidentally crossed and his girls will be taken. He was seeking assurances from me. I gave them..."

"And I gave you mine. The Weiners and your operations will never be bothered again. You have a very good roof."

Takhoyev turned the conversation. "Let's move on to the unfinished business. Come with me."

Takhoyev led me from the greeting room through what may once have been a spacious dining room. It was now general office space set for several others. It was richly appointed with cherry

270

and mahogany heavy furniture that included desks, a moderate conference table and credenzas.

In the back of the house was a full kitchen in stark white - white walls, floors and ceilings, white marble counters and cupboards and black professional appliances and cabinet hardware. But there was no cook. In fact, there seemed to be no one else in the place. There was no other sound but for the two of us.

Takhoyev led me around a corner to a set of stairs. To the right, the stairs went up toward the roof where he had taken me yesterday. But Takhoyev turned left and we proceeded down to the lower level. At the base of this brightly lit staircase was a steel door. He presented an access control card to the reader and entered six digits into a control panel. The heavy door clicked open almost silently.

For a space with no windows, it was brightly lit, and it looked very functional, and I noted that our voices seemed to stay right in the room. I guessed that it was acoustically soundproofed. There were three desktop computer monitors up and running and one large, wall-mounted monitor that seemed to be a live satellite map of central Moscow. The three monitors sat on a large cherry wood conference table ringed with chairs. A multi-button, speaker-telephone sat at each end of the table. The large burnished top was empty except for a small stack of green file folders. The top one had a red circular seal with the Russian Hammer and Sickle on it with three big red letters in the center "*KGB*". The script around the circle read *Komitet Gosudarstvennoy Bezopasnosti*, in Cyrillic. I felt intimidated. They were KGB files. Takhoyev motioned to the table and sat me next to the stack of files while he walked to a sidebar credenza and opened it. There was a large carafe of hot black coffee and a tray of pastries artfully arranged.

Takhoyev carried them to the table and said, "We may be here a while, so I have arranged for lunch. I think we should get you up to speed on just who we are dealing with, from my perspective anyway." He motioned to the files, "I see you have noticed the seal. Much of this has been declassified, so I can share it with you. The rest, maybe not so much." I wondered about *the rest*. Maybe Takhoyev would not share it, or he'd share it all, declassified or not. *God, I keep getting pulled in deeper and deeper,* I thought. *Was I now a spy?* I wondered.

Takhoyev separated the folders. Several of the green covers had a different stamp on them. "These are SVR" he said, "Not declassified, but important for you to know, so we can work on an equal footing."

How the hell did Takhoyev get access to all this information if he was retired from the service? And wouldn't someone know it was missing? Or did he sign it out and create a paper trail that might lead back to us both?

"First I need to clarify something for you," the Russian said. "Regardless of what you have been told, there are no missiles missing from the inventory. All ICBM warheads that should have been delivered under the terms of the Arms Agreement have been delivered. Cumulatively, each of the Plowshares Companies can account for every item of inventory that has been consigned to it, yours included. All have been accounted for. So lets not think of them as missing *missiles* or their payloads."

Takhoyev continued, "What *is* missing, and therefore making it very difficult for anyone to find them, is a handful of suitcase bombs."

I knew what suitcase bombs were from Walters at the CIA, and this confirmed what they had been telling me. I wondered if perhaps Takhoyev wasn't as well briefed about me as I had supposed. And I had to wonder which intelligence officer was spreading misinformation.

Yet, he continued to surprise me with the depth of his information. "Your Department of Defense is building launch scenarios in the event of a nuclear device being detonated on American soil. They are preparing plans to brief your president for his signature. The plans authorize nuclear retaliation against the Russian people, when the truth is our populace will have had nothing to do with it. Furthermore, the Politburo will have had nothing to do with it either. The Russian government has had nothing to do with the disappearance of these devices. It is not merely an *official position*. It is the truth."

I was beginning to see the larger picture. On the one hand, the Russian president would argue in advance they were not complicit in a possible attack on the United States. The President would have to accept the advice of his Secretaries of Defense and State as well as his Chairman of the Joint Chiefs. They would be responsible for developing a counter strike strategy, and for encouraging the president to see the Russian denial as a diversion. Regardless of the reality, if such an event were to occur in the States, the blame was already being laid at the doorstep of the Kremlin. I was sure someone in Moscow had that figured out and they were preparing their own retaliatory strike strategy.

When I thought about it, I could also see why so much energy was being dedicated to joint government investigations to find these devices. But what if the Russians found the devices first? Could they be trusted to return them to proper custody and inventory control? Did the Russians wonder the same about us?

Takhoyev continued. "Now that we have that out of the way, Michael, let's talk about the challenges. Originally, we started with a suspect list of several hundred people, from scientists, to developers, to contractors, to assemblers, to inventory managers to rogue Spetsnaz operators, even our own Special Forces teams. Frankly, the bombs were originally developed for the KGB and put under our custody. You can see how damaging that is. So, the list had to include some of my own people." *Oh, great* I thought. Do I need to add Takhoyev to the suspect list?

"These are not bombs with the explosive destructive power of an ICBM. Oh, certainly they have enormous force, but they are also dispersion devices. The radioactive material would be generated over large areas by detonating the explosive and letting the destructive force get the particles up into the air and spread along the ground and into the water systems. They will poison everything for miles with radiation, and render the areas uninhabitable for decades, if not centuries.

Regardless of what we call them, the devices are not very big and that is our next challenge. They are no larger than a twenty-liter fuel can, or your five-gallon can. As you can see, they could be placed inside another small container or just carried on the back of a terrorist to be set at their target of choice. Not only would there be fear and widespread panic once the nearby survivors knew their deaths were merely delayed, but there would be economic disruption as well, once an area was declared uninhabitable. Imagine, no access by anyone to your Wall Street or your nation's capitol."

Takhoyev then casually opened a file and turned it to me. "Regardless, you will need to know what these look like."

Inside were user diagrams of the devices, showing the optional shapes, sizes and dimensions. "They must be kept under constant electrical power at these connection points," Takhoyev said.

He showed me two small threaded terminals with caps. "The current from the power source must be fully charged for the device to detonate. So being near an electrical source for internal battery backup is a requirement. They must be cared for and attended to, to remain volatile. If the electrical source runs out, the radiological material would still be hot, but not likely capable of being detonated. There is no dead man's switch on the device. If a battery runs out, the device is merely incapable of being detonated until it is recharged. So, this works to our advantage. The devices must be stored somewhere that has electrical power if they are not to be used for a while." I saw no advantage for us there. Russia is a big place and as rudimentary as their electrical grid was, it was very large.

"Next we have the allegations that these weapons are missing, but we do not know how many are missing or where they are missing from. Originally, we developed some two hundred fifty of these units of varying yields and sizes. Some believe a few have already been deployed in caches in the US and Europe, just waiting to be detonated in the event of a war with your country. Our government denies that unconditionally.

"Several of these are also believed to be located in Sweden with a few allegedly having been found and detonated. Our government denies those are ours as well. Others were deliberately placed in three secret inventories in and around St. Petersburg and likewise distributed here in the suburbs around Moscow. Of the two hundred fifty units, roughly two hundred twenty-five can be positively accounted for. That leaves approximately twenty-five that are missing or are already deployed. If some are truly deployed, no one is admitting it, which makes it difficult for us to know how many are truly missing compared with what might be secretly in position.

"It also does not mean that any one person has them, nor does it mean that they are safe but unaccounted for. Worse, it could mean that some are safe, and some are definitely in the hands of arms dealers looking for buyers. We believe the latter."

I asked myself, *why was the CIA so interested in recovering these bombs when they didn't even know how many were missing? Was there some kind of present danger they weren't sharing with me??*

"And that, Michael leads us to likely suspects. We have been over and over these files looking at their backgrounds, and their access to the weapons, their political affiliations, wealth and health – both physical and mental."

Takhoyev held up a handful of files. "These names then made it to the key suspect list, and I have since taken them off the list, based on our investigations. This one," he held up another file, "was my first real suspect. But he made it through an intense interrogation, and we cleared him." He held up two more, "These two people are missing. They have slipped the noose, so to speak. Therefore, they are high on my list."

Then he held up the remaining personnel file. It was an SVR file – domestic intelligence. He slid it over to me and opened the cover. It was all typed in Cyrillic. "This man was not on our suspect list, because he is not one of ours. I have created the file based on information I received just days ago. The file has yet to be distributed for the very reasons you and I talked about last night." The photograph inside the front cover was perfectly clear. *So, this is what he looked like.*

I looked at his picture on the inside cover.

■ ■ ■ ■ ■

Oveshkin was a handsomely cut man with square features and an almost Germanic, Aryan look about him. It was easy to see why he would be accepted as a leader over the East German Stasi and why he would rise in the ranks of the USSR. The Stasi was a feared federal police agency staffed by Germans but run by the Russian military. Oveshkin managed the armory detail and ran off with a significant portion of the weapons and ammunition after the fall of the iron curtain.

I had received a pretty good briefing on Pavel Oveshkin in a confession from Natasha "Tasha" Krause, also known as Natasha Boryenko. Tasha was Oveshkin's young lover-accomplice in my previous German smuggling case. My guys on that caper had access to an Interpol file and the details became even clearer about her relationship and role with Oveshkin. From his photo, I also understood why a young, barely eighteen-year-old girl like Natasha, could be swept off her feet by this man over ten years her senior.

As soon as Natasha realized she was facing certain jail time for a raft of federal charges including smuggling and accessory to murder, she began selling Oveshkin out - in great detail. Especially since he had fled to Russia and left her behind to take the fall.

I wondered what was more impressive, that Oveshkin had managed to steal several tons of weapons from his superiors without them knowing it, or simply that he had the balls to try it. Either way, he was now a fairly wealthy civilian that never stayed in any one place for long. And he had also stayed off the KGB radar screen. Until now that is. I asked Takhoyev about it. "If he is your key suspect, why hasn't he been picked up for questioning on this? And how would he have access to the bombs anyway?"

"Good questions. I have been able to confirm that Oveshkin is an independent contractor of sorts and is very well connected to the mafia. Sergei Miloradov has him protected. Oveshkin and Miloradov have been doing business in arms for about a year. I guess that ties in with your investigation and may explain why he wasn't caught up in your net. He was floating between St. Petersburg and here and protected in both places.

"I have heard that Miloradov wants to bring Oveshkin into the mafia in a leadership role with a specialty in arms smuggling."

"Where did you hear that Vladimir? It could only have been from someone higher-up in the Bratva for you to know such a thing."

"Michael, I do not ask you to reveal any of your sources. So, do not ask me to reveal mine. You know how that works. Trust me, it is accurate."

I could only shake my head in wonder. His intelligence resources seemed wide and deep for a guy who was supposedly retired.

I said, "Let's suppose that he does come here, Vladimir. And suppose you will know when that is. What do we gain by scooping him up if we don't know where the bombs are? There is no way to know they are even in Moscow, or if they are in the country at all. Remember, he had a small arsenal in Germany in a little town called Plau am See. And no one knew it until we stumbled on it by accident."

Takhoyev replied, "I am presuming you learned about his warehouse by using some very good interviewing techniques. I have some techniques at my disposal too, Michael. The trick will be in getting him to meet with us, so I can use them."

279

I doubted Oveshkin would crack under Takhoyev's *techniques*. More significantly, I knew that Oveshkin was not going to accept an invitation to meet with Takhoyev and certainly not with me, the guy who busted up his operation and recovered his warehouse of guns in Germany. Oveshkin would just as soon kill me than meet with me.

"I think I have a way to get him to come to me." Takhoyev said. "And you my friend, are the bait."

We spent the rest of the afternoon going over the files. At this point, without any effort on my part, I knew I had become every bit the spy. But who was I working for, since no one would claim me?

■ ■ ■ ■ ■

Pavel Oveshkin was contemplating how his life had changed in the last few weeks since Sergei Miloradov required his presence in Moscow. Pavel was nobody's fool and kept a very low profile. Buyers in his dark market knew who he was. But no one knew where he was. If they needed him, he somehow found out and reached out to them to close their deals and always on his terms, his time and his place. He enjoyed being elusive and it did not get in his way of making money, it just kept him from being detained or killed. And having money allowed him to enjoy all the things of life unachievable by most others. He had built quite a business in arms trading and did not need the Bratva. But he was unable to turn down Sergei Miloradov's invitation to meet and talk. No one in his right mind would.

Pavel enjoyed his freedom to move from place to place and the inability for anyone to find deliberately him unless he wanted to be found. It terrified him that Miloradov had found him as easily as he had. He seemed to have a line on everyone.

So, when the mafia leader invited Pavel into his inner circle, he knew it was an invitation with only one answer. Miloradov was, in essence, taking over Pavel's' business but keeping Pavel in charge of the work but it had to be from Moscow where Miloradov could keep an eye on him.

Now that the meeting was mover, Pavel was unsure if he could see any benefit in moving to Moscow, but couldn't figure a way to say no. He didn't dare say no.

Miloradov was having trouble with the management of one of his most prosperous lines of business, one belonging to Fedor Davydov. His was to generate revenue through kidnap, ransom and extortion. There was no real downside to that business because if a ransom was not paid, the kidnapped women and children became assets for sale in the human trafficking business.

The only challenge Davydov faced was keeping his voysko in line. That was the responsibility of the brigadiers. And Davydov had dropped the ball twice. Miloradov was offering Oveshkin a succession slot and membership in the Bratva. He would be trained to replace his own boss.

In essence, Oveshkin was given a blessing to operate his arms business in Miloradov's territory and be protected by him while operating in other territories. He was also given a leadership position over a larger organization than he could ever have hoped to achieve. In exchange, he would give up a sixty percent share of his gun business. Of course, it didn't hurt when Miloradov sweetened the pot and Oveshkin agreed. To seal the deal, Miloradov also threw in a house in Moscow Central District. Greed soon overcame Oveshkin's misgivings and he agreed to the terms.

More importantly, Oveshkin's supply of arms and ammunition was running low. If Miloradov had known, he might not have added in the house, or even made the offer and Oveshkin was not about to tell his new Pakhan either. The house in a prime residential district in Moscow was already being outfitted with modern appliances, and a bar with a fireplace in his bedroom. Telephones were being installed for him in several rooms. It would be nice for Oveshkin to be able to say he owned such a property but he planned to spend no time there. He needed to be invisible to succeed and his plans did not call for a career with the Bratva that would end only in his death.

He wondered if Miloradov would be dismayed or pleasantly surprised to learn that his new partner was about to enter the world of arming terrorists with weapons they had only dreamed of. Oveshkin thought, *Yes, I am ambitious, but that is not a bad thing.* He rationalized that it was best to keep his own secret, since the transaction was in the works before Sergei Miloradov reached out to him. This sale was something he would not speak about, especially with Miloradov. And though he knew his life would be forfeit if he pulled off a deal behind his boss's back, he would nevertheless move ahead without his blessing or knowledge.

Pavel would have to manage *this boss of bosses* very carefully.

In the meanwhile, he had been ordered to meet with a brigadier named Fedor Davydov. From this one he would learn. He would squeeze him dry of information, but he would share nothing of his business.

CHAPTER ELEVEN

MY CALL TO BRINTON WENT as well as I could have expected. He was pleased to learn that Weiner had not violated the Foreign Corrupt Practices Act, and more importantly Transeget Industries, and therefore Brinton, were off the Bureau's radar on that account. He was a bit dismayed, though, that Weiner had expended so much unauthorized money to avoid reporting the extortion to the Security Department. It was company policy to do so.

Brinton wanted to be on record for taking the high road, deciding the incident had to be officially reported to the Bureau. He gave that responsibility to me and not the law department, saying he thought I could handle the communications with Maniaci without getting TI into a legal battle.

He also agreed with my recommendation to report my findings, as they stood, to Koval in Moscow. He was all about staying on the good side of the Feds and knew that it was my goal as well. The Bureau would also want to know what

285

Transeget Industries was going to do with Weiner. Brinton and I struggled back and forth over that.

The question revolved around returning Weiner to the States or leaving him in country, as if nothing had happened. If they repatriated him, what would TI do with him? I knew the decision about re-assignment was none of my business. But the questions were more complex than that. The unauthorized expenditures were a violation of the company's ethics policy. Weiner could be terminated, demoted, or re-assigned. There were so many individual options and so many combinations. But the illegal payments also constituted theft. Should he be prosecuted, should he be sued in civil court to recover the money? And then Brinton asked, "What do you think we should do with him, Michael?"

I had been asked that numerous times before. The answer was *it depends.* It depended on the severity of the violation. Was the act also a crime, and if so, was it a misdemeanor or felony? What was the financial loss or the damage to operations, or to the morale of the workforce? Would there be a customer relations or public image issue? And finally, what were the mitigating circumstances? But *it depends* was not an answer this CEO would tolerate. He wanted a direct response.

When I first entered the world of corporate security, I had just come from a career in law-enforcement. For me the answers back then were pretty simple. If you did the crime, you did the time, period. It had bothered me at first that there were vagaries in sentencing from judge to judge. I felt the more liberal judges were always finding exceptions to handing out maximum penalties. I felt conservative judges had it right. Then there came the Federal Sentencing Guidelines in an effort to ensure there was no racial or political bias in sentencing, particularly as to drug laws in a society that was becoming more permissive.

At first, I looked on the Guidelines with contempt as well. As far as I was concerned, it was the first step in lowering the social standards of personal responsibility. Eventually though, I came to understand the value of differentiating between a first-time offender and a habitual criminal. There was a place for determining if drug possession was for personal use or distribution. I got it. But it went against my grain. Weiner's was a perfect example of the moral dilemma of taking the act merely on its face.

I responded, "You know my position on these matters is pretty straight forward. But in this case, I am struggling. Weiner was briefed before coming over here how dangerous the place was. He was told of our policy that we don't negotiate with kidnappers and neither would the Feds. Knowing that, his boss and he had developed a slush fund for the financial cost of criminal activities. But when our speculation about Russian risk became a reality for him, it became a whole new ballgame of how to act.

"I believe that if the threat had been directed against him alone, we would have heard from him on the first contact. But when Rachel and Sarah were brought into the mix, all bets were off. Weiner went to plan B, and that was to pay these guys off with our money.

"We put this man and his family in harm's way and a worst case scenario happened to them. I think we need to take that into consideration."

Brinton followed, "So are you saying we should reassign him, no harm, no foul?"

"No," I replied. "I am thinking out loud with you. I think the risk is over. I believe we have built a very safe environment for him and the business if he wants to stay. Maybe he would like to stay and send his girls home. Maybe he wants them all to come home. What I am saying is these are real options in my mind. But I do have an opinion and frankly, I want him out of here. I'm sure you can figure out a soft landing for him back in the states or in some other less hostile country."

I didn't like this aspect of the job, but it came with my pay grade. I was recommending that Weiner and his family be uprooted again and moved out of Russia. "I'll handle it with him. I'll explain we are disappointed in his choices, but we understand why he made them. I'll let him know that there will be no next time if he fails to notify us in a similar circumstance. Then I'll tell him the choice is not his to stay or go. That he is returning to the states with his family as soon as I can get him out."

I knew the challenge would be to Brinton's team to find a comparable position for Weiner to land in. This was still big business and there are no completely happy endings when you end up costing the company millions of dollars, regardless of the circumstances.

Brinton liked the clarity of the response and the short rationale for it. "That's better," Brinton said curtly. "Do it."

"OK, Barry," was all I could say.

I asked him for permission to prepare evacuation plans if I needed them. A plan for me, for the Weiners, or for us both. He brushed that off and told me to coordinate that with our aviation unit. No problem having to arrange getting out of Russia, I'd call Walny myself and ask him to figure out the technicalities of flights and fuel. Brinton's mind was simultaneously dealing with me and the issues in front of us while it was reviewing TI's investments and operations across the globe. He would soon usher me out when he thought other problems outweighed this one, whether I thought we were through or not.

"Let's move on to the other issues." Brinton added. "We have to figure out how to deal with the Feds response on the issue of Weiner and what they saw as payments to P2K2."

I thought that was pretty straightforward and not too complicated. "We tell it exactly as it is. Weiner, and by association we, were victims of a mafia extortion plot involving our business and the kidnapping of his family. We're not in the United States and the Bureau has no official role over here as an investigative or protective agency. I'm not a lawyer, but I think I'm right about this. When you decide not to report a crime to the police because your life is in danger, or because that threat is immediate, such extreme duress might mitigate his failing to report a felony. On that basis, I believe we and Weiner are off the hook on that." I knew Brinton would be making a note to check that out with our General Counsel on both continents.

"And another thing, I think the Feds knew all along what was going on and were waiting for us to report the incident as a crime before taking any action. Given all that, I recommend we tell them what happened and let the chips fall where they may. And frankly, I don't think there will be any negative fallout. As to the other payment, let's keep in mind that it was the Feds who pointed me to that insurance agent to begin with. I don't expect any problem from them at all."

Brinton stopped me there. "About the insurance premium," he said, "that does not need to make it into your report. I am still not sure we are comfortable with doing business that way. I understand it and the Feds seem to informally accept it. But I don't like it." I waited to see if there was going to be any further discussion of it. There wasn't. Nor did he want to discuss the Information Technology issue. He was waiting for the Executive Vice President of IT and the European Council to report back to him on that. I would get any future marching orders, or reprimand, at that time.

"And that," he said, "brings us to the next matter. About the missing special inventory, where are we with that?"

I noted that Brinton was talking in the first-person plural. I wondered if he actually had some of his own skin in the game for some reason I wasn't aware of. I got the distinct impression he was still expecting results, regardless of telling me it was my call.

I could only say so much on an international phone call out of Moscow. I hoped Brinton could put together what I was going to say, even if I could speak only cryptically.

"I think I may have found a Sherpa to guide me with some search options. We may also have a line on someone who might have firsthand knowledge, but that is only speculation at this point. I'm putting myself in the hands of another person's expertise and his connections. I'm not sure anything positive will come of it, though. The number of downside outcomes is too great for me to give this much hope, but I'll run it to ground within reason.

"There is one more thing, Barry. If I understand the program correctly, we are not processing any materials from the missing ground equipment, only the airborne ones. Is that correct?"

Brinton's answer was very short. "Why?"

"Well, we are more or less helping our friends and there isn't too much business risk if we can't help them. We are basically trying to be good corporate citizens. Is that about it?"

" So, what's your point?" There was another question answered without an answer. There seemed to be a lot of that going on lately. I wanted to have it on record with Brinton, even if only verbally, so I pressed on. "I just want to know how hard I should be pushing this and what is at stake if I come up with nothing."

Brinton answered, "It's like I said before, I don't want you to take unnecessary chances, I don't want the company name dragged into an in international scandal and I don't want you to get hurt. But if you have a chance to help, pursue it. That's all I am asking. Remember, be careful and keep me posted." Then he disconnected the call. I was sure he was charging down the hall to interject his will on some other matter.

I was no further than when I started the conversation with him. I was on my own with any decision I made.

I began dialing my next international phone call.

■ ■ ■ ■ ■

The Moscow office of the FBI was situated in a non-descript two-story building just outside of Moscow Central District. As Sasha drove up to it, I noticed a building directly across the street that bristled with antennae. It could only be one of two things, another U.S. Federal building on Russian soil or a Russian electronic surveillance intelligence facility. Either way, I was also on that radar screen now. Literally.

Koval greeted me in the lobby and we proceeded through a series of electronically controlled doors, deep into a building that smelled like fresh brewed coffee throughout. He walked me into a locked, windowless, conference room and soon a hot cup of the black brew was placed on the conference table in front of me. The FBI logo was centered on the mug, as if it was necessary to remind me where I was. On the desk was a STU III phone. Koval dropped his blank, lined notepad and ballpoint pen on the table and began dialing what would soon be the encrypted connection.

As he began the dialing sequence, he said, "It's very early back in the States, as you well know. But Jerry has asked us to call first thing this morning for your briefing. He's most anxious to learn what you and Brinton have in mind. And in case you are wondering, this is also a sound secure room – our version of a SCIF. It's electronically enclosed, so we can talk in the clear here."

Given what had occurred at the Embassy, I wasn't so sure. I decided I would be as circumspect as the Feds would let me be, especially on the matter of Oveshkin and the bombs.

I wrapped my hands around the heavy, white, hot porcelain coffee mug and sipped slowly. I would work without notes and I wasn't ready to share Weiner's statement with them either. That way, Koval would be less likely to ask for a copy. I didn't like leaving my civilian notes in the hands of the Feds, or any law enforcement agency for that matter. That kind of thing came back to bite you regularly. I preferred to give them summary notes that had been first cleared by my law department. Today they were getting nothing.

Koval pushed the button for the speakerphone and Maniaci picked it up on the first ring.

The sound of Jerry's voice was converted into data bits then scrambled in a secure encryption algorithm. They traveled the four thousand, six hundred and sixty some miles from Newark to Moscow in mere seconds, where they were decrypted and rearranged into the correct order of bits and bytes. Although the sound was a digital reproduction, it bore the clear characteristics of his timber and tone. "Maniaci." He answered.

"Jerry, Tom Koval here, and I'm with Michael Christian. How are you this morning?"

The cordiality of the conversation ended abruptly. "I'm well. Guys, can you fill me in? I'm heading to Newark airport soon and I have a copter waiting on the roof so I haven't much time."

Koval nodded to me. In only ten minutes I summarized Weiner's predicament, our involvement with Takhoyev as an insurance broker, and the nearly immediate results of the disappearing mafia at the plant. No more trouble with those guys, it seemed. Maniaci pressed on. "What is it that Transeget Industries wants or intends to do now?"

I had it scripted and followed my lines as I had memorized them. "We will not be filing a criminal complaint with the Russian authorities against the mafia actors unless you need us to. Frankly, I don't want to drag out our relationship with them any further and I wouldn't expect any positive outcomes, even if we did.

"Weiner won't be disciplined, nor will we file a complaint to have him prosecuted or sued civilly to recover the payments. They were made to save his wife and daughter's lives and were made under extreme duress. Later this morning I will tell him he and his family are leaving Russia. We plan to let some single guy take the post until we get better established."

"That was easy," Maniaci said. "And what about the other matter," He asked.

This is where it got dicey. I began slowly, "The only lead I have is through a guy introduced to me by your people. I am willing to take this next step if you can tell me that I can trust him. I do not want to get my ass shot up or kidnapped just because he was a good insurance agent, but turned out to be more of *a different kind of agent*. And frankly, I would have thought you guys would be working directly through him and wouldn't need me anyway."

I heard only silence on the other end. Looking up, I saw a look of surprise on Koval's face as he asked, "What do you mean, *Takhoyev is a lead*?"

Maniaci asked on the other end of the phone, "Has he approached you about something?"

I realized that the conversation and information sharing Takhoyev and I had was apparently only between the two of us. It seemed to me that I had opened a can of worms here. I started mentally backpedaling as I framed my answer.

"Takhoyev said he thought I might be looking for something missing. I had guessed, and maybe incorrectly, that you or the agency had already tapped into him as part of your informal inquiries. I also guessed that he put two and two together and knew I was with a Plowshares company and would also be inquiring, if not for you, then for my company's own interests. Anyway, he said that he felt there were untrustworthy, competing interests in his government and preferred to work a backchannel in case he could find anything out. I don't really know what's in it for him and maybe that's the first question. To put your minds at ease though, we haven't done anything together and he hasn't reached out to me since we last met. I am thinking he is just getting his unofficial resources lined up in case he wants to use an informal approach to communicate with you."

I decided it wasn't an appropriate time to mention that I had seen KGB intelligence files on Oveshkin and other actors or that Takhoyev had them in his possession.

Maniaci answered, "You know we can't tell you what to do, Mike. So, let me answer your questions as best as I can. You'll have to decide for yourself.

"I think Takhoyev is a pretty trustworthy guy on the surface. Never forget that he was KGB, never. He may indeed have very powerful connections and access to great intelligence. But the moment he shares his interest in our research with his superiors, especially our items of interest, he will be at the mercy of political decision makers whom we don't know and can't vouch for. That should have a strong bearing on whether you can trust him or not. If you move forward with him, you do so at your own risk. Additionally, if you come up on anyone's radar screen, ours or theirs, you will likely get a tag on your file that will be tough to explain.

"We would understand of course, but it doesn't mean we could come forward and vouch for you. Not on a matter as sensitive as this. Since you are not acting as an agent of ours you would be on your own. And even if you were acting as an agent of ours, you'd be on your own as well. You know how that goes. Besides, we don't have any jurisdiction over there. Maybe you are working for the Agency, but not us. Here's the bottom line, Mike. We surely want your help but be careful. If you get your ass in a jam, well, I don't have to tell you how the Communists treat spies."

The cold war had demonstrated plenty of examples of each side dealing harshly with spies they captured. Many remained imprisoned for years while waiting on some diplomatic resolution before they were released. "No," I said. "I am not working for anyone. I am not even inquiring to see if anyone knows anything. I was only going along with Takhoyev's approach and maybe that was too much in itself. Hell, maybe I should just head back home." Here was the FBI, already categorizing me as a spy.

Koval took it from there. "We are not saying you should go home, Michael. We are also not encouraging you to stay. Nor are we vouching for Takhoyev on this matter. We are merely laying out some facts for you. It's your call."

"Well, Jerry. You asked about the other matter, so there it is. There may be a lead, but it is not my lead. If I can determine anything positive, I am turning it over to you guys. I can see where I'm in way over my head." I wished I hadn't brought it up at all. Now I had fewer answers than when I started. Again, I felt that even my friends, who had an agenda outside of my control, were playing me.

Koval told Maniaci he would call back after he saw me out.

"Tom, do you mind if I make a couple calls back to the States before I head out?"

Koval agreed and showed me to an empty room, outfitted with a phone. He politely waited outside while I dialed. Within twenty minutes I had that wrapped up and we headed through the maze of hallways and up to the exit.

On the sidewalk, I turned back to look at the building again. It bore no official markings, and could have been any small, old brick business office. I began to wish I was simply an accountant working at a desk in a small town in Kansas, rather than dealing with dark and dank undertakings, in a dirty city in Russia.

Sasha and I had seemed strangely at odds ever since he learned that I had the capacity to hire the KGB. We drove in silence as I opened the cream-colored, linen envelope that had been left for me at the front desk of the Metropol that morning. I had earlier tossed it in my briefcase when I was preparing for the meeting with Koval.

Inside was a linen stationary notecard, officially printed in Cyrillic on the front, in English on the back, and in Brushscript font. It was an invitation to dinner that evening as the guest of Vladimir Takhoyev at the State Kremlin Palace, inside the walls of the Kremlin. I could hardly believe it. The stated event was a gala Celebration of the United States and Russian Chamber of Commerce. I had never heard of such a thing. It didn't matter. There was no way I was going to turn down this once in a lifetime opportunity. I asked Sasha if he was available to drive there that evening. Again, Sasha had a look of wonderment on his face.

"You have been invited to dine at the State Kremlin Palace?" He paused and then smiled. "Of course, I will drive you. You big shot. Me big shot. What time boss?"

We worked out the details to have Sasha pick me up that evening in front of the hotel. Then I pondered silently for the rest of the ride to Weiner's warehouse.

■ ■ ■ ■ ■

Weiner was relieved when I explained he was not likely to go to jail or be fired. He asked for time to talk it over with his wife about staying. She was a brave woman, he said, and she and Sarah had traveled with Weiner around the world on other business start-ups. He wanted to explain the risk to her again based on what could have happened. In that context he felt relatively sure she would see the risk as greater toward Sarah and they would leave.

I told him there was nothing to talk about. "The decision is out of your hands Alex. You are not being terminated, but you are going back to the States. I have reported the details of your predicament to Brinton and he concurs. I think things are stable here for now, but I am not allowing you to take any more chances with your family and that's it. I will see to your transportation needs, and the company will take care of returning your personal property and your home furnishings.

"I'll let you know when you are heading out but tell Rachel to pack your passports and only enough clothing for her and Sarah for a couple days. Alex, she should do that today. We may have to leave on very short notice, so I want you all to be ready. You and she are to stand by at your home for my call. Under no circumstance are you to come back to the office unless I instruct you. Once you get to the States, you can buy what you need for the short term."

I could see he wanted to have a discussion about this, wanted to be in control of his family's destiny, but the look on my face told him there was no time for that. I instructed him to make no travel plans of any kind without checking with me first.

We then spent the better part of the day working out the last of his handwritten, in-depth statements. I wanted as much information as I could get to turn over to Tom Koval to add detail to their intelligence files on the mafia actors, and to give the Bureau the sense we were cooperating completely.

One good thing had come of my visit to Russia. There were no more antagonizing or ugly thugs parking down the street, terrorizing our employees. And although some other "bad guys" had replaced them, they appeared to be on a tight leash and on Weiner's side. Weiner also knew I had provided not only the muscle to protect him at work, but also the roof over his personal house.

We kept up a good pace stopping only for a short lunch break.

I went back to the hotel and got in a short nap before dinner. I wasn't getting much sleep on this trip and I needed the rest. Fitful and sleepless nights seemed to be happening more and more often as I traveled now. It could be the time-changes. It could be anxiety. It could be simply that I wasn't a kid anymore and needed more sleep. I welcomed the hard nap and the hot shower.

■ ■ ■ ■ ■

The Concierge at the Metropol presented me three tuxedoes for my selection, based on sizes I gave him earlier that day. The first I tried fit perfectly, and the size twelve patent leather shoes looked brand new. The shiny jet-black silk bow tie, matching cummerbund and cufflinks rounded out the package. I now felt properly dressed for dinner at the State Kremlin Palace. I decided I'd had enough of my bags being searched and threw a few necessities, some extra clothes and a jacket into my duffle and took it with me downstairs.

I tossed my duffle bag into Sasha's trunk and climbed into the car. I noticed that Sasha was looking very pleased with himself in a freshly pressed suit. "You clean up pretty good there, Sasha," I told him. He understood the humor and chuckled.

It was a very short ride from the Metropol to Red Square, but it gave me a few minutes to reflect. I had grown up during the height of the cold war. As a kid I had practiced *duck and cover drills* hiding under my desk. I had anxiously listened to the tests of the air raid sirens every Saturday afternoon at one o'clock sharp, in the event the Russians launched nuclear death upon the United States. I often thought one o'clock would be the perfect time to attack, because no one paid attention, but everyone worried. I prayed in church daily as a young boy when Kennedy and Khrushchev took the world to the edge of World War Three, averting it only in the last minutes of the Cuban Missile Crisis.

Of course, I had watched all the James Bond movies and knew the Russian code of *smert' shpionam* 'death to spies.' And now here I was, preparing to dine in the Kremlin Palace, with a KGB agent, while on the hunt for nuclear weapons. I didn't feel much like James Bond. I felt insignificant and out of my league, yet very excited as I prepared to enter inside the walls of the Kremlin. I made up my mind to do whatever I could, short of dying.

Sasha jumped from the car at the portico entrance to the Palace courtyard and opened my door with a flourish. He whispered quietly, "You very big shot," and winked at me as I was escorted inside the walls.

The State Kremlin Palace included a very large dining room capable of feeding a large convention audience, if necessary. At one time it was used to seat the bicameral houses of the Russian government. Inside, I could see other businessmen milling about, Russians and Americans alike, and most in tuxedos. My invitation had a table assignment and I found Takhoyev already seated and entertaining a small group of tuxedoed gentlemen all speaking flawless English.

Takhoyev rose and introduced me, in dialect-free English, to two men. It turns out they were also Russian "insurance agents" who were meeting their U.S. counterparts at the same table. Introductions and business cards were passed around. I noticed that as the men read my card, their eyebrows arched, and they looked inquisitively at Takhoyev. He explained that I was head of security for a very large company and had come here to help a business startup. And yes, I had indeed purchased a policy through him. The suspicion turned to polite smiles and a bottle of vodka was quickly opened on the table. The diners were filling in rapidly now.

As soon as everyone was seated, a Master of Ceremonies greeted the audience with stiff prepared remarks, and then introduced a couple of acts performed by the Moscow Symphony and a Russian Ballet troupe from the Bolshoi. Basically, the acts were praising and depicting vignettes of the long-standing friendship between the United States and the Russian business communities. Whenever such a phrase was sung or shouted, the Russian audience sneered and roared in laughter. It was obvious to all present that propagandists had written the words. It probably could have also signified that we were in league with untrustworthy business partners.

The MC called the dinner portion of the evening to order with a toast. *To Boris Yeltsin, our dear president, who could not be here with us tonight but I am sure that wherever he is, he is lifting a glass to us as well.* That was followed by another roar of laughter from the Russian audience. I leaned over to Takhoyev and asked what that was all about. He told me that Yeltsin was believed to be a raging alcoholic, and wherever he was at this moment, it was a virtual certainty that he was having a drink.

The drinks at our table flowed easily, with each person at the table offering a toast. The Americans toasted to mutual growth and partnership. The Russians toasted to a future of prosperity for their Motherland. It seemed as if each Russian at our table shared an inside joke about prosperity being reserved for them individually, and they could care less about their country. I began to get the distinct impression that the other insurance agents had a darker agenda and were derisive not only of their country as a whole but particularly of their American partners.

After dinner and before dessert arrived Takhoyev grabbed my elbow and said quietly, "Let us step outside for a smoke." I whispered, "I don't smoke." To which Takhoyev quietly replied, "Neither do I. Come."

Takhoyev looked around the pillared balcony and confirmed we were alone. Regardless, he spoke in a whisper, "The boys inside, they are all businessmen, no? Like me, we all come from similar backgrounds. In nineteen ninety-one Gorbachev decimated the KGB, or so he thought. He wanted to make certain they never again posed a problem to his executive branch. This was especially important to him because many of our leaders in the KGB had indeed conspired to overthrow him. When locking him in his office, inside these very walls, failed to generate the necessary national support, the officers succumbed to pressure and surrendered their cause. Some of those men are in this room, some at our table. Some are in jail and others ... well, some of the others are no more.

"The purge that followed was more civilized than it would have been in other decades, and Gorbachev appointed new executives, including Yeltsin, who sprung up to take Gorbachev's place."

"*Why do I tell you these things*, you must be asking yourself. Well my friend, like me, these gentlemen inside have been trained by our government in ways that make us capable businessmen. Everyone at our table has a background similar to mine. But not everyone here is my friend."

I knew Takhoyev was referring to them all being former KGB, as well as highly educated and field trained.

"Each of us is multi-lingual and speaks nearly accent-free English, the international language of business. We have all become experts on the economies and geo-political risk of the countries we monitored, and we have invested in as well as disrupted banking and business systems around the world. Those traits alone make us perfectly suited to be businessmen and to profit from our training, don't you agree?"

Takhoyev continued, answering his own question. He had a point to make but was taking his time. "Yes, it is so. And while we all have connections on the inside of the Directorates, we also all watch from the outside. Every time we ask a friend for a file, ask about a person of interest, ask about an opportunity, or ask who protects whom on the outside, our names are added to someone's list of people to be watched. Then, when we are made aware we are being watched, we have to pay someone else or use a favor to get our names off their list. Complicated, no?"

I began wondering where Takhoyev was going with this. But didn't have to wait long to find out.

"Today I have learned that both of us have been added to a list, you and me, Michael. My inquiry about Oveshkin put me on it. Your presence here as a Plowshares Security Director and then being seen with me has put you on it."

I felt my stomach tighten. This was what I didn't want to happen, and I had done nothing on my own, other than to listen to Takhoyev's proposal. That and maybe having seen a few classified KGB documents. *Damn*!

"What the hell Vladimir. This is exactly what I was trying to avoid. The last thing I want is to disappear because someone thinks I may be a threat to Mother Russia, or to his get rich quick scheme. And if anyone knows how to make people go away, it's you guys."

Takhoyev seemed amused. "Well, Michael I hardly doubt that we alone have, how do you say it, *the corner on that market*. Regardless, do not worry. I am already working on getting my name removed from the list, and with it, yours too. While this is not a regular occurrence, it happens enough that I think I can manage it."

I wasn't facing men with guns as I had in Germany. But this news was every bit as disconcerting, and I wasn't getting the warm fuzzies from Takhoyev's assurances. It met the standard warning criteria of *don't get hurt.* "That's it, Vladimir. I have nothing to show for my involvement, so I have no skin in the game. In fact, I haven't yet even made any effort and I am already on someone's shit list. Count me out. I'm through. I'll make arrangements to leave Russia tomorrow." At this point, I didn't see bailing out as being cowardly. It was more a matter of prudence.

"I think that would be unwise, Michael. First of all, it is late, and you are very unlikely to be able to make accommodations to travel on such short notice. Secondly, if someone wants you to stay in Russia where they can keep an eye on you, you will not be allowed to leave, even if you have a first-class ticket. But more importantly, we have a lead!"

As much as I wanted to take down Oveshkin, I knew it was a long shot. And long shots require an investment of time and a lot of luck. I felt I had run out of both.

"The fact that Oveshkin is a gunrunner just isn't enough." I said. "I'll pass along his name to Maniaci and Koval, or you can work with them as you please. Look Vladimir, I understand your passion to want to recover the packages safely. I feel the same way. But I don't need to be a part of the recovery. All you have is a name that interests us both and that is what got me involved. But there is not enough evidence that he even knows about these suitcases, much less has them. This may seem like a lead to you, but to me it is just raw intelligence. I am still going to try to get out of here tomorrow."

"No, Michael. I mean, we have a direct lead on him and a meeting he is having this late evening. Oveshkin has tried to slip his new handler already and he has been in town less than twenty-four hours. He has opted out of a dinner meeting with his new boss, the man in charge of your Mr. Weiner's extortion. It is only because I have someone inside that I know this. I would think it imperative we observe who it is that comes and goes to this meeting."

I still wasn't convinced but had to admit I was interested. "I guess I'm curious, but that doesn't mean I want to spy on the meeting Vladimir. I do not want to become anyone's spy or end up on a hit list because of it. You go right ahead. The link between Oveshkin, the suitcases and the meeting is just too tenuous for me."

"I have more information than I have let on Michael." Takhoyev teased. "In order to receive permission to attend, Oveshkin had to agree to two stipulations. He had to include his handler in the meeting, and he had to name the attendees. Oveshkin had no choice. The meeting was already scheduled and the attendees, who have come a very long way under dangerous conditions, will be leaving tomorrow. No exceptions and no chance to reschedule. So, tonight he is meeting with people from the camp of Abubakar Khasanov. Do you know who that is?"

"No, I'm afraid I don't. Care to enlighten me? And while you're at it, please let me know how this ties to our mission. I have conducted surveillances of meetings that turned out to be merely peripheral to our larger goal. They were a waste of time and resources."

Takhoyev began explaining, " Khasanov is a guerilla fighter from Georgia's Pankisi Gorge region. They have been at the heart of the secessionist movement of Georgia and of the Chechen people. He is a Muslim and a mastermind of the supply lines for the Chechen revolution. He is after weapons to arm his people and the radical Islamic fighters who have entered Chechnya, Dagestan, Georgia and North Tartarstan. They train, amass weapons and radicalize entire communities there. Tens of thousands of people have died at the hands of warriors armed from this region.

"We do not know if Khasanov himself will be there, or if this is merely an exploratory meeting of Oveshkin and Khasanov's minions. Regardless, Oveshkin is an arms dealer and I now have a direct link between him and rebel terrorists. In the past year, financed by the limitless funds of various Saudis, they have been responsible for over forty terrorist attacks in Russia. I want to validate this connection for myself. If I can do this, I will have a better future than I already have."

It seemed to me that Takhoyev already had a pretty good future. He lived well and seemed to have plenty of money. I wondered why he bothered to get engaged in these complex challenges when he apparently didn't have to, especially given that he could end up dead if he slipped up. Me too.

"But there is a bigger issue here Michael. It is big for Russia and could be big for you too. If Oveshkin has briefcase bombs and he passes them on to Khasanov it would change the dynamics of the terrorist battlefield. These weapons could be transported too easily into major population centers anywhere the terrorists desired. Imagine what last year's World Trade Center bomb could have done if it contained a nuclear yield. It wouldn't even have taken a truck. It could easily have been left in a trash dumpster behind the building or alongside a park bench in your mid-town Manhattan.

"Michael, I do not believe we have a choice. We must watch this meeting, just as we discussed before. If Oveshkin has the bombs we have to find out where they are and get them back, then I will help you get them back to the United States. If not, you have lost nothing but dessert with our friends at the dining table."

I was all for just going to Koval with the information and letting it run from there. But I didn't know where the meeting was or who all would be attending, only Takhoyev knew. I was beginning to develop an idea.

"Alright Vladimir. You have me boxed in. I'm ready, let's go." I started towards the exit.

"No, it is not yet time, Michael. I will pick you up in a half hour at your hotel. Get into some casual clothes. Something dark would be better. I will make your excuses when I go back in. And I will bring you some *pryaniki*, in case you are sorry we missed dessert. They are our very special cookies."

I just shook my head. I didn't feel at all hungry or humorous.

■ ■ ■ ■ ■

They watched in their small group as Takhoyev and the American went out onto the balcony. Slipping into his native language, one said, "You were right. He has gone off on his own with the American in a search for our bombs. I believe we must accelerate our plan to kill them."

The other two thought for a while before one said, "I agree. The American must be a spy for the CIA because Takhoyev would not select just any random businessman as a partner for this. And he works for a Plowshares company. His presence here cannot be a coincidence. We could do it in a matter of minutes and be back on time for coffee and cocktails."

The third, a colonel who seemed to hold the highest rank among them said, "I am not so sure. I agree that we need to kill them. But I do not agree as to the timing. Right now, we do not know what they know or don't. I think if they already had the weapons, they would not be here this evening, especially acting so casually. No, they may be looking for them but they have nothing. I think we should follow them closely and see what the American is up to. I want you to find out where they go and who they meet.

"I am also guessing the American has nothing to offer so I do not yet understand what Takhoyev is using him for. He must have a plan of his own for this American, otherwise his involvement makes no sense. I am wondering what Takhoyev has in store for him. No, do not kill them yet. Follow them."

"The American is inconsequential for the time being. We will kill him in due time and I will see that he cannot leave the country until we are ready to deal with him. In the meanwhile, see where Takhoyev goes and who he meets. If he knows where the bombs are, he may also know who stole them from us. He might just lead us to recover what is ours. If you have no other options, bring him to me and we will find out the hard way what he knows. If you find what we are looking for, kill them and bring us back our bombs. *Eto libo pogonya za dikim gusem, libo lovushka* 'this is either a wild goose chase or a trap.' I do not believe in luck nor do I believe we can spit into the hand of fate. Go now and do not lose them."

■ ■ ■ ■ ■

As I walked back into Red Square, I saw Sasha waiting in a long line, a dozen cars back. He tossed a cigarette to the ground and immediately brought the car around.

"So, boss, tell me. How was it?"

Too many things were rumbling around in my head and I didn't really have the time or interest for small talk. But I knew I couldn't offend Sasha. "It was amazing Sasha. They celebrated one hundred years of friendship between our two countries."

Sasha laughed. "It is the same joke on the streets as in the Palace. If you have money or cigarettes or nylons for me, I have been your friend forever. It does not matter if our missiles are pointed at each other at all times of the day and night."

"Exactly, Sasha. And that is why I am glad you are my friend." At that Sasha laughed heartily.

It was literally only a few blocks from the Kremlin to the Metropol, but I am glad I didn't have to walk it wearing a tuxedo. I would have stood out as an easy mark, and I got the distinct impression that Sasha didn't mind getting all gussied up to be paid full price for the short rides either.

As we pulled in front of the Metropol, I told Sasha I'd call him in the morning, and there was no need to wait out front before then. I grabbed my duffle bag from the trunk, made my goodbyes and entered the magnificent structure.

From the corner of my eye, I noticed two men who had been standing outside toss their cigarettes into the gutter and follow me in.

I decided I wasn't going to turn in my passport in exchange for the key to my room. I wanted to hang onto it in case there was a problem. I approached the front desk and asked for a house phone. The clerk pointed to a table in the lobby. Within moments a phone was brought to the table and plugged into the floor jack. I dialed Koval, who answered on the first ring. I decided I didn't give a damn if the call was being monitored.

"Tom, this is Christian. Don't talk, just listen. Things are moving too fast for me and I have no control over events. Our friend, the insurance man, has arranged for me to attend a party later this evening. Someone you and I know, but don't particularly care for, is going to be there. This bad actor is meeting with others that you might like to

312

know about, very high-profile foreigners. I am guessing I am an uninvited and unwanted guest. They would be very angry if they found out I was crashing the party, so my presence there must be a secret. Our guy is picking me up in front of my hotel in about twenty minutes. I think I already have a tail on foot. Two guys. Tom, I need you to watch me through this."

Koval said, "Jesus Christ Mike. What have you gotten into?"

I replied, "I haven't got time to explain. I think our friend is on to something. And even if it isn't directly related to our lost items, it is big enough to warrant you being in the wings. But he can't know you are there. Right now, it's just him and me. Can you do this or not?"

Koval said, "It will be nip and tuck frankly. It will take me that long just to get there if I break every traffic law on the books. I'll need time to assemble a crew and then to develop a strategy ..."

"For God's sake Tom," I interrupted. "I just told you, I am being picked up in twenty minutes. I hope to hell you are behind me when the smoke clears."

With that I hung up and headed to the men's room on the main floor. My leather jacket was in my bag along with a sweater. That was all the change of clothes I was going to get. The risk was too high that my passport would disappear if I left it at the front desk. I dumped the tux jacket and tie in my bag.

My two-man tail was sitting at a table smoking when I came out. They looked a bit surprised when they recognized I had changed.

I walked through the lobby and handed my bag to the clerk, asking the young man to hold it for me.

I figured I would never see my bag or the clothes again. I then rushed back to the grand staircase at the entrance to the lobby and waited at the top of the steps facing the exit below. The two guys following me almost knocked me over as they rushed through the doors. They didn't look like mafia types. And even though they practically crashed into me, I could tell these were professionals.

Without even a word of apology, they walked by me and down the steps to the curb. They didn't seem to be mobile, just planted there. I waited a few minutes before heading down to the luggage-lobby myself.

On schedule, almost to the minute, Takhoyev showed up in a black Mercedes. He pulled to the curb, leaned over, tossed open the front passenger door and motioned for me to get in. "Quickly, you are being followed," he said.

I slipped in and was about to ask how Takhoyev knew, when the car accelerated rapidly from the curb. We made a quick right and ran the stop sign at the next intersection. A car approaching on the through-street from the left cut off and hit the car that was following us. Both drivers got out and began shouting at each other.

"That should hold them for a few minutes," he quipped, casually. Then Takhoyev looked down at my pants, noticing the bottom half of the tux. He raised his eyebrows questioningly.

I explained. "I decided not to give up my passport tonight and changed from my go bag. I want to be able to get the hell out of here if I have to, Vladimir, and I don't want to be held up in the morning by some hotel perfunctory under orders from your FSK." I wondered if the tail we lost was Koval's people. But there was no way he could have gotten anyone there that fast. It looked like it was going to be just Takhoyev and me tonight. I would have to be very careful not to be discovered under any circumstances.

Takhoyev aimed a finger out his driver's window, "Look here Christian, to your left. Do you know where we are?"

I looked up and saw a large, yellow brick building to our left and an open square to our right. The building was maybe eight stories. There was a clock beneath the top parapet, but the hands were only at nine thirty-six. I didn't know if it was running late or just broken like everything else in Russia.

"This is KGB Headquarters. You may have heard it referred to as *Lubyanka*."

I was startled. "You are taking me to your headquarters, Vladimir? Why?" I was considering jumping from the car at my first chance. I had no idea the Metropol was so close to this spy agency headquarters that also served as one of the most feared prisons in the world. We were only five blocks from my hotel. I no longer felt safe there either.

"No, no, my friend. This is just where we ended up after we lost your tail. Relax. We are going elsewhere."

"Where are we going Vladimir? And what else should I know that you aren't telling me?

■ ■ ■ ■ ■

I could tell he had a lot going through his mind and he drove a while without answering me. I wondered what he was thinking. Was it about my ability to support him if necessary? Since he already knew my background, he knew I was fully capable of playing hardball and that I was a straight up guy without political influences. He also knew I was from the United States and working for a government contractor, and that he could not be entirely sure I wasn't some kind of agent. I may have been keeping my eyes and ears open for a couple federal agencies, but I was on no one's payroll.

Maybe he was playing me for some kind of sucker while he carried out his own plan. Or maybe he was just playing it safe. Either way, that left me out on a limb which is not a perch I am used to playing from. "Well?" I prodded.

He started slowly. "Today I was told about Oveshkin's meeting. I have been tracking him since he got to town a few days ago. He was on my radar screen merely as a gunrunner. But I have heard that he has had some dealings with the GRU, our military intelligence service. That is odd because normally there would be no need for that. Our people are perfectly capable of anything they want to do, without outside help. But Oveshkin has a reputation for being an inventory manager, "with discretion". He was hired by some rogue members of the service as a consultant to manage a single commodity from multiple locations. Much like he did in Germany. And we both know what he did there.

Their payments to him are completely off the books. His mission with them is supposed to be a State Secret. But even they have accountability requirements. He seems to have none and no file other than a basic intelligence report."

I could see exactly what Takhoyev was leading up to. Oveshkin was charged with reconciling the inventory of the East German Stasi's main armory system and repatriating all the weapons back to St. Petersburg and Moscow. He stole from the Russian army and ran off with thousands of guns and ammunition.

Takhoyev continued, "I and some of my compatriots feel he is self-dealing from our own armory now, and this time a bigger weapon. I think he may have the ones we are looking for. If he has, then he has balls bigger than a mule. It is one thing to steal from the Army. It is something entirely different to steal from the GRU. If we could prove it, he would be a dead man waiting for the lone bullet he would never hear.

"He does however have a very powerful protector. He has teamed with Miloradov. It seems Oveshkin is being groomed for a position in the Pakhan's group. None other than Miloradov himself has selected him. It makes me wonder whether he is Davydov's replacement or if he will run a separate enterprise. Right now, your friend's connection seems to be that he was supplying arms to Miloradov's organization. It would appear that he now wants to take Oveshkin's operation in-house. It would make organizational sense for

Miloradov to want to consolidate the arms dealing business under him. And it would extend his power within the other regions. I don't believe either Davydov or Miloradov has any idea that Oveshkin is making this side deal.

"And that, Michael, is how I know where the meeting is tonight, and I how know generally who is coming. This, my friend, is the fundamental intelligence that convinced me that we need to be there to observe and learn what we can."

This still seemed like more of a police action to me. "If we know where Oveshkin is having the meeting, why don't you just report this, have him taken out and recover the bombs?"

"One step at a time, Michael. I know where the meeting is. I think I know who he is meeting with. But I do not believe Oveshkin will bring an actual device to the meeting. That would be to his disadvantage. So, the goal is to find out when the actual transfer will occur and take the weapons from him there."

I could see this as possibly being a week or more of additional investigative time. I didn't have that luxury, and I didn't want to be here any longer than it took to get Weiner out of Russia. And it was still highly possible that Oveshkin could slip Takhoyev. "There are just two of us Vladimir. I don't see how we can keep him under surveillance until he leads us to his stash. Let's just grab him and take him out of the equation. That way, even though we don't know where the devices are, he can't get to them either. Probably no one could." It seemed like a clean alternative, given our limitations.

318

Takhoyev continued driving south on Leninsky Road, glancing frequently into the rear-view mirror. I could not make out the expression on his face, but his body language suggested he was worried about being followed. "You are right, of course, Michael. But before we come to any conclusions about next steps, let us get through the first one. Tonight, we watch and listen. Keep in mind that I have an eye on him at all times."

He shifted slightly away from me, reached under his jacket and pulled a Makarov semi-automatic pistol from his waistband. It was the same kind Oveshkin sold. This is what I had feared, a double cross of some kind. And here I was unarmed, and no one knew where I was. I tensed up.

Takhoyev noticed. "Relax, Michael. This is not to be used against you. It is *for* you." With that he turned the butt of the gun towards me and handed it over, pushing the tip of the barrel away from him. "Careful with that," he said. "It is loaded with one in the chamber. I believe the safety is on, but you better make sure."

I glanced down and confirmed the safety was on, dropped the magazine into my lap and cleared the round from the chamber. Then I checked again. It was empty. I jacked all the rounds from the magazine, testing the spring strength as I replaced them. The tension felt nice and firm, so I jammed the magazine back into the receiver and was pleased with the tight, solid snap as it locked into place. Satisfied I racked one back into the chamber and loaded the last round back into the magazine. I saw Takhoyev smile at the sureness with which I handled the weapon. "I should have known," he said. "You have done this before." Then he switched topics.

"We are almost there. There is a section of this road that is incomplete. That is where the meeting will take place. We will stay out of sight, so I expect no trouble. We watch, we listen, and we leave. But if something goes wrong, I want you to take no chances. These are people with a lot at stake. They will not hesitate to kill you, especially Oveshkin if he finds out you are here.

"If something happens to me, take the keys and get back to the hotel and call Koval. Better yet, just go right to the FBI building and wait for him there. You will need to get out of the country immediately. My car keys will be in my right-hand jacket pocket." I knew what he was inferring. Takhoyev wanted me to *take the keys from his body if necessary.*

In my mind, I retraced the route to where we were. It was pretty straightforward. This road would take me practically right back to the hotel. "Let's make sure nothing happens to either of us." I replied.

■ ■ ■ ■ ■

Takhoyev slowed. The highway conditions changed dramatically from paved concrete and blacktop to dirt. There were no warnings, no signs that the road had ended. It was as if all of Moscow knew that Vitaly Yefimov, the Minister of Transport of Russia, had run out of money at this very place in the road.

Roadside easements had ended, as had the few streetlights along the highway. Thick woods surrounded the small clearing and it was eerily dark. Rusted, abandoned front-end loaders and backhoes lay strewn about as if the workers had been told to go home and leave everything right where it was. The glass had been broken from their windows and it was obvious that scavengers had had taken anything of value a long time ago.

Takhoyev executed a tight U-turn, drove back onto the road and then abruptly off the shoulder. He slid the car deep into the woods, turned off the lights, grabbed a canvas bag from the rear seat and exited. "We walk from here," he said. Looking back over my shoulder, I could barely see the car even though I knew where it was. Nicely done.

It seemed Takhoyev had done his homework. Within minutes we were spread out prone on the soft twigs of poplars that had already lost the fluffy white "pookh" of their seeds. Knee high thickets provided the perfect concealment for us. We had a view of the entire open area of the equipment graveyard, even if we could barely see. I was hoping my eyes would soon adjust to the dark.

"We have about twenty minutes before I expect Oveshkin and his escort, Michael. A mid-level Bratva member who works for Fedor Davydov, Vadim Mirski, will be driving him. I am sure you know his name. Mirski is not a low-life. He is quite intelligent and manages millions in revenue for Davydov and Miloradov."

I merely nodded. I did not want him to know just how much I knew or who had provided me the briefing about the mafia organization structure.

Takhoyev continued his explanation, "Oveshkin is meeting tonight, out of sight from Miloradov. I am sure that he will try to shake his driver. Otherwise Davydov and Miloradov will be on to Oveshkin. Therefore, we cannot let him shake us. Understood?"

I understood but wasn't sure how we were going to make certain we kept an eye on my buddy from Germany. I had run plenty of surveillances when I was in the Organized Crime Task Force back in Detroit. But we always had at least six to ten cars. That is how we made sure we never lost our guy. Even in Germany, I had three cars. Now it was just Takhoyev and me in one car.

As I was mulling this over, I heard a car approach from our left. Given this desolate stretch, it had to be someone from the meeting. Takhoyev heard it too, dragged his duffle bag closer and unzipped it. He extracted a small dark object that looked like a small box camera. "*Nochnoy Pritsel* 'night sight,' " he said. It looked familiar and I had used them before, but this was shaped differently and a bit more sophisticated. "It has an active light intensifier. We will be able to see everything without any image distortion."

He reached back into his bag and brought out a small disk-shaped object and quickly assembled it to its mount. I recognized this too. It was a parabolic receiver. "We will also be able to hear all they say," he explained. "Well, I will. I am sure they will not accommodate you by speaking your English language." He drew out a wired headset and plugged it into the receiver and switched it on. "We are good for about two hours before we lose signal strength. Hopefully this will not go on too long."

My curiosity was peaked. I wasn't going to be able to hear a thing from here other than perhaps some murmurs carried on the wind. And unless my eyes adjusted, I wasn't going to be able to see much. "What will I be doing?" I asked. With that, Takhoyev reached in his bag and brought out a second night sight and switched it on. It was heavier and bulkier than I thought it would be. As I looked through it, I realized it had adjustable, telescopic capability and I could clearly see everything I scanned. It occurred to me that the car we heard had not entered the open meeting space. It must have occurred to Takhoyev too because he began scanning the woods on the perimeter of the area. "There," he said. Pointing across the field and into the tree line. "Stay very low."

I lay completely prone on my elbows and settled my scope in my hands, trying to get a bearing on what he was pointing to. He reached behind me and pressed on my shoulders. "Lower!" he whispered. It was uncomfortable, but soon I got the scope to a point where I could see out ahead of me with my chin practically in the dirt. And there they were.

Across the open area from us, two men were sitting cross-legged, watching the meeting area from slightly inside the trees. One had binoculars and was scanning the area also. I had no idea if they had night vision. Given how well we could see with ours, I felt very vulnerable.

CHAPTER TWELVE

PAVEL KNEW HE WAS PLAYING in a different league now, and the importance of it consumed him. It wasn't that he felt he couldn't compete. He had never been afraid of a challenge. Once he set his course to steal Russia's guns, he never looked back. He had become accustomed to lurking in the shadows, meeting in dark bars, back rooms or desert tents. He was no longer anxious of his customers. They had come to know him and to rely on him. He wouldn't say they trusted him. In this business no one trusted anyone. But he was dependable and true to his word and they paid on time, every time.

The only leverage he had with his customers was their constant demand for more weapons and his ability to provide them. He did not know how they could go through so many guns, but it didn't matter to him. As his limited inventory began thinning however, he had become concerned. He worried, that is, until Semenov reached out to him to confirm an invitation he had floated out months ago.

Ansar Semenov had Chechen origins. He was a Wahhabi Muslim but that was neither here nor there to Pavel. He had made a connection with Pavel through another customer. Semenov worked for Abubakar Khasanov, a powerful tribal warlord trained by, financed by and aligned with an emerging radical leader named Osama Bin Laden. And Bin Laden was playing all aspects of partnership with the Saudis, the Chechens and the Central Intelligence Agency.

Bin Laden used Khasanov and Semenov to wage a surrogate guerrilla war against Russia, financed by others. Financed by his own money and with some help from the Saudis, he trained his own armies in encampments throughout Southeastern Chechnya, the northern Middle East and small countries along the Caspian Sea. He founded a Sunni Islamist militancy he called al Quaeda, or *The Base*. Here in the hard-scrabble soil of the southern region of the former Soviet Union, he trained and armed his jihadists in preparation for his war against the western world.

As their armies grew, so did their need for weapons. More recruits were arriving at their camps daily. Disaffected and disgruntled, hungry and passionate, they came to be trained and fed, then to return to their homelands to take the fight there. Most came to join the Islamic fighting in the Middle East, not to join Semenov in his centuries old battle against the Russians.

If the radical Muslim proselytes stayed with the armies, they would be trained, clothed, fed and housed. They would have a cause they could believe in. This was more than they could expect at homelands, and their ranks were swelling.

Semenov had been given U.S. currency to buy the weapons. It did not matter to him in the least that the money came from the Saudis. So, as Semenov's and Khasanov's soldiers ran out of weapons, they came to Pavel for more. But Pavel had the same issue. He was running out of guns and ammunition, grenades and grenade launchers and these guys wanted more.

Oveshkin had hesitated to let anyone know he had access to something very special until he was positive he could safely sell it to them. It might mean he might become even wealthier, or it could mean his death. But Saudi money ran like water to him and he was a very thirsty man who was willing to take the chance.

He had hinted to Khasanov that he might be able to provide a weapon that could tip the revolutionary balance in their favor. It didn't bother him at all that he was Russian and Khasanov and Semenov were working with the goal of cleansing Russians from the world. Pavel saw himself as above all that nationalism. Besides the Chechens were closer to Iran than they were to Russia. The threat to Russia seemed unrealistic and remote. Most importantly, Oveshkin was first and foremost a businessman, and patriotism or loyalty did not factor into that description.

Pavel smiled to himself, *how easy was it that he came by these portable nuclear bombs?* It was his biggest secret and yet was so simple.

Interestingly, since nineteen ninety one, when Gorbachev disassembled the KGB and tried to rebuild it with loyalists, he failed to remove all the disaffected members.

A certain few of these former KGB agents, now attached to the SVR had access to the cache of man-portable nuclear bombs, paid for and made expressly for the KGB. Two hundred and fifty units sat outside the governance of the Third Directorate.

When Pavel returned from Germany as an arms dealer, certain members of the SVR got wind of it through the mafia.

Pavel openly explained to Miloradov how he had managed the inventory at the arsenal in Germany to his own advantage. Somehow word traveled further, to a few disaffected leaders of SVR which was now the foreign intelligence service.

In the process of conducting their own inventory some members of the SVR managed to secretly siphon off ten percent of the stock of nuclear bombs. A couple dozen of these were now outside the control of either the Politburo General Staff or the FSK Third Directorate, who shared the duty to ensure nuclear weapons never got into the wrong hands, except their own. They had a problem of their own now and saw Oveshkin as a solution.

They had secreted the devices away in several places. Only the crew that stashed their units knew where they were. Trust was in short supply and no team wanted to tell the others where any stash was. They agreed on a solution to use an outside, third party inventory manager who would report to a small group, with each team represented by two members. They cut a deal for Pavel to secretly work for them. In essence they were looking for someone, outside the government, who could keep track of an inventory scattered about Moscow. Some of the members wanted the bombs strategically deployed now. Others saw wisdom in waiting for the right conflict before using them. Oveshkin got connected with those who wanted them deployed now.

Pavel had discovered where all the units were when he became the arbiter of the inventory.

This was where the game got risky but he had made up his mind to move forward regardless of the stakes. He knew where their stockpiles were, and he was taking what he believed to be his share. He would have to steal from the KGB officers. This diverse group of officers was undecided where to position the bombs. They constantly bickered over how and where to sell them. They had trouble finding trustworthy buyers, or buyers with enough cash. And with so many of the units so widely disbursed, they never checked on their own hidden inventory.

So, when they asked Oveshkin for a solution, he suggested repositioning the units to be easily accessible yet hidden from discovery. They trusted Pavel to handle that for them until they could make up their minds how and when to use them and to decide if and when they could play nice together.

Pavel, however, was not an indecisive man. He was ready to pounce while the KGB officers paced in endless circles of indecision. He had purloined a supply of these units and stashed some right here in Moscow. It would make a transfer so easy.

All he had to do was get paid and train Semenov on how to use them. And he wasn't sharing his buyers with anyone, especially not the KGB or the mafia. Either would just as soon kill him and take his weapons for themselves. It was also why Pavel wanted no one to know where he was at any time.

Pavel knew that his customers were Muslim fighters. He was told they had personally met with the great and rising Osama Bin Laden to discuss jihadi tactics in the Chechen war against Russia. And tonight, he would be bargaining with them over the cost and delivery of a portable nuclear bomb. He still had to decide, if they had enough money, should he sell them all at once or trickle them into their hands? Perhaps, if they had enough money, he would sell them all at once and get out of the business. He was beginning to enjoy the idea that he would just disappear into an anonymous world of luxury.

For tonight, Oveshkin was well prepared and had all his talking points in order.

He reviewed the evening's agenda. Tonight, he would bring only the photos. They would illustrate a few of the bombs on display on a table with a white sheet as a background to the room. There would be nothing to reveal where they were being kept. He would show them just enough to prove there was a supply. The photos would show Oveshkin, holding one device up for inspection, to establish that he had access and control. Another would show the contents - one small nuclear warhead atop a canister containing a small detonator, its timer and its power supply. A photo would show the operating diagram. Not in detail, but with enough information that a buyer would see that this was real and within their grasp.

Oveshkin knew that this demonstration would be enough to not only whet their whistles, but it should be enough to satisfy his demand for a down payment. He would not be greedy, nor would he take less than an appropriate sum for a deal of this magnitude. Regardless of the amount of the deposit, he always delivered on his promise and the buyers knew that.

For the customer, the economic advantages were strategically as large as the tactical advantages on the battlefield. From that perspective alone, this was a much larger venture than any of his others combined. Just one device could do the work of ten thousand soldiers, maybe more. And the value of the psychological impact was immeasurable.

He wrestled with the numbers. A hundred thousand down and nine hundred upon delivery? Was that too much? Was it enough? He wanted to present the sale with a non-negotiable price. The Wahhabi Saudis were rich, and they believed in their cause. They had been seeking a chemical, biological or nuclear advantage for years. Now Pavel held it just outside their grasp and he planned to dangle it in front of them.

It was true that Pavel did not have much of his own money at risk in these ventures. In fact, he had no cost of inventory other than the low-rent storage building where he hid his weapons. He rented trucks for deliveries and that was about all the cost he had tied up in his business, especially since the arms and bombs were all stolen from the Russian government at one time or another. He had plenty of cash, but it was his rule - *never put up his own money in a deal, and always get the customer to cover the upfront expenses*. He saw this as the first in a short string of Saudi-backed purchases that would make him a multi-millionaire several times over, and all within a few short months.

He was a shrewd businessman who knew that where price was no object, and where decisions were made on desire rather than need, he could charge whatever he wanted. A million American dollars sounded like such a nice number and they would have to take it or leave it. Pavel's ego was as big as it could get, and he was riding on the confidence of a man who had never been seriously tripped up. He had overcome everything ever thrown at him. His only setback was in Germany, where his operation was disrupted, and his smuggling network shattered.

He had managed to avoid getting caught up in the arrests of his crew in Germany. One driver had been killed and another captured. His trawler captain had been arrested, and the Bundespolizei had confiscated his ship, leaving him only the weapons he had stashed in St. Petersburg and Moscow. He also had to leave a few pallet-loads of Kalashnikovs and Makarovs on the dock in Warnemunde and many more on a siding in Plau am See. He shook his head in anger and disgust thinking about the luck of that security guy from the States who stumbled onto his operation. It had cost him a small fortune and a very slick distribution route.

But Pavel was not a man to dwell on his mistakes. He focused on the present and how near he was to his end game. Soon Pavel Oveshkin would never have to work again.

For now, though, he had to figure out how to shake Vadim Mirski from tonight's meeting with Semenov. Mirski had insisted on attending, actually Fedor Davydov had insisted, but Oveshkin was prepared to disobey his first direct order from his new mentor. He was not yet ready to let anyone but his customer know that he had access to the highly sought and missing portable nuclear bombs.

This was his entry onto the big stage of arms dealing and he wasn't sharing it with anyone, not Davydov, Sergei Miloradov and certainly not with Mirski.

■ ■ ■ ■ ■

Oveshkin was deep in thought as they drove to the upcoming meeting. Although the stakes were high, there should be no trouble. He knew that he had both Khasanov's and Semenov's total attention. And tonight, showing the Chechen the pictures of the bomb would seal the deal. Oveshkin felt relatively safe in that regard. But there was still one area of exposure and it was sitting right next to him.

Mirski had been talking non-stop since they got in the car. Oveshkin had managed to tune him out while he planned, but his ears perked up when Mirski mentioned how an American security guy had interrupted Davydov's latest venture. *Surely it could not be*?

"What do you mean an American got in the way? How is that possible?" Oveshkin asked.

"Oh, it is possible, Pavel Oveshkin." Mirski replied. "There is a way and it involves building a roof over the business with someone else, someone perhaps stronger. I stay away from the details because everything is done at Miloradov's level. It is wise not to know too much. But this job was to be a continuing money-stream. I had researched myself and it should have been foolproof. Interestingly, Fedor Davydov warned me not to get too cocky, because nothing is forever. It appears he was right. But the American company had very deep pockets and the payments should have been rolling in for a long time. This Transeget Industries is huge, with businesses all over the..."

"Did you say Transeget?" Oveshkin interrupted.

"Yes, that's it," nodded Mirski. "Do you know it?"

It was that damned Michael Christian. It seemed impossible that Christian could have followed him here to Russia. No, it had to have been Mirski's venture that brought Christian. He pressed for more.

"This security guy, do you know if he is still here in Moscow?"

"I do not know, but I can surely find out. Why?"

Oveshkin wanted this so badly he could taste it. "Because I want to kill him. Yes, I want you to find out. And let me know the moment you find out where he is staying."

A flurry of options began crowding Oveshkin's mind. He certainly desired to kill Christian himself. He would love to pull the trigger for so many reasons, and all of them were based on vengeance. He might not have been able to spare his young lover, Tasha, a jail sentence in Germany, but maybe he could avenge her now.

And then there was the matter of the guns. Christian's investigation had resulted in the German authorities seizing crates of Makarovs and Kalashnikovs from Oveshkin's warehouses. And the American broke up the land routes through Germany, Belarus and the Ukraine. His entire network of operatives was either dead or in German prisons and all because of Christian. There was no doubt. Christian must die.

But Oveshkin was a businessman who knew he had to balance passion with reason. Nothing could get in the way of tonight's deal. This was the linchpin. If it worked, Oveshkin could be a multi-millionaire in less than a year.

"Let me ask you Mirski. If I wanted this security person killed, could your people do it?"

Mirski seemed to smirk as he answered. "Of course, we could do it. But the order would have to come from Davydov or from Sergei Miloradov. And I will warn you Pavel Oveshkin, be careful who you kill here. Everything is very complex. Start with Fedor Davydov, he will guide you. It is his responsibility to train you and teach you the Code. If he agrees, then he will decide who will do it, and when and how it will be done."

Oveshkin knew it would be cleaner to have the Bratva handle it. But if the opportunity presented itself, he would take the shot. Bratva be damned.

He considered his words carefully before he spoke again.

"This meeting I am having tonight. You do not need to be there. In fact, you will not be there. I do not want you to see who I am meeting because it is none of your business. You will tell me when we get close. Then I will drop you off and come back to get you when I am through. Is that understood?"

This is what Mirski had feared. He was supposed to not only drive Oveshkin here, he was supposed to not lose sight of him. Davydov was clear on that. Besides, when he escorted someone, he stuck with them. He was about to object when Oveshkin continued.

"My meeting is not for you Vadim Mirski, nor for Fedor Davydov. It is for Sergei Miloradov. You will not attend and that is not up for argument. Once I drop you off, you will not leave that area until I come for you."

And now Mirski understood why Davydov wanted to know where the meeting was going to be held. "I understand," was all that Mirski said. They were just minutes away as it was.

■ ■ ■ ■ ■

Ansar Semenov did not have expensive needs. In fact, he needed very little. His two priorities were revenge against the Russian people or any infidel for that matter, and an afterlife with Allah. The two goals were most compatible.

For centuries his Chechen people had been persecuted by Russians. It was more than mere political oppression. It was a constant march toward ethnic annihilation.

When he was visiting a widowed aunt and his cousins in the country, Russian soldiers came through his home village and killed all the males of any age. Old women were killed, and women of childbearing age were raped. The village was burned and anything of value was sacked or stolen. He returned home completely unaware of the atrocity only to find himself without a family. He walked the nearly twenty miles back to his aunt's home. She placed him with an Islamic school. The rest was an expected history.

His raw passionate dislike for the Russians was augmented with a hate for western culture in general. The skills of his youth changed from helping on the family farm and shepherding, to soldiering. He was fearless and ruthless in battle. His supervisors thought he might have a death wish but that served them well. He was adept at tactical maneuvering with his men and he was stealthy enough for guerrilla fighting.

He was taught the elements of insurgency - patience, target identification, analysis and research, mapping, simulation, preparation, planning and execution of attacks. And he was cleansed of any sense of civility when it came to striking. An enemy who could be so ferocious as to commit genocide and rape against his entire nation, including his family and neighbors, deserved no compassion - man, woman or child.

He was taught to pray, and he taught young children to pray. But mostly he taught them the spiritual benefit of cleansing the world of Russian infidels. He was an active recruiter of Chechen youth. His work was relatively easy. The rebel army had money and they used it to feed, house and educate, especially religious education. He recruited orphans and turned them into religious zealots. They would be the next generation of soldiers and suicide bombers. With his role came the responsibility of arming them for battle, literally.

Initially some of the weapons he obtained were recovered from the dead bodies of enemy soldiers, and others were recovered from his own dead warriors. Others came from theft of small arms stashes of other insurgent groups in outlying villages. Semenov knew that a soldier must be armed, and he made it a point that his men were always well equipped. Khasanov took note of this young man and groomed him as an arms specialist.

Semenov's only untimely incident of note was when he was attempting to disarm a bomb he found in a field. He was relatively successful. But when one of his subordinates was transferring it to the back of their truck, it went off, killing Semenov's soldier. Although Semenov survived the explosion, his face was badly burned and terribly scarred. His beard barely covered the wounds. But that lent him even more credibility amongst the new recruits. He did not see the explosion as an act of carelessness on the part of his dead compatriot, but rather as a further act of aggression by the hated Russians.

Semenov was beyond passionate in his revulsion of them. He was a zealot, and that made him even more valuable to Khasanov. Ultimately Semenov became so knowledgeable in the weapons of war that Khasanov included him in negotiations with arms dealers.

That was his role tonight when meeting with Oveshkin. Neither Khasanov nor Semenov cared for the Russian, but he was a necessity of war. He was their most reliable arms dealer - trustworthy, on time and affordable. Khasanov had clearly explained that Semenov's job was not to kill this Russian tonight, but to learn from him whether or not he had this "special weapon". If so, and if it was what Khasanov thought it was, it would tip the tide in favor of Khasanov and this *Bin Laden* they were working with. More than that, it would create an overwhelming margin of victory on the terrorism front. The Russian population would come to know what it was like to see entire towns slaughtered. Tens of thousands of Russian bodies would not make up for the genocidal devastation they had wreaked on Chechnya.

His people would dance in the streets at the news broadcasts of the death and destruction. Afterwards, the mere threat of a weapon hidden in a city or town would breed fear and uncertainty. There would be a pervasive mistrust in the ability of the Russian government to protect its people. Their citizens would be afraid to take the trains, go to work, or assemble anywhere. Commerce would halt, food could not be transported, and Russians would become even hungrier. So much so, that after only a few detonations, it could surely mean revolt across all of Russia.

Regardless of the price, a devastated Russia, and the possibility of the final Islamic Caliphate could become a reality in Semenov's lifetime. The Islamic center of authority was more important to Khasanov and Bin Laden than it was to him, and he knew that obtaining and demonstrating the weapons on the Russians was part of Khasanov's plan. And that suited him perfectly. This was what he lived for. Give Russia to him, and the rest of the world to Bin Laden.

But first, Semenov must positively identify what Oveshkin possessed. Then he had to ensure that it worked, and that Semenov's troops could deploy it repeatedly without assistance from Oveshkin. Khasanov had a plan to immediately distribute the weapons across the Islamic world so no single attack could ever devastate their stockpile. And

Ansar Semenov would be a critical part of the entire operation, Praise Allah.

He knew money would not be an object. They were very well funded and tonight Semenov had over one hundred thousand U.S. dollars with him, none of which was counterfeit. If Oveshkin demanded more, Semenov could honestly say, this was all he had. He felt very comfortable carrying this cash in the car. He had a semi-automatic handgun under his dark green fatigue jacket. The three other passengers with him were trusted soldiers, each armed with fully automatic weapons provided by none other than Pavel Oveshkin.

The directions to the meeting site were quite clear and easy to follow. He was mere minutes from the location.

■ ■ ■ ■ ■

Vadim Mirski was not accustomed to playing second fiddle to anyone but Fedor and he resented having to babysit a newcomer that no one knew anything about. Vadim was an extortionist and he performed that role with pride. He did not get his hands dirty with drugs or turf wars. He studied likely targets, did his research and presented the results to Fedor. Although Fedor made the final decisions, they were all based on Vadim's selections.

He may not have been an *Avtoritet*, but he was regularly included in the discussions about methods and payoff amounts. He managed the surveillance teams and the photography that frightened the targets. He oversaw the final negotiations with the victims, and he insured payments. He was a source of big money for Sergei Miloradov's organization and he knew it. Had it not been for a direct order from Sergei to his boss, he might have told Fedor he would not accompany this Pavel Oveshkin.

Making matters worse, Oveshkin knew nothing about safe places for clandestine meetings in Moscow. Mirski provided that as well. He could see where the learning curve for this man would be long and slow, and it would take quite a while for him to become a made member. So, it especially irked Vadim that he had to put himself out for someone who was not even Bratva.

Finding a rendezvous point was not difficult for Mirski. Extreme budget cuts had left The Third Ring Road around the City in a state of partial completion for years.

Once Mirski had told Oveshkin where the meeting was to be, Oveshkin had sworn him to secrecy about it. But Vadim's loyalty was to Fedor, not Oveshkin. So, he passed the location along to his boss as instructed. *Just in case*, as Fedor put it. He liked the idea that the boss might be backing him up should this Oveshkin try to pull a fast one.

He also knew from his briefing that Oveshkin came well recommended as an arms dealer. This kind of operation was new to Vadim and although he did not understand the details, he was not an ignorant man. He knew the weapons were illegal in some fashion. He knew there would be buyers and there would be profit for Fedor and Sergei. That was all that mattered. He figured that the newer Makarovs and Kalashnikovs, carried by all the men on his crew, likely came from Oveshkin. The source didn't matter to him, as long as the weapons were reliable. And they were, extremely.

The scowl on his face reflected his mood about being involved with Oveshkin. He was no one's lackey and he did not want to be involved in these dealings. He preferred strong-arming western businessmen into protecting their women. It was a much more respectable line of business. And he knew the services he provided made Fedor and Sergei happy. That was all that mattered. This business with Oveshkin was a distraction. And it was, frankly, not worthy of his time. If the going got rough, it would be just as well if Oveshkin never made it back. Vadim couldn't wait for it to be over.

CHAPTER THIRTEEN

NEITHER OF US SPOKE OR moved as we watched the two men hiding across the open field. It was obvious they hadn't spotted us, and it looked like they were setting up to get a good view of the meeting area, and maybe a clear shot.

I was scanning off to the right of the other observers when I noticed a barely discernable movement in the tall shrubs. I was going to ask if deer or other animals frequented this area when I saw two more men moving low to the ground. The humps of their backs were visible, but I could not see their faces. I was about to mention them to Takhoyev when he said, "I see them too. This is becoming a very busy place."

My night scope was doing its job well, observing them as they nestled into the cover. Before long, I saw a rifle protruding out and facing downward to the open area. Takhoyev said, "This is not good, Michael. We do not know who they are or their intentions. If they kill Oveshkin before we find the bombs, it would be disastrous." I was wondering more about the consequences of them killing *us*. I had another nagging question, *how did all these people know to assemble here?*

Before I could mention that to Takhoyev, we heard another vehicle approach the edge of the clearing from the left. It parked, with its engine still running, alongside the skeletal frame of a lifeless front-end loader. The car's poisonous vapors rose slowly from the tailpipe, enveloping it like a shroud.

The first two, directly across from us in the woods, turned their binoculars and rifles to the new arrivals. I could clearly see four men in the car. The driver seemed to be the only one unarmed. The others carried rifles of their own, upright in their laps. I waited for gunshots to riddle the car, but the reports from the snipers never came.

Takhoyev slowly reached back into the duffel bag, extracted a thin black tube and handed it to me. "You might need this," he said. It was a silencer. When he originally handed me the Makarov, it was dark in the car and I failed to notice that the barrel was threaded. I pulled my gun from my waistband and began screwing the silencer onto it. When I looked over, I saw him doing the same with his. I knew a little something about handgun silencers, and while the Makarov wasn't going to be totally silent, given its firepower, the source of the metallic clink it would generate would be hard to locate.

"Sit tight," he said. "I'll be right back." He then handed me the keys to his car.

"Don't forget what we talked about. If something happens to me, get the hell out of here."

I took his keys and said, "And just in case, Vladimir, I'll put these in my right-hand pocket."

344

With that, he began doing a perfect crab-walk, barely moving the branches of the thickets, and within moments he was out of sight. I slowly reached into Takhoyev's bag to see what other tricks he might have in there.

I could feel extra magazines for the Makarov's. By their heft, I knew they were full, so I grabbed two and slowly slipped them into my pockets. These guys had the advantage of reach with their rifles, but I had the advantages of stealth and surprise. And now I had plenty of firepower as well. With the crowd that was growing, it might come in real handy.

There were already ten people here by my count, and none of them was Oveshkin. Whatever he was up to, his secret meeting was anything but.

Within minutes, everything had gone still. The guys in the car had yet to emerge and the guys in the woods hadn't taken their sights off the occupants, literally. The other team seemed to be just watching and waiting. I slowly scanned the woods trying to find Takhoyev. In order for him to get behind the guys across the way, he'd have to navigate quite a wide circle around them. That would take time, and my guess was that Oveshkin would be here any minute.

It was approaching nine in the evening and for some inexplicable reason, meetings were usually called on the hour or the half hour. Don't ask me why, but that's almost universally the way it is. It was as if humans were programmed to stay within the cycle of their solar orbits. If Takhoyev was trying to get to a tactical position on these guys, he wasn't going to get back here on time for the opening ceremony.

A couple minutes before nine another vehicle approached with a sole occupant. It pulled right to the center of the clearing. Oveshkin emerged, leaving the car running and the headlights on. I immediately noticed that the headlight glare did not affect the image in my scope. Takhoyev had some decent technology.

As soon as Oveshkin exited his car, the four men from the first car got out and approached him. The three bodyguards hung back in a tight arc, their weapons slung waist high and aimed forward. The fourth approached Oveshkin. It was only then that I realized I had to turn Takhoyev's parabolic receiver back on. I missed the name of the other guy, if it was offered in the greeting. But now I could hear them. I wished to God I understood Russian.

Oveshkin sized up the Chechens and said, "Ansar, you did not have to bring all those bodyguards to meet with me. You know I am not going to rob you."

"I am not worried, my friend. And I am not here to kill you either. We have business to discuss. I understand you have a unique weapon to present to us and I would like to see what is so special about it. Show me."

Oveshkin noted there was no cordial greeting other than the overused expression *my friend*, which everyone tossed around, whether to a true friend or a mere acquaintance. He decided there was no need to stand around. He agreed, Semenov wasn't his friend and this was business, so he cut to the chase.

"I am not going to bore you with tall tales Ansar. What I have will turn the direction of your jihad to your favor."

Semenov cut him off. "I am already bored Oveshkin. Show me the weapon or I will leave."

Oveshkin sized him up a moment. Semenov was a fighter, so there was no bluff in him. But Oveshkin knew that Semenov was not the top dog in this process. If he returned without even seeing what the weapon might be, or if he had nothing to report, then he would be rebuked, if not shot.

Oveshkin pointed inside his car. "I will not reach in to my car with your gunmen pointing rifles at me Semenov. On the seat is my briefcase. Get it out and I will show you what you want to see."

Semenov reached in, withdrew the case and handed it to Oveshkin who placed it on the hood of his car. Pavel ran his fingertips over both four-dial combination locks and opened it. I could hear the sounds of the briefcase latches clicking open in my earphones.

Oveshkin reached into his jacket pocket, pulled out a small high-beam flashlight, switched it on, then handed it to Semenov as they peered at the contents of the case.

Oveshkin drew out a single photograph. "What is this I am looking at Oveshkin? You are holding a backpack? We have plenty. If there is something inside, get to it."

Oveshkin slid out the next photo. "What the hell is this?" Semenov exclaimed. "It looks like a missile warhead!"

Oveshkin's face contorted into a sneer. "That is exactly what it is you impatient fool. It is a low yield nuclear warhead." Semenov was silent as

Oveshkin produced the next photo. "This is its detonator pack and twenty-four-hour timer." He explained the next photo also. "This is the entire device outside the bag. You can see the warhead, the detonator pack, the timer and the battery source. The battery is rechargeable."

Semenov knew this would be no fake device presented in an attempt to rip off Khasanov. He was looking at a nuclear bomb and he was about to buy it. His mind was going non-stop with dozens of questions. He began rattling them off. "How do you keep it charged if you are putting it in the field? What is the yield? What is its destructive capability? Is it complicated to use? Is it safe? Have you tested one?"

Oveshkin knew he had hooked Semenov. He had given him just enough information to seal the deal, without giving him enough to try to cut Oveshkin out of it. He would not leave now without his down payment.

"I have complete instruction manuals, one for each device. But once you read the instructions you will see how simple they are to arm and to set the timer. Keep in mind, these are not toys and there is no test firing. There is no live demonstration. I know you have heard of these, and you must have wondered, *Does Russia really possess such a weapon? Is there really such a thing?* I assure you, Ansar Semenov, they exist. I have them and they are soon to be yours. There is merely the agreement on financing, and we can be on our way."

Semenov could barely contain himself, yet he tried to hold his composure in front of Oveshkin. When he concluded this deal then he, Ansar

Semenov, would be known forever as the man who freed the caliphate movement from impasse, who provided the ultimate revenge for his people and the man who set in motion the events that brought Russia to its knees.

"You have never cheated us Pavel Oveshkin. Therefore, Abubakar Khasanov has authorized me to take the next step with you. But I must warn you. You do not have enough protection in the world to hide from us if you double cross us. I do not look for a response from you. I am merely passing along a warning. The stakes are now too high. So, tell me, what is the next step? Will you take us to see the device?" Semenov knew he was authorized to make the down payment, sight unseen, if he felt the weapon was real and attainable. But he would feel much better if he saw and touched it.

Oveshkin had already anticipated Semenov. There was no circumstance where he would take anyone to see where the bombs were stored, and no one would see a device without paying for it. His reputation was solid. He had never run off with anyone's money without delivering the goods.

"No, Semenov, I will not take you to the device. However, you are merely two steps from owning it. The next step is for you to give me some good faith money. Just like always. I will then call you with a time to meet for the exchange. And at that time, I will take as long as you want to teach you how to arm your device and deploy it.

"As for your questions about destructive force. That is a tactical question. Your leaders are thinking about the strategic opportunity. The question is not how much physical *damage* can a

349

bomb cause. The question is how much *fear* can such a destructive bomb generate?"

Semenov was going over it in his mind. He wanted the answers, but he was beginning to believe that Oveshkin and Khasanov had already discussed this. Consequently, they entrusted him with the money.

Oveshkin said, "I will need one hundred thousand dollars now and with that, you are only a day or two away from owning the first device. And tell your boss that the balance is nine hundred thousand American dollars. And it must be good cash, not counterfeit. When you bring the rest of the money, I will turn over your bomb and train you." With that Oveshkin began stacking the photos. "Give these to your boss. And do not, under any circumstances, get caught with them. It would mean the death of us all." With that he placed the photos in the briefcase and handed it to Semenov. "My money?" He asked.

"In my car," Semenov said. "I will be right back."

Semenov was ecstatic. He was now only days away from giving his people the opportunity for revenge greater than they could ever have imagined. Their land would soon be free of all Russian influence.

Oveshkin felt the hair go up on the back of his neck. He knew that Khasanov and the Chechens needed him, and they wanted the bomb. But that didn't mean he wasn't afraid that something was wrong with this deal. Was this an FSK sting? Had he been set up? As he watched Semenov lean into the trunk of his car, Oveshkin's palms began to sweat as he thought through the possible outcomes. But when Semenov came back into full view, he was carrying only a briefcase.

Semenov set it on the hood of Oveshkin's car and opened it. The inside contained only tightly wrapped bundles of hundred dollars bills.

"Take them out." Oveshkin told Semenov. "Lay them on the hood where I can see them."

Semenov grabbed handfuls of cash. Each banded item contained one hundred, one hundred-dollar bills. Ten thousand dollars in each pack. Semenov arranged them in two rows of five.

Oveshkin grabbed each pack and riffed the bills. He saw nothing but hundred-dollar bills.

Semenov said, "Do you really think we would pay less than we agreed? It is all there Oveshkin. Not a dollar short."

Oveshkin put the cash back in the briefcase, snapped it shut and tossed it onto his front seat. This was not a moment for a western handshake to seal the deal. Instead he told Semenov, "Khasanov knows how to reach me. Tell him to call me when you have the rest of my money." Oveshkin knew that once Bin Laden realized that Khasanov's ragtag army had a nuclear device, he would seize it for his own purposes. And once he possessed it, he would salivate at the idea of owning more. Oveshkin smiled to himself as he thought about tripling the price for the other eight. Since none of the KGB knew where he had redistributed the units for them, it made him wish that he had taken them all.

In that moment, he made up his mind. When this evening was over he would take them all and disappear, even from Miloradov.

With that, Semenov nodded and turned back to his car, signaling for his men to join him.

■ ■ ■ ■ ■

Where the hell was Takhoyev? I glanced into the woods where the first two gunmen had been lying in wait. Either they had left or Takhoyev had put them down, but I couldn't see them. I scanned to the right and saw the other two making their way deeper into the woods. It looked like they were leaving as well. The buyer and his bodyguards were gone. Still no Takhoyev, and Oveshkin was getting in his car.

After what I had just seen, I just couldn't let him get away. If he escaped and delivered the bomb, the western world would be held hostage by jihadists. And there was no doubt in my mind many of the devices would end up planted in the United States. I saw Takhoyev's rendition of mutually assured destruction between Russia and the United States becoming even more real.

Given that Oveshkin was trying to sell nuclear weapons to terrorists, I began listening to a voice in the back of my mind telling me to take him out, right then and there. I knew cold-blooded killing was not in my DNA. I'd never murdered anyone and never shot anyone without justifiable cause and, until now, never even considered it.

But this was not a coffee house discussion about morals or ethics and difficult choices. No college professor was standing in front of an auditorium filled with eager but ignorant teens, guiding them down a path that had no answers but his own. This was real life and the stakes were about as high as they get. Could I possibly justify taking out Oveshkin? And even if I could, would I be able to actually sight in on his head, knowing that in the next instant the impact of the projectile would pulverize his brain and kill him? It wasn't as if I'd never shot anyone before. It was just that I had never assassinated anyone. Not yet, anyway.

I was very well concealed and felt pretty confident that no one would ever know who fired the shot, if anyone even heard it. Now that the attendees had left the area, other than Oveshkin and maybe Takhoyev, no one else seemed to be around. And if Takhoyev managed to witness it, somehow I felt it wouldn't matter anyway.

From a humanitarian perspective, if there is such a thing when you are talking about killing a guy, I knew Oveshkin would never hear or feel the round that hit him. One moment he would be planning the transfer of a nuclear device to a terrorist who would kill the people of his ancestors, and the next moment there would be nothing. His mind would not even register that it had no body or that his soul had abandoned it. He'd have no pain, no light airy space to walk towards, no dark corner from which to wonder what happened. No place from which his mind could ask a question and no recollection of even having lived, or of the fact that he had just died.

Relative to recovering the nukes, I felt I could report Oveshkin's demise by merely turning that information over to Takhoyev, if he too wasn't already dead. And as for not recovering the nukes, that wasn't why I was here anyway. Even if *we* never found the stolen weapons, it seemed no one else knew where they were either. The logic and the ethics of stopping him here and now became compelling. Maybe it was safer this way.

Still it came down to the basic question. Was I wired to kill in cold blood? I wasn't a government agent on some kind of secret mission, with a license to kill. I wasn't technically a spy, regardless of what I was doing now and I certainly wasn't being paid as one. This wasn't combat. My target wasn't a barricaded gunman nor was Oveshkin pulling a weapon on me or holding someone hostage.

But a free world could soon be staring down the nuclear barrel of a group intent on destroying them, and they wouldn't know it until it was too late. All of it began to make sense for me to take the shot.

I was thinking about my immediate options. Could I just shoot someone to ensure that nuclear devices never made it into terrorist hands? That was the crux of the question. As much as I liked to think not, the rationale was becoming overwhelming. I understand shooting an armed combatant. It made sense, whether in the law enforcement world or in a state of war. I can also see it as part of an intelligence operation. Hell, it went on all the time if you believed everything you read in books or saw in the movies. But now it was personal, and the dilemma was real.

I was a former DPD sniper and knew I could get a clean and accurate shot off. I could hear a voice, way off in the back of my mind, quietly cautioning me not to do this. It was warning me *you might be able to rationalize your way through this now, but afterwards grief and guilt will come crashing down on you. And when they do, they'll combine to destroy your very soul and haunt your dreams for the rest of your life.* The voice of right choices is always there, guiding you. And the voice of rationalization is always there, making any path you choose to follow, sound like the right one.

I was beginning to see a way my conscience could handle killing Oveshkin, here and now. The reasons why *I should shoot him* became heavier and heavier on the scales, tipping the explanations for why *I shouldn't shoot him* weightlessly into the air. I had to listen to one voice or another and I had to do it now.

I decided.

Staying low to the ground, I tossed all Takhoyev's gear in his bag and ran with it towards our car. I had to follow Oveshkin at any cost now. If I could get an eye on him as he drove, he wouldn't lose me. But if I couldn't, I would reconsider the shot at that time. If I thought I was going to lose him, I would kill him.

I was trying to stay quiet, but I knew I was crashing through the woods and grunting as I ran. I got to where our car was, or where I thought it was. But it was so well camouflaged I couldn't find it. My head was swiveling around when I heard a voice whisper, "Over here." It was Takhoyev, waiting for me by our car.

I unlocked the driver's door, tossed his bag in the back and was about to jump into the front seat. "Give me the keys," Takhoyev said, "I will drive."

We sat in our car with the lights out and the engine off, waiting for Oveshkin to leave the area. We seemed to have nothing to say. We were just watching and waiting. Within just a few moments,

Oveshkin drove by our hiding place and slowly rolled onto the tarmac, heading back toward downtown Moscow, staying on Leninsky.

Takhoyev waited until the car was almost out of sight before starting ours. He quickly backed us out of the shelter of the trees and fishtailed through the loose dirt with our headlights off. It was nearly pitch dark, but he deftly handled steering us back onto the road.

Suddenly Oveshkin braked and we saw the interior light in his car come on as someone ran up to the driver side door. He got out, ran over to the passenger door and hopped in. The other man got behind the wheel and they sped off.

Takhoyev let their car get a good lead on us again before he followed. This was not his first surveillance pursuit and it showed that he knew how to follow someone.

Oveshkin's taillights were visible less than a quarter mile ahead. Takhoyev continued to drive with our headlights off.

"Where the hell did you go?" I asked. "I nearly shot Oveshkin to keep him from getting away!"

"I am glad you didn't, Michael. We need to get those bombs and get them out of here."

"I thought about that Vladimir, but I also felt that if he got away, we'd lose him, and the bombs would get transferred. With him gone, nobody gets them."

He thought a while. "You would have shot Oveshkin?" He asked.

"Yes, I think so. I didn't know where you were, if you were dead or alive. I began worrying that he was getting away, that I couldn't follow him, and he might make the trade. I was getting my mind ready for taking him out."

Takhoyev drove a bit, and then glanced sideways at me. "Yes, Michael Christian, I believe you would have. Perhaps you aren't a spy, but you might make a good one."

"Vladimir, I wish you would stop talking like that. The last thing I want is to be your guest in Lubyanka prison." Takhoyev grunted as if the prospect did not appeal to him either. "Nor would I like to be your cellmate," he said.

Ten minutes ago, I was faced with the choice of killing Oveshkin and opted out of that call. But now, with time to think about it, I was still turning over a lot of options. Interestingly, the idea that I might go to jail had never been a part of the consideration.

■ ■ ■ ■ ■

We drove in silence the next twenty miles or so, passing no other cars and seeing none come in our direction. As we approached the Second Ring Road, closer to Moscow city center, traffic picked up a bit allowing Takhoyev to turn on our headlights and blend in with the other cars. If Mirski was driving, he seemed completely unaware of us, as his speed didn't change at any time.

An airport loomed off to our left. I had seen it as we drove to the meeting, but it didn't register at the time. It wasn't as large as Sheremetyevo, but it seemed quite capable of handling full sized commercial and passenger aircraft. "What is that?" I asked, nodding in its direction.

"It is Vnukovo. It used to be a local airport used almost exclusively by corporate executives and for secret flights by my people. It was recently privatized and is now majority-owned by private shareholders. Today it is mostly used by Eurasian travelers and private aircraft. Western passenger flights enter and depart from Sheremetyevo and of course, so do the large commercial carriers. Our customs inspection office is staffed heavier up there. I think someday this airport will be exclusive to private carriers."

I could not believe I missed this place coming down here. I must have been terribly preoccupied. We were now nearly back to Moscow center and I noticed Takhoyev closing the gap between Oveshkin and us. "I do not want to lose him in traffic. There aren't many exits, but the signs are nearly invisible, and they come up on one very fast. It is possible he could get off and we could miss it completely." As if anticipating my thoughts he continued, "Don't worry, I will not get so close that he will notice us."

I could tell his surveillance skills were sophisticated. Takhoyev was no amateur at following someone in a car. No matter what you saw on TV or in the movies, it just wasn't the same. You didn't get two cars behind the guy and "keep an eye" on him. You had to hang back. So far back, that you could barely keep track of the guy's car. Tail lights became your best friend and you soon learned their configurations in various makes and models, because the shape of the car soon became indistinct in the dark. But if you got too far back, then they became tiny little red dots without shape or size. It was a balancing act. And you

358

could lose a car if a driver made a sudden turn onto a short street.

Back at the Organized Crime Task Force, we had six to ten cars to run our surveillances. And we never lost a target. We'd position a few cars behind, so we could switch on and off, presenting different makes and model cars in the suspect's rear-view mirror. We had cars running on parallel streets, in case he made a sharp turn either way. And we were in constant communication with each other on a private police radio channel.

Better yet, if traffic got so heavy that we lost sight of the target for a while, we could call in the police traffic copter to keep an eye in the sky until we could catch up.

Here in Moscow, we had one car and no radio partner.

Takhoyev appeared well schooled in the technique. He was constantly checking his own rear-view mirror and he was anticipating the pitfalls of the road. He was right to take the wheel. I would never have expected the dark and virtually unmarked exits on this tarmac highway, even in the metropolitan area.

We were approaching the Inner Ring Road, the one that ran around downtown Moscow. The Moskva River cut through the southwest corner of the ring, running northeast for about a mile and a half, before turning back southeast and exiting the ring another mile and a half later. Looking at the river slicing through the ring on a map, it looked like a skeletal jaw.

"We must keep a sharp eye out here, Michael. With all the traffic, we could easily lose him." But before I could respond, Oveshkin's driver got in the lane to cross the Moskva River Bridge. If he continued, he would drive practically into Red Square. And in a short while, before I could even try to figure out our next move, their car pulled to the curb in front of the Moscow Hotel, There Oveshkin got out and began walking toward the lobby doors with his briefcase. His driver easily re-entered traffic and disappeared.

I grabbed the door handle to follow Oveshkin, when Takhoyev suggested, "Maybe you should drive around the block, Michael. He may know you. I will follow him inside." With that Takhoyev threw the car into park and jumped from the vehicle. I ran around to the driver side and got in. "I'll circle the block." I told him. But Takhoyev was already bounding toward the doors.

Navigating turned out to be pretty easy. Muscovites drive on the right side of the road here in Moscow just like in the States. And the one-way streets lent themselves to circling the large city block quite easily. But for what seemed like the longest time, when I reached the front of the building, Takhoyev was nowhere to be seen. After about five minutes, I began to worry. *Should I find a car-park and go in after them*? I decided to stick it out and keep circling, but the minutes seemed to drag by.

After two more trips around, Takhoyev came running down the stairs and jumped into the passenger side door. "Quickly," he said. "Go around the back to the parking garage and wait. He took the stairs down and I am willing to bet he has a car there."

I wondered how we would know which exiting car would be him. "When we get around back," I told him, "hop out and get as good a viewpoint as you can of the cars coming out. I'll drive down the street and wait. He can only turn right and that will put him right behind me."

I got into position on the street and looked back through the rear-view mirror at Takhoyev squatting behind a waist-high tree planter-box. The first car exited and turned up the street behind me. Takhoyev stayed in place. The same with the second and third car. But when the fourth car turned out of the drive, Takhoyev began running in a crouch, making a beeline for our car. He hopped in and slammed the door behind him. "That's him. He's in the blue AvtoVAZ."

"You mean the Renault?" I asked.

"It is based on the Renault, but it's an AvtoVAZ. For Christ sake follow it. And don't get too close." He said.

I looked sideways at him. "Really, Vladimir?"

By the time I got into the traffic lane there were two cars between Oveshkin and ours. His block-shaped horizontal taillights sat just above the bumper corners on each side and would be easy to follow. Our little parade was easily keeping up with the pace of traffic and Oveshkin was stuck in it as well.

It was close to midnight and cars still crowded the inner-city roads. He wasn't going anywhere in a hurry. As long as he didn't try to shake a tail, we should be ok. Downtown Moscow neighborhoods can be a myriad of highways crossed by small narrow streets. Takhoyev said, "Unless he is staying nearby, he will likely hit one of the ring roads to get out of the area. It is better than trying to cut through town."

We needn't have worried. Oveshkin turned onto Teatralnyy and hung in the right lane, keeping up with traffic and not trying to leapfrog cars. Usually that's a good sign in surveillance.

After about six blocks, he even used his turn indicator to signal his right turn onto Tverskaya. Perhaps even arms dealers did not want to be pulled over by the local police. This road was wider and Oveshkin picked up speed which was short lived. After about four or five blocks, the street narrowed again and Oveshkin got in line with everyone else as he continued northwest. In another mile and a half, the road widened again. And as if to demonstrate he was no longer patient with waiting for others, Oveshkin hit the gas as the name of the road changed to Leningradskiy.

It's at moments like this that things can go all to hell. Cars were jockeying for lane positions. Russian drivers were proving the maxim true, that only drunks and drug addicts would dare enter an intersection, even with a green light, without slowing to almost a stop. And there seemed to be plenty of drivers under the influence of something or driving with a death wish. Traffic controls seemed to mean nothing as cars ran through red lights without even slowing down. Between watching Oveshkin and watching out for someone trying to T-bone us, I was beginning to feel my adrenaline pumping. Takhoyev sensed it. "Don't let it worry you Michael. We either get hit or we don't. But do not let that bastard get away from us!"

My concern shifted back and forth between losing Oveshkin to getting killed. *Screw it* I decided. Hopefully Takhoyev had some juice around here.

I floored the Mercedes and it responded effortlessly and quietly. I drove through a crowded intersection in the oncoming lane, then slipped back into traffic three cars behind Oveshkin. He didn't change his mode of driving at all.

That was when I glanced back into my rear-view mirror looking for the cops. And that is when I saw the headlights of a car doing the exact same thing I had just done. It wasn't so much the fact that a Muscovite was trying to get to his destination in a hurry. But the driver actually crossed over into oncoming traffic, as I did, and then back onto our side of the road. Then he slowed and got in our lane about four cars behind us. I know a tail when I see one and I knew we were being followed. At some point, we had gotten onto someone's radar.

■ ■ ■ ■ ■

I was alternating my gaze from Oveshkin to the mirror. Every now and then, Oveshkin would pass a slower driver then return to the slow lane. And when I followed suit to keep up with Oveshkin, so did our tail car.

"Vladimir, are you aware of anyone that would be following us?"

At that, he sat up straighter. He had the presence of mind not to turn around, but he did look out his passenger side mirror. Then he dropped the visor and tried to angle it to see behind us. "Why do you ask?" He replied. I guess I was hoping for either a *yes* or a *no* answer.

I explained my observation. He seemed to accept that I was neither hallucinating nor over reacting. "Can you make out what type it is?" He asked.

I explained that all I saw were its headlights and it was too dark to see the form of the car. I told him I couldn't make out the number of occupants either, but based on the wide spacing of its headlights, it looked like a full sized car and not a small Lada.

"No," was all he said. Then he reached behind his back and slipped the gun from his waistband, holding it in his lap. Its silencer was still threaded in. "Keep driving and don't lose him. In about nine kilometers, we will come up on Khimki and the MKAD." As the highway veered right, the name changed again to Leningradskoye. I reached behind and pulled my Makarov out also, sliding the silenced barrel between my thigh and the seat, using the weight of my leg to hold it in place while I drove.

"The MKAD?"

"Yes, there will be a bridge over a small river just before we get there. The MKAD is the Third Ring Road and you will see the signs. Oveshkin's meeting with Semenov was at the southwestern end of the road, where it was abandoned. If he is heading east or west, he will exit just up ahead. Hopefully he will use his turn signal again."

"I can keep an eye on him Vladimir. I am more worried about our company. Given their distance behind Oveshkin, it is unlikely they are following him. And since there seems to be no one else now in sight on this road, I think odds are good they are following us. But who are they and why would they be following us?" My mind was trying to keep it all

364

sorted. Then I had a thought and it wasn't comforting.

"Remember earlier at dinner when you said that we were on someone's list? Did you manage to take steps to get us off that list? And the list we are on, is that the kind of list where we just disappear, and the matter is forgotten?"

Vladimir's countenance was severe. He was deep in thought, which was not very comforting for me. We were coming up to the bridge over the river. It seemed more like an industrial canal, but there was a freighter plying it as we drove over. The water seemed mercurial and moved languidly off the vessel's bow, silently creating a gentle wake like beaten black molasses.

Soon we would be at the MKAD exits.

Oveshkin was not giving any pre-indication of his intentions. I noticed that street lighting had gone from bright in the city, to subdued in the suburbs to non-existent out here. If there were clouds in the sky, I couldn't see them. I could barely see the shadowy outline of a dense, dark forest off to our left, on the other side of the river. The treetops and the sky were indistinct, as if both had lost their identity.

I recalled the area. It was on the way to Weiner's warehouse. I remember thinking on my ride from there to the Metropol, how backward this country was. Power lines ran alongside the roadway on poles set less than six feet from a road with no shoulder, no lane markings and no curb. Drunks, addicts and the normally arrogant Russian drove this road. None of them had any regard for traveling a safe speed, whatever the hell that meant to them. Most of these guys could never pass a high school driver's training test back in the States.

How did we ever get to a point where we fear them? I supposed the answer could be found in the thousands of nuclear warheads sitting atop their Inter-Continental Ballistic Missiles and pointed at every major city center in the United States. And all that technology was turned over by Americans, who willingly or unwittingly gave the information to KGB spies, much like the guy in the seat across from me.

Oveshkin continued past a series of the MKAD's very intricate cloverleaf exits and stayed on the main highway. Takhoyev broke his silence. "He is on the way to the airport. It is only about six miles to the Sheremetyevo exits. This could get complicated quickly."

Complicated quickly? He hadn't answered my question about our tail car, or if he might be aware of their intentions. That was the problem I was worrying about now, as much as losing Oveshkin.

As Oveshkin drove on, and as our tail car stayed right with us, Takhoyev answered, sort of. "We are in way too deep now to let Oveshkin get away. He cannot be allowed to board an airplane. And no one or nothing can be allowed to interfere with our mission. Do you understand what I am saying, Michael? A moment of decision may be fast upon us. I hope your resolve will be as good in reality as it was a moment ago in theory."

I still had no clear answer, but I now had a sense that the car behind us may not contain the good guys. I began arranging the options in my mind.

Kill or capture Oveshkin before he was allowed to board a plane, in a major international airport? Not just any international airport, but one in a communist country. And what if the car behind us engaged us? Do we shoot it out, regardless of where we were? I resolved that if they started popping shots off at us, regardless of where it happened, that they were going to be in for a hell of a surprise. Under any set of circumstances, if Oveshkin tried to board a plane, it was going to be ugly.

Maybe we could just try to strong-arm him into our car. I didn't know where that would get us, but maybe not killed and maybe not having to kill him. But what about the other guys? I saw nothing good coming out of them being here.

In any shootout scenario, I could see us being arrested for sure, if not gunned down in the process. And what if Oveshkin was merely approaching a gate to greet a passenger or buy a ticket? Do we kill him anyway? What if he had a device stored in an airport locker? We could be mere steps away and never find it if we took him out. This was not the way we would do things back home. But I guess I knew I wasn't in Kansas anymore.

I was beginning to think a good option was to snatch him and try to pry the information out of him. Maybe the airport parking lot was a good place to grab him. Whether rough interrogation is something for Takhoyev, or we turn him over to the *real* KGB, the GRU or the FSK, didn't matter.

I'd already breached the cautions I had been given. *Don't put yourself in harm's way*. But like Takhoyev said, and I had to agree with him, we're

367

in way to deep to stop now or to let Oveshkin sell one of these devices to terrorists.

Oveshkin ignored the first airport exit, choosing to stay on Leningradskoye rather than get off at Mezhdunarodnoye. "What is he up to?" Takhoyev murmured. Behind us, I saw the headlights ignore the exit also. But they were of less concern to Takhoyev than were Oveshkin's intentions.

Looking right and left I saw a series of dirt roads on this unlit portion of the roadway. They wound worm-like towards old, run down, single-family houses and storage yards with empty, corroded trailers that seem to have been dropped and forgotten. I drove past several scrap metal yards, with sagging, corrugated sheet metal fences. And what may have once been a series of active machine shops, now sat derelict beneath tin roofs with gaping doorways. Less than twenty-four hours ago I drove this road, or rather Sasha did, to talk with Weiner. We were now less than a mile from our warehouse.

There were only three cars moving along this quieter stretch of the road, Oveshkin's, ours and the car behind us. I had dropped back about a quarter mile on our guy, and so had the tail car on us. Oveshkin seemed to be the only one unaware he was being followed. He was either mighty careless, aware we were there and didn't care, or so single-minded in his plan to deliver the device that he was oblivious to us being on his ass.

Without any signal, Oveshkin turned right onto Sheremetyevo Road. "This street runs on the north side of the airport to the warehouses and storage lots. This could be very good Michael."

I killed my headlights and, as we approached the intersection, I guided my turn into it without touching the breaks. I could see Oveshkin's tail lights ahead and closed the gap to two football fields. In my rear view-mirror, I could see our tail car go past the intersection. Hopefully we had shaken them, and I let Takhoyev know. His eyes were focused on Oveshkin. For as chatty as he had been these last few days, he was solemnly quiet now.

CHAPTER FOURTEEN

OVESHKIN COULD PRACTICALLY TASTE THE money in his briefcase. It was all he thought about the entire way to his storage building. The end of living and working in shadows was within his grasp. So were the millions he craved.

He knew the Saudis were financing both the Chechens and this Bin Laden. As soon as they detonated the first of these units, they would want them all. In the meanwhile, he would continue to provide Miloradov all the guns he needed until it was time for him to disappear. The short-term sales would give him enough cash to live very well these next few weeks or months. He couldn't envision Semenov and Khasanov's people being in possession without wanting to use it right away.

But attacking a specific site involved them following their tried and true ritual of developing a list of viable preliminary targets. That process of studying and selecting could be weeks or it could be days, if they had already begun the analysis.

No matter the outcome of the first bombing, they would crave more. They would want to create increasing fear and destabilization, and to prove the attack was not a one-time capability. And in Semenov and Khasanov's case, they wanted to murder as many of their enemy as they could.

Indeed, Oveshkin could afford to be patient. He was standing on the brink of millions of dollars that spent very well anywhere in the world. His final destination did not reside in some nether reaches of the cold and bleak Russian landscape. He could go to St. Moritz or to Monaco, to northern Italy or Austria. His possibilities were endless. In the meanwhile, he knew it was time to decide where to go once he sold the first bomb, and it most certainly would not be anywhere in Russia.

His reverie was disturbed by the sound of a large passenger plane on its landing approach from west to east, behind him. He glanced into his rear-view mirror and seeing no lights, turned left onto a dirt road.

He drove past open yards with parked trucks gathering frost on their windshields. The temperature was dropping quickly this evening. He came to his building.

It was perfect for him. It had electrical power and a propane backup generator that could provide both heat and electricity. But he got his main power from the local service. He kept the building heated at all times in cooler weather to keep his weapons at sixty degrees. That way it wasn't so warm or cool that he had to worry about humidity gathering in the metal components.

More importantly, he wanted to ensure a continuing supply of power to the RA-115s bombs. Otherwise he had nothing of value to offer. He was not well equipped to find new power sources or to recharge these unique batteries if they died.

He parked his car close to the wall, grabbed his briefcase and entered his building. He flipped on the banks of lights, turned off the alarm system, and then reset it, arming only the perimeter doors, so he could move about.

He entered his small office and fired up the space heater, set his briefcase with the money on his desk and opened it. He was very pleased with this evening's results. He extracted all ten of the small packets, set them onto his desk and sat down.

Reaching into his drawer, he pulled out a bottle of Stolichnaya and poured a small quantity in a tumbler and sipped it. He randomly grabbed a wrap of bills and slowly riffed them again. Each packet contained ten thousand dollars in one-hundred-dollar bills. He sipped again and flipped through the other nine packets.

He didn't doubt Semenov. The money would all be there, but he counted it anyway. He held the bills close to his face as he counted, breathing in deeply, knowing that a thousand people had touched, handled and caressed this money before him. Every bill had its own story of joy or sadness, of celebration or corruption. The scent excited him.

When he was through, Oveshkin pulled his Makarov from the desk drawer, checked the magazine, confirmed the safety was on and slipped it into his waist band. Then he swiveled his chair around to the wall and the five-foot safe welded to steel braces in the floor. He twisted the dial back and forth four times and the tumblers dropped into place. He gave a quick turn to the three-spoked handle and the door slid open quietly.

Most of the shelves contained stacks of money. There were piles and piles of American dollars and each stack contained ten thousand dollars. Oveshkin smiled to himself. This was his getaway money. No Russian banks for him, just piles of untraceable U.S. currency. He picked up a fistful of bundles off the desk and placed them in the safe, repeating the process until all ten were in there. And having a second thought, he grabbed about an inch of hundred-dollar bills from one pile and stuck them in his pocket.

Tomorrow night he would head back downtown and indulge his pleasures. He would go back to the room Miloradov put him in at the Moscow Hotel. He would have room service bring up appetizers and plenty to drink. He would get some of the best cocaine from one of Davydov's men. Light, fluffy, easy on the nasal passages and easy on the places where the girls liked it dusted.

Then he would indulge himself with the high-end girls he fancied. These whores knew every trick in the book and seemed to enjoy them. And for the money he would spend on them they would play all night. This is how he, Pavel Oveshkin, would live for the rest of his life, but first things first. He pushed the safe door closed.

■ ■ ■ ■ ■

I had seen Oveshkin make his turn, but by the time I got to the intersection, his car was gone.

"Son of a bitch!" Takhoyev exclaimed in perfect English.

I cruised very slowly, looking up each dirt alley that we passed, seeing more of the same old, cold buildings and derelict vehicles we saw earlier, at the end of Leningradskoye. Then one of them caught my eye. It was so close to the building, I almost missed it in the shadows. I could see only the windshield glass reflecting a distant yard light. And the glass wasn't frosted.

Takhoyev got out of the car without closing his door and walked over to get a closer look. He returned quickly. "That's it!" he said. "The hood is still relatively warm." I glided the car past the corner, let it cruise to a stop without using the brake and slipped it into park.

I could feel my heartbeat quicken as I considered the possibilities. "Vladimir, I think we've found the place. I can't think of any reason why he'd dump his watchdog at the hotel and then head all the way out here to a cold warehouse after grabbing a briefcase full of money. Can you?"

"I can think of several, Michael. But none of them are as valid as what you believe. I have to admit, I agree with your conclusion. But you know there is only one way we are going to find out. It is not like we can leave here, muster some forces and return.

"We have to keep Oveshkin under watch and if the weapons are here, we have to make sure they stay here until we can figure out what to do with them. If he leaves, we would have to leave the weapons here and follow him. I would hate to think of abandoning them at this point."

"Agreed, Vladimir. So, what's say we get a look inside? It's the only way we can confirm things one way or the other." As I turned off the engine, Takhoyev reached around into his bag and grabbed an extra ammunition magazine. He looked at me. "I've already got a few, thanks." I said.

We exited the Mercedes and quietly pressed the doors shut. Taking gentle steps, so as not to scrape the gravel surface, we approached the building. I saw a problem right away. There was only one window about eight feet up and Oveshkin's car was parked below it.

Without thinking about it, I slipped off my rented shoes and climbed onto the hood of the AvtoVAZ and leaned up to look in the window.

■ ■ ■ ■ ■

Oveshkin walked from his office to the main warehouse and stood there looking at his space. It was very likely that in less than a few months he would be out of here. But for now, his local office was here, and he was pleased with his domain.

The steel girders were rusting, but still strong and stable enough to hold the building solidly in place. The roof was good and that was a plus out here. The windowless pedestrian door was constructed of solid wood and was steel clad inside and out. The truck roll-up door was heavy-duty aluminum and was locked from the inside. A tall pile of wood lay in one corner, remnants of packing crates that previously held some of the Makarovs, the Kalashnikovs and their ammunition.

376

Oveshkin personally supervised the installation of the alarm system the day after he bought the building. He was proud of the fact that he thought about adding a separate zone for the perimeter. Since there were these front door and back doors, he did not want to be surprised by anyone while he was inside. Not with this inventory. But he refused to have it monitored by an alarm company. The last thing he needed was for the police or a guard to enter the building, see something he shouldn't and trace these guns back to him. The whole purpose was to would alert him inside.

The building was actually much larger than it seemed. Shortly after acquiring the space, he had a one hundred thirty square meter space walled in at the northwest corner with a steel pedestrian door and an overhead door added. He also had an electric, five-digit combination lock mounted on the inside steel door.

He added a propane-operated forklift. Tonight, he would not need it, but in the old days, Anatoly and Gennady would manage the offloading of the weapons from the truck they drove from Germany. They'd use the forklift and slip the crates of weapons into the secure room. Now Anatoly was in a German jail and Gennady was dead and buried in an unmarked grave somewhere in Germany. *That fucking security guy did this to me and now he is here in Moscow. If it is the last thing I do, I will see him dead or kill him myself.*

Oveshkin gathered his composure and walked to the secure area. He entered his code and opened the steel door. He reached inside and flipped three switches for the rows of overhead industrial lights that buzzed to life, brightly illuminating the space.

■ ■ ■ ■ ■

I saw Oveshkin exit what appeared to be an office with no windows. The partially closed door prevented me from getting a view inside. He walked to the center of the warehouse and seemed to be looking around. Had he heard us? There wasn't much in there, maybe we were wrong. All I could see was a forklift and a pile of wood.

Oveshkin walked to a corner and I could see right away there was a wall of cinderblock enclosing an area that looked to be about fourteen hundred square feet. It took up quite a bit of space. Had he not walked over there, I might not have seen how the interior measurements differed from the outside of the building. Then he unlocked and opened a steel door. In a moment bright lights illuminated the inside.

And there they were.

The back wall was lined with floor to ceiling steel racks filled with long rectangular and short square boxes. Dark green ammo boxes were stacked against one wall. On the left wall I could see wooden crates with the lids still nailed on. If the boxes were full, there had to be hundreds and hundreds of Oveshkin's guns in there.

There were three steel tables sitting in front of steel racks of handguns and rifles. On the tables were nine burlap bags looking exactly like the photographs Oveshkin showed Semenov. Electric cables ran along the floor and then to the inside of each device. We had them!

I jumped down off the car.

"Vladimir. They are here. I saw hundreds of guns in boxes and crates and plenty of ammo for them."

"Yes, yes. But are the bombs here? Did you see them?" He asked.

"Yes. Well, I did not actually see a device outside its bag, but I saw nine bags exactly like the ones that Oveshkin showed his buyer in the woods. And the bags are full. I believe each detonator is fully charged. If I was a betting man, I'd say our nuclear bombs are in the bags.

"I saw him unlock the door to an interior storage area where the guns and bombs are. Vladimir, it is like an armory in there. He also has a forklift charging in there and a pile of junk wood. Otherwise, the place is clean. He came out of an office, but I couldn't see inside it."

As I was explaining this to Takhoyev, I was drawing the interior of the building in the dirt with a piece of broken glass I found on the ground. The light out here was terrible, but we could both see well enough.

The obvious question now was, *what were we going to do about it?*

CHAPTER FIFTEEN

WE KNELT THERE TRYING TO figure a way into the building without getting ourselves killed. Our odds of quietly entering through the steel door were minimal. The racket would surely tip him off and ruin any chance we might have of surprise. It might be stretching our luck to get back on top of Oveshkin's car to keep an eye on him, yet we needed a better lay of the land. "I'll take a walk around back and see what's there. We might find a more vulnerable point of entry, or his office may have an outer window we can work open." I told Takhoyev. "I'll be back in a minute. By the way, now that we know where the devices are, try to refrain from just killing him if he comes out."

There was no smile on his face as I headed off around the far corner of the building. I felt pretty confident that Takhoyev would have no qualms about killing Oveshkin. Nor did I think he worried about such ethical dilemmas. For me, the perfect outcome was to seize Oveshkin and take him captive. If there were other bombs at other locations, he might see making a deal for his life as

381

a favorable option in exchange for revealing their locations.

It didn't help our likelihood of success that the front of the building was so secure and that it was very dark out here. The airport was only about a thousand yards to the south of us, but its lights were all facing inward. This must have been a low rent area of storage buildings and warehouses, because there were no other lights and most buildings were either empty or running with their lights out, to save money. In fact, Oveshkin's was the only one on the block that had its lights on, inside or out.

I thought about our facility, only about eight blocks away. It was well lit, front and back and all the doors were secure and alarmed. We had blocked in all the ground level windows to prevent snooping, as well as to eliminate any weak points in the perimeter walls. So far, the only weak point I saw here was the window over Oveshkin's car.

I turned the corner to the short side of the building, hugging the walls as I walked. I was careful of each foot that I set in the dirt. I wanted to make no sound that would alert Oveshkin. There were no doors or windows on this side, but there was an exhaust vent only a couple feet off the ground. Its opening was four by four and had a steel, wire-mesh screen in front of it with a three bladed fan and motor mounted inside. The fan wasn't turning, but its construction was too sturdy for us to try to force it. This was not a way in.

I turned the next corner and walked into a narrow alley bounded on the left by a high concrete barrier. The long north wall had another vent about eight feet off the ground. Without some kind of ladder, we weren't getting in there either. In the center of the wall I found another windowless, steel pedestrian door and an overhead door. Both looked like they were frozen in their hinges. The dirt in the area hadn't been disturbed in months, maybe longer. Even if they had been viable entry points, I had no idea where they led in the plant.

I turned the third corner and was walking along the short wall. This one also had a vent the same size as the other, but no windows. The only vulnerable way in seemed to be the front window. And that was sure to expose us in the process. As I approached the front of the building, I heard two sounds. One was of a car engine quietly idling. The other was a voice and it wasn't Takhoyev's.

Someone was talking so softly, I couldn't understand what was being said, but the tone was low, guttural and menacing. The guy was speaking a universal language and I didn't like the sound of it. I thought he was one syllable away from shooting someone. And the only other person out there in the open was Takhoyev. I pulled the Makarov from my waistband, transferred it to my left hand and quietly flicked off the safety, as I edged half my face around the corner

■ ■ ■ ■ ■

Takhoyev was standing with his hands open at his sides and his palms facing a stranger who had his back to me. Vladimir was indicating that he was not a threat and not holding a weapon. I figured he was buying time and hoping that his fate wasn't

383

already sealed. So far, the other guy, who was standing about arm's length away, hadn't called his bluff or tried to search him.

Then the scope of what I was seeing became a bit clearer. The guy standing at the front of the car with his gun on Takhoyev was the passenger. His car door was slightly ajar, and that seat was empty. The brake lights weren't on, which told me that driver had the car in park. I could see him with his left hand on the wheel. The other was below my line of sight. There were just the two of them.

Takhoyev began talking calmly, but he barely got started, when the gunman fiercely struck him across the face with the butt of his gun, sending Takhoyev to his knees. The gunman brought the barrel of his gun directly to Takhoyev's head and I saw his gun-arm stiffen as he braced for the kill shot.

Without hesitation, I raised my Makarov and squeezed off a nearly silent shot. The gunman's head jerked from the impact of the slow, heavy round that turned the inside of his skull to mush before it blew out the other side. He slumped to the ground onto his knees in front of Takhoyev. It looked like the two of them were praying. At that moment though, only one of them was capable of a requiem. The other had lost his chance for all time.

I put the second shot through the rear passenger window to clear it. The driver instinctively looked in my direction and raised his gun to fire. But his fate was already determined. I took the next shot through the open window with lethal effect. His head snapped back against the driver's window post and then fell forward to his chest.

I rushed to Takhoyev who was still on the ground holding the side of his face. "Get up." I said quietly. "We need to get away from the front door." I helped him rise but had to practically drag him to the side of the building.

Even in the dark, I could see he already had a terrible welt on the side of his face.

"You okay?" I asked.

"I will be fine." he slurred. "Thank you. I would be dead if not for you."

I still hadn't processed the fact that I had just killed two men. I was trying to keep focused on our next dilemma. Had Oveshkin heard, and if he did, would he come outside and see us? "Vladimir, do you know these guys?"

"Yes. But I am losing my touch, I am afraid. The one on the ground walked up behind me and I did not even hear him. The other pulled up after this one got the drop on me. You have met them too."

I never really got a look at these guys, but I only knew a few people here in Russia. I didn't think any of them were capable of executing Takhoyev. "Who were they?" I asked.

"You met them at dinner tonight at the Palace. They too were insurance agents and sat at our table. I introduced you to them and another of the group." That may have been the case, but I didn't recall any names, besides, it no longer mattered at this point. I had just killed two KGB Agents.

"They were colleagues of mine at the KGB and members of the General Staff. Their group shares responsibility with the Third Directorate for ensuring nuclear weapons are not misused. I think I see what their role may have been in all this. They must have been part of the group that siphoned off some of the devices. It appears they want their stolen weapons back and were following us to see if we would lead them to the bombs."

"And he was going to kill you? Why?" I asked.

"Because when he held me at gunpoint and asked where you were and where the bombs were, I knew he was going to kill me regardless of my answer. I was on their list and so were you, Michael. You turned the corner when I was about to tell him to go fuck himself." It wasn't lost on me that Takhoyev was going to take a bullet rather than give me up.

"So, were these the guys who were following us?"

I was also about to ask if we were on anyone else's list, when the front door to the warehouse opened a crack. A rifle barrel protruded through the opening. Oveshkin would have to open the door much wider to get a look at the full scene, otherwise he would not be able to see us, the idling car or the bodies. If he did, this might be our only chance to get inside.

■ ■ ■ ■ ■

Oveshkin heard a car pulling up slowly, practically outside the front door. He stood perfectly still waiting for it to pass through the alley to the next unit. It stopped. He listened intently. He thought he could hear voices, but they were too muted to make out what they were saying. He had no idea who they might be, but if they didn't move on, it could be bad.

He went back into the storage area and grabbed a Kalashnikov automatic rifle from the shelf, tearing off its oiled and waxed protective paper. He wiped it down with a rag and then knelt in front of an ammo can and flipped open its latch. He grabbed two magazines and began quickly feeding sixty rounds into them. When full, he rammed one into the receiver of the weapon and racked the bolt to chamber the first round. Deliberately, he flipped the safety off and set the selector to the center fully automatic position. He pocketed the other magazine and walked out into the warehouse, turning off the lights and making his way more by recollection than by sight. It was ominously dark in that area.

He turned off the alarms and unlocked the front door, opening it a crack. From the slight angle he had, he couldn't see much. His car seemed undisturbed. He extended the barrel of his rifle out a bit, opening the door a bit further. Now he could see a body lying in front of a car. *What the hell?*

He slammed the door shut, locked it and retreated back into the storage room, turning off most of its overhead lights. He pulled the armory door partially closed and knelt alongside it, waiting inside. From his vantage point, he had concealment and hopefully some cover. But he only had a partial view of the outer storage area.

It was entirely possible someone could force that front door. It may take a while. But if they got in, he would have to expose himself to defend his space. The overhead door to the gunroom was already locked, but it was the most vulnerable entry point. Big as it was, it was only secured by a brass padlock. He grabbed a few more magazines for the

Kalashnikovs and began loading them for extra firepower.

There was no way out and no one he could call. Even if he could get to a phone, he couldn't call Miloradov. He would not want to give up his cache of weapons nor would he be able to explain the bombs. Whatever this was about, he would have to handle it on his own. As tense as the moment was, he was relatively calm. He knew he had the advantage and whoever was outside had lost the element of surprise.

Although it didn't matter why someone was already dead, it was a curious fact. Was the shooter already gone? Maybe the incident had nothing to do with him. Moscow had become a hostile place and killings were widespread, with bodies being left everywhere. Oveshkin did not believe in coincidences, and he was not about to take any chances. If someone was after him, they had better bring their best team. He was armed with tons of weapons and ammunition, and he knew how to kill.

Then he realized that sword cut both ways. He turned to look over his shoulder again. In the dim glow of the remaining lights, he was looking at a room full of explosive ammunition. Any stray shot, especially a tracer, could set off a massive blast. But that was the least of his worries. There, in plain view, was a table full of nuclear devices. If either cache of weapons went up, he would be dead in an instant. Even though he had not been a man of prayer since his youth, the words escaped him, *St. Matrona, save me.*

Pavel Oveshkin was not a pessimist. Other than that one slip up in Germany, he had outsmarted everyone to get where he was. He knew he was a superior strategist in every way and now he was about to become a multi-millionaire. Whoever was outside his door was not going to disrupt that plan. He was willing to kill to protect his vision and he did not feel the least bit of fear.

■ ■ ■ ■ ■

We crouched perfectly still in the dark. Oveshkin had closed the door without exploring the entire front area. The assailant's car was still idling quietly. "Get me back to our car." Takhoyev whispered.

There was no doubt he took a hard blow. It must have been like getting hit with a steel pipe. I guessed he was done for the night, even though our business wasn't finished. He was wobbly on his feet at first but seemed to gain strength as we walked back to the Mercedes. He pulled me to a halt along the way as he picked up his assailant's gun.

I opened his Mercedes' front door for him to sit, but he shrugged me off. He went to the back door and dragged his duffle bag out onto the ground. He pulled out a few more magazines and handed me two more. I could see where this was going. We were not calling for reinforcements. He was not calling the GRU to turn the matter over to them and it looked like I was not calling Koval.

"Look Vladimir, we have Oveshkin locked in there by himself and I have seen the bombs in there with him. He is not going anywhere. I think before we do anything drastic on our own, we should call someone to back us up."

"And who do you propose we call? I cannot call the GRU or the local police. And you have seen how greedy and dangerous my colleagues are. They just tried to kill me. So, tell me. Who do we call, your Koval? You know that I cannot do that on my own, with the possibility looming over me that I might be executed for turning these devices over to the FBI. The way I see it, we have to get the devices ourselves. And then, as we discussed, I will help you get them back to the States and into your reprocessing facilities. That was our deal."

I remembered the "deal" as he put it. But at the time, I was thinking maybe all I had to do was get my hands on the intelligence. Then I could turn that over to Koval and he would take it from there, with Takhoyev or without him. Now I was parked outside a warehouse in Moscow trying to figure out how to breach a secure building, with no element of surprise and an armed gunman waiting for us if we tried to enter.

We were way past the warning *Do not put yourself in harm's way.* We were now at the *Don't get your ass shot off* words of wisdom.

Takhoyev grabbed a shoulder bag from inside the duffle and slipped in his extra magazines. He grabbed two small canisters and tossed them in his bag too. "What are those?" I asked.

"A surprise. We may need to even the odds a bit," was all he said.

I didn't like being out in the open like this and suggested we sit in the Mercedes and talk about our next steps. I started the car and turned on the heater and the defroster, put the car in gear and

390

slowly coasted further away from the building, towards the entrance to the alley. If Oveshkin heard us, he might think we were leaving. Whether he did or not, a few seconds hesitation on his part could play to our advantage.

We had to have more of a plan. I may have been an American, but I was not about to live up to the image of "cowboy" and go charging through the front door, guns blazing. The odds were not in our favor. Oveshkin had an armory in there. Besides, it was a steel door.

"I have an idea." I said to Takhoyev. He looked at me in anticipation and said, "I hope it is better than mine, which is for us to drop in through the window with a lot of firepower trained on Oveshkin."

Oveshkin had the advantage of hiding behind protective cover. I knew he would have fully automatic weapons at his disposal and all the ammo he could ever want. But that paled in comparison to another outcome. All I could think about was a stray round going off in there. Even if all we did was ignite a firestorm of ammunition, it would likely kill us in an instant. Not to mention detonating a nuclear bomb. I didn't know if it was possible to go fully nuclear from a ricochet. I supposed it could, but it needed a full detonation to do that. On the other hand, the slow radiological release in such close proximity would kill us in a few days or weeks, rather than instantly. Climbing through the window, amidst a hail of bullets both ways, didn't seem like a plausible alternative.

"Here's what I am thinking, Vladimir."

■ ■ ■ ■ ■

Oveshkin was good at waiting. He would not allow himself to be forced into making the first move. If someone wanted to get in here or to get him, they would have to take the first step. The way he figured it, there were only a few ways in. There were two steel reinforced pedestrian doors that were locked from the inside. There were some fan vents, but they were practically impenetrable. There were two heavy-duty, aluminum overhead doors as well. One was on the back of the building, but it was so immovable that Gennady and Anatoly couldn't open it to offload the arms crates. No one was coming in the back.

Although the outside overhead door was vulnerable to a determined attack, he had a distinct shooter's advantage if someone tried to pry their way through either of those front doors. He could just shoot rounds through them all day. So, he guessed that the easiest way for someone to enter was to climb through the top window in the front, one at a time. That would be a deadly mistake. Even if one got through, he would still have to unlock the door from the inside for the others. By then Oveshkin would have killed him.

He got up from his floor position, loaded another Kalashnikov and placed it, with two extra loaded magazines, on the opposite side of his door. His last level of retreat, if it came to that, was at the table with the bombs. If they decided to shoot it out there, *then damn us all to Hell*, he thought. He thought back to all the money in the safe, just one room over, and became even more determined to survive.

But in case it didn't play out that way, Oveshkin had a final plan. He reached across the steel table for an instruction manual.

■ ■ ■ ■ ■

Takhoyev listened passively, with no expression on his face, as I outlined my plan. When I was through, I sat up a little straighter in the front seat of the Mercedes, awaiting a response.

He leaned further back in his seat, rubbing his temples.

"So, your plan involves a diversion. What a unique idea."

His sarcastic response revealed he was getting a bit testy and I wondered whether it was because my plan was so desperate or if he was just reacting to getting whacked in the face with the barrel of a gun just minutes ago. Either way, I felt he was justified. "If you have something better, I am all ears Vladimir."

"No. I have nothing better and my own plan was more reckless. Whatever we do, we have to act right away. It will be light in a few hours and traffic will pick up. When that happens, our options will be very limited, and the advantage shifts further to Oveshkin. I also do not know if we should expect more of *my friends* to follow soon. Let us get moving."

"Alright Vladimir. I'll wait here in your car. You take the other one and I'll keep an eye on the place. But I promise you, if he pokes his head out the door, I'm unleashing a barrage at him. I no longer have any hesitancy about shooting him."

While I waited for Takhoyev, I decided that I was at a disadvantage sitting in the car like this. I had no real cover other than the windows of the car, and with the car running I was not exactly hiding. I turned off the engine, disabled the interior lights and got out of the car. I could feel the cold air now as evening had turned into early morning. I zipped my jacket tighter to my neck and rearranged my spare magazines, to give me easier access without them falling out of my pockets if I had to do any running. It was then I noticed what I was wearing. The morbid humor of my situation became starkly clear. I was about to engage in a paramilitary action wearing borrowed patent leather shoes, a tuxedo shirt, pants held up by suspenders and a cummerbund. In an effort to gain some semblance of respect if someone found my body, I unclasped the cummerbund and tossed it in the car.

The building was still dark inside and no one poked his head out the door anymore. Oveshkin was waiting it out as if we weren't even out here, or maybe because we were. Either way, we were at a stalemate and our team was about to break it. Takhoyev was gone no longer than twenty minutes. In that time nothing had changed.

He pulled alongside the Mercedes and the three of them got out.

"Michael, I believe you have met my men before. They tell me they pointed their guns at you the first day. They still think the look on your face was very funny." I nodded at the two men who had greeted me so dangerously, the morning after I paid Takhoyev to protect Weiner's enterprise.

He had driven over to our warehouse and pulled them off protective duty there. Bringing them back here doubled the size of our assault team and added significantly more firepower. They had automatic rifles whereas all we had were semi-automatic pistols.

I wanted to make sure they fully understood that this was not a massive firefight where they could spray rounds wherever they chose. Yet we couldn't let them know what was in the building besides conventional weapons. I had to leave that explanation to Takhoyev. We certainly wanted an overwhelming rain of bullets in the breach phase, but they had to be very carefully placed rounds. I did not see where they carried any more ammunition than what was loaded in their magazines. Our Makarov handguns and their Kalashnikovs fired different caliber ammunition so there would be no lending of rounds in an emergency. Each of us had to make every shot count. Takhoyev and I decided that the key rule of engagement was to take out Oveshkin if they got a clean shot. We couldn't take a chance of us all being killed in an attempt to get Oveshkin free of the nukes.

Takhoyev knelt on the ground and we gathered around him. He began making the same drawing of the building as earlier, referring to his scratching in the dirt and occasionally pointing to the building for confirmation. I assumed he was explaining the plan I had made earlier, as he spoke to them in Russian.

During the initial assault, the primary goal was to get Takhoyev and me inside the building by means of their covering fire. Then we would lay down the next cover fire from inside, for them to follow us in. Once inside, we would make one final attempt to get Oveshkin to give himself up. If he refused, we would all take up closer positions, again using alternating cover fire. Eventually one of us would get a shot and take him down. I think each of us knew, when it came to a close-in shootout, someone in our group was going down too. The odds were too great against us. I think secretly, without naming names, we each hoped we weren't the guy going down.

I looked at our two new warriors. There wasn't a hint of fear or hesitation in their eyes. They seemed to have a great deal of confidence in Takhoyev. It was obvious he had commanded them before. They seemed totally committed to the plan which I was beginning to think might work.

I looked at their Kalashnikovs, the trusted weapon of the Russian army. They were not silenced or suppressed. They would be very loud going in and louder still once we got inside. But this was a Moscow suburb and gunfire was not going to be a shock to the neighbors. We nodded to each other and prepared to make some noise.

I had designated one of his men to stand on the hood of Oveshkin's car and lay down a steady burst of gunfire from the window at the doorway to the armory room. I was counting on the fact that Oveshkin would still be in there. If not, then our odds of success got worse.

Takhoyev's other soldier was tasked to get back into the car we had commandeered and crash it through the overhead door. I could see where the latch and lock mechanism were located on the left side of the door. Although it was only minor it would provide extra reinforcement to the strength of the door. His goal was to back up across the alley and then use the car as a battering ram, hitting the door to the right of center, where the panels would be the weakest. All we really needed was enough room to get inside. Anything else was gravy. Takhoyev tossed his duffel bag into the back seat and nodded to his soldier sitting behind the wheel.

Takhoyev and I took up our positions alongside the door, ready to follow the car inside or squeeze by it if necessary. It was a one-time opportunity. If this didn't open the door, we were back to square one.

I nodded to the driver and to our sniper who shot out the window glass and then opened fire towards the armory door. The driver punched the accelerator and the car lurched forward. I really didn't expect what happened next. The sound of metal on metal was both screeching and explosive, to the point I couldn't even hear the gunfire any longer. The lower panels of the door peeled inward and wrapped themselves around the hood of the car as it continued completely inside the building.

Takhoyev and I had to run into the warehouse without any cover at all because the car had gotten in so much farther and faster than we anticipated.

He broke to the right and used the car for cover until it crashed into the office wall.

I broke to the left and got behind the engine of the forklift. I had a better line of sight than Takhoyev, but still did not have a shot at Oveshkin or even the inside of his room. I could see our sniper at the window, training his gun sights on the doorway. Every now and then I was startled by the pop of a single round, meant to keep Oveshkin from getting a visual on us or making one of us a target. He was pinned down. He must have known any hope of escape was futile at this point.

Takhoyev peered above the hood of the car. His driver had crawled out the passenger door and was crouching alongside Takhoyev who looked at me questioningly.

I held up my hand motioning for him to hold off a bit while I sized things up.

■ ■ ■ ■ ■

Oveshkin had been rehearsing imaginary assault schemes in his mind. He envisioned different options, but each came down to gunfire coming at him from within the building. He assumed that somehow the assailants would make their way in, regardless of his overwhelming arsenal. But each of his second stage scenarios involved assailants on the right and on the left of his position. He figured it would be easier to take out the gunman on the right first, as that would be more aligned to his field of vision. He had also guessed that he would receive the second wave of their cover fire from there. His plan was to lay down heavy automatic fire, pinning that gunman in place. Then he'd switch positions to the other side of the door and work on those assailants. He was feeling better about his tactical situation the more he rehearsed the choices. He loaded a few more magazines and set them in place.

He heard a sound and he knew something was up. But he did not expect what happened next.

From the upper window a hail of automatic gunfire rained down on his position in the doorway. He wasn't exposed, but his instinctive reaction was to duck farther away from the door for additional cover. The incoming fire was deadly accurate, and he could not even get his weapon around the corner to return fire without being hit for sure.

Then there was an ear-splitting sound as the exterior overhead door gave way to the impact of a car crashing through it. The powerful force did not tear the door free of its mounts and rollers, but the panels gave way as the car plowed through them and smashed into the wall of his office.

That was his first indication that he may not be able to defend his position. The gunfire stopped and he tried to get his head around the corner to see what was out there. As soon as he moved in that direction, single shots banged off the doorframe inches from his head. All this had happened in a matter of seconds and he had not been able to fire a single round.

Oveshkin had hoped for more than this. He had known it was going to be difficult, and he correctly assumed that if the building were assaulted, there would be gunplay. That was not a worry to him at the time. He was ready for that challenge. He did not however anticipate a small army being out there, armed with automatic weapons. Nor did he assume a breach so daring as to take a twelve-foot door out by using a car as a battering ram. He recognized he had made the gravest mistake of any battlefield commander. He had underestimated his enemy.

Now all he could do was wait to see what happened next. In any case, he was not being taken out of here alive to be a prisoner for the rest of his life. And that life would be very short for so many reasons now. He was holding a hundred thousand dollars of terrorist money and they had nothing to show for it. He had engaged in a transaction about which his new patron, Sergei Miloradov knew nothing. He had, in effect, gone behind the back of one of the most powerful Russian mafia Pakhans. And he was in possession of nuclear bombs he had stolen from the KGB. He was a dead man unless he got out of here completely free. There must be a way.

He retreated to the steel table.

■ ■ ■ ■ ■

Oveshkin, as far as we could tell, was alive and pinned down with more weapons and ammunition than he could handle. He was relatively safe for the time being, as long as he did not try to rush us or change his vantage point.

We, on the other hand, had achieved only the first phase of our plan. The next was going to be tricky. It involved me getting to the other side of the room while our sniper pinned down Oveshkin. That would give me a better line of sight into the room and a likely shot. Although I had an apparently good marksman at the window, there were about twenty feet of open space I had to cross before I could get to the cover of the woodpile on the other side of the warehouse. Oveshkin would have a better line of sight and minimal exposure. My timing had to be perfect and his had to be less so. Otherwise ... I didn't want to think about *otherwise*.

"Oveshkin," I shouted. "Listen to me." I motioned for Takhoyev to translate. He understood and spoke my lines immediately. "There is no way out and you are surrounded. You can make this easy or difficult. Extend your empty hands through the doorway and walk out. We will not shoot you."

Takhoyev translated, but looked at me as if to say, *do not promise what you cannot deliver.*

We waited for Oveshkin's reply. The ball was in his court. Oveshkin's answer was unresponsive.

"I speak English. And now I know who I am dealing with. You are not Chechen or Bratva and you are not GRU or FSK. So, we finally meet, Michael Christian."

Takhoyev looked at me and smirked, as if to say *it looks like he has you figured out.*

Oveshkin continued, "There may have been a time I would have considered cutting a deal with you, when I thought you were Bratva. And I would have held out for a deal that eliminated torture and death in a Russian prison when I thought you were GRU. But now there is no deal, Michael Christian.

"You killed my people in Germany and put others in prison, one of whom was very dear to me. You confiscated a million dollars in arms from my warehouses and ruined my entire operation. I am not surrendering. Come and get me if you want me, Christian. But it may not be as easy as you think. I may have a surprise for you."

401

Oveshkin had hoped against all hope that there would be a way out, that they would slip up somewhere and he could make a getaway. But now he knew that wasn't going to happen. For the time being everything was at a standstill. They were outside his door and he was inside with no exit.

That damned Michael Christian was here and making demands. *Was he leading a commando team? What the hell brought him to my doorstep? Had Christian been following me all this time*? Just listening to his voice made Oveshkin's blood boil as Christian suggested surrendering. There would be no surrender.

Oveshkin couldn't believe his bad luck. Then he thought no, this was not luck or coincidence. It was fate. And maybe fate was bringing him the chance to get his revenge.

He had failed to act quickly enough in Germany by telling Anatoly to hold off for a day when his friend wanted to kill Christian. The result was the destruction of his organization. He wanted to kill Christian so badly that his hands trembled but it looked like he had lost that opportunity again. His entire focus had to be on a plan to get out of this without being killed.

He tried to figure out what he could offer them in exchange for his freedom. But he had nothing.

There were all these guns, but they practically belonged to Christian now anyway. No, the guns were not bargaining power. At least not with that God damned Christian.

Then there were the bombs. He had made a mistake with them. Normally he separated his stashes to ensure that he did not run the risk of losing everything in a single raid. Until recently, he had done that with the rifles and pistols. It had almost been a trademark of his.

But he was never confident of having the bombs in more places than he could effectively watch. It was the mistake the KGB had made, and it was how he got access to the devices on the table. Now, because of Christian again, he was about to lose them and the millions of dollars they represented. Even more, he was about to lose his financial freedom when it was just within his grasp.

He had one bargaining chip left, actually he had nine of them, but he needed to use just one.

He laid out the instruction manual and opened it to the section marked *Setting the RA-115s Device Detonator*. As he struggled to open the top of the nearest backpack, he began breathlessly responding to Christian.

■ ■ ■ ■ ■

I heard Oveshkin's refusal to surrender, but it sounded like more bluff than reality. He sounded winded to me but I couldn't tell if it was from excitement or fear.

Or maybe it was something else. Then I realized what was going on. He was stalling because he was up to something else.

I motioned to Takhoyev that I was going to try to take up that position on the other side of the room, which would require his sniper to lay down some cover for me. Takhoyev nodded but held up his hand motioning for me to wait. He pulled open the back seat of the car and dragged out that old duffel of his. He reached in then held up two of those canisters he called his surprise. He held two fingers to his lips as if smoking. Takhoyev had smoke grenades. He never ceased to amaze me with his forethought. Either that or his go-bag always contained guns and grenades and not undies and shirts.

He pressed himself against the outside wall of the arms room and began walking slowly and quietly toward Oveshkin's doorway. I began to worry that Oveshkin might just reach around the corner and pop Takhoyev. But Vladimir was past that decision point.

I crouched and got ready to run across the warehouse to the other side. The door I had to run by was open only about a foot, but it seemed to be wide open as I sized up my chances.

I looked up and saw our sniper lean into his sights. I looked back at Takhoyev just in time to see him pull the pin from the smoke grenade, its ping audible in the warehouse as the lever released. He leapt into the air, his arm easily reaching above the seven-foot pedestrian door and tossed it over the top. Instantly, smoke began to fill that smaller room and obscure the area outside it.

I took off running and never even looked in the doorway as I passed it. There was only brief cover fire from our guy and no shots from inside. My ears were ringing but I was safely on the other side. When the room cleared, I would be looking right into Oveshkin's smoke-filled hideout. Hopefully he wasn't looking down his sights right back at me.

I clambered behind the wooden scrap pile. I needed to be able to see him clearly, yet I also needed more than concealment. I needed cover. I looked back up at the sniper position. He was gone from the window. A few seconds later, I saw him enter through the broken overhead door and take up a position behind the forklift that I had just vacated.

There were four of us inside now and this had worked out better than I thought. Takhoyev had dropped back to the car along with the guy who drove it in. They had no clear shot but were perfectly concealed in case Oveshkin decided to rush out. They would have the best angle if he came out shooting. While the forklift was fairly good cover, it didn't offer his guy much by way of a clear shot without exposing himself. I had the best vantage point but would be exposed each time I tried to take a shot.

It wasn't ideal, but it wasn't bad either. We had managed to get inside the building before daybreak. And given the lack of sirens outside, we had done it without alerting the authorities. There were other considerations that might affect how much time we had to bring this to a conclusion. If Oveshkin was working with the Bratva, would they come looking for him? Did they even know where he was? And if Takhoyev's buddies from the GRU knew how to find us, had they communicated that to others in their group? Time still was not on our side.

My thoughts were interrupted by the sound of a large motor from within the armory room. The smoke that was hanging in the air was being pulled into the room. But more than that, it was being drawn into the room and right out through one of the large wall fans. In a matter of moments, the room would be free of smoke. I would be forced to keep my head down or run the risk of having it blown off, if Oveshkin got a line of sight on it.

Takhoyev reached in and sounded the car horn twice. When I saw him, he was signaling the guy on the forklift. He swung his arm in large circular motions with his index finger extended. To me, that looked like the signal to regroup near Takhoyev. But I no longer had a smoke covered path along the front of Oveshkin's door. Takhoyev's guy nodded in understanding, but rather than run over to him, he hopped onboard the forklift, unplugged its charging cables and started it.

It was the same plan we used to enter the building, but with a lot less cover for the driver. Takhoyev and the guy with him took up a position alongside each side of the overhead door to the armory. The lift operator turned the forks toward the tall door, engaged the forward gear and waited. As if on cue, the other three of us dropped our partially used magazines from our weapons and inserted full ones. I stood up behind the crates and leaned across the top with my Makarov extended, sighting in on the door. As soon as the smoke cleared, I was going to open fire. I figured that would be the beginning of the assault on the room. Hopefully, none of my shots hit anything but Oveshkin. If I didn't have a shot at him, I'd have to put the rounds high and into the wall. I couldn't take a chance on setting off an ammo explosion and I sure as hell didn't want to detonate a bomb. The smoke was thinning. It would be just seconds now.

■ ■ ■ ■ ■

Who were these guys, Oveshkin wondered? And how the hell did Christian get to a point where he could muster a small strike unit with automatic weapons and smoke grenades in Russia?

It didn't matter. Oveshkin knew he had few choices and none of them were good. Escape was no longer an option, and neither was surrender.

He could not be taken alive and would not be. He could not allow himself to be taken to Lubyanka prison. That would be a fate worse than death. Perhaps they would just hold him at a cabin in the woods until they were through torturing information from him. Wherever it happened, he was eventually sure to tell them everything they wanted to know.

They could even force him to give up information on Miloradov and his organization. Perhaps he could convince them not to bother torturing him. Since he would give up what they wanted anyway, maybe it was smarter not to suffer through it. Regardless, when they were through with him, the outcome would always be the same. *They* would kill him or Miloradov would. When he was no longer useful, his lifespan could be measured in mere minutes, days at the most.

His dreams of wealth, and all it could buy, were over. The luxurious clothes, the exotic cars, the large mansion and the caresses of young girls were gone forever. The thoughts of those things no longer brought him joy or hope. If his future could be measured in less than days or weeks, then he had no future. There was only now. Tomorrow was no longer a concept for him.

Oveshkin took a deep breath and recommitted himself to the present. He was still in charge of his own destiny, even if only minute-to-minute. He reduced his remaining goals to two.

First, he had to ensure with the utmost certainty that he would not be taken alive. Secondly, he had to be positive that Christian died in the process. *That son of a bitch has brought me down. The least I can do is take him with me.*

Soon the wall fan would have done its job. He stood over the steel table, following the instructions exactly. Within seconds he had armed the bomb that would guarantee his final wishes. Damn them all. May they join me in Hell.

His prayer to the devil was interrupted when he heard the forklift motor start. He knew they were about to assault his position. He reached under the detonator, set the timer for three minutes, tucked them both under the bomb and drew the bag closed. He grabbed his Kalashnikov and trained it on the overhead door.

■ ■ ■ ■ ■

The smoke was clearing in the room and I could vaguely see Oveshkin's form moving about the steel table. There could only be one thing he was up to and it scared the hell out of me. I saw him lean under the table and raise something onto it. Then he leaned back onto the table behind the

408

bags of bombs. With only my Makarov and no scope, I didn't have a shot at the small target he presented.

I saw my team looking at me, waiting. I could see the far corner of the room and put two rounds into it at the ceiling, hoping the ricochets would rattle upwards. And that set off the action on our end.

The driver held his foot on the brake as long as he could while revving the engine. He had the forks lifted about three feet off the ground when he released the brakes. I was expecting the fast rush of a ton of steel into the door, but the machine just lumbered to it. I fired two more rounds into the room and saw Oveshkin duck.

The forklift hit the overhead and never stopped its slow march into the room. It pushed the door from its lower brackets and forced it inward. The driver engaged the lift drive and the forks began raising the door into the air. That was when his body was riddled by the jacketed rounds that passed through him and into the wall behind him.

I should have realized it, but only at the worst time did it sink in. These wooden scraps were no cover at all from those rounds. If Oveshkin knew it was me behind these broken crates, I was done for. Then I saw Takhoyev rush through the overhead door to the right and lost sight of him. His partner followed him with his Kalashnikov on full-automatic and was blasting away at Oveshkin! Had he forgotten what we told him in the heat of battle? I saw the storage racks behind Oveshkin rattle from the rounds hitting them. The angle was definitely aimed upward, but the rounds had to be flying pretty damned close to the tabletop.

Then I heard shots from the far right, individual pistol shots. Takhoyev.

Oveshkin turned to his left and seemed to be adjusting his firing toward Takhoyev. I clambered over the crates and ran sideways toward the entrance. Oveshkin heard me charging the door. He turned, saw me and changed his mind about Takhoyev. He rose practically to full height and looked right into my eyes as he aimed down on me. I let go three quick shots and knew they all had effect. But so did Takhoyev and his soldier. Oveshkin jerked and twisted as he took full and half-jacked, hollow point rounds from all three of us. He was dead before he hit the floor. It was crazy what he did. If his wish was to commit suicide by firing squad, then he accomplished his goal.

Takhoyev ran from the room back to the forklift and cradled his friend in his arms. There was no response from the dead soldier. Although in my original scenario I calculated that at least one of us would be killed, I was saddened that someone had actually died, even though I didn't know his name. A member of Takhoyev's team had joined a battle he didn't ask for and died fighting bravely, at the mere request of his former commander. But there was barely time to dwell on that. Takhoyev walked back into the armory and was assessing the damage and Oveshkin's corpse.

"Vladimir, Oveshkin was standing at the table working on something when we hit the door. I am sure he was setting one of these."

"God, no! But which one?" He asked, frantically looking at the nine satchels.

"He was standing at the far right of the table, Vladimir. So, I would ignore the first four on the left.

410

We have to start on the right. Vladimir, you take that one." I said, pointing the one farthest right. I grabbed the middle bag and yanked it open. All the lights were out except the green, charged-battery light.

"Not this one." Takhoyev said as he tugged his open.

I grabbed the next bag and slid the cord open and my heart rate exploded. The device was lit up like a Christmas tree.

"This is it Vladimir. You and your guy need to get out of here."

"Michael, this is a nuclear device. Where the hell would we go?"

The enormity of the problem set in. There was nowhere to go and if we couldn't find the timer, much less disable it, we were going to fry in a nanosecond of it going off. There was no choice but try to deactivate the bomb.

I didn't know where the detonator was and said so. "The manual is written in Cyrillic, Vladimir. Find out where the detonator and timer are and then see if you can decipher how to disarm it. Meanwhile, I will look."

I tried to recall the pictures Cross and Walters had shown me in Brinton's office, and Takhoyev's diagram from the secret files in his office, but that all seemed so long ago. At the time, I didn't think I was being given a crash course in how to disarm one. But there was something I did recall about the devices. They needed constant power to keep the batteries charged.

"Vladimir, have your guy find the electrical circuit panel and shut off all large circuits. That should kill the battery supply's primary power." It was a long shot, but if we were lucky, one of these cells might be bad and not generate enough power to activate the detonator. Takhoyev said something to him in Russian and he ran off.

I grabbed the device and tried to pull it from the satchel. It was bulky and heavy, and felt like it weighed over fifty pounds. "Grab the bottom of the bag Vladimir." I said. I lifted the device and he pulled on the bag. It came off like a shoe from a wet boot, slowly but steadily. As the device came free, I saw the timer and the detonator, which was flashing red. The timer was counting down, one minute and fifty-eight seconds.

I'm a process-oriented guy. I've even been told I'm a linear thinker. So, I was trying to remember the order of detonating explosives, even though I had no training. "You know anything about these Vladimir?" I asked. He shrugged and said, "Only what I have seen in your movies."

"Knife?" I asked. He reached in his pocket and pulled out what looked like the Muscovite version of a Boy Scout pocketknife and handed it to me.

"Really?" he asked, as I opened the blade. "You are just going to start cutting wires?"

What else was I going to do? All I could think was we had to remove the power source from the detonator or we had to remove the timer from the detonator.

The nuclear payload was exactly as pictured. Although much smaller, it looked like any other nuclear tipped missile, not that I had ever seen one live before. It was tubular and conical at the top and appeared to be made of a polished stainless steel and brass-like metal. At its base though, was a cylindrical appendage tightly threaded onto the payload. I figured that to be the detonator but it didn't look like the picture I saw back in New Jersey. At the detonator's base were two bare connecter screws tightly clamped down on a red and a black wire, just like my light switch at home. There was nothing sophisticated here and perhaps that was by design - keep it simple in the field. As I talked out loud, Takhoyev seemed to be nodding in agreement, but he was also immersed in reading the instruction manual.

Those wires from the detonator led back to the timer. And it too had two wires, a red and a black one leading back to a large case that must have been the battery power source.

I looked at the timer.

"What have you got for me Vladimir? We have only about ninety seconds!"

Takhoyev had been quickly leafing through pages, like he was cramming for the most important test of his life, and he had failed to study. He looked at me with a look of disappointment and grave sadness. He said, "It may be booby trapped."

Everything took on a new dimension. It was no longer a matter of guessing the right color and the right place for a cut. Now it was a matter of accelerating our deaths by a few seconds.

In wiring a light switch at home, you can use either the red or the black wire for power to the switch. But that was a light switch in the United States. What about a nuclear device made in Russia? What was the color code? And what if they intentionally switched the colors as part of a fail-safe?

For the first time, I noticed the tremor in my fingers. *Don't get yourself killed*, sounded like hollow advice.

I slipped Vladimir's knife under the battery pack wires. *Why not go for both*?

I thought of Alice at home. Was she out with her friends, home reading, or in the basement working on her stationery crafting? Was she peacefully asleep? Was she wondering where I was or when I was coming home? I felt an extreme sense of loss, thinking I had let too much time on the road get in the way of giving my wife the attention she deserved.

Then the enormity of it came over me again. What of the thousands of Muscovite husbands and wives, home in their beds this morning with their children sleeping in the next room? What of their futures? This device, with the force of one thousand tons of explosives, wasn't the extent of the damage here. There were nine of these devices and all of them would go off simultaneously if I guessed wrong.

"What the hell." I said to Vladimir.

He shrugged his big shoulders, "What the hell." He said.

Suddenly, the lights to the entire building went out.

Failing to find the right breaker on the circuit panel, our warrior must have made a decision to turn off all the lights. Thank God.

In the dark, I saw an anomaly. Under the red wire leading from the power source, a small, faint red light pulsed at the rate of a heartbeat. Without hesitation, I cut the red wire.

414

CHAPTER SIXTEEN

THE TIMER HAD STOPPED AT thirty-six seconds. On the opposite wall, I could see the light of dawn breaking through the fan blades and fluttering weakly, as if beaming brightly no longer mattered. Takhoyev and I stood there not knowing what we should be looking for.

Although we were both pleased to be alive, something was definitely not right. The device was not the calm green color that the other eight were. There were still circuits, about which I knew nothing, that were showing red or green. I had no idea what that meant. Should we leave well enough alone since I had cut the power source? Or had I?

We had less than thirty seconds to either randomly cut more wires or let the clock run out on us and find out.

"Takhoyev pointed at the device. "Cut, cut!" he exclaimed.

Right or wrong, I had no idea. But he had trusted me to cut whatever wire I chose a moment ago. Now I trusted his instincts.

I began cutting red and black wires randomly. This was truly high stakes Russian Roulette. With each slice, I thought we would die and not know it. Each time my knife tore through the thin weave of wires in a slim rubber sheath, I could see thousands of strangers dying in their beds. When I got down to the final wire, I didn't know if I was worried without good cause, or if the gods had played a terrible joke on me, leaving my death to the last cut. I took what I thought might be my last breath and prepared the final slice. Takhoyev put his hand over mine and nodded. Together we yanked the knife through the last wire.

Instantly, all the lights on the device went out. We waited what seemed like an hour but was surely no more than a full minute. Nothing happened.

I set his knife on the table just in time to receive a massive bear hug from my new best friend, Vladimir Takhoyev.

Adrenaline and emotion rushed through my veins. I was not a soldier or a spy. I was a security guy conducting an investigation. How the hell did I let this get so far out of hand?

One of Takhoyev's friends was dead. Oveshkin was dead. We were sitting on an arsenal that could power a small nation to prominence and we almost used it to destroy much of northern Moscow. I was trying to find a focal point where I could get back to some semblance of control.

I pointed to the body hanging off the forklift. "I'm very sorry, Vladimir. What should we do about your friend?" I asked Takhoyev.

I could tell that he too was assessing what we had done and what had almost happened. He turned to his other friend, placed a strong hand on his shoulder and said something in Russian. Our sniper nodded, reached across to me and shook my hand and went over to the forklift and sat there.

Vladimir began, "I have known Vasiliev since he was assigned to my command nine years ago. He was not quite a young man, maybe more boy than man. But being a warrior changes a young one to a man. I saw something special in him and advanced him into the lower ranks of my KGB unit. Through it all, I knew one thing for sure. He obeyed orders without hesitation. He was loyal to our country and he was loyal to me. I am not a man of excess emotion, but his death makes me sad."

Then his mood changed. He had regained his sense of composure in an instant, as if he had already spent too much time being vulnerable.

"Michael, I told you when we began this arrangement that if we found the devices, we had to get them out of Russia and to your facility in America. What is your plan?"

I thought to myself, *my plan?* Hell, I barely had time to sleep these last few days, much less plan a movement of nuclear devices out of one of the most tightly controlled countries in the world. I had taken some random steps to that end, but I would hardly call them a plan.

"I actually have an idea, but it is very fluid. I will need more of your help and Tom Koval's too. But first, help me take the rest of these bombs apart."

We pulled the devices from their satchels and disconnected their power sources in the same way we decommissioned the one Oveshkin made live. We placed the payloads back in their satchels and

417

left the guts on the floor. We then searched Oveshkin and the rest of the building.

He had some keys, a pistol, his identification papers and a wad of cash in one hundred-dollar denominations, thousands of dollars. Takhoyev took the cash and we left Oveshkin's body on the damp, dirty floor.

■ ■ ■ ■ ■

Takhoyev and I entered Oveshkin's small office. It was starkly furnished with a swivel chair, a beat-up grey steel desk, a lamp with no shade, a ceiling light with a wire safety cage over it and a wall safe that was welded to the wall and the floor. It appeared locked. We were running out of time and there was no way we were going to be able to crack a locked safe. "Are you also a safecracker Vladimir?" I asked, jokingly.

"Not a specialty of mine," Takhoyev answered as he pulled on the door lever. To both our surprises, the door swung open. *Mater' Bozhya*, he exclaimed. Mother of God!

In the safe were stacks and stacks of United States hundred-dollar bills. There could have been a million dollars in cash in there, maybe two. Takhoyev went to grab a stack. "Wait!" I shouted. "Don't touch them yet." He looked at me sternly. "Oveshkin is dead. What does it matter now? This is ours, Michael. These are our spoils."

"Let's think this through first Vladimir," I said. "It is very likely that the money on top has at least two sets of fingerprints on it."

"It doesn't really matter, Michael. It will spend just as easily, and it will deposit in an offshore account just as easily also." Takhoyev said.

"Vladimir, we have a mess to clean up here and we have to leave a plausible scene no matter who finds it. The top stacks of money are very likely from Oveshkin's buyer. It's the down payment money. I know his prints are on the stacks because I saw him arrange them for Oveshkin on the hood of his car. Of course at least one other set of prints will be Oveshkin's. Any good forensic review will link the two of them. It will also link the two of them to the bombs and to the guns. It confounds the investigators with an unsolvable mystery as to the whereabouts of the warheads. It suggests that Oveshkin was an arms dealer for terrorists. But it could also set a false flag for everyone to follow as to the bombs.

"We would also have all these guns to dispose of. What the hell are you going to do with them? Cart them back to your house?" I saw Takhoyev's eyes close slightly as he thought about the possibilities.

"I am not a gun runner, Michael. God knows I could figure a way to move these. But that is not my thing. The cash, however, ..."

I wanted to hold him off on that. "Let's get to that in a minute. Who would come looking for Oveshkin? Your two friends who ambushed you last night, who are they?"

"They are former KGB and are now with the GRU." Takhoyev revealed. "I know both of them. I can see where they could easily have been part of the group responsible for stealing those bombs for their own use. What I can't know is whether or not

419

they were acting in an official capacity or in their own interests. If the former, then we are in a file somewhere and may even be known as the subjects of their surveillance. If that is the case, their disappearance will be very bad for us and I will have to work very hard to get us out of that file. If they are on their own, then our slate is clear.

"I also know that Oveshkin was working for Miloradov and that Davydov was grooming him. They will miss him when he does not show up on schedule today or when next summoned. Mirski will surely have to report dropping him off at his hotel last night. But he will be in the clear. I think Davydov could care less if Oveshkin disappears. Miloradov had big plans for Oveshkin, so he will certainly be looking for him. Right now, none of their trails leads to us."

"Then, my question for you Vladimir, is *who should find these bodies and the guns*? And which scenario works best for you?"

Takhoyev thought a moment. "Well, the question should be *which works best for us both*? We still have to get you and your new toys out of Russia."

He continued, "I am well connected to Miloradov and Davydov. I would not call it a relationship of friends, but of mutual satisfaction. It is a business partnership and sometimes those are stronger than friendships are here in Russia.

"The Bratva are very strong and nearly invulnerable, even to the Moscow Police. They are not that safe from the FSK or the GRU, no one is really. But Miloradov has one thing in his favor and that is *plausible deniability*, relative to Oveshkin's activities with Semenov."

"Are you saying that we should report this to the FSK?"

"That is exactly what I am thinking. Let them find the bodies outside. They will keep this very quiet. Only neither you nor I will report it. I will have my man report it, saying he heard a large gunfight. Even if no one responds for hours, I will have my man keep watch to ensure no one but the FSK will enter.

"They can find the GRU bodies outside and Oveshkin's inside. They can find the guns and make a connection, accurate or otherwise. And when they find the power sources and the instruction manuals, they will draw their own conclusions about Oveshkin and Semenov and the bombs. Maybe they will conclude the rebels ripped off Oveshkin and possess nuclear warheads. This could leave us very clean."

"I think I can add to that, Vladimir. Let's get rid of all the auxiliary parts. Let them believe all the bombs are intact and gone, leaving only an instruction manual on the floor."

"Wickedly brilliant!" Takhoyev replied. "Now about our money," he added.

"My friend, you can take all you can handle. None of that is anything I want. But I think we should leave some of the money from tonight's transaction for them to find. With that, the FSK will have the money, the fingerprints and the identity confirmation they will need.

"We have some work to do yet Vladimir. But let's get this mess cleaned up first. Everything can go over to our warehouse for now. I may have to call Weiner for the key." I said.

Takhoyev surprised me. "That won't be necessary. We have a key." I looked at him in disbelief. "Why do you look surprised? Do you think we would be unable to get inside a building I was protecting? Of course, we have a key."

We began loading up the warheads and the satchels of parts into the trunk of Takhoyev's big Mercedes. He had found several canvas bags and a small box to put his money in and those got tossed in the trunk and back seat as well. We were running out of room in the car. They would have to make a second trip to recover the body of their comrade.

As the three of us rode the few blocks to the TI warehouse we were silently lost in our own thoughts about the last hours.

■ ■ ■ ■ ■

We drove the car around to the rear and opened the overhead door to the warehouse. I watched the alley to make sure we were alone as Takhoyev backed the car into the cargo bay. It took longer than I thought before we removed the money and the all bombs onto the floor. Then we got busy right away repackaging the payloads with their original works, the detonators, timers and power sources for each. Nothing was hooked up, but each was intact as could be, without making them more dangerous than they already were.

It wasn't lost on me that I was in possession of nine nuclear devices and as crazy as that was, I couldn't dwell on the insanity of it. My focus was entirely on how to get them the hell out of Russia without ending up in one of the most feared prisons in the world.

While we worked, Takhoyev said to his man, "Use my car to go back to the warehouse. Watch from a safe distance so you are not seen, but make sure no one but the FSK enters. Once they arrive, get the hell out of there. He then reached into a canvas bag and handed his man a thick packet of hundred-dollar bills. This is for any cost you incur but, I want you to take care of Vasiliev properly. Keep the rest, but make sure to do right by Vasiliev." His man nodded and was heading to the door. Takhoyev grabbed him by the arm and turned until they were face to face. "And remember, for the sake of your life and those closest to you, you can tell no one, ever." Their eyes locked for a moment and there was the slightest nod in complete understanding.

When we were alone, I asked Takhoyev, "Do you think we can trust him?" He replied simply, "Yes." Then I saw it again. Takhoyev's mind withdrew from the room for a moment as he came to a difficult decision. I knew this was not the time to press for clarification.

We climbed up the stairs to Weiner's office and I dialed him at his home. "Alex, It's time. Gather your family and pack only the clothes you will need for two days. Try to get everything into no more than two carry-on cases. Bring your passports and whatever cash you have on hand, then meet me at your warehouse back door in two hours. Do not go outside your house until you are ready to come here."

He must have had so many questions that came with the uncertainty of being in someone else's plan without having any control over it. I knew just how he felt. "Alex, we talked about this. It is now time to leave. I have a company plane ready, but we have to hurry." He answered uncertainly that he understood and before he could think of more questions, I hung up.

Then I made my next call. He answered on the first ring. "Are you guys ready?" I asked. I explained the change of plans and was told they could manage them. We agreed to meet as planned, still on time in two and a half hours.

Then I called Koval. This is where it got a bit dicey. Okay, really dicey. Takhoyev had been specific. The bombs could not go to the U.S. government. As the Legal Attaché, Koval was one of the few official faces of the our government in Moscow. And regardless of the good work he had done with the Russian police and intelligence agencies, he was still an American. I was about to burn up all my favors, and he might have to burn some of his.

When his aide answered and told me Koval was in a meeting, I gave the guy my name and said, "This is an emergency. Go into the meeting and tell Koval that I am on the phone. I don't care if he is meeting with the American Ambassador. Interrupt the meeting, and get him to the phone now. I can assure you, he'll be very disappointed with you if he finds out you didn't put my call through to him. I'll hold. "

I didn't have to wait long.

"This had better be good, Michael. I was in a meeting with ..."

424

I didn't give him a chance to finish. "Tom, please listen, then maybe I can answer your questions. The Weiners and I have to leave Russia now, right now. The Bratva will be looking for us soon, and the heat will be on big time. Additionally, I think we may have somehow gotten crosswise with the FSK and the GRU. I don't think they have figured out it's me specifically they are looking for, but that realization will come to them pretty soon, and I can't wait around to find out. Tom, we need to get out and it has to be now, today. And we can't afford to go through customs or anything like that or I will likely be in Russia longer than you." I stopped to catch my breath and Koval jumped right in.

"Whoa. Wait a minute. What the hell have you done?"

"Tom, you know one of the reasons why I'm here. I am afraid I asked one too many questions, crossed a line I shouldn't have or pushed too hard somewhere. I need to get out of here and it has to be under the radar, literally."

I could tell Koval was about to object again, as he should. Everything the Bureau does is according to some protocol. There was no contingency for which the FBI hadn't written a procedure. It took the creativity and guesswork out of making decisions in the field, and with it a lot of liability. I was sure my request was covered somewhere and the answer, by the book, was very likely *No*.

Takhoyev grabbed the phone. He began talking immediately, not waiting to find out if Koval was listening or already speaking. And it was all in Russian. I couldn't understand a word he said except I heard *Christian* several times. Koval's translation skills must have been damned good, because Takhoyev barely stopped to take a breath as he practically shouted into the mouthpiece.

It was a long conversation, if a monologue could be called that. After a while Takhoyev stopped and waited, holding the phone to his ear. His head bobbed several times as if in silent agreement. Whatever was said, it must have ended to Takhoyev's satisfaction because all he said was, "*Da, Spasibo.*"

He handed me the phone. "It's me," I said quietly.

"Jesus Christ, Mike! What happened to your plan of not getting in harm's way?" I was about to answer when he said, "Don't bother with an explanation. I don't want to know and I sure as hell don't want you on record with an answer. I can meet you all at Sheremetyevo in three or four hours. I might be able to get the four of you on a flight, but I don't think we can avoid customs or immigrations. It will be a real crapshoot. And remember, respecting my badge is a mere courtesy here. I have no real authority, especially if the FSK gets a burr under its saddle."

I felt terrible about pushing him, but there was no choice. "I don't want to seem ungrateful Tom, but that's not going to cut it. I need more than that. I need you to meet me at Vnukovo where I'll have the TI jet already on the ground and fueled. I'll have Alex Weiner and his family there in about two and a half hours. They'll be traveling with about a dozen small bags, but I can't take the chance of going through customs, not us and not the bags. My pilots have a flight plan cleared back to New Jersey. I need to hit the tarmac, load the Weiners, their gear onto the plane and we need to get the hell out of here before the flight gets grounded. I cannot stress how urgent this is. Tom, you are our last hope to ensure our safe exit from here. Can you help us or not?"

The line was silent for the longest time.

"This is probably going to cost me a posting to Nowhere, Idaho, but I'll do everything I can. I'll meet your car outside the gates of the Fixed Base Operator's office at Vnukovo and escort your car in. There'll be no way around it, so we'll still have to check in with the FBO manager. It's at that point where we either do or do not get you out of here. I'll do my best, I just hope it is enough."

"Tom, Sasha will not be driving me. I will be arriving in a small TI ten passenger van. It won't be a vehicle anyone would expect. Will that be a problem?"

"No. That will be fine. Now I must hang up. I have several calls to make to try to set some kind of clearance in motion for you. Wish me luck."

And with that he hung up.

CHAPTER SEVENTEEN

TAKHOYEV SAID, "I WILL drive . You cannot afford to be stopped by the police, speaking only English." I saw no point in arguing. Takhoyev had already stood by me in a situation about as bad as it can get. I welcomed his help.

"Let's get busy and make these bags look as much like cargo as we can. I want them in the van before the Weiners get here." I said.

The canvas satchels already looked like soft-sided luggage bags. I guess that was the point of the design to begin with, to make them seem innocuous. I just wished the cloth wasn't military green. I found plastic Transeget Industries shipping tags and wrote a brief description for each bag. I labeled them *Assembled and loose reject parts* and threaded zip ties through the tops, tightly snugging one tag to each bag, effectively securing them from being opened casually.

I told Takhoyev I was worried about bringing the detonator explosives on board the plane. He laughed right out loud. "You have nine nuclear warheads and you are worried about explosives?"

But then he agreed that the explosives were likely more unstable than the warheads. So, we got into the next discussion, which was whether or not I needed to travel with all the other components. I decided that I really only needed one complete set of parts, but not assembled. I was pretty sure that the Agency would like to see what those parts looked like and how they were configured. I also grabbed one user's manual.

We set about unpacking the bags and stripping all but one down to just the payloads. Then we repacked and retagged them and secured the tops. In short order, we had stacked the nine bags neatly into the cargo area of the van. It looked like I was hauling gear for a small hockey team, minus the sticks, of course.

And now we just had to wait for the Weiners. They would be here within the hour.

We sat quietly for a while. I was mulling over the next steps and what we might encounter. Frankly, I was going over several *what could go wrong* scenarios and it was depressing. The list just kept getting longer and longer and I was running out of acceptable alternatives. I was thankful that Takhoyev re-opened the conversation. "What are the chances I could convince you to stay here with me in Russia?"

He must have been able to tell by the look on my face that I was dumbfounded. I couldn't wait to get the hell out of there. He chuckled. "I know, I know. You don't speak the language. And it is very likely that the Bratva and others might soon come looking for us. But I can't imagine having a better partner and I will genuinely miss you. You have very good instincts, you can make difficult

430

decisions, and you are an honest man, Michael Christian. These are very good qualities for a partner, no?" It was my turn to laugh.

I appreciated what he was saying. I realized that I was very comfortable with Vladimir Takhoyev. And despite the warning of, *trust no one,* I trusted him with my life, and I knew he trusted me with his.

"I have a different idea Vladimir. How would you like to come work for me? I am certain that your country's economy will blossom soon. And when it does, my company will expand its footprint here very quickly. I'll need someone on the ground with your special skills and connections, with your knowledge of the players and your access to them on all sides. And most of all, I will need someone I can trust. I have a pretty good budget you know and could pay you quite well. "

Takhoyev laughed robustly as he kicked a small bag on the floor. "Is your budget this good, my friend?"

We both knew it wasn't.

"You can call me at any time, Michael. I will be there for you. And maybe you could do the same for me in America?" These are the kind of promises one reads about in novels or hears in a gangster movie and the words just slipped out, just as naturally as can be. "I will Vladimir. All you have to do is call."

"Help me with these," he said. He picked up some of his bags of money and I grabbed the box of cash as we walked the flight of steps. It would take a couple trips to get them all up there. He set them in Weiner's office under and behind the desk. "I do not think your friend will be using this space again. So, for a few hours, it will be my office." With

431

that we left the office and Takhoyev locked the door with his own key.

We made nervous small talk about contingencies, agreeing that we would need a lot of luck to get through all the possible obstacles. Takhoyev mumbled something about one more enemy he had to deal with but never finished the sentence. I knew he was talking about the third KGB agent who wanted us dead, but I said nothing.

We grew quiet again and before long, I heard Weiner pull up outside the rear of the building.

■ ■ ■ ■ ■

Alex, Rachel and Sarah arrived right on time at the back door, and I ran down the stairs to open the overhead. "Pull inside," I instructed. The Weiners looked stressed and like they weren't talking to each other.

Rachel started right in on me. "Mr. Christian, Alex told me we are leaving now. Right now. Do you have any idea what I had to go through to get Sarah out of school, to cancel the sitter, to tell the maid not to come today? And then I had to pack. You could have given us at least a day or two of advance notice to put our things in order. Is all this urgency really necessary?" I looked at Weiner. Had he not explained to her that we might have to leave in a hurry? He shrugged his shoulders as if to say, I told her, but it doesn't matter. I wondered if Weiner ever told Rachel about the kidnapping threats.

I could tell this was more than just the jitters that accompany a major move. We were literally fleeing another country and they were not sure why. At least Rachel wasn't, and I really wasn't in a position to tell them everything. I could leave them here to find their own way home, or I could leave with them as promised. I knew it was selfish, but they were my cover to get the bombs out of Russia.

"You sounded rather ominous on the phone, Christian," Weiner said.

I felt like a traitor, bringing them into this without telling them about our special cargo and the additional risk they were facing. But it seemed the only way out right now. Besides, if we cleared customs at Vnukovo, we were practically home free. If not, they could honestly claim ignorance of my intentions. "Look Alex, I told you we might have to get out in a hurry. Well that time and circumstance is now. I believe we have all the bases covered. Everything is in motion and now I just need to get us all to the airport."

That was when Takhoyev started up the van. "This is my friend, Vladimir. He will be escorting us to the airport." I pulled open the rear door. "Load your things in here." Takhoyev opened the side door for Rachel and Sarah while Alex loaded the two small bags. "What's all this?" Alex asked.

"That is something the company has asked me to bring back with us." I answered, noncommittally. I slammed the rear door shut, held the door for Weiner and closed it behind him when he got in. Takhoyev pulled the van out of the garage and I locked the overhead door behind us. When I hopped in the front seat, Takhoyev had the van rolling before my ass hit the cushion.

Only then did I realize that I still had my Makarov in my rear waistband. I quietly slipped it out and put it in the glove box hoping to do so secretly. Rachel saw. "Is that going to be necessary?" she asked. I could hear the tremor in her voice. "That was a *just in case* piece that I brought along last night for something." My answer was purposefully evasive, but abrupt enough that she knew better than to ask why. Takhoyev raised his eyebrows at my response. It was obvious that with the Weiners in tow, I was no longer going to be able to pull a gun out for any reason. I think he also knew that whatever we encountered, resistance and flight were out of the question. The ball was in Koval's court.

■ ■ ■ ■ ■

We were approaching Vnukovo Airport from the northwest and still had to drive a couple miles around the east side of it to get to the FBO office. I wanted it to take forever, but even following the minimum speed, we were outside the gates in no time.

When we passed it the previous evening, the airport didn't look as large as it did now. Instead of there being only the east-west runway we drove by last night, I now noticed a second runway running northeast and southwest. I pointed it out to Takhoyev, who explained that at one time, there was only one runway, but the airport is the closest to Moscow, so a second runway was added for the nineteen eighty, twenty second Olympic Games.

It shouldn't have made a difference, but I began to worry that this was no mere bush airport, and would likely have a police station inside it. And it surely had customs and immigration officers and probably an FSK officer or two assigned here. I was beginning to second-guess my choice of a quiet departure airfield but it was too late now.

We were riding along the south border of the airport, approaching the short entrance road to the FBO offices off Leninsky Highway. We were here at the agreed time but Koval wasn't. Takhoyev sensed it too and drove past the gate without slowing. "Where is our boy, Michael? This is not good. If he is not here, we must return to your warehouse. There is nowhere else to go right now." I kept looking back at the FBO entrance as we drove farther south and wondering if our only opportunity had slipped away. I had no backup plan to get us to our plane inside the fence. I immediately dropped the idea of crashing through the gate. If we weren't shot immediately, we surely would not be allowed to board the aircraft anyway.

As the building was about to disappear from my view, I saw a black Chevy Impala turn the corner from around the back of the FBO office, race toward the gate, while flashing its headlights. It had to be Koval. Who else would be driving a Chevy in Moscow? I called out to Takhoyev, "He's here! Go back, turn around!" Takhoyev slammed on the brakes and pulled on to the shoulder. He navigated a sharp U-turn and headed us back toward the gate driving down the median grass.

Koval and another man got out of his car. The other guy, wearing a blue uniform jacket, slipped a magnetic key into a slot and the gate opened for us to pull in. I hopped out and shook Koval's hand heartily. "I thought we had missed you or something had gone wrong. Boy, am I glad to see you." I said.

Koval had only a partial smile going when he introduced my passengers and me as guests of his. I was too tense to get the guy's name, but I knew from the explanation he was the FBO manager. He jerked his thumb as if to say *pull inside.*

Takhoyev pulled the van inside the gate and the manager used his key again to close it. Koval translated as the FBO manager said, "Your plane is here, and your pilots are on-board. There are just a few formalities. Come inside and bring your passports."

I looked at Koval with a sense of dread. He said to the manager, "I will have the driver pull them around."

When we got to the runway side of the FBO office, I could see our large Gulfstream still in the hangar with the stairway down and the cargo door open in the rear.

We got out of the van and I said to Koval, "I'd like our driver to begin loading our luggage," as I gestured toward the plane. That was more for the benefit of the FBO manager who appeared not to understand English. Koval translated.

"Nyet, dokumenty, Papers," he said. Koval made a big show of getting the passports from each of us and handing them to the FBO manager. He then nodded to Takhoyev to take the van to the plane. "Nyet!" the manager said when Takhoyev put the van in gear. The only reason I could imagine for not letting us begin unloading was that the next step would be an inspection of our cargo.

At that point, Takhoyev slammed the gear lever into *park* and stormed out of the van.

He rushed the FBO manager and reached into his jacket. Dear God, I thought If he shoots or even threatens the FBO manager at gunpoint, we will have fighter planes all over us before we reach the edge of Russian airspace.

But Takhoyev pulled a leather wallet out of his inside pocket. In it, I could see the gold shield of the former KGB. He spoke very quietly to the man, held him face to face by his lapels and shoved the badge in his face. It might as well have been the Makarov. It had the same effect.

The manager handed Koval the passports and backed away from Takhoyev. "*Pozhaluysta, nyet.* Please, no," he repeated. Then he averted his eyes away from Takhoyev. Takhoyev harshly gave what must have been a warning to the manager, and then told us, "Get in, now." We needed no further encouragement.

As we got in the van, I noticed that the manger was riveted to his spot. He did not look up and he did not walk away, just kept his eyes on the concrete between his shoes. As Takhoyev drove the fifty yards to the plane, he quietly said to me, "I told him to not look up and to stay right there until I got back. You will not have to worry about him giving an alert to the tower or anyone else. He and I will be spending time together until you are safely out of our airspace. But tell your pilots to speed it up on the front end."

Walny had climbed down the aircraft steps and was waiting for me when we arrived. He nodded toward the Weiners, "I'll get their bags, you get them on board. Ankers has the cockpit and we will

437

be finishing the preflight checklist once you are all seated. I'll get us the hell out of here as fast as we can." I walked over to them and told Weiner to get on the plane with the girls. Just as they were about to board, Takhoyev yelled, "Wait!"

As he approached Weiner, he reached into his back pocket. I wondered what he was going to do next. He said to Alex, "Take this. You might need it."

With that, he handed Weiner a bound packet of hundred-dollar bills. Only Takhoyev and I knew at the time, it was ten thousand dollars. "You and your family have been through a terrible time. Consider this a rebate on a portion of your insurance premium. This is for you and your family only and there will be no record of it." With that he gave Weiner a brief handshake and walked away. I wanted to acknowledge his generosity, but he averted his glance from me as he joined Walny and Koval at the back of the plane.

As I walked up, Takhoyev had already begun setting the bags at the foot of the cargo conveyor. He told Walny, "This one is a bit heavy and it is very fragile."

I reinforced that, " Make sure the green bags won't rattle around at all if we catch any turbulence, this one especially. They're the most valuable pieces on the plane." Walny didn't ask. "I'll put it in last and make sure it is properly lashed down."

This time I told him, "Bill, I'd like to help you with that." He wasn't offended, but I am sure he wondered what could possibly be so important.

It looked like we were out of immediate danger for the moment. I had the Weiners on board. I had their bags and our cargo loaded and soon to be tied down. Takhoyev had the FBO manager scared out of his wits. All we had to do was get airborne and out of Russian airspace. Then I got my next setback.

"I'm going with you, Michael." It was Koval. I was about to interject with denial or at least surprise, but he wasn't having any of that.

"This is non-negotiable. I won't even discuss it with you. So, find me a good seat and have your pilot add me to the manifest, under my name if he has to, but not my credentials."

I was stunned. It didn't make any sense to me at all. "What do you mean? Why are you on the flight? Are we going to be under arrest in New Jersey? What the hell is going on?"

Koval said, "I'll tell you privately when we all get onboard, but I'm making this flight with you or you are not leaving. It is as simple as that."

Walny overheard the whole thing. "What's going on? Who is this guy and are you authorizing him on board or not? We need to get going."

My choices were pretty clear. I had none. "This is Special Agent Tom Koval of the FBI, United States Legal Attache to the Russian Police. He has nothing better to do this afternoon and he'd like to take a joy ride with us across the Atlantic Ocean. He weighs about two hundred pounds. Do you think we can accommodate him?"

Walny knew this was most unusual. I had been in a few dilemmas where he had to fly me out in a hurry before, and with minimal paperwork. But this was quite unorthodox, even by those standards.

"Let me recalculate given the additional cargo. But I don't think it'll be a problem, since we are way below our maximum weight capacity. Somehow I get the impression we won't be claiming this other passenger anyway, will we?" He didn't wait for an answer. "Climb aboard," he told Koval. Then he walked toward the cargo hold with me. As I looked back, I saw Takhoyev and Koval shake hands firmly before Koval disappeared inside the Gulfstream.

"What the hell, Mike?"

"Bill, if I told you," and I pointed to Takhoyev, "this one would shoot me."

Takhoyev approached us and Walny began loading bags up into the hold. I'd join him there momentarily.

I reached out and grabbed Takhoyev's hand. "I can't thank you enough, Vladimir Takhoyev. You have saved my life and the Weiners'. You've built a roof over our business. And now you are ensuring safe passage for our cargo and us. What can I say? I am going to miss you my friend."

Takhoyev said, "We had an agreement and we have both honored it. But let's face it, you have increased my fortune immeasurably and you have saved my life. I know your company has other businesses here. Consider them protected as well.

"There is one more thing, in case you were wondering. By the time you land in America, I will have cleaned up that other loose end for us. You will recall there were *three* insurance agents with us at dinner. Maybe our last friend will have a change of heart and tell me where the other devices are, if he knows."

He was right. I had completely forgotten, and when he brought it up, a sense of dread came and went. If Takhoyev could get the location of the bombs he would, and he would take care of getting us off *the list*, very likely with extreme prejudice.

He paused as if looking for more words. "Do not wait, Michael Christian, for a need to arise for my services. I would like it very much if you would just call me. It would do me good to hear a true friend's voice."

I was moved by his gesture. I knew Takhoyev was KGB and could be as cold and brutal as his assignment called for, and it would not cause him to flinch or think back on it. "And call me too, Vladimir. I would like it as well."

We shook hands firmly, as friends, both knowing we would likely never see each other again.

■ ■ ■ ■ ■

Walny and I were securing the bags when he saw the tags. Bill knew there was no way we would be using the Gulfstream to transport rejected parts. He held up a tag as if reading it then looked to me. Not so much for an explanation, but as if to say, *I'm not even going to ask.* And the look I returned said *Thanks, and please don't.*

We secured the outer and inner cargo doors and walked into the main body of the cabin.

I was surprised to see Kathy Stillman there, retracting the stairs at the front and securing the hatch latch from inside. She had already briefed the Weiners, and little Sarah was enthralled with everything aboard the aircraft, but mostly with Stillman. The look of awe never left her little face as she watched Kathy moving about in her perfectly fitting, flight attendant jacket and skirt, with the gold TI logo embroidered over the breast pocket.

The Weiners took the rear-most seats and were holding hands, as if to comfort each other. Koval and I took seats further up front, adjacent to a small conference table.

Stillman moved between us and said, "We'll be airborne in about ten minutes, unless you two or the FBO have any more surprises. After that we will be about twenty more minutes reaching our cruising altitude. Once the captains give me the okay, I'll begin serving our first meal and beverages. I'll bring you coffee shortly and if you would like something stronger, we have that as well." Then she put her fingertips lightly on my shoulder and said, "We are very glad to have you safely on board again, Michael." I noticed she did not call me Mr. Christian, and for some reason, I blushed.

Koval caught it and watched intently as Stillman walked back to her seat in the galley. "What was that all about?" he asked.

"Absolutely nothing." I replied. "We have traveled together before. I am sure it's just a courtesy." Koval looked at me, trying to decipher my straight face.

I needed to change the subject. "Now that we are all one big happy traveling family, would you mind explaining what the hell you are doing on board?"

He wasted no time. "You're asking *me* what the hell? Did you think I was going to let you leave the country on a private aircraft carrying nuclear devices? Are you crazy? What the hell were *you* thinking? You were only supposed to get any intel you could and let us know! Not interdict an arms dealer and leave a body count for the FSB to find. And then there's the little matter of you driving around in a van, full of nuclear bombs! So, let me ask you again, what the hell?"

The big jet was taxiing very quickly onto an active runway. The pavement tar strips made a staccato sound as the wheels slapped over them. It was as if the pilots couldn't wait to get out of Russia either. With its twin Rolls-Royce engines, it wouldn't take long for this baby to get off the ground, once we got clearance from the Tower. There were two remaining milestones we had to cross, and the first was getting final approval to take off. The second was getting safely out of Russian airspace.

I was about to object to Koval's accusations, when he held up his hand. "Don't bother. Vladimir told me everything. We knew about his agreement with you and had to decide, do we use you to recover as many devices as we can and get them in our custody, or do we let Takhoyev decide how to deal with them?"

It still wasn't clear to me why Takhoyev wouldn't just turn over the devices to the Bureau.

Koval continued. "We have talked about this at the highest levels, and not just here in Moscow. Jerry was leading those talks in the States since before you left New Jersey. None of us, not even Takhoyev, knew where the devices were. We suspected the Bratva, but it wasn't until your man Oveshkin turned up that we felt there might be a connection.

"You know that we have no jurisdiction here and the Agency is persona non grata everywhere in Russia. Takhoyev worried that he might have been considered a defected agent if he worked directly with either of us. We didn't have many choices until you came along, and that is how we decided.

"The agreement we reached with him is about the same agreement he reached with you. We both want these things out of Russia. Takhoyev and we agreed that you were the best likely middle ground, since he was operating without any official backing and we had none."

It didn't escape me that my participation had been decided without me being involved in the conversation. I wondered if Brinton had known too.

Koval continued, "We had no idea where you guys ended up after our car lost you in the crackup outside your hotel. So, when Takhoyev took the phone from you this morning, he explained what had happened and what your plan was. At that point, I knew I had to get you guys out and also had to be on this flight with you."

Koval switched topics for a moment, "By the way, since we are in a tell-all conversation right now, Takhoyev says you are quite the shot and saved his life. Do you care to explain?" Then he quickly reconsidered, "Please don't. It's better for me not to know. He thinks very highly of you and insisted we uphold our end of the bargain."

I was happy not to have to tell a Federal Agent about shooting anyone. "And what bargain was that?" I asked.

"These warheads will not end up in the hands of either government for deployment. The nuclear content in the devices should have been included in Transeget Industry's inventory of sub-rosa units to be reprocessed into energy grade, but these never made it. Well, here they are. I am just along for the ride to make sure they get to your plant.

"To that end, once we get outside of Russian traffic control, we will have your pilots file a couple of new flight plans. Our final destination will not be New Jersey, but we'll be going to your reprocessing facility in Tennessee. Our local office has already briefed your plant personnel to expect you, and they are prepared to receive your cargo when you land. The Bureau will also provide them an escort on the ground until they are safely within your facility.

"There's more," he added. "Once we clear Russian airspace we'll have a fighter-escort the rest of the way, and at that time I'll be giving your crew additional new coordinates."

"Should I be starting to worry?" I asked.

"No," he replied. "We just won't be refueling at London's Heathrow, as they planned, because we'll be rerouting you directly to Spangdahlem, Germany. It's the home of the U.S. Air Force's Fifty-Second Fighter Wing. We've already been cleared to land and refuel there, but no one will be allowed to board or deplane. You'll probably want to let your guys up front know that. You might want to tell the others, as well."

I could see the logic of the new plan and agreed to support it, if there were any problems up front.

I didn't tell Koval however, that I had no intention of returning to Teterboro with this hot load either, so I already had Walny file that flight plan to Tennessee, although not from Germany. I couldn't wait to see the expression on my flight crews' faces when our new *guest* began giving them all new flight coordinates. I wondered too what the Weiners

445

and Stillman would think when they saw our plane being escorted by military aircraft.

I steered us back to the bigger issue, because I still had a lingering question. "I was under the impression there were a couple dozen of these devices that had gone missing. If that count is close to being accurate, what are you planning to do about the other fifteen or so?"

Koval seemed less than convincing when he answered. I couldn't tell if he was struggling for the right words or just trying to be careful what he revealed to me.

"You're right about the count. We had it as twenty-four or twenty-five units that had been stolen from the General Directorate's governance, and now we can account for only nine of them. I would love to think that Oveshkin had taken them all, and that the secret of their whereabouts went with him to the grave. But the accepted wisdom is that several different former KGB officers collectively have the bulk of them and the few Oveshkin had were all he managed to steal from them.

I'm afraid we are going to have to work the intelligence out further on that to see if we can find the others, or at least learn who might have them. As of right now, we're no further ahead than if we had not recovered these at all."

I told him we might have a possible lead on the others. "The two guys, who might get found by the FSB at Oveshkin's warehouse, were KGB agents I had met at dinner at the Palace. Takhoyev introduced them to me, and there was a third one with them, a colonel. What I don't know is how Takhoyev will deal with that one. But given they wanted us dead and actually tried to kill us, I can only imagine what Vladimir will do. He too realizes there are units still out there and he may try to convince the last guy to make a dying declaration in good faith. Who knows?"

As if he didn't care to be on record discussing possible torture or worse with me, Koval turned the conversation away from those possibilities. "Do you need anything else from me to satisfy your crew?" he asked.

Koval's explanation for being on board was pretty succinct, made perfect sense and it fit a narrative I could easily explain to Brinton, if forced to. I was beginning to like his no-nonsense style.

I also could see right away where he couldn't let these warheads just fly out of Russia on a private aircraft, without any security controls, regardless of my past work with the Bureau. I was going to keep an eye on Mr. Tom Koval, Legal Attaché. He might be a good fit in my organization and, unlike Takhoyev, my budget could probably accommodate him.

I was sure we would have several hours to engage each other in conversation and tall tales about his work, my work and his career aspirations, before we dropped off our cargo in Tennessee. I was going to use that opportunity to conduct his employment interview, without bothering to tell him.

I saw Stillman approaching us gracefully from the galley. For some reason, my eyes were drawn to the flash of a thin, gold bracelet over her nylon-covered left ankle. When I looked up, she was looking right into my eyes. I know I hadn't done anything wrong, but I felt as if my eyes had committed some wholly inappropriate act. For the second time in the last half-hour, I blushed.

If she noticed, she seemed unfazed as she walked up alongside me, leaned in close, placed her hand lightly on my shoulder again, handed me a crystal tumbler and whispered, "I know you didn't ask, but here's your favorite, Crown Royal on the rocks." As I took it, she grazed her fingertips over mine.

Other Books
By
Mike Saad

The first of the Michael Christian Mysteries, **A DAY LATE,** is an international crime novel set in post-cold war Germany. Meet Michael Christian for the first time, as he takes on a smuggling-ring operating in Germany, Poland and Russia while using his plant's customs-paperwork, trucks and employees to seemingly legitimize their cross-border activities.

The bodies begin to pile up, while Christian works to solve the case before the Russians add his body to the count. Available on Amazon as a Kindle e-Book and in paperback format.

Released in August 2018, A DAY LATE enjoys all Five-Star reviews!

Here's what people are saying about it:

"Beautifully written"
"This book has it all"
"Sounds as if it has been ripped from some secret file"
"Great TRIP!"
"Interested the entire time"
"Intrigued til the very end"
Extremely suspenseful"

Book three of the Michael Christian series opens in London, England, where he travels to discover who has been stealing blank checks from the corporate register. The signatures have been forged to buy nearly a half-million-dollars in gold.

What starts out as a simple theft case, evolves into a global terrorism-financing scheme. This book is in-progress and is expected to be released in the fourth quarter of 2019.

WANT TO LEARN MORE?

You can keep up with Michael Christian, sign up for advance notice of book releases, and learn more about the geographic and historical settings and characters at http://www.mikesaadwrites.com.

You can also read Mike Saad's personal musings and professional biography, by visiting his blogs and webpages. You will also find a few short stories, fact and fiction, about Mike's experiences as a decorated officer on the Detroit Police Department.

Access all this and more at www.mikesaadwrites.com.

Made in the USA
Lexington, KY
20 April 2019